THE GALAXY BOYS AND
THE SPHERE

The Galaxy Boys and The Sphere

By

Andrew Steele

JANUS PUBLISHING COMPANY
London, England

First published in Great Britain 2007
by Janus Publishing Company Ltd,
105-107 Gloucester Place,
London W1U 6BY

www.januspublishing.co.uk

British Library Cataloguing-in-Publication Data
A catalogue record for this book is available from the British Library

ISBN 978-1-85756-677-2

Cover Design: Jarett Greene
jarettmanx9000@yahoo.com

Printed and bound in Great Britain

Dedication

For my daughter Amanda – the most amazing young woman in the galaxy. And for my sons; Robert, William, Matthew and Kristopher – The Galaxy Boys. Whenever each of you are not with me, I miss you like we are solar systems apart.

Contents

Escape

Far from Earth, on the other side of the Milky Way, in a part of space devoid of planets and sparsely lit by stars, a small, silver spaceship sought its escape.

Barrelling down on the sleek vessel, a massive, dark warship relentlessly fired orange bursts. Every shot missed, but each one was close to hitting, dead-on.

Suddenly, the great beast hit its mark and the silver ship vanished in a streak of light, leaving the heavens deathly quiet.

Meanwhile, in New York City, on Earth, there was no such thing as deathly quiet, as New York is one of the noisiest places in the galaxy. And, at that precise moment, it was even noisier for two boys because, inside the tunnel, the one into which they had run to escape from a gang of bullies, a rumbling locomotive's thunderous horn cracked the still air as its oculus light pierced the tunnel's darkness.

Short of breath from running and sheer panic, Rob scampered up on to a ledge beside the tracks, snagging and ripping his jeans as he did so. Without slowing, he rolled up against a cold, hard wall, and from where he lay, he looked out and gasped at the sight of his brother attempting to follow him.

Fear laced Will's heavy breathing as he struggled to claw his way up on to the ledge. Rob lunged, grabbed his hand, and gave a firm yank. But Will was stuck, dangling with his feet a foot off the ground below. Rob pulled harder while Will desperately kicked at the wall.

A blinding light flooded the tunnel. The air was split again by a thunderous blast from the locomotive's horn, which forced a panic-stricken scream from Will's gut before he found a firm footing. But it was not as firm as he'd first thought as it slipped away beneath him.

Suddenly, Will shot up in the air, as though he had been thrown and landed on top of Rob, knocking the wind out of both of them.

The noise was unbearable. The vibration of the train's steel wheels rumbling over the tracks shook every bit of the passage. It seemed as if the tunnel would cave in at any moment in a cloud of dust, and a pile of rubble would cover Rob and Will's crushed bodies. Fear gripped them as they realised that no one would ever find them. With their eyes shut tight, their teeth clenched and their hands clasped over their ears, there they remained – brave to the end.

Having barely escaped the dark warship they were still a long way from Earth. From the co-pilot's seat, Katia peered sideways at her robot as she kneaded the ends of the armrests with both hands ...

"We're not going to make it, are we, Keb?"

Katia knew very well that due to sheer computer intelligence, a robot could pilot any spaceship and could do so whilst baking cookies. Of course, she would never order Keb to do such a thing, but it was fun to dream about it. However, in spite of her robot's abilities, it looked every bit as though the robot was concentrating hard on piloting the ship.

The robot turned its head and said, "We have made it this far, young miss," and returned its attention to the ship's controls.

Katia often imagined she could see human emotion in Keb's metallic face, especially in his glasseen eyes, although she knew that wasn't possible. Though human in shape, robots were machines and did not have emotions; they just received and processed data, then responded logically or as ordered.

To Katia, the dark blue of Keb's eyes could look both warm and friendly, or, at other times, seem as cold as the vast emptiness of space from which the glasseen was mined. Few robots had eyes like Keb's – only the newest and most advanced models did – but Katia thought Keb's seemed different.

Katia still suspected that there was something wrong with the ship, so she persisted in her questioning.

"Will we make it to Earth?"

The robot turned its head again to look at her. Katia's long, brown hair always seemed to hang neatly, framing her round face, complementing her eyes. Only ten years old, she was a tall girl and mature beyond her years. That maturity came at a price, with her position in life, or rather, that of her mother. Katia, the daughter of a galactic senator, knew of life's dangers early on. That's what Keb was for; to be a loyal companion and a tireless protector.

"The ship is badly damaged, young miss," said Keb. "It will not withstand entry into Earth's atmosphere."

The robot stared at Katia for a moment, and then turned its attention to the ship's broadly-curved view-screen and continued, "We will have to land on Earth's moon and from there, receive help from Earth's ranger."

In Katia's mind, Keb had always been a male robot; a classification that her mother had once called 'silly but sweet'. 'Robots are machines,' her mother would say, 'no more'.

But Keb had been manufactured with a deep, gentle, male voice, perfect for a robot that must combine the firm care of a young girl with a loving, fatherly tone. Katia's mother had ordered him that way, betraying her own insistence that Keb was just a machine.

"Robots are supposed to protect humans at all costs," said Katia in a matter-of-fact tone as she watched Keb. "But I know I might not survive this ... It's not your fault if I die, Keb. You've done everything you could ... "

Keb looked from the ship's view-screen, which was filled with the star-speckled blackness of space. Katia thought she saw a look of anguish cross his metallic face.

" ... and since I know I might die," she continued, "I would feel better if you could just tell me what's wrong with the ship, Keb."

A high-pitched signal sounded suddenly and the cockpit went dark. Katia gripped the armrests more tightly; she could feel her heart pounding. She knew how unforgiving space travel could be, and that with little or no warning, in an instant, a problem in space could bring an end to one's life, like a puff of breath extinguishes a candle.

The emergency lights came on, casting the cockpit in an eerie, red glow. Keb had returned his attention to the ship's controls and was now tapping directives on the computer console.

"You do not need to fear, young miss," said Keb, in a calm voice – the only voice a robot ever used. "Given the ship's damaged state, in preparation for our next pass through thin-space, the computer is automatically shutting down unnecessary systems in order to conserve power."

Keb tapped a few more keys and a holographic map of Earth's solar system appeared above the control console.

"The last impact was well aimed," he continued. "My manoeuvre was anticipated. It is fortunate we entered thin-space the instant the blast hit the ship, as the severity of the impact was diluted as we left our attackers behind."

Keb glanced at Katia, as though checking on her, before continuing, "I am not sure as to the extent of the damage to the ship, young miss, and we must make one more pass through thin-space to reach Earth's system."

Katia continued to watch Keb through the red glow in the cockpit. Then a smile came to her and she relaxed her grip on the armrests.

"You're being a sneaky robot, Keb," she said. "You still haven't said what's exactly wrong with the ship."

Again, the robot turned its head to stare at Katia, with its glasseen eyes taking on a strange, dark-red hue reflecting from the emergency lights.

"A robot cannot be sneaky, young miss," said Keb. Returning his attention to the ship's controls, he continued, "I am programmed to respond promptly and precisely to questions, commands, and events."

Katia studied Keb for a moment as she thought about what to say next. Controlling a robot could be difficult for those unaware of the intricacies of manipulating an advanced machine. It was especially so with a robot like Keb that was designed to think independently, to solve problems, and to protect Katia at all costs.

But then it came to her; she knew what to say and spoke with a firm voice, "I think you are being sneaky, Keb, in a robot sort of way. I also know that my mother strengthened your basic robotic program to protect humans, with a priority command to protect me. That's why you won't tell me what's wrong with the ship. You think I will come to harm by knowing. But I won't. Maybe another child, but not me. You of all robots should know that by now ... " Katia took a deep breath, and then continued, "I know how to override my mother's command if I have to. So please, tell me what's wrong with the ship, Keb. Don't make me command you. I don't ever want to treat you like that. It would hurt my feelings to do so."

Her carefully chosen words worked. A far greater harm would now be inflicted upon her if Keb did not tell her what was wrong with the ship, because her feelings would be hurt should she have to force him to do so. Again, Katia thought she could discern a look of anguish on the robot's metallic face. Or was it the eyes? Something was very wrong. She knew for sure, now.

"Air is leaking from the ship, young miss," said Keb in his ever-calm voice. "As I have said, we cannot land on Earth, and as you know, the Earth's moon lacks an atmosphere."

"Then why must we go to Earth?"

"Because, of all the planets under your mother's rule, she trusts Earth's ranger above all others. Also, Earth is inhabited by a civilisation that does not yet know of life outside its own system. For that reason, it is protected under the Galactic Settlement Treaty and is less likely to have Boargen spies. Besides, young miss," continued Keb, after tapping a series of control keys, "we would have the same problem with our ship no matter what our destination. And regardless of our destination, with the cargo which we are carrying, we must hide well and trust few."

At the mention of the precious cargo with which she and Keb were entrusted, Katia craned her neck to look towards the back of the ship. Though out of sight, she knew it was there, safe for the time being from the evil Boargen leader – Admiral Slatter.

A bleep sounded and the holographic image above the control console began to pulse.

"We are ready to make the last pass through thin-space," said Keb, the pulsing holograph of the solar system reflecting in his glasseen eyes.

After a moment, cracking a slight smile, Katia said, "I know we'll make it, Keb. I'm certain of it now." And she was ...

Moments later, the sleek, silver ship vanished from space in a streak of light.

Tunnel Vision

With the rumble of the train now a distant sound, Will was the first to remove his hands from his ears and open his eyes. A faint glow from the city's lights outside the near end of the tunnel barely reached where they lay on the concrete ledge. Rob still had his eyes closed and his hands over his ears when Will sat up and nudged him with his foot.

Opening his eyes slowly, one after the other, Rob sat up and looked around. His eyes, wide-open, and his lips, firm-set, betrayed the concern he held for their close call. At ten years old, Rob was the oldest of four brothers. He was tall and thin with hazel eyes, and had a child's version of his father's straight-ridged nose. His blonde hair was kept regularly trimmed, which was strictly demanded by the nuns at the orphanage.

Looking wide-eyed at Will, he remembered why they were in the tunnel in the first place, and whispered, "Do you think we lost them?"

Though sixteen months younger than Rob, Will was almost as tall. He was thicker-boned and tough-looking, but with a more boyish nose. One could see the boy's mother in his face. His hazel eyes tended to lend themselves to a lighter shade of blue, as though there was a light shining inside his head, brightening his eyes from within. Will's light-brown hair had a tendency to take on a life of its own and he had a smile with a dimple on his left cheek that melted even the strictest nun's conviction for neatly trimmed hair.

With a dubious look, Will said, "I bet they didn't think we would ditch in here with a train coming."

He glanced from one end of the tunnel to the other and shivered. It was damp and cold, and the darkness stirred up a fear in him that made him want to run towards the nearest light. With some effort, he stayed put and remained calm.

He continued, "We should get going ... "

Despite his desire to get out of the dark, Will pointed towards the dark end of the tunnel.

" ... That way. I don't think we should go out the way we came in."

Sliding on his rump towards the edge of the ledge, Will dangled his legs over the side, ready to jump down on to the tracks. He felt Rob grab his shoulder and looked back.

"It's really dark that way," said Rob, his voice expressing the very fear which Will now felt. "What if another train comes ... ?"

"I'll risk the long way out before I face that gang again," answered Will. "I don't think they wanted to play baseball with those bats." Will stared towards the dark end of the tunnel. "And I don't hear another train coming. We'd hear it ... don't you think?" He glanced back at Rob, seeking reassurance.

"I suppose you're right," answered Rob, doubt tingeing his voice.

Feeling braver and encouraged by the strong desire to get back to the orphanage and into a warm bed, Will leapt down on to the tracks. He turned to look up at Rob, and then said, "If we don't go now, we just might have to dodge another train."

That was enough to get Rob moving. He slid to the edge of the shelf, dangled his legs over, and jumped, landing near his brother beside the tracks. As he brushed his hands off on his jeans, he glanced at Will, who was staring at the ledge wall.

"What are you looking at?" he asked.

There was no reply. Will simply kept staring at the wall. Rob nudged him and Will jerked his head to look back.

"What's up, Will? What are you looking at ... ?"

Returning his attention to the wall, not really knowing himself what he was looking for, Will hesitated, and then answered, "I don't know. I was just looking for what I stepped on to get up on to the le..."

"Hey ... ! You ... ! Punks!" echoed a voice through the tunnel.

The brothers shot glances towards the tunnel entrance, just long enough to see six youths standing there, silhouetted in the dim light. Baseball bats dangled menacingly by two of the boys' sides. There was no choice now as to which way Rob and Will could leave the tunnel.

They ran towards the shadows of the dark end, sprinting through the pitch-black.

The gang of six gave chase.

Since Rob could run faster than Will, he made himself stay at a close second. That proved to be difficult, because the dreadful echo of the stampeding boys behind them made his and Will's predicament sound even worse than it truly was, and made him want, so very much, to run faster.

Finally, appearing as a small, dim circle in the distance, the other end of the tunnel came into view. Though initially the world outside had seemed so far away, Will and Rob found themselves bursting, suddenly, from the tunnel.

Then, without warning, Will stopped dead, and Rob had to dodge so as not to run headlong into him. Skidding to a stop on the gravel of the railroad bed, Rob turned and lunged back, grabbing at Will's arm to drag him on.

"Come on, Will!" he said, in a raspy, breathless voice. "What are you doing? They're gonna get us!"

But Will was unmovable. He stared back into the tunnel, listening with unwavering attention.

Then Rob became aware of panicked yells from the gang of boys coming from within the tunnel and stopped tugging.

"They just bats bro'! Jus' knock 'em out o' the air!" yelled one of the boys in desperation, his voice echoing.

Cacrack!

A flash lit up the tunnel like there was a mini lightning storm inside. At that moment, Will caught sight of what looked like two silver disks buzzing over the heads of six crouching figures. Rob blinked, unsure of what he saw.

Sounding alarmed, the voice of one of the boys in the gang echoed through the tunnel.

"Ow! What the – that wa'n't no bat, bro'! And it 'aint lettin' us go but back where we come!"

Another boy's voice echoed, "Those punks sicced somethin' on us!"

The sounds that emanated from the tunnel over the next few moments were incoherent cries of continued panic as the gang retreated towards the other end of the tunnel. As they went, whatever had attacked the gang continued to dog them as the tunnel flashed with an eerie glow several more times.

The tunnel grew quiet as Rob and Will stood there listening and watching. Soon, all they could hear were the sounds of New York City both near and far – a never-ending city voice of hustle and bustle; a sound that the brothers had become used to during the past year in the orphanage, on Thirty-ninth Street, Brooklyn.

Feeling Rob's tug on his sleeve, Will turned. "Did you see them?" he asked.

Rob stared at Will.

"I didn't get a good look at any of them," he said. "Does it matter? Hopefully we'll ne … "

"No! Not the lug-heads that were chasing us!" snapped Will. "Th … those things that chased them away!" Will pointed towards the tunnel. "Didn't you see them? They were like … like little flying-saucers!"

Rob followed Will's pointing finger, staring.

"You had to have seen them, Rob! I didn't imagine it … ! And, something helped me up on to that ledge, too!"

With an apologetic look, Rob tried hard to remember something similar that he had seen back home, in Oregon, so long ago. But now, he was tired and just wanted to get back to the orphanage and into bed. Now that their immediate problem appeared to be over, he worried that their absence from their beds would be discovered.

"I saw something," he said. "But I didn't get a good look at it."

"At them!" said Will, his frustration coming out in his voice as it grew louder. "There were two of them … little silver things flying around … like big frisbees! You had to have seen them!"

Desperate, Will stared pleadingly at his brother. Rob peered into the tunnel as though he might be able to get another glimpse of whatever had chased the gang away. Only now, there was nothing but a dark void.

"I did see something," said Rob, "I did. And although I didn't get a good look at them, I'm sure I've seen something like that before … "

"Exactly!" Will danced around excitedly, looking as though he was going to run back into the tunnel at any moment. "I've seen those things before," he said, staring back at Rob. "I just can't remember where ... like they're from a dream ... or a movie ... or something ... But they're real. They're real … right, Rob?"

Reaching out, Rob tugged on Will's sleeve. "Let's get out of here," he said, now feeling very tired. "We can talk about this later."

Glancing back to be sure Will was following, Rob started walking. Hesitating, Will followed, still staring back at the tunnel until he stumbled on a railroad tie, which brought his attention to the long walk home.

High above, two silver objects followed the boys as they made their way through the city streets to a magnificent, stone church surrounded by colourful, blossoming bushes and majestic, blooming trees. Next to the church was the orphanage: a small, brick building unremarkable in architecture. The window to the brothers' room on the third floor was accessed by an old, creaky drainpipe, which they would have to climb. Neither boy considered the orphanage home; it was just where they slept until their parents returned.

It seemed to Rob and Will, that where they lived was always noisy until, that is, they wanted to sneak about. And of course, the only time they could sneak about was at night, which was always quiet, even in a place like New York – very inconvenient for sneaks. Only this time, it seemed even quieter than usual as they made their way to the back of the orphanage. Of course it would be; after the ear-splitting, bone-jarring noise in the tunnel, any other sound paled in comparison.

They had climbed the drainpipe many times during the past two years, including during the winter, when the metal pipe was freezing cold. They knew it by heart, and where it would creak if weight were placed on the wrong footing.

11

Will went first. He climbed, effortlessly, to a third-floor ledge and, hugging the wall, slipped inside the open window. Seconds later, he popped his head out and indicated for Rob to follow. Duplicating Will's moves, and in about the same amount of time, Rob reached the window and climbed in.

The brothers paused to look out – a habit of sneaks – to be certain that no one had seen them and then turned to head for bed.

"Aaah!"

They jumped in alarm at the sight of a small figure standing at the centre of the room. The moonlight cast an eerie glow upon the creature, which the boys then realised was none other than their little brother, Matt.

Will had been born sixteen months after Rob, and eighteen months later, Matt had arrived. Matt was cute to the core, with big, round, hazel eyes set in a round face. When he smiled his eyes smiled – three smiles in one – which he now gave as his older brothers tried to calm their heavy-beating hearts and catch their breath.

"What are you doing up?" whispered Rob, irritated. "You almost scared me to death. How many times do I have to tell you not to sneak up on me like that?"

Will chuckled.

His smile fading, Matt said, "I didn't wake up for no reason. A couple of clods made an awful racket climbing up a drainpipe and through my bedroom window."

"It's not just your bedroom, Matt," whispered Rob, louder than he knew he should. Pulling his shirt over his head on the way to his bed, Rob breathed out in frustration as he walked past Matt and said, irritably, "And talk quietly ... you'll wake up Kris."

"Like you haven't already made enough noise with your girly shrieks," whispered Matt, under his breath.

Shrugging at Matt, Will began pulling off his own shirt as he walked towards his bed.

In spite of the age differences between Rob, Will, Matt and their youngest brother, Kris, who was sixteen months younger than Matt and, at present, asleep, the nuns had decided to keep the brothers together in the same room. This arrangement worked well as four beds fitted nicely in that particular bedroom: two opposite walls housed two beds each, paired a few feet away from each other. The door, flanked by closets, filled the third wall. And the window, flanked by dressers, occupied the fourth. The room was very orderly, as was the orphanage in general.

Matt walked over to Rob's bed and plonked down on the end just as Rob was pulling on his pyjama shirt.

Wide-awake and curious, Matt asked, "Where'd you guys go tonight?"

Rob frowned, then said, "Go back to your bed, Matt. We'll tell you about it in the morning."

Unfazed by the attempted brush-off, Matt stayed put, staring up at Rob with alert, round eyes. "Kris said we got a weird e-mail today," he announced.

Rob was about to ignore his brother and slip under the covers in spite of Matt sitting on his bed, but his curiosity made him hesitate. Instead, he ended up sitting on his pillow and staring across the room at Kris, who was snoring lightly and slept through anything.

The youngest of the four brothers, Kris resembled Rob the most, which meant he also resembled his father, as Rob was very much the young version of their father. At six years old, Kris's body was beginning to grow long and lean. But his face – cuddled-up with his pillow as it was – retained some of his toddler features, including a button nose. Kris shifted slightly, ending his soft snoring, and scrunched his lips into the pillow, pushing them into a crazy shape.

While Rob usually wore pyjamas in bed, except on the warmest nights, Will almost always slept in shorts, except on the coldest nights. Tonight, as Will sat on the edge of his bed, watching the exchange between Rob and Matt, he was wearing a pair of soccer shorts.

"Who sent the e-mail?" he asked.

Matt looked from Rob to Will and said, "First, tell me where you guys went tonight." He looked back at Rob. "I noticed you ripped your jeans."

Breathing out through pursed lips, Rob glanced at Will, who was looking rather droopy-eyed, then stared back at Matt, who sat there, waiting expectantly for the exchanging-stories deal to be accepted.

"Matt," he said, "we're really tired. Our story will be a lot more exciting if we tell it to you in the morning, after we've slept."

Nodding in agreement, Will slipped under his covers, flopped down on his pillow, rolled over, breathed in deeply, exhaled, and was out for the count. Rob, too, slid down, squeezing his feet past Matt, kicking him a bit.

"We'll find out about the e-mail from Kris in the morning," he said, yawning as he rolled over and snuggled into his pillow.

Rob suspected that Matt would want to claim the glory by recounting the contents of the e-mail. His suspicion was confirmed when, after a moment, Matt said, "OK, I'll tell you."

Trying not to seem too eager, Rob rolled back to face him.

Matt began. "Mother Superior ate lunch in her office today, so Kris had to wait until she went for her evening bath to sneak on to her computer. You were the last one that checked the e-mail two weeks ago, so there was a lot of junk that had to be downloaded. Kris said it took forever."

Rob listened, patiently, but he was tired and it was difficult not to hurry his brother along.

Taking a deep breath, Matt shifted his position, and then continued, "The e-mail was addressed to all of us, which is weird. And it wasn't from any of our pen-pals. Kris tried to run a trace on it but he was wary that Mother Superior might catch him, so he got out of there."

Scowling in thought for a moment, Rob then asked, "Kris said he was trying to trace where the e-mail came from?"

"Yeah ... I mean ... I don't know why, but that's what he said. How do you trace an e-mail?"

Rob looked perplexed as he said, "I don't know how to do anything like that. Kris is smart, but I don't know how he would learn how to do that either, or why he would even want to."

"Maybe it's because of what the e-mail said."

Rob stared at Matt, expecting him to continue, then, when he didn't, said, "Well? What did it say?"

"Oh … yeah. It said for us to get home, fast."

"What?" Rob barked as he sat bolt upright. Realising he had raised his voice, he leaned in closer to Matt and, in a hoarse whisper, said, "What do you mean, it said to get home fast? Who would tell us to do that?"

Matt shrugged, and then said, "Maybe that's what Kris was trying to find out."

Rob's mind spiralled, searching every bit of his thoughts for a reasonable explanation. After a moment, he lay back and stared at the ceiling …

The next morning, as Rob awoke, he felt fuzzy-headed and his body was heavy. Having no idea when Matt had gone back to his own bed, or when he, himself, had fallen asleep, he sat up and stared out the window, remembering the e-mail. He wanted little more than to go home, even if he had to live with a kooky, old grandmother – he missed it that much. And he knew it was the same for his brothers, too.

Why would someone – apparently no one they knew – send an e-mail telling them to get home, fast? And how would they do such a thing anyway? Maybe one of their pen-pals was playing a trick on them. If so, it was a mean trick. But the very notion of going home had raised Rob's hopes. And now, as his head cleared, he could no longer contain his excitement.

With a streak of light, the sleek, silver spaceship appeared in Earth's solar system and raced to meet the moon. Keb had programmed the computer to send a distress signal the instant they came out of thin-space. That done, the ship's computer would repeat the message every ten minutes until they received a reply. Now, the robot had to get the damaged spaceship to Earth's orbit in one piece; a task that could prove impossible as the ship was disintegrating.

Keb was not worried about himself. Although a robot understands the concept of death, it does not experience death as a human, or any other intelligent being of the universe, does; a robot either functions or does not. Barring physical damage or a debilitating system failure, Keb could survive on the Earth's moon – even without a ship as shelter – as long as his power-source continued to function, which, in his case, would be about 496 years. It was Katia for whom the robot was concerned. With air leaking from the ship, the young girl had just 307 hours of breathable air remaining. If the ship held together and they reached the moon, Katia's life would then depend on a rescue from Earth.

Once on the moon, there was no way, that Keb could ever know whether help would arrive or not. Unknown to him, Earth's galaxy ranger was not receiving their distress signal, because the ranger, Rob Roar, was missing.

What on Earth?!

"Rob Roar ... !"

Rob's eyes grew wider as he gasped and sat up straight, staring at the bedroom door. Crowded around him, discussing the mysterious and exciting e-mail, his brothers froze.

" ... I want a word with you, young man!" Sister Greta's voice boomed from down the hall, as her footsteps neared the brothers' bedroom.

As Rob watched the door, he braced himself for the berating words which he knew were coming.

Heavy, echoing footsteps arrived outside the door with a final scuffing of feet. The door opened, revealing a determined-looking, pudgy-faced, heavy-set woman dressed in a habit – Sister Greta – holding out a pair of jeans.

As they were not the targets of her glaring eyes, Will, Matt and Kris sat still. Seated on Rob's bed, they watched Sister Greta with rapt interest. Rob now wished he had done what Will always had after ripping a pair of jeans – lost them.

Holding open the gaping rip in the jeans for the boys to see, Sister Greta approached. She boomed again, in a stern voice, "What sort of mischief have you been up to now? And don't you look up at me with those innocent eyes, young man! It won't work on me!"

She looked, for a moment, as though she was done. But then, she continued, shattering the short but complete quietness, giving the brothers a start.

"The other sisters may think you're the sweetest thing since honey on toast! But you haven't fooled me, Rob Roar!"

With Sister Greta quiet once more, the brothers stared at her, not sure if she was going to start up again.

She didn't disappoint, barking, "Well?!"

The boys jumped again.

Rob swallowed ...

Sister Greta's eyes remained unblinking.

" ... well ... I ... um ... "

"He crawled over the fence to get a ball, yesterday," Will cut in, "and snagged them on the way back over."

Squinting as though she could see through Will's explanation, Sister Greta switched glances between Rob and Will a few times, before resting her suspicious gaze on Rob.

"Is that what happened?" It was a statement rather than a question.

She returned her hard look to Will. "At least your brother doesn't try to hide his mischievousness by throwing his jeans away."

Will's eyes strayed, betraying him.

"Ah ... yes ... I see I'm right. Fine then. You two will have a sewing lesson today. Meet me in the laundry in half-an-hour." With that, Sister Greta turned on her heels and headed for the door. "And don't be late."

Closing the door behind her, Sister Greta left the room as it was, except, that is, for the now shell-shocked brothers.

Rob was the first to close his mouth. The others followed suit, in close succession.

"Well," said Rob, "that wasn't so bad." He looked at Will and gave him an exaggerated smile, "And we get to have a sewing lesson," he continued, cheerfully. "That could be fun."

Will's jaw dropped; this time in astonishment. Then, sneering, he said, "Don't be a sissy, Rob! I don't want a sewing lesson!"

Rob shrugged. "Look," he said, "forget the sewing lesson for now. We've got to decide what we should do about that e-mail."

"What do you think we're going to do about it?" asked Will, still sneering. "It's not as though we can just hop on a bus and go home."

Sitting up straight, Rob leaned in close to his brothers and spoke, low. "Look, school's out. What if we could get Mother Superior to send us home for the summer?"

"Coool!" said Matt, his round, hazel eyes gleaming.

Kris's face brightened with wonder.

"Tuh! And what about Aunt Hilary?" asked Will, frowning. "You think she's gonna let us get that far away from her death-grip? Not a chance."

"Will," said Rob, "don't be such a killjoy. We can do this."

Downcast, Will shrugged and took a deep breath. "I just don't want to get my hopes up," he said. "I can barely even remember what home looks like, it's been so long." Will pointed at Kris. "He was only five when Aunt Hilary … "

"Aunt Hilly … " Matt cut in.

" ... Aunt Hilly, dumped us here."

Rob put a hand on Will's shoulder and spoke while switching glances from brother to brother. "Look, Father went missing almost two years ago. And Aunt Hilly made Mother's life miserable with all those police and that big investigation, blaming her for his disappearance ... "

"I remember all that," said Matt, in a subdued tone.

"Me, too," added Kris.

Still looking from brother to brother, Rob continued, "Mother always promised us she wouldn't give up looking for Father. And she was gone a lot of the time, too. You guys know none of that stuff Aunt Hilly said about Mother is true … "

"That witch was never nice to Mother," said Will, frustration tingeing his voice. "Even when Father was around, she always gave Mother dirty looks."

"Maybe Mother and Father are in trouble somewhere. Or maybe we gotta face up to it that they're both dead." Looking between Kris and Matt, who had both dropped their heads, Rob said, "Sorry, guys." Then, more upbeat, he continued, "But someone sent us an e-mail telling us to get home, fast. And I say we owe it to Mother and Father to do just that." Rob gave Will's shoulder a little squeeze and a shake. "What do you say, Will? We can't let Aunt Hilly get the better of Mother like that."

Will remained cool.

"I want to go home," whispered Kris, looking sad.

"Look," said Rob, "there has to be a way to get Aunt Hilly and Mother Superior to let us go home. I'll figure that out and, Kris, you can figure out where that e-mail came from."

Kris nodded.

"I'll sneak into Mother Superior's office with you tonight and you can show me what you're talking about ... OK?"

Kris nodded again, "OK."

Turning his attention to Matt, Rob continued, "Matt, you can keep watch while we're in Mother Superior's office."

Matt nodded, and then said, "You got it."

Will was still downcast. Rob nudged him.

A moment later, a look of determination overtook Will's depressed mood. He looked up, and then quietly said, "Let's go home."

Later, while Rob and Will were learning rudimentary sewing techniques from Sister Greta, Kris took Matt down to the basement. He wanted to show him a toy he had just finished building from scraps scavenged from Mr Cain's junkyard. Several months earlier, Kris had found a crashed, remote-controlled aeroplane stuck high in a tree at the park around the corner, which had given him the start he needed.

Outside in the courtyard behind the orphanage, holding a small duct-tape-wrapped, makeshift box with two toggle switches and an antenna sticking out of it, Kris watched the sky as he manipulated the toggles. Matt stood close by, looking up, transfixed on a silver saucer that looked like a miniature UFO flitting about the church roof. A number of other children stood nearby in a loosely gathered group, also watching the flying object with great interest. Included, were Tic and Talk, skinny, twin eight-year-old brothers with curly black hair, thin noses, and black-rimmed glasses.

Watching Kris, beside him, Matt asked, "Can I try it?"

Kris gave Matt a quick glance, and then returned his attention to the flying-saucer. "Uh-uh," he said. "It's not that easy."

"It doesn't look that hard," said Matt after a moment, looking up to watch the saucer. Then, looking at Kris again, he said, "C'mon, I'll give the controls straight back if I can't fly it. What can happen ... ?"

Kris gave Matt a searching look, then said, "Alright, but give it right back if there's a problem ... OK?"

"You got it," said Matt, rubbing his hands together.

With that, Kris held the controls out in front of Matt and explained, "The left-hand toggle controls the RPM of the motors, which makes the saucer go up when you push the toggle forwards, and down when you pull it back. The right-hand toggle controls the pitch of the motors, which will make it go more or less in the direction you push the toggle ... "

Kris's speech quickened as the excitement over explaining his flying-saucer's design intensified. Finally, someone he could tell about his accomplishment.

" ... Now, that can get confusing, because the saucer can rotate a little, in spite of my having installed four fans. Two, with opposing rotations to the other two ... You see, what I really need to do is install a ... "

"Kris ... Kris," Matt cut in, "slow down. My brain'll get clogged up with all the stuff you have to think about. What do I do if the thing rotates?"

Kris glanced at Matt, disappointed that his explanation had been cut short. He turned his body a little and pushed the toggle to the left. The saucer, too, moved in the same direction.

"It's easier to keep track of it if you just rotate with the controls until you and the saucer are in sync," Kris said.

Matt reached over and carefully grasped the controls. Kris hesitated, and then released his hold and Matt was in control of the flying-saucer. He pushed the right-hand toggle a little to the right. The saucer, too, moved in that direction. Matt turned, adjusting his position to place himself in sync with the flitting, silver object. Kris took a deep breath.

Molly Polanski was a husky twelve-year-old girl with long, tangled black hair and one continuous eyebrow across both eyes.

She was a little ugly, and not very nice. She did not live at the orphanage, but a few blocks away on the nicest street in the neighbourhood, just two houses down from the park. Molly always made sure the children at the orphanage knew just how special she was because she had parents that loved her enough to keep her.

It was her arm that Matt saw, out of the corner of his eye, swiping Kris out of the way, knocking him to the ground.

Taken aback, Kris yelled, "Hey!" as Molly lunged at Matt for the remote control.

However, Matt was quicker than his pursuer and ducked out of the way

"Ugh!"

But unfortunately, he had ducked right into Molly's little sister, Patty, who was not so little when ducked into.

At ten years old, a smaller version of her older sister, Patty Polanski had to try to be as nasty as Molly. Or at least, she put on a good show of it, just to impress.

Anyway, when Matt bumped into Patty, he caught her off-guard and she failed to grab him before he tucked and ran. He had, by this time, lost track of the flying-saucer and, because the toggle that controlled the speed of the motors had been knocked back, the saucer was now a silver streak, diving for the courtyard.

As Kris climbed to his feet, he looked up, gasped, then uttered, "Jumping jitterbug!" as he saw his flying-saucer streaking towards the ground. "Matt! The ship!"

More and more children poured out of the orphanage and appeared in the courtyard with each moment, to see what all the ruckus was about.

With Molly making another threatening advance, Matt, still gripping the controls in both hands, dodged away from her and looked up. Panicking at the sight of the saucer racing towards him, he thrust his thumbs against the toggles, pushing both up, hard.

The silver streak whined as it seemed to strafe the now panicking, screaming, ducking and diving crowd, as it shot back towards the sky.

Kris yelled out, "Don't let it get out of range!"

With his full attention on the flying object, Matt was just toggling back both controls and adjusting the direction of the saucer's travel, bringing it back towards the courtyard, when he heard Tic and Talk yell out in unison.

"Matt, watch … !" But no more needed to be said because, at that moment, he felt a vice-like grip on his left wrist – Molly Polanski, continuing the attack.

"Kris!" barked Matt, as he held the remote control out towards his younger brother, in his right hand, while he used his left arm to fend off Molly.

Then, Patty was there between the two brothers, approaching with a menacing look, leaving Matt no time in which to wonder why there had to be two Polanski girls, before he was looking for someone else to whom he could hand the controls.

That's when he saw Tic and Talk standing beside each other as though they were one, which was just about the case, as each was so skinny it took two of them to make one, regular-sized youth. Without time to consider, Matt tossed the remote control in an over-armed motion above his and Molly's heads, towards the twins, calling out as he did so.

"Tic … Talk … catch!"

Tic, whose real name is Mick, and Talk, whose real name is Mark, are identical twins. To describe one, is, therefore, to describe the other, except that Tic's left eye occasionally develops a tic when he gets nervous; and under the same circumstances, Talk tends to … well … talk. Tic's and Talk's clothes hung loosely on their skeleton like bodies. Their large heads had a tendency to seem even larger with their thick-lensed, black-rimmed glasses, which served to magnify their eyes to double the size, making Tic and Talk look somewhat owlish.

And it was owlish that the twins looked now as the remote control soared through the air towards them. Tic's left eye began to tic as he moved towards the object in preparation for catching it, and Talk began to talk.

"You got it, Mick! You got it! It's OK, Mick, you got it!"

And sure enough, Tic made a neat catch of it.

"Good catch, Mick! Nice going! Wow! That was spectacular! Couldn't have done better myself, Mick."

But Tic was distracted from his brother's praises because, at that moment, his rapt focus was on the flying-saucer, now diving towards the crowd in the courtyard for a second time. Even the tic in his eye ceased as, with his eyes wide, magnified by the bottle-like lenses of his glasses, he fiddled with the two toggles, trying to figure out how the thing worked.

With Tic's random jerking adjustments to the toggles, the saucer lurched up then down, and from side to side, but continued to barrel towards the courtyard and, as it appeared to Tic, straight for him. He began to crouch, ready to allow panic to take over in the form of a dive for the ground.

Kris was holding on to Patty's wrist, tugging back to keep her from grabbing Tic when he, himself, caught sight of the saucer.

"Tic, push up on the toggles! Quick!" he yelled, above the mix of excited screams now emanating from the onlookers, many of whom were now scattering.

Some of the crowd squeezed, one after the other, back through the doorway of the orphanage.

For Matt's part, he had now jumped on to Molly's back, his hands clasped over her eyes as she stumbled in circles trying to shake him off.

This was when Jerome Casper – the church's janitor, a tall, slender man with a rich, dark complexion – followed by Rob and Will, exited from the side door of the church to see what all the ruckus was about.

"What on Earth … ?" he began, and would have continued to say, " … is going on out here?" But, at that very moment, he had to duck to avoid the one-foot diameter, silver flying-saucer that shot towards his head. He jerked around to see the object skip once on the church's roof as it raced skyward once again, before uttering, "What on … "

With mouths agape, Rob and Will watched in disbelief. They were seeing one of the mysterious saucers in the daylight, in full view, only this time, with other people witnessing the same thing; including an adult.

Will was especially enthralled, his eyes aglitter with excitement. Any doubt in what he had seen the night before was erased. He now knew the saucers were real. He was sure he was witnessing a real, unidentified flying object; sure proof of life elsewhere in the galaxy. Had it been one of the flying-saucers that had helped him up on to the ledge in the tunnel? He certainly thought so. But if so, why?

With Mr Casper's arrival on the scene, Patty ceased struggling to reach Tic – Kris in hot pursuit throughout – and stood watching the saucer soar upwards. Kris slipped past her, running towards Tic, and grabbed the controls from him.

By the time he was working the two toggles to bring the object under control, it was just a mere glittering speck in the sky.

In the background, Kris heard Talk encouraging him from a hiding place under one of the courtyard picnic tables. "You got it, Kris! You can do it! Get it under control, Kris!"

While Rob and Will stared upwards, they hesitated, and then migrated to stand one on either side of Mr Casper. Looking up, squinting, transfixed on the object now coming back towards him, Mr Casper was astonished at what he saw.

Matt released Molly, slid off her back, and watched the saucer descend. Molly took one last look towards the sky, and with Patty close behind, they both slunk around the corner of the orphanage and were gone.

Talk crawled out from under the table and walked over to stand by Kris and Tic's side. Now calm, Kris directed the saucer towards a landing.

"You did it, Kris! Good going! That's the way! Knew you could do it the whole time!" came Talk's encouraging words, as the whirring saucer set down on the pavement in front of them with a gentle, tiny scrape.

Incredulous, Jerome Casper walked over to where the silver saucer now lay on the ground. Kris stood next to it, holding his duct-taped control-box and stared up at the man curiously. Rob and Will slipped past Mr Casper to stand near their youngest brother. Matt and a number of recovering children came forwards to join the congregation. No one spoke. Still incredulous, Mr Casper moved his gaze from the sleek saucer to Kris.

Kris had never spoken with Mr Casper much beyond a shy greeting. He was captivated as he realised how very alert the man looked: the whites of his eyes in contrast to their dark brown irises and his dark complexion, were pearl-white. The lines on Mr Casper's face combined with hints of grey in his otherwise shiny, black hair to suggest that he was an older man. But Kris had noticed that the janitor always moved around with ease, and that he seemed to work tirelessly to keep the church and orphanage buildings in good repair. So, to him, he seemed young. In fact, Kris wondered now as he looked up at the man, how Mr Casper somehow looked familiar; like a long-lost friend.

"Where on Earth did you get that thing, young man?" asked Mr Casper, interrupting Kris's study of him.

"Yeah, Kris," added Rob in his big-brother, authoritative voice. "Where did you get that?"

Rob and Will were both experiencing profound, emotional swings. Upon seeing the flying-saucer above the church, the two older brothers had thought they were seeing something from outer-space. This had brought them both a feeling of spectacular astonishment, mixed with excitement and anticipation. Now there was a list of new emotions bound to the new mysteries – none of them easy to figure out – the uppermost one being as to how Kris had managed to fly two of the remote control toys at the tunnel last night. For Rob and Will, deep confusion was setting in.

"OK, big brother," said Mr Casper, glancing at Rob, "how about you be a kid for a few minutes and let me ask the questions?" Mr Casper watched Will stoop to get a closer look at the now grounded saucer, and he then returned his gaze to Kris, who was looking up at him with disarmingly bright, hazel eyes. In a kind voice, he asked, "Did you build that yourself?"

They all stared at Kris with bated breath, impressed.

Unsure whether it was safe to smile, Kris just nodded.

Pausing from his inspection of the saucer, Will looked up and said, "It doesn't say 'made in China' on it or anything," and his brows lowered in concentration. He asked Kris, "How did you fly two of these? And how did you get them to the tun … Ow!" Rob had given Will a swift kick on the shin.

Will shot a sore look at his older brother who was sending him a stern look, and realised that he had been about to make a huge blunder by asking too many questions in front of too many people; and worst of all, in front of Mr Casper.

Clapping his hands together, in a raised, authoritative voice, Mr Casper said, "Right, everyone – except for the Roar boys – head to the dining hall. Lunch'll be ready about now."

At that moment the bespectacled Mother Superior, followed by Sister Anne and Sister Chloe, exited from the brick building followed by the remainder of the children at the orphanage.

Sister Anne, an ever-jubilant woman with a beak-like nose, was almost always smiling. But her smile was uncertain as she, Sister Chloe and Mother Superior approached the congregation; a smile diminished by a slight look of concern.

Sister Chloe was the youngest of the nuns at the orphanage. Of light-brown complexion, there was something fittingly angelic about her and her face was free of worry-lines as she stood next to Matt. He looked up and smiled at her, his eyes brightening.

Never one to be left out of a gathering of any sort, especially one in which the children may need to be disciplined, Sister Greta exited the church through a side doorway. She paused to see what the commotion was about before joining the crowd. Everyone was now present.

With wire-rimmed glasses riding low on a soft nose set on a soft, wrinkled face, Mother Superior was the next person to speak. Her voice was rich and seemed to sing the words as she spoke.

"If I am to understand what I have heard the children say … we have been visited by the Polanski girls," she said, with raised brows, "and, a UFO."

Looking over the top of her glasses and smiling, her cheeks puffing up, she looked around at the children, and then glanced down at the saucer before continuing, "The Polanski girls appear to have vanished ... but for once, the UFO is still around for someone of repute to witness its existence, thank God!"

There was silence for a moment as Mother Superior stared at the grounded object. Her eyes then found their way to Mr Casper. Just as he was opening his mouth to speak, Sister Greta broke the silence.

"If the two younger Roar boys have been stirring things up, I have time for more sewing lessons this afternoon."

Mother Superior did not remove her gaze from Mr Casper, as she said, "It does not look like anyone has been being mischievous to me, Sister Greta. And besides, your sewing lessons are of value even to those who have been good. Perhaps there are some children that would, indeed, like to spend time with you after lunch, today."

Sister Greta smiled proudly and nodded enthusiastically.

Still looking at Mr Casper, Mother Superior continued in her singsong voice, "I am sure Mr Casper has some things the Roar boys could help him with this afternoon. Let us have the other children head for the dining hall and we will serve that delicious lunch that Sister Anne and Sister Chloe have prepared for us all."

At Mother Superior's words, Sister Anne and Sister Chloe, arms outstretched, herded the children like sheep across the courtyard towards the orphanage. Sister Greta followed, leaving Mother Superior with Mr Casper and the Roar brothers.

"This is not one of yours then, Mr Casper?" asked Mother Superior, pointing down at the gleaming, silver saucer.

Upon Mother Superior's arrival, having given up the inspection of the toy, Will now gave them his full attention. He shot glances back and forth between Mother Superior and Mr Casper, refusing to miss one detail of their conversation.

Mr Casper shook his head and gestured to Kris, "I told you he was a brilliant lad."

Will glanced at the grounded saucer, then from one adult to the other. A look of surprise appeared on his face. Now, he knew for sure.

Their faces all screwed-up, Matt and Rob worked on catching up with Will and coming to some sort of conclusion.

Kris's careful study of Mr Casper did not waver.

"As I have seen yours flitting about from time to time, during the middle of the night," said Mother Superior, with a raised eyebrow, "I assume, so has at least one other youngster." She lowered her head and gazed over the top of her glasses, which now rode even lower on her nose, down at Kris. "And, I gather something, Mr Casper," continued Mother Superior, "has come up which requires you to bring these young boys up to speed?"

Mr Casper shrugged, and then nodded.

"I knew it!" said Will, as he danced around. "I knew I saw a couple of these things flying around!" He turned to face Rob. "You see, Rob? Mr Casper has a couple of remote controlled flying-saucers. Kris just copied them."

Will felt as if he would burst from the excitement of everything coming to light. It was a feeling similar to receiving a wonderful gift for your birthday, making you want to jump with joy, which was pretty much what the others witnessed Will doing next.

Rob's thoughts were mixed. Nothing was making any sense.

The look on Matt's face showed that he, too, was at a loss about all this; more so than Rob.

Kris's mouth expanded with a slight smile. Now he knew for sure that there was something more to Mr Casper. He was also sure that the silver saucers he had seen flying around the church and the orphanage during the middle of the night, belonged to the janitor. But what were they?

Mr Casper noticed Kris's look. Mother Superior did, too, and grinned.

With humour in her voice, Mother Superior said, "Take them, Mr Casper, and tell them what you must so they don't have to figure it all out on their own."

Mr Casper stooped to pick up Kris's toy, but Mother Superior had more to say. As he stood, tucking the saucer under his arm as he did so, she continued in her singsong voice, "I trust you, Mr Casper, to remember that they are just children."

The Fix-Its

The Roar brothers followed Mr Casper, who carried Kris's ship tucked under one arm, down a long, brightly-lit staircase to the church's basement. They zigzagged through aisles of shelves on which were stored boxes and things like candlesticks, all highly organised and sorted into lengths. As the brothers followed, they noticed that everything was dust free; even the candlesticks were polished to a shine and the floor appeared to be spotless.

They reached a long wall, in the centre of which was a door. Mr Casper opened it and, with Rob in the lead, he ushered the boys through the doorway.

Inside, the brothers promptly bumped into one-another, as Rob, astonished, had stopped dead. The windowless room was brightly-lit, filled mostly with machines and tools, although in the corner, was a couch and a well-padded chair and a large, low table. Like the aisles of shelves, this room was also very clean and neat. In fact, the place was shining from floor to ceiling as though someone had polished every surface. Everything was aglitter.

Mr Casper entered and closed the door behind him. He slipped past the gawping boys and walked to a workbench, where he placed Kris's toy. Watching his young guests, he reached for a wheeled chair, pulled it towards him and sat down.

Knotted together and rubbernecking, the brothers shuffled towards Mr Casper. He chuckled at the look of awe on their faces.

"I've been waiting for a year to have a reason to pull you guys aside." While the others continued looking around, Rob looked at Mr Casper, who continued, "I was kind of hoping your parents would be back by now … "

Will, Matt, and Kris snapped their attention to Mr Casper.

"You know something about our parents?" asked Rob, his voice trembling slightly.

After glancing at their older brother, Will, Matt, and Kris, now hooked, settled their attention on Mr Casper, who was nodding.

"I've been your parents' friend for many years; your father's for even longer. I promised your mother I would keep an eye on you lot while she was gone. But I never thought anything like this would happen … your parents disappearing and all." Mr Casper lifted his brows. "And I know how dangerous life can be."

"Do you know where they are?" asked Rob, a mixture of pent-up sadness and a new sensation of hope affecting his voice.

Mr Casper chuckled and Rob scowled.

"In our entire, vast galaxy," said Mr Casper, "it's easier to know where your parents are not. And I'm very certain they are not here, on Earth."

Not on Earth, each of the brothers thought.

Angrily, Will said, "That's crazy!"

"Yeah," said Rob. "Are you trying to tell us our mother and father are on Mars, or something?"

Putting up his hands, Mr Casper said, "Hold on. It's OK. Give me a chance to explain." He took a deep breath and sighed. "I promise," he continued, "it'll all make sense. But first … Socket … Wrench … come on out here … "

Mr Casper looked towards the other end of the room where there were yet more banks of shelves filled with tools. The boys followed his gaze, each of them startled to see movement.

"From what I understand, you two haven't been as sneaky as you think. I suspect each of the Roar boys here have seen you at least once. And Kris here has made a pretty fantastic model, so he must have seen you plenty of times."

As Mr Casper spoke, from the other end of the room, hovering about four feet off the floor, came two thick-bodied, sleek, silver flying-saucers, both a bit larger than Kris's toy.

Mr Casper watched Rob Roar's sons' eyes grow wider, but not through fear. Their response was pure joy as their mouths gaped in wonder.

"Jumping jitterbug!" uttered Kris.

Mr Casper looked up in thanks and took another deep breath.

As Socket and Wrench approached, the barely audible hum of their motors was hardly noticeable in the still silence of the room. The two objects came to a hover in front of the boys, at about eye level.

"Guys, that's Socket on the left, Wrench on the right."

The brothers were uncertain as to how Mr Casper could tell the two objects apart; the hovering machines looked identical. Their metal surfaces were both shiny and a little clouded, like stainless-steel. With the exception of what appeared to be a map-work of fine, almost indiscernible lines and two elongated oval slits about four inches apart on the outside edge, Socket's and Wrench's bodies were smooth and curved, thick in the middle, and tapered to rounded edges about two inches thick. They looked every bit like little flying-saucers.

The boys thought they knew what the elongated oval shapes were, until both Socket and Wrench blinked, which made the boys jump. Socket drew closer to Kris and blinked again. Kris giggled. Enraptured, he reached for the hovering machine with an extended finger. The others watched along with Wrench.

Startled, Kris took a step back, his eyes having grown wider with further surprise, when, with a 'psssht', sound like a whispering release of air, a small, metal arm extended out from the left side of Socket's body, at the end of which was a splayed hand with four fingers and what looked like an opposable thumb.

Mr Casper chuckled, which drew an uncertain glance from Kris. He motioned to the boy to continue, "Socket just wants to shake your hand."

Licking his lips and hesitating, Kris reached out with his finger. Socket wrapped his little, metal hand around it and gave it a gentle squeeze and a shake. Kris looked over at Mr Casper, who was smiling, and beamed.

"What are they?"

Wrench extended an identical arm and gave first Rob's, and then Will's, finger a squeeze and a shake.

As Mr Casper opened his mouth to answer Kris's question, he paused to smile at the sight of Matt grinning from ear to ear, as Wrench and the boy shook hand to finger.

"R – B – eleven-ninety-twos," he said. "R stands for repair, B stands for bot, and eleven-ninety-two stands for how many mistakes the robot masters made before they got it right. I call Socket and Wrench 'Fix-Its'."

Kris sobered, his ever-present curiosity taking over as he asked Mr Casper, "What's a 'robot master'?"

As the brothers gave their undivided attention, Mr Casper explained: "All robot masters are Mindinee – Mindinee who have been entrusted with the knowledge of designing and manufacturing robots; specifically, robotic brains. Any robot built by someone other than a robot master would just be a trashcan. Also, a robot built by someone other than a robot master would be considered to be among the most egregious crimes against civilised society, and would likely carry a severe punishment."

"Hey, Socket … Wrench, come over to the bench and open up," said Mr Casper, as he waved the fix-its over.

Their little arms snapped closed and the two machines darted to the bench so fast that the boys blinked from the sudden movement and almost missed the action. Then the brothers understood what all the barely perceivable lines on the fix-its were, as, upon touching down on the bench, the saucers fractured along the lines and began to transform: with a quiet hissing sound, two feet and legs extended. The familiar arm appeared, accompanied by a second, opposite the first. A torso formed and lengthened, and a short, thin neck extended from the shoulders, pushing up the elongated oval eyes, which now appeared large on a head that looked like a smaller version of the original saucer body.

By the time Socket and Wrench had finished metamorphosing, they remained identical and stood there on the bench, as two-foot-tall, slender, silver, almost humanoid robots. The Roar brothers stood still, mouths agape, staring in awe.

"Coool!" said Matt, transfixed by Socket and Wrench, who stared back with apparent, equal interest.

The brothers broke free of their awed state, moved closer to the robots, and began studying them with varying degrees of intensity.

Breaking the quiet that had enveloped the room, Kris asked, "What is their source of power?" He stepped closer to Mr Casper with a thoughtful look on his face, "And I don't see any air intakes or an exhaust, so how can they fly?"

Having moved even closer to the robots, Rob, Will, and Matt continued to study Socket and Wrench. They had discovered that the two fix-its were built of a tubular metal, skeleton-like frame, the parts of which met at complex joints that looked as though they could bend in any direction. They had been trying to see inside, in-between the skeletal framework, deep into the impossibly complex, three-dimensional, two-foot-tall machines. But their eyes crossed following the intricacies and their minds became clogged up, trying to make sense of the map-work, of what must have been millions of parts.

Kris's questions to Mr Casper caught his brothers' attention and they looked towards him, each with the same question on their minds.

"How could the robots perform like that?" said Rob.

"Yeah," said Matt, "how the heck did those things fly like that?"

"I don't see any batteries or motors," added Rob.

"Yeah, nothing's making any sense," added Will.

Mr Casper chuckled and said, "You boys are going to have a lot more questions than that." He looked from Roar boy to Roar boy. "But first, I want to talk about your mother and father, and about why we need to get home to Oregon, fast."

The brothers shot confused glances at each other, and then returned their attention to Mr Casper.

"You sent us that e-mail?" asked Rob, his face screwed-up.

It was Mr Casper's turn to be confused. "What are you talking about?"

Rob looked around at his brothers, then back at Mr Casper and said, "We got an e-mail that told us to get home, fast."

His brows raised, Mr Casper's eyes twinkled brightly against his dark skin, which seemed to shine, like everything else in the room, as though everything about the man was spotlessly polished and impeccably cared for.

"How did you guys get an e-mail address? You don't ... ugh ...." He waved his hand. "Never mind. I know you've been sneaking around. It shouldn't surprise me you've figured out a way to access e-mail."

Leaning forwards, knitting his brows and speaking in a more serious tone, Mr Casper continued, "But I didn't send you an e-mail. And I'm the only one that should know about the need to get you boys home. How on earth would someone else know that, let alone your e-mail address?" Mr Casper shook a finger, as though counting the things about which to be concerned. "First, we need to find out where it came from."

"Kris said he can do that," said Rob, as Kris nodded.

"Oh yeah? I suppose that that shouldn't surprise me, either." Mr Casper leaned back in his chair, reclining a bit, his eyes searching the ceiling as though looking for answers there. "We should treat that e-mail like a warning," he said. "Someone knows something I don't ... " Mr Casper's voice trailed off. "And that's not good."

Without warning, Socket and Wrench hopped off the bench and walked towards the far end of the room, where they disappeared behind a row of shelves filled with boxes and assorted power-tools. Mr Casper stood and ushered the brothers to move behind him. As they did so, they peered up at him, confused and afraid.

The sound of knocking broke the quiet, startling Mr Casper and the Roar boys.

His body tense, Mr Casper bravely called out, "Come in."

After a pause, the door slowly opened ...

Sister Chloe, carrying a tray of food and a pitcher of milk, entered the room.

Mr Casper and the boys exhaled simultaneously and, after an awkward pause, rushed to relieve the sister of her burden. With the tray set on the table, Sister Chloe smiled, beaming at Mr Casper and each of the brothers, in turn ...

"Mother Superior said that men and boys can forget to eat; sometimes. There are three flavours of ice-cream for dessert, and plenty of it, so don't worry about missing out. Come and find me when you want some ... OK?"

One would think Sister Chloe's smile could not have expanded more than it was. But just then, it grew even broader, highlighting her youthful face and white teeth. "Enjoy," she said, and left.

They served themselves salad and parmesan-chicken. With the Roar boys on the couch and Mr Casper in the chair, they settled down to eat.

Re-emerging, Socket and Wrench returned to the workbench where they paused and glanced over at Mr Casper and the boys. One of the robots pointed up at Kris's toy saucer. "Bleep-blip?"

Looking at Kris, Mr Casper asked, "Do you mind if they check out your fine work?"

Kris shook his head.

The fix-its leapt, effortlessly, on to the counter and folded to half their height – in a sort of crouch – one on either side of the saucer. Together, they reached out and picked it up. Next to the robots, the saucer looked very much like a toy. Socket and Wrench then set off in a soft series of bleeps and clicking.

With food still in his mouth, Rob spoke, thickly. "You said you would tell us about our parents."

Mr Casper swallowed, and then said, "I will. But first, let me tell you about the reality of life; a reality that only a few, here on Earth, know about ... OK?"

The four boys nodded.

With a tinge of mockery, Rob and Will said, "OK," as though they pretty much knew everything there was to know about life.

"Good," said Mr Casper. He took a deep breath before beginning. "Let's see now ... As far as can be seen from the Milky Way – the galaxy in which the Earth's solar system exists – there are about 125 billion galaxies in the universe. Some say the universe goes on forever and has no defined boundaries. Others go further to suggest that there are yet more universes beyond our own. Our galaxy – the Milky Way – is but only one of those 125 billion galaxies. Are you guys following me?"

"Yeah," said Rob, a little impatient. "But what does that have to do with our parents?"

"Huh … well … everything," said Mr Casper. "And for that reason, it's worth starting with the big picture and narrowing things down to us, here, on Earth. That way you can begin to understand just how small, alone, and vulnerable Earth really is, and why I can't possibly know where your mother and father are."

Impatient, Rob shrugged.

"Anyway," continued Mr Casper, "there are billions of stars just in our galaxy alone; our sun being but only one of those billions. I think you would be hard-pressed to find a scientist here, on Earth, who researches the mere possibility of such things and that doesn't believe in some way, that there must be other, habitable planets in our galaxy … And, in fact, guys, there are over a million registered, habitable planets. There are also others that are not registered but that surely some must know about, and, undoubtedly, millions more habitable planets to be discovered."

The boys had all stopped eating. One after the other, they placed their plates on the table. Mr Casper took a bite of salad and watched his audience as he chewed.

"So, you're saying you know about things living on other planets?" asked Will, doubting it was true.

Swallowing, Mr Casper then said, "Not things, Will; people … humans, like us … and other intelligent beings … and, actually … yes … also creatures you could call things."

Rob, Will, and Matt stared at Mr Casper, not ready to believe it. Rob opened his mouth to speak:

"Where is the planet the Mindinee live on, Mr Casper?" asked Kris.

Of course, it was all true. It all made sense.

Mr Casper studied Kris, surprised, though he knew better.

He replied, "You don't have any trouble believing this stuff do you, Kris?"

Kris shook his head.

Mr Casper grinned, "Good ... Good ... Well, the Mindinee live on a planet called Mindin in a solar system about as close to the centre of our galaxy as you can get without getting cooked ... I was there once when your father and I picked up Socket and Wrench, and another robot your father named Dynak." Mr Casper sat up straight and, with excitement in his voice, continued, "Boys, you wouldn't believe what the night sky there is like. The stars are so close to one another towards the centre of the Milky Way that Mindin's night sky is incredibly bright."

"Can I go there someday?" asked Kris.

Mr Casper laughed uproariously. His laughter subsiding, he chuckled as he said, "You're really not afraid of any of this stuff, are you, young man? You're just ready to jump right in and go for it."

By this time, Kris's infectious curiosity was beginning to work on his three older brothers' scepticisms. Any doubts were seeping away as they began to believe that what Mr Casper was telling them was all very true.

"Anything's better than being stuck in this place," said Will, feeling brave.

Glancing from brother to brother, each nodded in agreement.

Mr Casper eyed the boys, and then spoke: "Huh, you may find that not to be true. But, it's important to have you guys know everything I'm now telling you, because ... "

Mr Casper sat up straight and glanced at each boy in turn, his voice becoming more urgent.

" ... we don't have any time to waste. There's a desperate emergency at hand and our help is needed as soon as possible."

"What kind of emergency?" asked Matt, whose attention had wandered to the two robots still looking over Kris's toy.

"We'll get back to that in a bit," said Mr Casper. "You're not really going to understand the emergency and what we can do about it until you know who your parents really are. Listen, guys ... your parents are not farmers like you've been led to believe all these years ... "

The brothers stared at Mr Casper, at a loss as to what he could possibly say next.

" ... they're galaxy rangers."

Will knitted his brows, concentrating hard on figuring out the meaning of what he had just heard.

Matt's right cheek was scrunched up as he tried to figure out exactly what a galaxy ranger must be.

Kris's eyes gleamed with wonder as he grasped the concept.

Rob was angry.

"One of your mother and father's responsibilities is to represent Earth," continued Mr Casper. "To protect the planet and the surrounding solar system if the need should arise. But a galaxy ranger is much more than that. A galaxy ranger works to ensure peace in the galaxy. Your parents can be called on to mediate in a dispute between planets, or even to protect a planet … or an individual, for that matter. They are both galactic police officers and politicians."

Rob felt himself becoming hot. This was ridiculous!

"No!" he barked, as he jumped up from the couch.

Socket and Wrench looked over from their fiddling with Kris's toy. Rob's brothers, wide-eyed and uncertain, stared up at him.

His voice shaky, Rob continued, "I've seen Mother and Father working in the fields! I've ridden in a tractor with Father! You're playing a trick on us! They're dead, aren't they? Just say so! Why won't anyone just tell us?"

Standing there as he was, Rob began to feel embarrassed about his outburst and self-conscious that everyone was looking at him. But, for almost two years, he had been hoping his father would come home. Then, a year ago, his mother had also failed to return. Now, here comes this maintenance man telling him his parents are galaxy rangers. He'd had enough!

Rob looked over at the robots. Socket and Wrench were staring back at him, unmoving. Even with his doubts, he knew all of it was true. He remembered noticing strange things back home: there had been a mysterious, white helicopter that had made only a whisper as it flew. But he had seen it – usually late at night when there was a full moon, adding light to an otherwise dark sky, or sometimes early in the morning as the sun was rising.

And then there was that time he had wandered far out into the fields with Will – much further than usual. They had seen their father driving the tractor, tilling the land. But when they had waved to him for a ride, he had just waved back and driven on. It had certainly looked like their father driving the tractor; but there had been something strange about his appearance. Oddly, it had not seemed like him. Now, it all seemed like a dream.

Glancing at Mr Casper, apologetically, Rob sat down.

"Sorry," he said. "I know you're telling us the truth ... "

Mr Casper took a deep breath, and then said, "Don't worry about it, Rob. This is a lot of stuff for you guys to take in all at once. I'm sorry I couldn't tell you all this a long time ago."

"How do you know our parents?" asked Will.

"I've worked with your father from the beginning; since the time we met in the marines before he became a galaxy ranger. Your father was an air-jock. I was a mechanic. When your father met your mother, she moved in, they got married, and my repair work doubled." Mr Casper smiled as though a distant memory took him outside the room for a moment.

"I don't remember ever seeing you," said Rob, doubt still remaining in his voice.

"I saw you and Will every once in a while when you were very young," said Mr Casper. "But with the Boargen occasionally stirring up trouble, things got busy and your mother and father were always flying out, which gave me a lot of work to keep the ships in good order. Plus, your father moved the base out to the coast, so, eventually, I was never around." Mr Casper smiled, "But your mother and father always showed me pictures of you guys ... "

"So what's the emergency?" asked Will, now feeling very mature and important.

"Yeah," added Matt and Kris.

Rob remained quiet and observant.

Leaning forwards and grabbing a piece of lettuce from his plate, Mr Casper popped it in his mouth as he sat back in his chair, chewed and swallowed. Then he said, "Since yesterday, distress signals have been sent from a ship that eventually crash-landed on the moon."

He took a deep breath, sighed as he exhaled, and continued, "At first, I thought it had to be your parents. I got pretty excited about it. But the ship is registered to the Peridians; specifically, to the Peridian senator. The signal specifies that there are two aboard – a girl, and a robot."

Mr Casper eyed the brothers. "You boys are going to have to go and get them ... well ... at least one of you, anyway."

Blank faces stared back at him.

"You're going to have to learn how to fly, so you can go and retrieve the girl and her robot from the moon."

Blank stares continued.

"And there's not much time. Their ship is bleeding air."

Incredulous looks returned on the three older brothers' faces. Kris still appeared to be taking it all in his stride, as though he foresaw no problem with learning how to fly a spaceship.

"How?" asked Rob, an edge returning to his voice. "How are you going to teach us how to fly a spaceship? And why can't you go get them yourself?"

"Don't worry about how we're going to do this," said Mr Casper, as he held his hands up to encourage calm. "There is a lot to learn, but there are ways to accelerate the learning process. You'll find out about all that when we get home."

The room was quiet for a moment; then Rob persisted, "So why don't you just go and get them?"

"Yeah," added Will and Matt.

Kris still sat there, listening and absorbing everything.

Mr Casper inhaled through clenched teeth. "Uh ... I get seriously airsick, guys," he said, as he looked away, noticeably embarrassed.

"Yeah, but you could handle a little airsickness to rescue someone ... couldn't you?" asked Kris, eyeing Mr Casper with a slight smirk on his face because he suspected there were more revelations to come.

Mr Casper continued, avoiding eye contact with the brothers.

Mumbling as he spoke, he said, "Well, it's more than just airsickness. I ... I'm prone to panic attacks when I fly." Mr Casper hesitated, and then looked up at the Roar boys. "I can fix anything. But I can't fly. You boys are going to have to rescue that girl and her robot."

It seemed to each boy that there were endless questions to ask, but exhaustion had set in and there was no more energy left in them. It also seemed that there were endless impossibilities. However exciting, the new reality which Mr Casper had shared with them came with a heavy burden. How could they, mere boys, ever really save the girl trapped on the moon?

After a short period of quiet, a whirring sound from across the room drew everyone's attention. Kris's toy saucer was hovering. Socket and Wrench were standing on the bench, watching it.

"Blip-cli-cleek," one of them said.

"Cleek," the other answered, then folded, and took off to join the toy.

Kris jumped up and walked over to stand near the hovering machines. The second fix-it also folded and took off, joining the other and Kris's saucer.

"They're flying my ship!" said Kris, excited.

With Mr Casper and the Roar boys watching, the fix-its flew around the room with the toy saucer for a while, until yawns brought forth the end of a long conversation. Mr Casper would speak with Mother Superior the next day about getting the brothers back to Oregon. The brothers would try to find out the origin of the mysterious e-mail. As Socket and Wrench were having so much fun playing with Kris's flying-saucer, the toy was left with them.

"Have things really come to this, you guys," Mr Casper asked Socket and Wrench later that evening, as the three of them sat lounging on the couch, one fix-it on either side of him, each matching his flopped-down posture. " ... to rely on Rob and Mara's young boys in a time of crisis?"

Socket and Wrench didn't answer. They couldn't. Fix-its were not designed with speech capability. But they loyally remained next to Mr Casper, listening.

"Rob and Mara told me if anything ever happened to them that it was up to me to decide when to bring their children into the fold ... Huh! And a crisis we now have," he said, dropping his head back, resting it on the back of the couch. Socket and Wrench copied him.

"But those boys are still so young," he continued. "How are they going to learn how to fly those ships in such a short period of time, even with KNIAs help ... ? And what about that greedy aunt of theirs? I still can't figure out how that witch managed to get control of the Roar estate. Fortunately, she knows nothing about her brother and what he really is. I guess we should count that as a blessing. But she's going to make it nigh on impossible to get those boys out of here and back to Oregon. And Mother Superior's going to have me on a skewer for this ... Or, maybe not. She's an amazingly perceptive and accepting woman. She probably knows more than she shows ... Ugh ... and the galactic senate is going to think we're dizzy from a lack of oxygen when they find out the new Earth rangers are children."

But Mr Casper knew the galactic senate was of little concern because, though he had never heard of children being galaxy rangers, out there in the rest of the galaxy, children of all ages were doing equally important things. Age was seldom a deciding factor; it was intelligence, maturity, and the will to do it that counted.

It was only here, on Earth, that children were held in status as children, until a certain age. Then again, there were exceptions, even on Earth. But those exceptions were few and far between, partly, Mr Casper suspected, because Earth people had difficulty in understanding that maturity was a lifelong growth. Immaturity did not stop at a given age, and maturity did not start where immaturity left off.

Yes, the Roar brothers were perfectly capable of accomplishing that which would be set before them. But could a basic galactic education be achieved in such short order, even with a mind-link with KNIA? Could KNIA teach the Roar brothers how to fly those spaceships in time to save the girl trapped in her ship on the moon? It had to work. Mr Casper had a feeling that the well-being of the galaxy hinged on rescuing Katia.

To Get Home, Fast

There was no light in Mother Superior's office, save for that cast by the computer monitor which set three young faces, huddled close together, aglow. Kris's fingers raced across the keys as though he was old enough to be an ace typist. Rob and Will watched, trying to follow what was happening on the monitor.

"Wow, Rob, look at him go," whispered Will.

"Yeah, no kidding. Kris. How did you learn to type so fast?"

Kris's fingers continued tickling the keys a little longer. Then he hit the return button, sending the hard drive to work, and rested his hands.

"I've been sneaking on to the computer during the middle of the night since we got here," Kris shrugged and whispered, "so I've had lots of practice. Plus, I make sure the computer is running smoothly for Mother Superior ... "

"I thought you slept like a rock," said Rob, staring with some confusion at Kris, who returned the stare and smiled.

"I pretend a lot."

Hiding in a corner in the hall next to Mother Superior's office, Matt was keeping a lookout. It was his job to alert his brothers should someone come out of one of the nearby bedrooms.

However, it was not the footsteps of a child coming out of a bedroom that startled him, but the sound of someone coming up the stairs. This was a problem, because the door to Mother Superior's office was in plain view of the stairs which meant that there was no time in which to warn his brothers.

He had no plan or diversion when he walked from his shadowed hiding place to the middle of the dimly-lit hall at the very moment that Mother Superior and Sister Greta arrived on the second floor.

Inside the office, code scrolled from the bottom to the top of the monitor.

"What's going on now?" asked Rob.

As the monitor reflected in his eyes, Kris whispered, "I can't find an origination server for that e-mail." He glanced at Will on one side of him and then to Rob on the other. "Whoever sent it hacked into the system. Now I'm trying to see if I can find any trace of the sender, sort of like looking for a fingerprint or something like … "

They suddenly became alert when they heard Mother Superior's voice in the hall. They stared at the door, certain that she would enter at any moment. There would be no explaining this away, that was for sure.

There was no point in trying to run for it either, because there were only two possible escapes, neither of them any good. The most reasonable escape was through the storage room next to the office, but that exit led to the hall. Surely they would be caught if they tried to escape that way. The other, involved certain bodily damage as there was no drainpipe outside Mother Superior's office window.

But they needn't have worried as the door never did open. Instead, they heard a quiet version of Mother Superior's musical voice say, "You see, Sister Greta, it's just our darling Matt stumbling about up here."

In the hall outside the office, Matt strode past Mother Superior and Sister Greta. His arms were raised a bit in front of him and his eyes were open just enough to see where he was going, which was towards the stairs. Mother Superior was smiling. Sister Greta frowned.

"Yes," said Sister Greta, "but what is he doing?"

Mother Superior clasped her hands in front of her, smiled adoringly, and said, "I believe he is sleepwalking, Sister. We should follow him."

Pointing at the space under the door to Mother Superior's office where a light-blue glow could be seen, Sister Greta said, "But Mother Superior, there is a light on in your office."

Grasping Sister Greta by the arm and bringing her along, Mother Superior began to follow Matt. "Oh don't worry about that, Sister. I probably just left that silly computer on. I'll shut it off later, after we've watched over our little wayward sleeper."

In the office, the activity on the monitor ceased. The brothers had been holding their breath. They listened a moment more, then, convinced Matt had saved them, they exhaled at length.

Kris stared at the monitor. Will and Rob stared at Kris.

"Jumping jitterbug," whispered Kris, after a moment.

The room was quiet save for the hum of the computer.

"What is it?" whispered Rob.

The cursor blinked on an empty screen ...

"Kris," Rob pressed, "what's going on?"

Kris was sure there should have been some hint of where the e-mail had come from, even if he could only discover the general region where the system had been hacked into, as would be the case if the e-mail had been sent from a cell-phone.

"Kris!"

"It was sent from nowhere." Kris looked at Rob. "It's just as if it appeared out of thin air ... "

"So that's it?" asked Will, frustrated. "We can't find out who sent the e-mail?"

Kris tapped some more keys. The monitor cleared and the computer began to shut down. Then the monitor went black and the brothers were left in darkness.

Downstairs in the kitchen, Matt opened the freezer door, flooding the immediate area with light. Having heard Mother Superior and Sister Greta follow, he knew they were there in the shadows nearby. Then he heard Mother Superior whisper, "Yes, Sister, I suspect if one can walk in one's sleep one can also eat in one's sleep."

It took Matt some effort to refrain from giggling over his delight at the thought of eating ice cream in his sleep. Why-oh-why had he never thought of this before? But of course, opportunity spawns discovery. And for Matt, he had never before had the opportunity to eat ice cream while he slept. With the freezer standing open, he was now faced with a fantastic set of choices: what flavour should he have?

He reached for the strawberry one.

As Matt savoured his ice cream and his brothers snuck back into their bedroom, 24 of the 307 hours of air which Katia had remaining in her ship on the moon had been spent. Her only hope was for the Roar boys to get home, fast.

Early the following morning, the air was dry and had a slight chill to it, like the feeling you get when you are in the countryside far away from the smog of city life. Except that, as Rob awoke, he could hear the sounds of New York – alive and well. Feeling a tug on his ear, Rob became fully awake and sat up with a start. With deep breaths, heart pounding, and recalling the previous day's events, his eyes adjusted to the morning light and a fix-it came into focus.

It hovered at eye-level beside his bed with a small piece of rolled-up yellow paper clasped in its extended hand. Rob hesitated, figuring it was a note from Mr Casper, and accepted it as the robot pressed it closer. He unrolled the paper and read:

Meeting with Mother Superior this morning.
Any luck with the e-mail?
Mr Casper.

Rob peered up at the fix-it, which now held out a pen in its little, metal hand.

"Now how did you do that?" he asked under his breath, noticing that the pen was the one from the drawer in his nightstand.

He took it and added his own message to the note:

No luck.
Rob.

As Rob rolled up the yellow square of paper and handed it back to the fix-it, Will stirred, opened his eyes, and sat up. He stared, sleepy-eyed, at the hovering robot, which turned, extended its other arm, and waved its little hand at him. Will waved back as he yawned.

With Matt and Kris still fast asleep and Rob and Will watching, Socket, or Wrench – neither brother could figure out which one it was – headed for the open window. To their astonishment, the fix-it vanished. But not completely, as the boys could still see the faint blur of the saucer shape in the air, as though it was a ghost. As the fix-it left, Rob and Will rushed to look out of the window. They could just discern a shimmering shape soaring up and over the church roof. Then it was gone.

Later that morning, Rob was sitting on the couch in the recreation room watching TV, when Will came in carrying a thick turkey sandwich with lettuce hanging out. Noticing what Rob was watching, Will stopped, abruptly, his sandwich poised in front of his open mouth.

"Why are you watching that?" he asked.

Without looking up, Rob sniffled, and then answered, "She could make it if someone would help her."

Will lowered his sandwich a bit, revealing a stunned face. Staring at the television, he was bewildered that Rob was watching something so stupid: a lost, dirty, tired-looking collie lay on a city pavement. Streams of people rushed by as though the dog was invisible.

"Rob, that's a really lame, ancient TV show. Mother and Father probably watched it when they were children." Will knitted his brows, "Ooh, scary thought. And it was just as lame then, too. You've got to get with the times, brother, and watch something new and hip … you know, something with too much violence for young, impressionable minds like ours; or something with degrading humour. Then you'd be laughing instead of lame … which could translate to sissy if you're not careful."

Will took a deliberate bite of his sandwich, and, with his mouth full, continued, "Besides, those old shows are too predictable. Lassie always makes it, usually with one-minute left to the end, just before the tunnel collapses or the boat blows up." He swallowed. "Did you know, Lassie's really a male dog?"

As Will took another bite of his sandwich, Rob looked up at him in disgust and said, "What do you mean she's a male dog? Lassie's a female."

Will shook his head as he swallowed. He said, "They used male dogs to play the part of Lassie because male dogs have fuller, more brilliant coats." He pointed at the television. "'She's' a 'he'."

As the collie raised its head and whimpered at someone who had finally noticed it lying there, Rob reached for the remote and turned the television off.

"Do you have to ruin everything?" he said, sneering at his brother. "I'll never be able to watch that show again without thinking I'm watching a complete fake."

Giggling, Will said, "The show is a complete fake."

"Well, next time, just keep it to yourself."

Will shrugged and took another bite of his sandwich. As he chewed, he said, "We should have stayed behind before this." He held up his sandwich. "We have the run of the kitchen."

As they often did during the summer, the sisters had taken the children to the park for a picnic. Though the Roar brothers always looked forward to picnic days – because it usually meant plenty of watermelon and a game of baseball – today, they had stayed behind, hoping they would soon find out that they would be going home. Everything else paled in comparison to that possibility; even watermelon and baseball.

Will swallowed, then cocked his head and asked, "Where're Matt and Kris?"

Rob snapped, "Upstairs."

Scowling as he thought about it, Will said, "I didn't see them upstairs."

"They're in the storage room."

Will opened his mouth to say something, but all that came out was a weak, "Oh."

Upstairs, in the storage room, the two younger Roar boys sat on the floor next to a copy machine, above which was a window that provided a view of the street below. There were two entrances to the small room: one from the hall, and the other from Mother Superior's office. Every wall surface not occupied by a door or the window was lined with shelves, floor-to-ceiling, filled with everything from cleaning supplies to pencils and erasers.

"Go fish," whispered Kris, smiling greedily down at the selection of matched cards he had accumulated, which numbered to substantially more than Matt's winnings.

Matt worked his lips into a distorted shape, making his nose wrinkle. He whispered, "Hiding with you is too frustrating. Next time, I hide alone."

Next door, Mother Superior's office was dominated by the presence of a large, thoroughly distressed desk, which, from its appearance, could have been around since Jesus himself. A computer rested on one end of it; the only hint of the room existing in the twenty-first century. Like the storage room next door, this room, too, had shelves lining the walls. These shelves, however, were filled with very old books; some of them large enough to give anyone second thoughts about trying to pick one up.

Mother Superior was seated behind the old desk in an equally old and creaky chair. Behind her were two windows with a view of the same street as the window in the adjacent storage room. Bright daylight glared into the otherwise dark room making it difficult for Mr Casper, who was sitting in an old, winged chair opposite, to see Mother Superior, as everything facing away from the windows was in shadow. This placed him in a sort of spotlight, which made his position under Mother Superior's careful scrutiny even more uncomfortable. He imagined this was her intent, and he was convinced that she was paying attention to every expression that crossed his face, even when he was pan-faced.

" ... and there is no one else on Earth, Mr Casper, or on any other world that can help that poor girl?"

"No, Mother Superior. The fact that she and her robot have fled in to this system, suggests that there are problems elsewhere. In any case, I would not risk forwarding the distress signal."

Mother Superior's chair creaked as she stood. She walked around the desk, and towards the other end of the room.

"I know they are extraordinary boys, Mr Casper. I knew that even before you arrived and … and, challenged my belief in my God."

"I … "

"No. Don't apologise. Learning that there are millions of inhabited worlds out there, many of them inhabited by humans like, or similar to, us, and many others, inhabited by beings other than humans … challenged my faith, initially. For a short time, I despaired I would never recover the original strength of my convictions. But I did. Indeed, my faith is stronger today than it ever has been and I have you and those boys, and all the … knowledge I'm privileged enough to hold in confidence, to thank for it."

Mother Superior took a deep breath and strode back to her desk. Perched on the corner of it opposite the computer, she looked down at Mr Casper. His dark skin glistened from the sweat on his brow. The natural light pouring through the windows caught the scattered, grey hair woven in his dark hair.

"I'm encouraged by my belief that God has set the Roar boys' destiny in motion. And, I'm honoured that I may play a part in that destiny, however slight my role may be. But my faith might be shaken again, Mr Casper, if any of those boys come to harm."

Mr Casper could see profound concern reflected in Mother Superior's eyes.

"As you've said, Mother Superior, there is something extraordinary about those boys. And no wonder. They are the sons of an amazingly capable man from Earth and an equally amazing woman from the planet, Mindin, of whom … "

In the storage room, the card game ended abruptly. Matt and Kris stared at each other, saucer-eyed, completely blown away. Their mother was from Mindin? Well, then that made the Roar boys …

" ... but I can't deny I'm not concerned," continued Mr Casper. "I am concerned I'm making a mistake."

"Good!" said Mother Superior, as she stood. "I'm glad you said that. Too much confidence on your part would make me even more worried." Mother Superior eyed Mr Casper, then asked, "Will your fix-its continue their vigil over them?"

Excitement sparked in Mr Casper's eyes as he sat up straight. With great conviction, he said, "Even if the fix-its aren't with them, there will be more technology to keep those boys safe than stars in the sky. Now, what about their aunt?"

Raising a finger, Mother Superior said, "Aunt Hilary will be a major obstacle which will not be easily negotiated. Getting this by her will require stealth, fortitude, patience, and God's will."

Mother Superior stabbed her finger towards the storage room door and added, "Shall we have the Roar boys join us for an 'approach the Aunt Hilary' tactical meeting?"

Mr Casper smiled, unsurprised that Mother Superior had also seen the subtle movement of shadows visible through the space under the door.

Walking over from the desk to the storage room door, Mother Superior said, "I hope, Mr Casper, that amongst the things you teach the Roar boys, will be a finer technique of sneaking around."

Grasping the handle and squeezing, she whipped open the door.

Sitting on the floor, each holding cards fanned out in one hand, Matt and Kris found themselves looking up at Mother Superior standing there in the open doorway.

Of course, the timing of Mother Superior's arrival at the storage room door was unfortunate because it was at that moment that Matt was finally winning a hand. For Kris's part, he was not a bit worried about losing the game. Rather, he was concerned that he and Matt were now in big trouble. He wished now, that he had let Matt handle the surveillance solo, because Matt was better suited to getting into trouble. And, Matt always seemed to be able to come up with something to do, or say, during an uncomfortable moment, such as this, when he said, "Go fish," as though that would convince Mother Superior that he and Kris were just playing an innocent game of cards; and that it was purely coincidence that they happened to be doing so in the storage room next to her office during an important meeting.

Mother Superior raised an eyebrow at the two blonde-haired boys looking up at her with bright, hazel eyes, working their audience with their best rendition of pure innocence.

"Why don't you two 'go fish' for your brothers and bring them back here," she said. "Mr. Casper and I would like to speak with you."

Matt needed no further prompting to give up the game. He took his chance for escape from, or at least the postponement of, a thorough scolding. In perfect sync, he and Kris gathered up the cards, stood, and, without looking back, rushed to the hall door, flung it open … and were off at a run.

Soon after, all four Roar boys were gathered in Mother Superior's office, standing side-by-side, according to age and height. Mr Casper remained seated in the winged chair, looking confident. Mother Superior had returned to the creaky chair behind her desk and was looking rather less confident because she knew the Roar boys' aunt well enough to know that there would be obstacles to come.

"I wonder," began Mother Superior, "in what form my relationship with you … children … will be in the future. I see, four young boys standing before me. Yet, Mr Casper tells me that you are bound for an adventure that, some would say, belongs only in a fantasy story."

The boys exchanged hopeful glances.

"Yes," said Mother Superior, "I am willing to let you go. But we must now convince your Aunt Hilary, who cares very much for your well-being."

Mother Superior raised an eyebrow as she looked over the top of her glasses at each brother in turn; each of them betraying with varying, humorous looks that they thought rather little of their aunt's version of caring for their well-being.

"Do either of you have any ideas for persuading your aunt to let you go?" she asked, with a slight smile.

Rob looked down the line of brothers, each of whom looked back at him. Late into the night, they had discussed the problem of convincing Aunt Hilary to let them go home. Although they knew that their aunt had cried poor, passing that off as the reason she had dumped them unceremoniously at the orphanage; the truth was far different.

Aunt Hilary was their father's sister. With her brother's disappearance, she believed that she was the first in line to usurp control of the modest wealth he had accumulated; regardless of the fact that the boys' mother, Mara Roar, owned everything equally with their father. That had been the reason for the grief Aunt Hilary had brought upon Mara when Rob had gone missing. If Aunt Hilary had been able to prove that Mara was the cause of Rob's disappearance, then Mara would have been jailed and Aunt Hilary could have taken control of everything.

One can imagine Aunt Hilary's difficulty in containing her glee upon Mara's subsequent disappearance almost a year later. A minor investigation had been conducted which had been cut short by Aunt Hilary's insistence that Mara had been suicidal and that it was a good thing that their mother had not harmed the children before, by jumping into a nearby ice-cold river, or off the edge of a two-thousand-foot precipice, for instance. Aunt Hilary had moved decisively to have herself named as the executor to the Roar estate, which had given her complete control over Rob and Mara's land, house, money, and the boys. Then, she delivered the Roar brothers, with one small suitcase each, to the orphanage, taking her own two spoiled daughters on a two-month vacation through Europe and moving into a much finer apartment, not too far from Central Park, on her return.

Rob looked at Mother Superior and nodded.

"Well, as far as we know, no one has been working the fields at the farm," said Rob. Mr Casper smiled – the youngsters were sharp witted. "And," Rob continued, "if that's the case, then we could suggest to Aunt Hilary that we should go home for the summer and learn how to work the fields, so we can make the farm profitable rather than the unproductive land that it is at the moment."

Mother Superior and Mr Casper both looked proudly at the older Roar boy, with a glint in their eyes. Standing upright, his blonde hair neatly parted to one side, Rob looked every bit the lawyer, pleading his case.

Again, Rob looked down the line of his brothers, who nodded their approval, before smiling at Mother Superior with a mischievous grin.

"I mean, after all, we wouldn't want Aunt Hilary paying for our upkeep with her own money. We could help out with the exorbitant cost of raising us by working ... you know ... pay our own way."

There was a smile blossoming on Mother Superior's face. Then, she burst into uproarious laughter as she leaned back in her chair, the chair creaking as she did so. Immersed in quiet, body-jiggling laughter, Mr Casper slowly shook his head as he rested his cheek in his hand, his elbow propped on the arm of the chair. The boys exchanged uncertain glances.

"Don't look so concerned, youngsters," said Mother Superior, her laughter subsiding. "Mr Casper and I are laughing because I scolded him earlier for suggesting the very same thing you just did." The brothers exchanged glances again. "Only, Rob, when Mr Casper suggested it, the plan did not sound quite as innocent as your eloquently introduced version. Bravo."

Hesitant smiles of relief appeared on the boys' faces. Still resting his head in his hand, Mr Casper gazed with pride at them. Mother Superior stood from her creaky chair and walked to one of the windows, looked out at the street below for a moment, and then took a deep breath as she turned back to face the others.

"I'm walking a thin line between being a responsible Mother Superior on the one hand, and a responsible citizen of the galaxy on the other."

The brothers exchanged quick glances, and then looked at Mr Casper, only just realising that Mother Superior knew everything. Mr Casper smiled back and nodded for them to pay attention.

With a grave look, Mother Superior continued, "No matter what you may think of your aunt, she is your legal guardian and you should respect her for that. It is advantageous for you boys to remain in your Aunt Hilary's good graces. If not, she could make things difficult."

Mother Superior returned to her seat. The chair's creaking echoed in the pervasive silence of the room as she sat, with no outward appearance of even having noticed the noise.

"It is my responsibility to keep you – as you are still children – on the straight and narrow. That is the best way I can protect you. It so happens that I believe in what you must do." Raising a finger, she continued, "but I expect you to always be mindful of your responsibilities here on Earth."

The brothers nodded, solemnly, each beginning to understand the immense responsibilities settling on their shoulders.

As they lay awake that night, unable to sleep, each wondered what the vast galaxy was really like. And each wondered if they would ever find their parents in that vastness.

Mr Casper also lay awake much of the night, thinking. That night, Katia had just 259 hours of air remaining. That meant that Mr Casper had just short of eleven days to get the Roar boys to Oregon and to teach them how to fly spaceships. And, as if he needed more to worry about, there was that mysterious e-mail to consider. Kris had said that it appeared to come from nowhere. In the complexity of the galaxy, something like that was as much a mystery as it was disturbing. Mr Casper wondered whether whatever had taken first Rob Roar away, and then Mara, might also take away their sons. Could the girl on the moon be an elaborate trap?

Aunt Hilly and Her Hat

There had never been an invitation for the Roar brothers to visit Aunt Hilary for dinner or anything like that, so they had no idea what her apartment looked like on the inside. But if they had ventured to guess, they might have assumed she lived in a rather garishly-decorated place; an assumption that would have been correct.

Even though they had never seen the inside of Aunt Hilary's apartment, Rob and Will had, however, seen the outside, as they had stopped by whilst on one of their middle-of-the-night excursions. She lived in a very nice apartment building, on a very nice street, in a very nice part of New York; not too far from Central Park. And, of course, that is not a place where one short on funds, as Aunt Hilary always claimed to be, would reside.

There were three obvious reasons for the lack of an invitation for the Roar boys to visit their aunt's apartment: firstly, being that Aunt Hilary was sure that boys – especially such uncultured wretches as the Roar boys – would destroy anything they touched. Secondly, that she was sure that they would plead to move in with her. And thirdly, that even though she thought the brothers were idiots, she was paranoid that they would become smart enough to figure out that she was spending their parents' money by the bucket-load, and someday be able to do something about it.

Like her apartment, miles away, garishly decorated is how Aunt Hilary was dressed upon her arrival at the orphanage the next day; the day after a very long night. For the brothers, it had been a night of endless anticipation, contemplation and dreams of home and beyond, and of their mother and father. For Mr Casper and Mother Superior, it was a night of endless worrying – or at least, a night of no sleep worth mentioning. Aunt Hilary on the other hand, had slept just fine.

She was not a fat woman, but was perpetually swollen, creased in the middle by her custom-tailored, tight, gaudy clothes. Tipped slightly to the front and to one side, was an equally gaudy hat. Her tailor was obviously insane. As for Aunt Hilary's state of mind ... well ... what one saw is what one got.

As Aunt Hilary clumped down the hallway lead by Sister Anne, she was followed by what could best be described as two small clones: her twin daughters, Lucy and Martha.

At fourteen years of age, Lucy and Martha were each miracles; not in the usual way one thinks of a child as being a miracle, but ... you see, they were ... well ... never mind. It's as simple as this, really: like mother like daughter.

As Aunt Hilary approached Mother Superior's office, although she held her head high with her nose in the air, it was obvious that she was not happy about being in such a place. Lucy and Martha walked to the rear of their mother, one on either side, also with their noses held high. As they passed Tic and Talk, who had positioned themselves in order to spy on events for the Roar brothers, the sisters lowered their bulbous noses just long enough to glance sideways and sneer in contempt at the two scrawny boys; the Polanski sisters were outdone here.

In stark silence, the Roar boys waited, lying on their beds staring at the ceiling. Elsewhere, Socket and Wrench were seated on the counter in the workroom below the church, watching Mr Casper busy himself by pacing back and forth. Mother Superior, meanwhile, was ready, sitting behind her desk, plying herself with unimportant paperwork, when there was an expected knock at the door.

"Enter, please," she said, her musical voice strong and authoritative to those standing in the hall outside.

Earlier that morning, Mother Superior had said to Sister Anne, "There are times one must set the stage to keep the advantage. To allow the Roar brothers' aunt to dominate the meeting this morning could reap an unsatisfactory outcome in this case, and not just for the boys. And, in this case, that would be failing to serve the greater good."

Sister Anne did not know to what 'greater good' Mother Superior referred. But that mattered not, as Sister Anne liked it best when good prevailed. And she was also not above enjoying seeing someone like the children's aunt squirm a bit in God's house. Noticing the three visitors swallow nervously, she smiled, knowingly.

Sister Anne swung the door wide, stood to one side, and gestured for the three guests to enter. Looking stony-faced, her nose still in the air as though she used it for guiding herself by smell, Aunt Hilary entered with her daughters at her heels.

"Thank you, Sister," said Mother Superior. "Would you please ask Mr Casper to join us when he can?"

"Yes, Mother Superior," said the sister, as she left, pulling the door closed behind her.

Back in the hall, Sister Anne stood against the door with her eyes closed, and took a deep breath. As she exhaled a long, relaxing breath – her prayer for everything to turn out as it should – there was no way of knowing that her prayer included a young girl trapped in a spaceship on the moon.

Katia was, at that very moment, listening to Keb explain that there seemed to be a problem with the Ranger's availability. A message from Earth mentioned only that action was being taken to ensure their rescue but that there would be a delay.

Opening her eyes, Sister Anne looked down the hall, noticed Tic and Talk still standing there looking as nervous as ever, and whisked towards them.

Mr Casper knew someone was coming when Socket and Wrench hopped off the counter and walked to the back of the room to hide amongst the shelves of tools. He hoped, of course, that it was good news, or at the least, a request for him to join Mother Superior in her meeting with Aunt Hilary. He opened the door, and there stood Tic and Talk. One of them – Mr Casper could never tell the two apart – with a clenched hand, raised in preparation to knock. Both boys were out of breath. They stared at him, flustered and speechless.

"Well?" he snapped, uncharacteristically.

Startled, looking up at Mr Casper with wide eyes, made larger by their thick-lensed glasses, they stepped back. Then, still a little out of breath and stumbling over his words, one of them said, "Sister … uh … Anne … uh … asked us to come and … and get you. She said uh … to tell you that … uh … Mother Superior," he breathed, "is ready for you."

Mr Casper pulled the door closed as he exited the room and, with Tic and Talk following at a jog, he walked briskly through the maze of shelves towards the stairs.

Minutes later, he was standing in Mother Superior's office, facing Aunt Hilary and her daughters for the first time. Aunt Hilary peered at him, somewhat aghast. The two smaller versions of the strangely-dressed woman were staring at him as though they thought he might be an alien.

Mr Casper wondered at that moment how much fun it would be to arrange a meeting for the aunt and her two daughters with a gorp. A gorp is a creature from the planet Moxy which has a tendency to expectorate a most nasty, thick gunk at intruders; a substance not too much unlike the slime left behind by a snail or a slug. Only, the slime from a gorp remains semi-fluid for weeks; it is not easily removed and the gorp can produce quite a lot of it in one spit.

"Ms Peskin," said Mother Superior, "this is Mr Casper, the man who has offered to watch over the boys should you see fit to send them to the west coast for the summer."

Mr Casper leaned forwards, placing his weight on one foot, and reached out to shake Aunt Hilary's hand as he said, "Plea … "

But the look of revulsion on the woman's face intensified as he leaned in and, without moving her feet, she managed to tilt away from his hand as though she had already heard of a Moxy gorp and assumed he was one.

Clearing his throat, Mr Casper stepped back and gazed awkwardly at the two chubby daughters, who continued to look at him as though they were quite sure that he was, indeed, an alien.

It was quiet as everyone stared at Mr Casper. Mother Superior raised her brow. Aunt Hilary hesitated, and then dragged her gaze from Mr Casper to Mother Superior, before leaning over the big desk to speak to her in confidence. Mother Superior leaned in close, to listen, her chair creaking as she did so.

"He's black!"

The complete silence was broken only by Mother Superior's creaking chair as she leaned to one side to peer past Aunt Hilary and over the rim of her glasses at Mr Casper, who appeared to be doing his best rendition of a wax likeness of himself.

After a moment's consideration, Mother Superior returned to her former position with a creeeak! She looked up at Aunt Hilary and said, "Yes ... he is, isn't he?" She leaned in closer to the woman, creeeaking again. Knowing that there are times when one must work with narrow-minded people, she thought it wise to divert the conversation. She said, "Mr Casper is a fine caretaker. He has been very handy with the repairs around here. And I hear he is quite good at farming," Mother Superior whispered as she continued, "and he works for board and lodgings."

The part about working for room and board was true, because Mr Casper had, indeed, requested no fee for his services at the church, other than to eat the fine meals the sisters cooked and to have a comfortable bed in which to sleep. It was the part about board and lodgings that clinched it for Aunt Hilary. This Casper character would be a cheap farmhand and babysitter.

It's a good thing Mr Casper is a gentleman. And it's a good thing he was committed to getting the Roar boys home. Otherwise, having been dismissed by Aunt Hilary with a flip of her hand, he would have promptly, without hesitation, arranged a speedy trip for Aunt Hilary and her offspring to Moxy to meet a gorp. She had grilled him with questions such as: "Do you know how to farm?" and "Can you teach four stupid boys how to work the farm so I don't have to provide for you also forever?" before hiring him. Furthermore, she advised him that he would be paid nothing but board and lodgings for the work expected of him.

As Aunt Hilary had rented the Roar family home to a woman and her two children – otherwise known to Aunt Hilary as a peasant and her rats – the Roar brothers could not return to live in their own home. Therefore, the next option was for them to live with their grandmother – known to Aunt Hilary as her insane old mother – who lived in a small house not too far from a small, boulder-strewn mountain which poked up in the middle of the farm.

Having finally consented to them staying with the old grandmother for the summer, she decided that the boys would have to share one small bedroom; Mr Casper could sleep outside with the animals for all she cared. After all, it would be a good way to keep an eye on the four truant brothers, as the crazy old grandmother would unwittingly report everything the little farmhand-wretches were doing. And what they were supposed to be doing, of course, was making Aunt Hilary more money by making the farm productive.

Later, Mr Casper was in his room packing and using words stronger than the Moxy gorp with each item he thrust into his suitcase. At the same time, in the main hallway on the first floor, the Roar brothers stood against the wall in a sort of military line-up as though awaiting a troop inspection.

Aunt Hilary, Lucy, and Martha, followed by Mother Superior, reached the first floor and Mother Superior gave the boys a hidden thumbs-up; their hearts skipped. Aunt Hilary would have walked straight past the brothers without saying a word, except that she stopped abruptly having just passed Will and, without so much as turning her head, ordered in a snobbish tone, "Tell the nuns to cut your hair. You look like a slob."

Lucy and Martha snickered.

Each brother was thinking pretty much the same thing as Matt and Kris had, of course, told Rob and Will what they had heard whilst hiding in the storage room. Knowing that their mother was from the planet Mindin helped now, as each of them smiled slightly at the thought of their Mindinee mother returning to straighten things out with Aunt Hilly.

Like a parade of colourful circus elephants, Aunt Hilary, Lucy, and Martha clumped-clumped-clumped down the hall, out of the building, and towards a waiting taxi.

It is at moments like these, that a person may wonder at the timeliness of what would otherwise have seemed like completely natural changes in the weather except, in this case, for the extremity of the change. A stiff breeze kicked up very suddenly – actually, it was quite a gale – and disrupted the orderly exit by almost blowing the aunt and her daughters off their feet. This caused the three to have to do a little dance to maintain their balance, which, as one can imagine, was quite a hilarious sight. The wind blew Aunt Hilary's colourful hat away, down the street – never to be seen by her again – and relentlessly rearranged their hairspray stiffened hair so that by the time the aerated threesome reached the cab, they looked as though they had been hit by lightning, or otherwise electrocuted. Their hair had turned into giant cotton-candy-looking tangles, perfect for nesting birds.

Inside, Tic and Talk had joined the Roar brothers at the window. Bunched up, looking out, they watched as Aunt Hilary and her daughters struggled to stay afoot. At first, the boys had some difficulty containing their snickers, but then, in spite of Mother Superior's presence, they lost all restraint and broke into side-splitting laughter. They sobered only enough to duck out of sight as Aunt Hilary glanced towards the orphanage before following her daughters into the cab.

Mother Superior remained poised, though with some effort as her cheeks flexed to keep a smile at bay.

As the taxi drove away, laughter turned into gleeful cheers, congratulatory shaking of hands and hugs all round. Mr Casper appeared at the far end of the hallway holding up five aeroplane tickets.

Later that night, in her office, out of sight of the children, Mother Superior would share a more tension-relieving laugh with the sisters as she told them of the heavenly wind that had cleared the pavement of its debris.

The Roar brothers were going home. But by that evening as they tried to get some sleep in preparation for flying out in the morning, Katia also lay sleepless, aware that she had just ten Earth days before her ship would have no air left.

The following morning, the Roar brothers and Mr Casper drove away in a taxi, leaving behind a fanfare of well-wishers, including hugs from Mother Superior and the sisters and the gifts of a plastic compass and a small flashlight from Tic and Talk.

As the taxi moved along the city streets, each brother was reminded of their arrival in New York two years before. Their faces had been plastered to the car window, looking out at the endless maze of streets with their endless rows of buildings, the throngs of people, and the thousands of cars, trucks, and buses. With their arrival being preceded by the disappearance of their mother only a couple of weeks before, the experience of moving to New York had been doomed as a dismal one. The first miserable days had turned into miserable weeks, which, in turn, had developed into miserable months.

But as time had passed, the Roar brothers' resilience came through and their moods had improved. Matt and Kris had taken to enjoying the attention that the sisters gave them, especially that of Sister Chloe – she was the nicest – and Rob and Will had discovered the drainpipe outside their bedroom window and the subsequent freedom which that path of escape provided. Of course, they knew now that the fix-its had helped them a few times. They might otherwise have had a few serious injuries ... or worse.

Though New York would never be home, there were good memories associated with the orphanage, and they would miss it; a little at least. But they would not miss the oppressive humidity of the summer months and they would not miss the constant noise, even if they had become used to it by now. They would not miss the fear of running into gangs of thugs while exploring the city. They would not miss the feeling of being under Aunt Hilary's thumb. And – not that the girls rated as high as Aunt Hilary on the scale of unpleasantness – they would also not miss the Polanski sisters.

They were stopped at a light when Rob said, "I think someone's following ... "

"Don't!" said Mr Casper. "Don't look back, not all at once. And, when you do, don't look directly at him. I noticed him outside the orphanage yesterday."

"Who is he?" asked Matt, as he pretended to watch a motorcycle drive by, but managed to catch a glimpse of a man wearing a dark suit in a black car just one car behind them.

"I don't know who he is yet," said Mr Casper. "Just pretend you haven't seen him."

After a moment's silence, and pretending not to see their follower, Kris said, "I snuck into Mother Superior's office last night and sent a reply to that e-mail."

A brow raised, Mr Casper said, "Tell me you didn't say something like ..." he shrugged, "we're on our way."

Kris giggled as he said, "That would have been kind of stupid." Sobering, he continued, "I told the sender that the e-mail came through all garbled and that he could send it again. I wrote a bug and attached it to the message which will track the reply, if there is one."

Mr Casper patted Kris on the shoulder and said, "Brilliant."

By the time they reached the airport, their follower was nowhere to be seen. It seemed to take forever to check in. Then they had to get through security. Mr Casper went through unmolested. But the toy saucer in Kris's knapsack caused great concern, so the highly trained security staff performed a thorough check of all four Roar brothers' bags. And, as if checking the boys' bags missed qualifying as a superiorly professional, sophisticated, and advanced security tactic, the very wise and thorough security staff captain decided that a check of the brothers themselves was in order.

Mr Casper stood by, smiling broadly at the sight of the four youngsters standing side-by-side spread-eagled, thinking, if airport security only knew who they were searching. Of course, they were searching Earth's future galaxy rangers.

It was during the spread-eagled search that Rob noticed the man in black standing in a corner, almost out of sight. He passed his observation on to spread-eagled Will, who, in turn, passed it on to spread-eagled Matt beside him, who then passed it on to spread-eagled Kris, who was following every detail of the search with rapt interest.

They mentioned their sighting to Mr Casper on their way to the gate. He had also seen the man. The search of the Roar brothers' bags had not been a random one, as Mr Casper had noticed that several pictures of Kris' toy saucer had been taken.

By the time the five travellers had boarded the aeroplane, what with the memories they would carry with them for evermore of the stone-faced security guards searching the suspicious-looking boys and all, they were in high spirits as they found their seats and stowed their bags. Mr Casper took an aisle seat. Kris sat next to him, with Matt at the window. Rob and Will took seats in the row behind, although no one had taken the aisle seat next to them.

The man in black was not seen boarding the plane. But the relief felt over his absence was short-lived. Mr Casper looked around as though he had just noticed he was inside an aeroplane. His usually rich, dark skin suddenly drained and became rather dull. Mr Casper's hand trembled slightly as he fumbled in his shirt pocket. Pulling out a small bottle, he gazed at it, then relaxed and breathed a sigh of relief.

During this brief moment of the evident fear showing on Mr Casper's face, the four brothers had stopped all activity to watch him. Rob and Will peered forwards over the backs of the seats, wondering what a panic attack looked like and what they should do about it if it was.

Mr Casper had explained to the boys that the bottle was filled with an elixir that would knock him out for the duration of the flight; longer if he was not awakened. That was what the stuff in a smaller bottle he had given to Rob was for. Upon landing in Oregon, Rob would open the bottle and hold it under Mr Casper's nose which would revive him.

Mr Casper now looked supremely confident as the plane, its engines winding up, was pushed back from the gate on to the tarmac. He nodded to the brothers and uncapped the bottle. It was at that moment that a flight attendant breezed by and knocked his elbow, sending the small, open container flying, where it landed on the floor at Matt's feet.

A look of utter panic crossed Mr Casper's face. Eyes wide, Matt quickly unfastened his seatbelt, lunged forwards, and grabbed the bottle off the floor. Mr Casper looked agitated as the boy handed it back to him. Returning to his own seat, Matt stared at the distraught man. Breathless, Rob, Will, and Kris watched as Mr Casper stared at the bottle, and then looked around at them.

"This ... this was the only one I had left," he uttered, in a shaky voice. He looked again at the bottle, said, "God, I hope there's still enough," and downed what remained of the liquid.

It was not enough elixir to knock him out. But it was, however, enough to give him the giggles. As flight 192 flew from New York to Portland, a funfest developed at seat 17C as Mr Casper went from being dopily mellow into bouts of hysterical laughter.

Upon the first signs of his hilarious state, the Roar boys had decided that they needed to make it look as though he was responding to their jokes, and otherwise conversing with them. One hour into the flight, however, this task had become quite tiring, as there were other things they could have done during an exciting aeroplane ride, like eating the airline food that everyone complains about but eats anyway. Therefore, the brothers agreed to divide the remainder of the flight into half-hour-long 'Mr Casper' watches.

It was two hours into the flight when Kris noticed Mr Casper pull something that looked like a tiny cell-phone out of his shirt pocket. The man giggled incessantly as he pushed a series of buttons. Kris thought that it was probably a bad idea for Mr Casper to be pushing buttons on an electronic device during a time of delirium. He reacted quickly, pulling out an interesting airline magazine from the pouch on the back of the seat in front of him, opening it at a picture of a gorgeous beach with a happy couple walking along it, and thrusting it in front of Mr Casper. Mr Casper immediately dropped the electronic device – showing just how well advertising works – and Kris grabbed it.

Kris looked around: Mr Casper was cooing at the picture in the magazine. Matt was asleep and Rob and Will were playing cards. And the passengers sitting nearby, having decided that Mr Casper must be a New Yorker which explained how he was acting, were all now occupying their time. That left Kris feeling alone as he returned his attention to studying the little device.

The calming effect of the magazine worked better than Kris could have hoped as, without warning, Mr Casper dozed off and began snoring. Then there was a tapping on the window besides Matt ...

Socket, or Wrench – he couldn't tell which – was outside, keeping pace with the plane, inches from the window, looking in and waving at him with its little, metal hand. Not knowing what to do, Kris smiled, waved back, then abruptly reached across Matt and yanked down the shade. Then he shot darting looks around to see if anyone else had noticed the robot.

Only Rob and Will had, as the fix-it was then tapping at their window. Panicking, Rob yanked the shade down and looked at Kris with a 'what do we do now' sort of look.

The fix-it refrained from visiting other windows. Instead, it tapped again on the window next to Matt. Kris nudged Matt awake, took another quick look around, and then raised the shade a little. Rob did the same with the one next to him. The boys crowded around their two windows enough so that it would have been impossible for the other passengers to see past them.

Kris held up the little communicator for the fix-it to see and gave the robot a thumbs-up. The robot returned the thumbs-up.

It was at that moment, that the brothers saw the second fix-it flying erratically high above the aeroplane wing, as though it was only just keeping up with the plane and struggling to do so. Only this fix-it, was wearing Aunt Hilary's colourful hat which, of course, explained its erratic flight.

The second fix-it descended and, unfolding, it landed on the wing. With both hands, it gripped Aunt Hilary's hat as it struggled to walk, leaning into the incredible wind as it did so. But the speed at which the jet was travelling and the resulting air-stream rushing over the wing finally got the better of the robot and the hat was ripped from its grip. The fix-it stared back as though mourning its loss, watching the spot of colour fall behind, then turned to look at the brothers and gave the closest thing it could to a shrug.

"Aaah!" a woman screamed. "There's something on the wing!"

The brothers all waved their hands for the robots to go away.

After the panic-stricken passenger had been convinced by the captain that the boys were correct about it being the sunlight reflecting off the wing, the remainder of the flight was uneventful. The elixir having finally had its intended affect, Mr Casper remained asleep until the plane was pulling up to the gate and Rob held the open bottle under his nose.

Upon waking, Mr Casper had no memory of his lack-of-elixir state and the resulting in-flight fiasco. Later, as they collected their suitcases, the brothers told him in great detail about everything that had happened. Mr Casper, of course, was mortified over his drunken behaviour, and shocked when the boys told him that he had called the fix-its, and that one of the passengers had seen one walking on the wing, after which Aunt Hilary's hat had been blown off its head. But none of it seemed to matter as much now that they were in Oregon and home was only a four-hour drive away.

A Kooky Grandmother with Cookies

With each boy occasionally switching the suitcase he was carrying from one tired arm to the other, the Roar brothers followed Mr Casper to a lower level of the airport car park. Once there, Mr Casper stopped and looked around, trying to remember where he had parked.

"You left a car parked here all this time?" asked Will, astonished, as he, too, stared into the endless sea of metal hulks.

Mr Casper set down his suitcase and patted at his pockets, then stopped, looked at the boys, and in his own defence said, "I didn't know I was going to be gone for so long. Which one of you has my communicator?"

Turning so his knapsack faced Mr Casper and cocking his thumb over his shoulder, Kris said, "It's in the outside pouch."

Unzipping the pouch, Mr Casper reached in, pulled out his communicator, and began tapping a series of buttons. The guys figured that maybe he was calling one of the fix-its to help find the car. But a fix-it was unnecessary as, upon punching the last key with an exacting gesture of finality, Mr Casper looked up. At that very moment, there was a whistling call echoing from somewhere in the car park. It sounded like someone whistling for a dog.

Looking down at the boys, who each gave him a curious look, Mr Casper shrugged and said, "I didn't think it would be a good idea to have the car come to us. Someone might notice it driving around without a driver." He looked out across the car park, smiled, then continued, "I love it when computers have a sense of humour."

Stooping to pick up his suitcase, Mr Casper glanced at each boy and then started across the car park in the general direction of the whistling car. As he walked, he said, "We better get there and quieten that thing down before the place is full of dogs."

One after the other, the brothers picked up their suitcases and, leaning awkwardly to one side to balance the weight of their burdens, they followed at a brisk walk. The whistling persisted; a shrill echo.

With the weight of their bags and the car's incessant whistling, it seemed to take forever before they saw a long, white SUV with tinted windows; it was a vehicle that dwarfed the other cars around it … and none of the other cars could call a dog.

A man wearing a suit and tie and carrying a briefcase walked by, staring at the whistling SUV. Walking a fast, straight line to the vehicle, Mr Casper nodded as he passed him. Turning to look back as he walked, the man was startled by the brothers who, one after the other, said "Hi" as they walked by in quick succession.

"OK. OK," Mr Casper whispered, harshly. "You've made your point. You called, we came."

The whistling persisted.

Mr Casper continued severely, "Quiet now! You're drawing attention to yourself!"

The whistling stopped, abruptly. Mr Casper looked around to find the curious man watching from the next row of cars. Waving, he smiled at him. "Everything OK over here," he said.

Mr Casper returned his attention to the SUV and the man turned and made a hasty retreat.

Opening the SUVs rear hatch, Mr Casper tossed each suitcase in, one after the other, as it was handed to him, caring little for the order of things. As he closed the hatch and moved towards the driver's door, the brothers split up, two on either side of the SUV, and walked along its length. Because they simply had to touch the vehicle's body – as there was something odd about it – each boy discovered how very dirty it was. After all, it had been parked at the airport for two years.

As Mr Casper settled into the driver's seat, the brothers climbed in; Rob in front with Mr Casper, Will behind Rob, Matt behind Mr Casper, and Kris in between Will and Matt. The guys were quiet, alternating between staring at the dirt on their hands and staring at each other, feeling a little lost. Mr Casper glanced beside him at Rob and then turned to look back at the others.

"Well don't look at it like it's toxic," he said. "It's only airport grime. Just brush it off on your jeans."

Mr Casper turned back to face the steering wheel and reached out to push buttons on the unusual dashboard.

As the Roar boys brushed their hands off on their jeans, the dash lit up and the vehicle came to life with an almost imperceptible hum. This prompted the brothers to look around and notice that the inside of the SUV was different to any car in which they had ever been. In fact, it was more like the inside of a futuristic aeroplane. And unlike the outside, the inside was very clean.

Then, startling the brothers a bit, the seats contracted, moulding to each boy's body, making each feel almost weightless. They were all, instantly, very comfortable.

"Wow, cool," said Matt as he joined his brothers in looking around for seatbelts.

"No seatbelts, guys," said Mr Casper. "Each seat has its own restraining field, like the reverse of a repulse field. It'll hold you in whatever position you choose, even in an accident. That's why your seat is so comfortable. It lends a feeling of weightlessness."

"What's a 'repulse field'?" all four boys asked at once.

Mr Casper looked beside him at Rob, and then turned to look back at the others.

"It's just what it sounds like," he said. "It's a field that can repel just about anything fired at whatever the field is protecting."

"So, will my seat's restraining field also keep something out?" asked Kris, looking down at his seat.

Mr Casper nodded and faced forwards as he said, "Yeah, like if one of your brothers tried to punch you. But not something fired by a weapon. That would require a lot more energy."

"Well," said Rob, "what if we were in an accident and a piece of the car broke loose and came at us?"

Shifting the vehicle into gear, Mr Casper turned to look out of the rear and began backing out of the parking spot. He shook his head and said, "The vehicle itself has a repulse field. Not many things on Earth can hurt us in here, especially not an accident with another vehicle." Having backed out and stopped, Mr Casper smiled, and said, "You guys like country music?"

The brothers all shrugged and nodded. It had been a long time since they'd heard country music, as one was unlikely to hear that sort of music in New York. Mr Casper twisted back and pressed a button on the dash. Country music filled the cab, and they were off.

Before long, they gained some distance from Portland, before leaving the Cascades behind as well. They travelled across dry country, through croplands, wild grasslands, and over dry, rocky, hilly country towards Harney County. Mr Casper had turned off the music and cracked open the windows so the only sound in the car was that of rushing air and their passage over the road.

Approaching home as they were, the four brothers were feeling an almost forgotten peace. But it was a strange mixture of happiness and sadness. Mr Casper could understand the boys' quiet moods, for he also felt a certain disjointedness, returning after what had become such a long time away.

"Mr Casper," said Kris, breaking the relative quiet, "you said it took one thousand one hundred and ninety-two tries to make Socket and Wrench. Did you mean that?" The other three boys tuned in to listen.

Mr Casper peered in the rearview mirror at Kris. "Is that what I said?"

"Mmm," Kris nodded.

"I was just kidding then. The robot masters are always making improvements to a design. Eleven-ninety-two is probably just the upgraded version."

"Oh," Kris nodded.

As it appeared that Kris was preparing another question, Mr Casper continued to divide his attention between the road ahead and the rearview mirror, waiting. Rob, Will, and Matt, used to Kris's endless curiosity, also waited.

"Mr Casper?"

Knowingly, Mr Casper smiled, "Yes, Kris."

"It doesn't seem like a robot should need to blink, yet Socket and Wrench do."

"Mmm," Mr Casper nodded. "With all those moving parts, fix-its are very complex robots. They require constant lubrication. That's what they're doing when they blink." He drummed his fingers repeatedly on his thumb. "They're collecting moisture from the air. And from that, they manufacture the lubricant they need."

"Wow," said Rob, "that's awesome."

Will and Matt agreed.

Kris squinted, concentrating. "What if the air is dry," he asked, "like it is in Oregon?"

Shaking his head, Mr Casper answered, "That doesn't matter. Robots store plenty of reserves throughout their bodies. But they're always topping-up the supply anyway."

Satisfied for the time being, Kris again said, "Oh."

One after the other, the brothers returned their attention to the scenery outside.

Mr Casper's gaze lingered on Kris's reflection in the rearview mirror for a moment. Then he returned his full attention to the road ahead. As he drove, the list of problems that must be solved before they could rescue the girl on the moon flooded his thoughts. First, he would have to figure out how to keep the grandmother convinced that the boys were working on the farm while they were actually being groomed to rescue Katia. And second, was the nagging question as to whether the young boys could be taught how to fly in such a short period of time. Even if it was conducted by KNIA.

And then there was still that mysterious e-mail. Mr Casper was sure there would be no reply. He was also sure there would be no luck in tracing it. And what of their mysterious shadow? Mr Casper had first caught sight of the man outside the orphanage two days ago. Then he had followed them to the airport, and, whilst there, he had managed to have the Roar boys searched and have photos taken of Kris's toy saucer. As careful as Mr Casper had been, things seemed to be unravelling. Did it all lead to one thing? Or was it all purely coincidence?

Another hour had passed. Kris and Matt had fallen asleep. Mr Casper glanced beside him at Rob, then back at Will, and said, "We're coming up to the town of Narrows. After that, it won't be much longer before we turn off on the road to the farm. You guys want to stop in town for dinner?"

Will nudged Kris and Matt awake. They all agreed they should eat in town. Mother Superior had cleared their arrival with their grandmother, but from what everyone knew about the old woman – she was apparently a little senile, or something – they decided that arriving well fed would be a good idea.

The local diner had a reputation for serving the best burgers in Harney County, so they each ordered one, with a plate heaped with fries, for dinner.

The sun was low in the sky when they turned on to a dirt road that would lead them up and over a hill towards the western horizon. Soon after, Rob spotted two objects flying towards them from the south. Socket and Wrench appeared alongside the SUV, much as they had with the aeroplane, only this time, their only concern was for the Roar boys and Mr Casper to see them.

As the vehicle moved along the road, stirring up a wake of dust, the fix-its, one on either side, flew just above and to the side of the hood. One of them reached out with a little hand and appeared to sample the dirt coating on the SUV. It then appeared as though the robots nodded to each other in agreement. What happened next was a thrill to watch. As the vehicle continued to race along, the fix-its passed over every inch of the body, leaving a shiny surface in their wake. It became clear to each boy now, as to how the church and the orphanage were always so clean.

"How did they do that?" asked Will, astonished.

"Yeah," added Matt as he craned his neck to look outside at the vehicle's newly polished body, "how?"

Mr Casper chuckled. "Robots are sources of tremendous amounts of power," he said. "Some of them can focus that power in exacting ways called a manipulation field. The fix-its are designed for the specific purpose of repairing and maintaining, and cleaning is part of maintaining. They have the ability to use their manip' field to pluck a microscopic speck from the most sensitive surface without disturbing a thing. That's basically what they just did to the outside of this vehicle. They plucked the specks of dirt off, and did so with amazing speed."

"Hey," said Rob, "is that how one of them got my pen out of my drawer without me seeing it?"

"Yep, that's how," Mr Casper nodded.

"Mr Casper," said Matt after a moment, "how do you tell Socket and Wrench apart?"

Glancing back at Matt, Mr Casper returned his attention to the road ahead. With humour tingeing his voice, he said, "I can't tell them apart. They're exactly the same. I just call them Socket or Wrench and they both answer to either name."

The brothers glanced at each other, dumbstruck at first, then they shrugged and giggled.

Will looked ahead, watching the fix-its keeping pace with them. "We saw the one that delivered the note all but disappear. How do they do that?"

"Oh, well, that's called cloaking," answered Mr Casper. "It's another sort of field, using the same technology as the repulse field, the manipulation field, and the restraining field. The cloaking field disturbs the light reflecting off the body's surface, mixing things up to confuse its appearance. An object with a cloaking field can just about disappear. It doesn't work as well in a lit environment, but at night, or in space where the background is usually dark, a ship – or a fix-it for that matter – can virtually disappear."

They crested a low hill with tall, golden grass as far as the eye could see on both sides of the dirt track and Mr Casper pointed forwards. Ahead, was a small, white house set amidst an oasis.

Socket and Wrench flew away. Except for the sound of the vehicle rolling over the dirt road, all was quiet as the Roar boys craned their necks to see ahead. The brothers knew they had seen their grandmother from time to time, on rare occasions, but none of them could remember her. Only now, it was as though they had never met her and each of them felt very nervous. Each of them also began to wonder why they had so seldom seen their grandmother, as her little house was within an easy drive from where they had lived.

As they neared the place, though the quaint little house with shutters had never been home, somehow home was exactly what it looked like. It felt that way, too, in each boy's heart, as they pulled up next to a white picket fence.

They were all climbing out of the vehicle when they heard a sweet, high-pitched voice call out, "You're here! All of you! And I've baked some cookies!"

It was Grandma Roar, walking along the brick path from the house to the driveway, her arms outstretched in preparation for the first hug.

She seemed anything but 'kooky'. Or at least, that was how Rob saw it as she wrapped her arms around him and squeezed. Grandma was a tall, slender woman, and walked tall as though she was much younger than her grey hair – pinned up in a bun – and soft, slightly aged face, suggested. She was a lot like Mother Superior, only without glasses, and rather than a habit, she wore a long, flowered dress and a white apron with frills around the edges. She looked every bit like the perfect image of a grandmother from an advertisement in a home and garden magazine.

"Oh look at you!" she repeated, as she hugged each boy in turn. When she reached Mr Casper, she stopped for a moment to study him, and then moved forwards while saying, "Oh and you can have a hug, too, Jerome," she said, as she hugged him. "And some cookies, if you've been a good boy on your trip ... "

Ha, if she only knew about the flight, thought Rob.

As they followed Grandma to the house in single file, with Mr Casper taking up the rear, she spoke over her shoulder, "Isn't my home just beautiful? I never have to do anything to it, not even to weed the garden. It's as if little elves turn up in the night and keep it all pretty for me."

The boys all looked back at Mr Casper and mouthed, "The fix-its?"

Mr Casper nodded and looked around the yard with pride. As Grandma walked past some roses she reached out with a loving touch and caressed a yellow one as they arrived at the front door.

Inside, the little house was as clean and neat as the outside. And it smelled fantastic, with at least two tantalising smells of good cooking. As they made their way to the kitchen, two extraordinarily large healthy-looking cats – one was gold with orange stripes and the other was caramel-coloured with dark brown paws – arrived, slaloming around and rubbing up against the visitors' legs. As the boys kneeled to pet the cats, Grandma introduced the felines. "This is Tiger and Lion. They are the sweetest little things," she said.

'Little' was a huge understatement. With their keen eyes, they looked as if they could take down a small deer. However, the two cats were, indeed, very affectionate, as they began purring in appreciation of the attention.

"Now," said Grandma, "I've made you boys a delicious stew with dumplings."

That was the first tantalising smell.

"And I've made you some chocolate-chip cookies for dessert."

That was the second tantalising smell.

As the setting sun burned the tops of the mountains in the distance, the guests ate their second dinner of the night. One would think that two dinners would be a bit much, but as they all finished substantial helpings of the delicious stew, it seemed after their long day of travelling that two dinners was exactly what the doctor ordered.

After dinner, a large plate of cookies and a pitcher of milk filled the centre of the table. Grandma settled into her chair with the very large Tiger on her lap and she looked lovingly at each boy in turn, as each took a cookie. As Rob had thought earlier, his brothers and Mr Casper were thinking that Grandma was no 'kook', for as she watched them, there was a sharpness in her eyes that suggested there was something more about her than just being another sweet old lady and a great cook.

From where he sat with a nearby door cracked open, Rob could see into an adjoining room where there was a computer, behind which were shelves full of books. The computer was on, and streaming up the screen were strange characters in groups that looked like words; a foreign language perhaps, or a code of some sort. Whatever it was, though he could see it well enough, the text was unreadable. Rob shot a surprised look at his grandmother, a look that went unnoticed by all but her. She smiled back at him. Could it be, Rob wondered, that Grandma had sent the mysterious e-mail?

"Well," began Grandma as she looked down at Tiger, who looked much too large to be a lap-cat. Smiling dearly and stroking his head, she went on, " … now, Hilary said something about you boys coming out here to do some gardening or to mow some lawns, or whatever it was she said."

The four boys glanced at Mr Casper, who looked back at them and shrugged.

"Frankly," she continued, "I don't know what your aunt is talking about. She's such a city dweller … isn't she? … Thinking the countryside needs to be mown." Grandma looked up. "She is such a great aunty that she's concerned that you're well cared for and that you have enough to do. But things just seem to take care of themselves around here, so I don't think you'll need to worry about any yard work. When she calls to see how you're doing, I'll tell her everything is just grand and that you're out there doing what you came here to do." She smiled, "How's that?"

The boys and Mr Casper looked around at each other, shrugging and nodding, trying to appear unsurprised and as though what Grandma had said was a most reasonable thing to do.

"That … uh … that sounds just fine, Mrs Roar," said Mr Casper, as he looked around at the brothers and then back at Grandma. "In fact, we thought perhaps we might not be around here much and that we might do some travelling around; see the sights, do some camping maybe, but you could tell Aunt Hilary that … "

"Now that sounds just grand," said Grandma, standing as she placed Tiger on the floor. Walking into the kitchen, she continued, "No point in hanging around here doing nothing but playing checkers and reading boring books. No sir. Boys need to get out and explore." Confused, the brothers stared at Mr Casper. Grandma's voice became hard to hear, as though she had stuck her head in a cupboard. "Just be careful where you camp. There've been quite a few tremors recently."

Mr Casper shrugged at the brothers, then gestured an 'I don't know' with his hands. It all seemed too easy. Everything Grandma was saying could very well be interpreted to indicate that she knew all about everything.

There was much banging around going on in the kitchen during this time, then Grandma called out, "Your father – now I wonder where he's gone off to – and your mother ... " A symphonic clanging of pots and pans drowned out a few words. " ... so perhaps you boys should go look for them ... " Bang-Clang-Clong. "Anyway, your father keeps camping gear out in the shed here. Always seems to think having a few extra things stashed around in different places is a good idea. Don't know why. Guess that's the boy scout in him. Always prepared he is. So's your mother. No one on Earth like her."

After a bit more banging in the kitchen, there was complete silence for a moment. Then, Mr Casper and the boys were startled when Grandma poked her head through the doorway and said, "You know, I've completely forgotten where your mother is from." There was a blank look on her face as she thought about it. Then her face brightened, and she continued, "When you boys get a chance, perhaps you should go and look up some of your relatives on her side. Bet they'd love to meet you." Grandma looked around at her guests and added, in a stern voice, "Well don't just sit there! Bring those cookies in here and we'll pack them for your trip." She disappeared back into the kitchen and the clanging and banging resumed. "And bring that pitcher of milk, too. Goodness! What, does it take a woman to get a man moving around here?"

Grandma sent Rob and Will out to the shed to get the camping gear. It looked like there was more in the shed than just the average camping equipment, but they did not take the time to get a close look; it was dark now and though neither wanted to admit it, both got a little spooked by the still, night air.

Later that evening, Grandma rushed them out, inviting them to stop by as often as they wanted for a hot, home-made meal. As they reached the SUV, she asked the boys to remind their father when they saw him, to visit his dear old mother more often. Grandma smiled and added that the boys should also tell their mother to come by for tea sometime. She then kissed and hugged each farewell.

Back in the SUV, they all remained quiet, trying to figure out how the dear old lady could be so 'kooky', or whether she knew about everything that was going on.

The farm had very much become a lawn that had not been mowed for two years. The dirt track they drove along was so narrow that it was more like a path and the four-foot tall overgrowth on either side brushed against the sides of the SUV. Mr Casper had turned on all the vehicle's headlights. In addition to the powerful headlights were floodlights that, when not in use, folded into the roof. So the road ahead of them and the fields to either side were illuminated in a brilliant, white light. Outside the beam of light was total darkness, as if outer space began there.

Socket and Wrench joined them again, flying in and out of the lit area. At one point, they saw a large, grey coyote on the track ahead. In the fringe of the light, its eyes glowed red as it looked straight at them before slipping into the overgrowth. Although the drive seemed long, it was exciting. And although the brothers had yet to learn where they were going, they were free from the orphanage and their adventure had begun in earnest.

Then, ahead, was a gleam of silver reflecting back at them. Socket and Wrench raced forwards, and by each fix-it's mini-floodlight, the robots could be seen buzzing around a building, flickering in and out of view like giant fireflies.

As they drew closer, a huge, metal structure – a giant shed of sorts large enough for storing farm equipment – came into view. In fact, that's what the Roar boys figured they would find inside: farm tractors and other equipment. But as they got closer, something seemed wrong about the shape of the building. Then the brothers heard Mr Casper say, "This doesn't look good, guys."

As they pulled up, the vehicle's lights illuminated in crisp detail the large, dark boulders and rubble scattered around, partly covering the building. The corrugated-metal roof looked as though it was partially collapsed. The huge building was built up against a massive, monolithic rock outcrop. It was a section of the side of this outcrop that had collapsed. It appeared that the tremors Grandma Roar had mentioned had been severe enough to shake some rock loose.

With the SUV parked up, its lights shining on a door larger than one would think necessary to drive a tractor through, Mr Casper got out of the vehicle and headed towards it. The Roar boys filed out, stood staring for a moment, and then followed Mr Casper to an entrance door to the left of the larger one. In one complete motion whilst landing, the fix-its unfolded and walked to meet them.

The seven of them stood there in silence. No one made a move. Mr Casper and the robots just stared at the door as though waiting for someone to open it from inside. Then, Mr Casper looked down at the fix-it closest to him and asked, "Can you fix this?"

The fix-it looked up at Mr Casper, made a sort of shrugging motion and emitted tones that sounded like 'I don't know'. Then it returned its attention to the door and kicked it.

A green light came on and scanned Mr Casper from head to toe. Then, with a quiet 'psssht', a small, green, lit keypad appeared from the wall next to the door.

Mr Casper glanced down at the fix-it, who looked up at him, chirped, gave a nod of finality, and then resumed staring at the door. Glancing around at the Roar brothers, Mr Casper said, "Remember that, boys. Sometimes, brute force gets results."

He tapped a series of keys on the lit pad. With a hiss, the door opened. Mr Casper entered, followed by the fix-its, then the brothers. Except for the vehicle's lights shining through the doorway, it was dark inside. Then, two beams of light, one from each robot, scanned the vast space, illuminating the farm tractors parked alongside opposite walls. There was a wide path down the middle between the tractors to the other end of the voluminous structure. Where the building met the rock outcrop, the roof had partially caved in and there were small boulders and mounds of dusty debris piled up against the rear wall. The tractors parked closest to the cave-in were covered with rubble. Two of them looked damaged.

Taking a deep breath, Mr Casper said, "This is not good."

Socket and Wrench sauntered off to investigate.

"It looks like only two of them are damaged," said Rob.

Mr Casper shook his head. "It's not the tractors that are the object of my concern, Rob," he said. "There's a door buried behind that rubble. And that door is the only way into the cavern, and the only way to get the helicopter out."

"Helicopter?" asked Will, after a moment.

Looking down at Will and then around at the others, Mr Casper said, "Since we had to see your grandmother first, I figured you boys could use the helicopter to get to the new base on the coast. It would be better to have it there anyway, in case we need it. But now we're in a bind because, by now, Katia has only about two hundred and eleven hours of air left; just less than nine days. Wasting another day driving to the coastal base is not good use of our time … " he trailed off, "or hers."

As Mr Casper had explained to the Roar boys who Katia was and the severity of the risk to her life, they clearly understood that any potential for wasted time needed to be faced with an air of urgency.

Mr Casper took another deep breath which, quiet as it was, sounded loud.

"Yeah," said Will, wondering what all this about a coastal base was, "but … "

"Socket," Mr Casper interrupted, "what about that air vent?"

One of the fix-its folded abruptly, turned off its light, shot past Mr Casper and the boys, and flew out of the door.

Turning and walking to the wall between the big door and the doorway through which they had first entered, Mr Casper punched in a code on another green-lit keypad. With a long hiss, the big door slid open.

Flying through the newly-gaped opening, the fix-it returned as abruptly as it had left. Hovering beside Mr Casper, it produced a holographic image of a vent with a grid cover that looked like it was made from very thick metal. Next to the vent, was a keypad like the one they had used to open the doors. As Mr Casper and the Roar boys watched, what looked like a solid rock cover closed over the vent and the keypad was gone.

Eyeing the fix-it, Mr Casper asked, "Can you get in?"

Still hovering, the fix-it performed the equivalent of shaking its head, "No."

"Can I get in?"

The fix-it again shook.

"Did you ask the computer at the main base?"

The fix-it nodded.

"And no luck?"

He looked away before the fix-it shook 'No' a further time.

Mr Casper eyed the pile of rubble at the other end of the huge shed.

"See what you two can do with that mess. The boys and I have to get some sleep," he said to the fix-it.

Turning, he walked outside and Socket flew to join Wrench, who had already started moving rocks. The robots exchanged clicks and bleeps as the brothers stood watching, each boy thinking that perhaps they should help. But then, the robots started firing bright orange beams in bursts at the rubble. What sounded like sharp pops was followed by scattering fragments of rock, amidst a thick cloud of dust.

"I don't think we can help with that," said Rob, as he turned and walked out, followed, one after the other, by his brothers.

Laying out on the ground the space-age equivalent of cowboys' bedrolls, some distance from the noise of the robots at work in the shed, Mr Casper and the Roar boys settled down under the starlit night sky. As they lay on their backs waiting for sleep, a slight, warm, dry breeze stirred the night air.

Rob sat up and looked over at Mr Casper. "Mr Casper, how well do you know our grandmother?"

"Not that well," he answered, glancing at Rob. "I didn't even know where she lived before your father finished building that little house for her a few months before he disappeared. Why?"

"I was just wondering if maybe she sent us that e-mail."

Mr Casper laughed, "Not likely, Rob."

Rob did not agree with Mr Casper, but let the question go and asked, "What about that guy that was following us?"

Mr Casper glanced at Rob again and said, "I suspect we'll see him again sooner rather than later. But by then, I should know who he is. All I know now is that he's taken an interest in you guys, and Kris's toy saucer. I suspect he's looking for a fix-it but doesn't yet know it."

Rob and Will exchanged stares. That gang in the tunnel might have gotten a good look at Socket and Wrench and reported it.

It was quiet for a while until Matt said, "Mr Casper?"

"Yeah, Matt."

"When Kris and I were in the storage room listening to you and Mother Superior, you mentioned our mother." Mr Casper turned his head to look at him. "It's true about our mother, right?"

Mr Casper answered, "I didn't want to overload you guys with too much in the beginning. Sorry you heard it like that. A slip of the tongue. I gather you've already told Rob and Will." Matt nodded and Mr Casper returned to gazing up at the stars. "Well, guys, your mother is, indeed, a Mindinee."

"That's where the robot masters are from. Right?" asked Matt.

"That's right," said Mr Casper. "In fact, that means you boys have relatives on that world."

"Wow, cool," said Matt. "That means some of our relatives are aliens."

"I think Grandma Roar might be an alien, too," said Will.

Everyone laughed except Rob. The foreign text he had seen on his grandmother's computer begged for an explanation. But even if Grandma Roar was not the sender of the mysterious e-mail, she was no less a mystery, at least to Rob.

And All Fall Down

The next morning, Rob was the last to wake up. Alert, he sat up and looked around to see everyone was gone. He crawled out of his sleeping bag, slipped his shoes on, tying them, and hopped to his feet. The first thing he noticed was that the rock debris had been cleared from the roof and the ground around the metal structure and there was now a huge pile at the edge of the field.

"Wow," he said, under his breath.

Hearing voices echoing inside the building, he headed off to see if the cavern door was open. Inside, his brothers and Mr Casper were standing in front of the newly cleared, but closed, cavern entrance. His footsteps echoed as he walked along the wide, tractor-lined aisle, and he noticed the concrete floor for the first time. There had been too much debris on it the night before.

Rob was fully immersed in a yawn, when he looked up and noticed small streams of sunlight slipping through splits and holes in the crunched corrugated roof as he reached the others.

Through his yawn, he managed to squeeze out a tired, "Can we get inside, now?"

Will, Matt, Kris and Mr Casper, rested but dishevelled from their night's sleep, without looking at Rob, collectively said, "No." They stared at the door, which would not be opened by sheer will-power alone. Socket and Wrench were there, too, also staring at the door. One would have never guessed by looking at the two fix-its that they had worked all night moving a small hill of rubble.

"Oh," Rob began, "wha … "

"The door's jammed, Rob," said Will, glancing back at him. "We can't get in."

"Oh, well what about that vent?"

"There's a cover that closes when the vent is approached," said Mr Casper. "This is an old base so although there's a keypad up there, the method for getting in that way – even if it is possible – isn't stored in the coastal base computer."

Socket and Wrench turned abruptly to look out through the large open doorway. Then, in one fluid movement, they folded their robot bodies to become saucers and began flying towards the door. But then, without warning, they dropped, clunking to the floor as though they had lost power, startling Mr Casper and the boys who turned to see what was up.

Remembering how the robots had responded just before Sister Chloe had arrived with dinner the night they had met the fix-its, the brothers watched the doorway. They expected to see someone enter. No one did; only glaring sunlight flooded in.

But then, there was a hint of movement. A mere suggestion of a shadow of a creature the size of a dog or a coyote. Puffs of dust were stirred up just outside the doorway. Something on four feet was walking next to the building.

Then, close to the ground, a dark-complexioned face peered inside. It was not, however, the face of a dog or a coyote. It was a boy. He rose and stood in the doorway. The glaring sunlight made a shadow of him until he took a few steps in. He wore baggy khaki trousers, with oversized pockets, low on the legs. Bulky boots bunched the trousers up at his ankles. An oversized, faded blue shirt that looked like it could be his father's hung below his hips and a faded red baseball cap with some sort of insignia on it was pulled low, all but hiding his face.

It looked, for a moment, as though the boy was going to run away. Instead, he waved to someone outside and was joined by a tall, slender, dark-complexioned girl wearing blue jeans and a tank-top. A canvas bag like an overgrown purse hung via a long strap from her right shoulder. They all stood still and watched as the newcomers approached, side by side. None of them could think of anything to say in the face of such unexpected company.

"We know how to keep the rock on top of the hill from closing," said the boy, as he and the girl came to a halt before Mr Casper and the Roar boys.

They both looked to be of African-American decent with medium-brown skin. The boy was about Will's age, nine years old, though with his baggy clothes, it was difficult to tell for sure. His faded red baseball cap had the NASA insignia on it. The girl appeared to be the boy's sister and about twelve years old. Her eyes were big and bright, and her hair long and thick.

Uneasy, Mr Casper chuckled, "Wha … "

"Are those the things we saw flying around?" the girl finished, as she pointed at the fix-its. As her brother eyed the Roar boys, she looked up at Mr Casper and continued, "I was watching one of them earlier this morning, when it turned into a robot."

Sputtering as he chuckled nervously, Mr Casper looked, wide-eyed, first at the boy and then the girl and said, "How … "

"We have a telescope," said the boy.

Mr Casper pointed at the girl, "You live in the Roar house?"

"Yeah," she said, "and my room faces this way. I saw that thing that looks like a vent … " she pointed upwards, "the first week we were here."

As he turned away to stare at the jammed door to the cavern, Mr Casper ran his hand over his hair and breathed out, whistling through pursed lips. Under his breath, he said, "Rob and Mara disappear, everything falls apart, and then the whole world knows our secret."

The boy walked over and stooped next to one of the fix-its, then pushed at it with a finger. "So how do you make these things fly?" Mr Casper spun back to face the boy and his sister. "Do they have a light on them, too? Because we saw something flying around that opening up there last night."

Putting his hands out to plead his case, Mr Casper said, "Look, you really can't stay here. We have a lot of work … "

"They're made of a strange metal, Kaya," said the boy, as he looked up at his sister. "Mother would want to see these."

The girl stared down at the motionless saucer.

"Please," Mr Casper pleaded with the girl, "your name is Kaya?" The girl nodded. "You really should take your little brother and go home, Kaya, so we can finish up here."

Eyeing Mr Casper suspiciously, Kaya said, "My brother's name is Sean." She looked around at the damaged tractors and the crumpled section of roof. "It doesn't look to me like you're going to finish anything around here very soon."

She glanced from one to the other of the brothers, each of whom had been watching the exchange of words with interest. Then she returned her gaze to Mr Casper, smiled shrewdly, and continued, "We've known there's something strange about this place since we moved here; especially when we saw that weird aeroplane flying around. Sean thought it was a UFO."

Mr Casper's eyes grew wider.

"We haven't told anyone about this place," she went on, "not even our mother. So you can trust us." Kaya gave Mr Casper a pleading look. "We can help you clean up the mess." She looked around. "You did all this, last night? We know you weren't here before that, because we … "

"I know, I know," Mr Casper chuckled, still a bit uneasy, "you have a telescope."

"Uh-huh," Kaya nodded, cheerfully.

Running a hand over his hair again, Mr Casper took a deep breath as he looked at the Roar boys. He could see their recognition of the humour in the predicament in which they now found themselves. That is, all except for Will, who looked unfriendly.

"Don't tell them anything," said Will, giving Sean a nasty look. Sean returned the look and Kaya frowned. "Tell them and everyone will know."

"That's not fair, Will," said Rob, nudging him. "If we can be trusted, so can they. Besides, they've already seen plenty."

Turning to appeal to his brothers, Will said, "We're here because of our parents. They're not."

Rob stared at Kaya and Sean, considering.

"I think we should include them," said Kris. "We don't know what we're doing yet. We might need their help."

"Yeah," said Matt, with a mischievous smile, "if we screw-up something we can blame it on them." Rob, Will, and Kris giggled. Matt looked at Sean, who shifted to stand next to his sister. "I'm just kidding. It's alright with me if you stick around." Noticing Will scowling at him, Matt shrugged, "Sorry, Will."

Placing his hand on Will's shoulder, Rob said to him, "Come on, Will, ease up. You've got to be able to trust people."

Will jerked free and walked away.

Mr Casper frowned in thought, and then said, "You know, we have a way of knowing when people are approaching this place. How did you two sneak up on us?"

Sean smiled and his face brightened. He said, "We found out about that opening you guys were talking about … what is that thing, anyway?"

"Errr," Mr Casper paused, not wanting to answer the question, before relenting, " … it's a vent."

"Oh, Yeah, that's what Kaya thought it was," said Sean, in a matter-of-fact tone. "Anyway, the rock doesn't cover up the vent if we creep up to it looking like animals. We crawled here wearing those." He pointed at Kaya, who flipped open her bag and pulled out a pair of bunny ears.

Mr Casper's brows lifted in surprise. He said, "You crawled here, all the way from the house?"

Kaya and Sean giggled. Sean said, "No, not all the way. We followed one of the irrigation ditches. Then, once we got closer, we crawled the rest of the way."

Breathing out through pursed lips, with his hands on his hips, Mr Casper then said, "Huh … so two children snuck up on Socket and Wrench, then."

Kaya and Sean cocked their heads, in an inquisitive look.

Studying the two newcomers, carefully considering his next move, Mr Casper continued, "Everything that's going on here is incredibly important; more than you can imagine. I think we could use your help." He pointed at the ears, "… and, your bunny ears. But you've got to promise to keep everything a secret."

"Promise," Kaya and Sean answered in unison, without hesitation and with great sincerity.

As the Roar brothers had been just days earlier, Kaya and Sean were now treated to the same exhilarating introduction to Socket and Wrench, after which they were enlightened with the same awe-inspiring knowledge of the diversely inhabited galaxy. Though brimming with questions, each accepted it in their stride with a great deal of excitement and a strong sense of purpose. After all, they had thought their endlessly boring days on a quiet farm in the middle of Oregon would never end. But then, in the face of their diminished expectations, those boring days had, quite literally, come to an end.

The Roar brothers knew how Kaya and Sean felt. It was sort of a relief that there was more to life than homework, television, computer games and endless city streets for the brothers, and endless fields for Kaya and Sean. As it had for the Roar brothers, for Kaya and Sean, life had became completely exhilarating, if not a little scary.

Completely exciting and a little bit scary is what breaking into the cavern through the vent would be. But first, the security system would have to be fooled into thinking that whatever was approaching was an animal and not a human.

Still sulking, Will was fourth in line behind Kaya, Sean, and Rob as they made the climb; Rob, lugging a coil of rope. Matt and Kris followed Will. Mr Casper had stayed behind for fear he would be too large to fool the sensor into thinking he was an animal and therefore be treated as a threat.

They reached a point, just feet away from where a sensor would trigger the rock cover to close if approached by human or robot. From there, they could see the green-lit keypad on which it was believed a code could be entered to open the vent.

Kaya pulled out one of the sets of bunny ears from her bag and placed them on her head. She tossed a second set to Sean. Then, with the Roar brothers watching, Kaya and Sean crawled towards the vent. It worked. The vent cover remained open.

Mr Casper had given Kaya the code he believed would work – the same one he had used to gain entry into the large garage, below – and, which was now written on her arm in black ink. She tapped the code on to the keypad and … 'psssht' … the vent opened.

Looking back at the Roar brothers, Kaya waved at them to come forwards. With all six of them at the opening, they crowded together to look in. A gentle, warm breeze ushered out and caressed their faces. It smelled like mountain air, only a bit stale.

Separating himself from the bulky coil of rope with a grunt, Rob began to lower an end, hand-over-hand, down the vent shaft. Kaya took the other end and tied it around a huge boulder, nearby. The rope was so long it seemed to take forever to uncoil until finally, it hung, anchored to the rock, and faded into the pitch-black of what seemed like a bottomless pit.

They all looked at one another. It was that sort of unspoken question between them as to who was going to go first. Will broke the stalemate. Scowling at the others and without saying a word, he crawled over the rim and lowered himself into the shaft. Holding on to the rope with a vicelike grip that turned his knuckles white, he stared out, wide-eyed. Then, slowly, he lowered himself.

They could hear him descending; the clunking of his feet, knees, and elbows on the steel wall of the tube echoed to the surface. The rope moved a little, like a fishing line with a fish on the end.

Matt entered the tube next, then Kris, then Sean, then Kaya. Rob followed last, peering out one last time before descending into the darkness.

With all six of them hanging from the rope, descending to the cavern through the long, narrow vent, everything seemed to be going well.

But then, they all stopped dead to listen. Then they heard the familiar 'Pssht' echo from above … the vent hatch was closing.

No one had thought about that.

There was a slight tug on the rope as it was cut, clean through.

"Jumping jitterbug!" said Kris, before he and everyone else screamed as they began a long, dark fall, in what could otherwise have been one heck of a fun ride down a long tubular slide.

One would think the combined echoing screams of six children in a hollow tube above a vast and empty cavern, would have been heard around the galaxy. One would also think that this could be the end of it all – the end of the story – with each child, one after the other, falling to his and her deaths on the cavern floor. Or perhaps they would survive, as the vent might empty them out shallow, sending each child, one after the other, sliding across the floor.

What actually happened is this: bursting like a cannonball, Will popped out of the vent from a hole in the ceiling high above the cavern floor.

As he fell, screaming as he went, he felt himself brush against something. Then he felt his weight being fully supported, before he was slipping, once again, down something like a chute and across the floor in a cloud of grey, powdery dirt.

He was aware of the sound of screams from his brothers and the two intruders, followed by a sliding sound. Then, someone bumped into him.

Looking up and squinting through the dusty air, Will saw what had caught them: it was two identical light-green, thick-framed humanoid robots, each about the size of a large tractor. The machines stood close together and held between them what looked like a huge sheet in the shape of a giant slide.

The others sat up from their various awkward positions and looked around. One after the other, they noticed the robots and the sheet-slide.

"What are those?" asked Kaya, as she stood, looking up at the massive things.

"Duh! They're robots," said Will, as he got up. "What do you think they are? Tractors?"

The others began brushing the dust off themselves as they got to their feet, looking up at the machines as they did so.

Cooperating as two people would when folding bed linen, the robots proceeded to fold the huge sheet into a neat bundle and placed it on the floor near the cavern wall. Then, with a sound similar to that which Socket and Wrench made when transforming only deeper in tone and much louder, the two large, light-green robots promptly transformed into light-green tractors.

Will was dumbfounded. Kaya glanced at him with a smug smile on her face. The others did an admirable job keeping straight faces, which proved difficult. His frustration building, Will walked away.

Rob called out, "Come on, Will, it is sort of funny; them turning into tractors and all."

But Will would have nothing to do with reason. He walked past a pearl-white helicopter tucked in the shadows and continued on towards the large cavern door.

The sparse light in the otherwise dark cavern seemed to glow from several spots on the ceiling, like nightlights. Though the place seemed very much like a cave, it had been hollowed out by human technology rather than by natural forces, so the surfaces were almost smooth and the ceiling was symmetrically vaulted. The vent high above seemed far away to those standing on the floor looking up. The thought of what could have happened if the tractor-like robots had not caught them gave each one a chill.

"We better go get that door open," said Rob as he followed Will, studying the helicopter as he walked by, realising he had seen it before.

The others followed. But Kris, unable to control his curiosity, did not. He walked straight for the sleek helicopter and swiped a thin layer of dust off the fuselage with his hand. He looked up at the rotors, which he figured must be retracted as they were mere stubs. The entire helicopter including the rotors, was pearl-white. Even the windows were the same colour, making it impossible to see inside.

At the same time, Will had opened one of two access panels beside the large cavern door and was trying, without success, to turn the heavy wheel by himself. His face was red with effort as he grunted.

Rob and Matt arrived to help Will as Kaya and Sean went to the other side of the door and opened the second access panel. Kris joined them just as they threw their weight into turning the wheel. With great resistance, the wheels moved and a thin line of light appeared at the bottom of the door.

Four sets of little metal fingers appeared from underneath, lifting the door upwards. With all six youths exerting their strength into turning the wheels and with the added help of Mr Casper, Socket and Wrench, the amount of light flooding across the floor, grew.

Soon, there was enough room for the fix-its to dart under the door. Then, though one would think there was little more about the two robots in which one could be astonished, astonished was just what the children would be when they discovered why Mr Casper had named the machines Socket and Wrench.

One of the fix-its gestured for the boys and Kaya to move away from the wheels, as the other fix-it metamorphosed into what looked like a giant socket and clamped on to one of the wheels. The first fix-it then transformed into a straight, thick rod, like a ratchet wrench, and plugged into the other. There was an ear-piercing whine which made everyone cover their ears and grimace, as the fix-it functioning as the socket was spun with blinding speed, raising the door the remainder of the way with little effort.

Mr Casper stood there with a bright smile. "Good job everyone," he said, as he entered the cavern. "No problems, huh?"

The children exchanged glances with a few brows raised, a few slight smiles, and a few deep breaths.

A Helicopter in a Tube

One of the fix-its set to work, readying the helicopter for flight – which mostly meant cleaning off the dust – and then repairing the large cavern door. The other fix-it, with the help of the two tractor-robots – which Mr Casper referred to as farm-bots – began repairs to the huge steel shed outside the cavern.

All six children followed Mr Casper at a brisk pace from the cavern, down a short passageway, and past several large storage rooms filled with what looked like spare parts. Eventually, they reached a control room that looked like one big computer with a bunch of monitors, like a miniature NASA space-centre.

With familiarity earned over time, Mr Casper plopped down in one of the seats and began pressing buttons and toggling switches. The computer consoles lit up and the room began to hum. Monitors flickered on and were then filled with the image of a robot's face staring back at them.

"I am Keb," said the robot, after a moment. "We are relieved you have made contact with us."

Everyone stared, transfixed, at the image of the metallic face. Then a girl squeezed in next to the robot and smiled, as though this was just another call from familiar friends.

"Hi, I'm Katia," she said. "You have no idea how many games of Creose we've played. Playing with a robot is no fun because a robot always lets a human win." Mixing her cheerful smile with a frown, the girl continued, "Are you guys having trouble with your ship? Would you like me to tell you how to get the thing started?"

Chuckling, Mr Casper said, "No. No thank you, Katia. We can get the thing started all right. It's just … well … " Mr Casper passed his hand over his hair and rested it on the back of his neck.

" ... it's going to take us a few more days to get to you. Minor problems down here."

As though just noticing the six unobtrusive observers standing behind Mr Casper, the girl surveyed the scene, sobered, and asked, "Aren't they a little young to be galaxy ranger recruits?"

Mr Casper glanced behind him, then returned his attention to the monitor and said, "Yeah, but they're willing to learn a thing or two anyway."

Looking past Mr Casper at the others, Katia said, "I'll get to meet all of you when I get to Earth." Returning her attention to Mr Casper, she continued, "Can you bring something to eat when you come? I've had about all I can stand of the ship's rations."

At that moment, Mr Casper noticed that the robot, Keb, seemed to be studying him and the children behind him, with a look that gave him a bit of a chill. He shivered and smiled, "We'll bring something good for you to eat on your trip to Earth. See you in a few days."

"One more thing before you go," said Katia, her cheerful face growing serious as she straightened. "You must be wondering why we're here."

Mr Casper also grew serious and straightened in his seat. "I am," he said. "I expect something serious is happening out there."

Katia glanced at Keb, and then returned her attention to her audience. "We have something with us that the Boargen want. They must not find us."

"We'll do everything we can to help you, Katia," said Mr Casper, knowing that part at least, was true. "Just hang in there."

A worried look came over her face, and then she said, "You do know about our air supply?"

"Yes," said Mr Casper. "And we will get to you before you run out of air; even if we have to flap our arms to do so."

Katia relaxed and she smiled. "I'd like to see that."

"We'll see you in a few days," said Mr Casper. "Contact us any time you want."

"OK. Bye," said Katia, as she bounced out of sight, now back to her cheerful self. The robot was left studying Mr Casper and the children for a moment before the contact was broken.

Mr Casper was used to the glasseen eyes on the newest and most advanced robot models, as Rob Roar's robot, Dynak, had them. But there was something strange about the Dynak/Keb model. He just couldn't put his finger on it.

"Mr Casper?"

"Yes Kaya," said Mr Casper, as he swivelled in his seat to face her.

"That girl, Katia, she's human."

"Ah, yes," said Mr Casper, "she is. And you were probably expecting a little green girl with two big, purple eyes and two antennae with little round nubs at the ends."

Kaya stared at Mr Casper for a moment, and then said, "But humans evolved here, on Earth."

"There you have it. You have just stumbled on one of the many great galactic mysteries," said Mr Casper, holding up a finger. "The galaxy is full of humans that look just like us. And it is also full of humans that have different physical characteristics than us; like very large eyes, or pointed ears."

"Like Spock on *Star Trek?*" asked Matt.

"Or elves?" asked Sean.

"Yep," said Mr Casper. "Very similar, only real. Evolution has played its part on a galactic scale; not that evolution is the only possibility. Many believe life is too miraculous and complex to rely on one explanation for it all."

"All this could sort of upset a few people here on Earth," said Kaya.

Mr Casper laughed, "Yeah, there's always someone who thinks he knows everything and will try, and often succeed, in selling it to people as the one and only reality. But with the miraculous complexity of life, the chances are decent that everything is a combination of many true things; which means that many different beliefs and theories may be right all at the same time. No one person has to be wrong for another to be right."

"But … so Katia looks like she could be from Mexico or Spain or someplace like that," said Kaya.

"That's true," said Mr Casper. "But Katia is from Peridia."

"What do the guys that are causing all this trouble look like?" asked Will.

"The Boargen?" said Mr Casper.

"Yeah," said Will. "What do the Boargen look like?"

Mr Casper stared at Will for a moment, and then said, "They're one hundred per cent human. But keep in mind that the Boargen are not the only trouble-makers in the galaxy, and not the most dangerous, either."

During the following hours, the pearl-white helicopter, now sparklingly clean, was pulled from its corner and readied for flight. The building was repaired and the big farm-bots were ready for their next task, working the fields, operating a fleet of remote controlled farm machinery that had been sitting idle in the great shed for the last two years. The farm would be active once again, and it would be completely automated as it had been in the past, managed by the two farm-bots.

What happened next should not have been such a surprise, but it was. The Roar boys were loading their suitcases into the helicopter while Mr Casper was explaining to Kaya and Sean why there was no way he could sneak them to the coastal base, as he could not risk their mother knowing. The next moment, Socket and Wrench abruptly collapsed to the ground, just as they had earlier when Kaya and Sean had snuck up on them. Mr Casper jerked his attention towards the cavern entrance.

"Oh no," he said. "Not again."

Yes, again. A tall, slender, dark-complexioned woman stormed into the cavern. She wore a red coat with the NASA insignia on it. And she was wearing bunny ears. There was no doubt as to who she was.

"Mother!" said Kaya and Sean in unison.

Eyes wide, Mr Casper stared at the woman as she approached and then stopped a few yards away. She stared back.

"Jerome Casper?" she said, staring at him through disbelieving eyes.

"Adia?" he said, surprised. "Adia Rashida?"

Adia quickly closed the remaining distance to Mr Casper and the children. Looking at Kaya and Sean, she said, "I'm impressed that you figured out how to get so close to this place."

Mr Casper passed his hand over his head in his usual, nervous motion. The Roar boys watched, intrigued, whilst Will grew more frustrated and impatient.

Adia frowned, reached out, and snatched the hat off Sean's head, which brought forth yet one more unexpected event: Sean's hair fell to his – her? – shoulders, and then a little beyond.

"How many times do I have to tell you to stop dressing like a boy, Shani. You look awful in those clothes."

"Shani?" Mr Casper and the Roar brothers sang out in unison.

Will rolled his eyes and slowly shook his head while breathing out in frustration.

Brows raised, Adia glanced at Mr Casper, and then looked back at Shani.

"You told them your name was Sean, huh?" she said.

Shani nodded.

Will nudged Rob and said, "He's a she, just like in Lassie."

Rob peered at Will. "But you said Lassie was a male dog passed off as a female."

"Close enough," said Will, sneering at Rob, who looked away.

"Um," said Kaya to her mother, "you two know each other?"

Turning her attention fully on Mr Casper, Adia nodded, "We know each other. But right now, I want to know what's going on around here." She pointed at the helicopter and looked all round the cavern before returning her strict gaze on Mr Casper. "What is all this?" she asked, raising a finger, her bunny ears jiggling atop her head. "And don't try to give me any drivel, because I have all the strange things that have been going on around here on tape, including your arrival yesterday."

Mr Casper breathed out through pursed lips. "Oh-boy-oh-boy-oh-boy. Rob is not gonna like this." Then, noticing the bunny ears on Adia's head, he chuckled.

Adia scowled.

Mr Casper pointed at the quivering ears.

The boys and girls laughed ...

Being a scientist, Adia accepted her introduction to the fix-its and everything Mr Casper told her about the galaxy with ease, as though she pretty much suspected it all anyway. In an eagerness to help in any way she could, she would give Mr Casper her video footage, which included shots of the strange craft which Kaya and Shani had seen snooping around the rock outcrop.

Mr Casper was confident that Adia and her daughters could be trusted implicitly, so he offered to allow Kaya and Shani to join the Roar boys at the coastal base. It would be a great adventure for them, and one not to be passed up. Adia agreed, only she forbade the girls to leave Earth's surface. And finally, she invited herself – much to Mr Casper's apparent pleasure – to join them on the weekends when she was not on duty at a nearby NASA observatory.

In spite of her calm demeanour, Adia grew concerned when she discovered that Kaya and Shani would be flying to the coastal base in a helicopter piloted only by its onboard computer. That concern was quickly alleviated, however, upon her close inspection of the aircraft, which left her confident that her daughters would be perfectly safe. As for Mr Casper, he would drive to the coast, arriving later that day.

With the children settled in the helicopter, their seat restraining fields activated, the aircraft's engines wound into life with a shrill noise. The rotors' whop-whop caused bursts of pressure in the cavern air, its deep echo magnifying the sounds. The rotors turned, causing a great wind that encouraged Mr Casper and Adia who were clinging to each other, to watch the launch from outside.

For those inside the helicopter, the turbulent noises outside were muffled almost to a whisper. Seated in the pilot's seat, Rob looked out nervously; not just about flying in an aircraft piloted by a computer, but because the cavern doorway seemed even smaller now that the helicopter had to fly through it on autopilot. Will sat in the co-pilot's seat thinking much the same thing, determined not let his fear show. The others, Matt, Kris, Kaya and Shani – her hair now tucked back into the hat so that she looked like a boy again – all appeared to be relaxed. Of course, they would not be the first to be crushed should the helicopter fly head-on into the cavern wall.

Feeling the restraining field in his seat strengthen, Rob shot a look at Will, for reassurance.

"Coool," Matt said from the back, as the helicopter lifted from the ground and hovered for a moment.

Then it listed forwards and moved towards the cavern doorway. Rob and Will, eyes wide, squeezed their armrests as they pushed back against their seats – definitely a white-knuckle moment. The building anxiety of those in the back added to the accumulated apprehension filling the cockpit. Then the helicopter launched forwards, slipped through the cavern doorway and the great shed and, bursting into the sunlight, shot skyward.

Through clenched teeth, Kris managed to utter, "Jumping jitterbug!"

Rob looked down as the helicopter banked towards the coast. A glint of light caught his attention and he thought he saw something in the tall grass below. Whatever it was though, was gone before he got a good look at it. His belief that it might be a person was then forgotten, replaced by a profound sense of pride and a subsequent reverie over seeing his family's farm spread out below, now spotted for miles in every direction with a dozen rivers of dust … the tractors were at work.

It had been a holographic image – Rob accepted, without a doubt now – that he and Will had seen of his father in a remotely operated tractor, that day in the field. His father had been off someplace else; perhaps even absent from Earth. It was the tractors controlled by the farm-bots that would farm the land; not the Roar boys. Rob felt a sense of great joy at that moment as the helicopter soared ever higher. There was something far greater in life than what people like his aunt represented. Rob was worried whether Aunt Hilary would ever find out about all this.

Now very high up, the helicopter slipped through a wispy layer of clouds. Rob realised then just how little sound he could hear – just a whisper – not even a hint of the engines screaming and the rotors whop-whopping. Mr Casper had explained that once the engines had fully powered up, a whisper technology would all but eliminate the noise that the aircraft produced, making it audibly disappear. The need for the helicopter to be silent made complete sense, as its cloaking field made it invisible at night and just a shimmer during the day, so it could not be easily seen or heard.

Relaxed now that the helicopter had levelled off and was racing towards the coast, Rob and Will exchanged glances, then peered behind them. Quite comfortable, Matt, Kaya, and Shani were talking happily. Kris was looking up at something, wholly absorbed. Rob and Will craned their necks to look out their windows, too. The rotors were retracted as they had been in the cavern, only this time, they spun at a blinding speed. Stubby wings had sprouted low on the fuselage, making the helicopter seem more like an aeroplane.

"Mr Casper said this thing can fly faster than most of Earth's military jets," announced Kris. Rob and Will turned again to look back at their youngest brother. Matt, Kaya, and Shani also looked at him, Kaya with adoration. "And that's really saying something," he added, "because for the most part, this is a helicopter."

"But why have a helicopter?" asked Shani. "Why not some really fast aeroplane or spaceship or something?"

"Well," began Kris, sounding mature beyond his years, "I think it's because something that looks like an aeroplane would have to land at an airport so as not to draw attention. A helicopter can land anywhere, including our farm, without being too unbelievable."

"Hey, look!" said Matt, pointing out the window. The others moved quickly to look out. The Oregon coastline was passing beneath them. Then the helicopter abruptly dropped and began a fast descent, spilling towards the ocean with what seemed like reckless speed – yet another white-knuckle moment.

With the coastline far behind and the sea racing towards them, the children all began to worry that something must be wrong. The helicopter then banked sharply, turning until it faced land as it was still diving.

Just when one would think that a hysterical scream was in order, as the helicopter appeared to be plunging straight into the ocean, it levelled off, just feet above the surface. They were so close; if a fish had jumped out of the water in front of them it would surely have been the first time a sea creature had been run over by an aircraft.

Racing just above the water as they were, and not having slowed in the least, the children now began to think the helicopter would fly straight into the coastal cliffs.

Then, what they had feared was going to happen before they had levelled off, happened without warning: the helicopter plunged into the ocean.

"Ahhh!" they all screamed.

"Jumping jitterbug!"

But there was no impact. No splash. No flooding of the helicopter. Nothing like that. Now, they were racing through a tunnel in the sea; a tunnel with no visible structure holding back the water. It was as though a giant drill had bored a hole through a gelatine ocean.

In their fixated states, none of the others noticed that Kris, now relaxed, smiling and looking all around with great interest, was taking it all in as fast as he could. His attention rested for a moment on the rotors above, still retracted and spinning at a blinding rate.

Becoming comfortable with the visual sensation of racing through the ocean tunnel, Rob relaxed enough to look beside him at Will.

"How could Mr Casper have forgotten to tell us about this somewhat important detail of our flight?" he said.

In fact, at that very moment, Mr Casper was packing the last of some things into the SUV and wondering the very same thing. Glancing at his watch, he then shrugged and muttered to himself, "Oh well, too late now."

Slowing, the helicopter passed from a tunnel of water into a tunnel of stone. The children were surprised, once again, when they popped from the tunnel into a vast and bright futuristic cavern with several spacecraft positioned to one side. The helicopter set down, ever so gently, within a yellow circle on the hangar floor and the engines shut down, leaving the cockpit still and quiet.

Having felt his restraining field release, Will leapt from his seat and rushed to the cockpit door. Opening it, he hopped out of the helicopter and stood there looking around, amazed at what he saw. The others filed out behind him, gawking at their new surroundings.

Here, unlike the smaller cavern at home, the exposed rock was smooth as if it had been polished. Light seemed to emanate from everywhere. It was as if every surface in the entire place glowed. It was also warmer, unlike the coldness of the cave where they had been a short time ago. In spite of the vastness of the place, it felt comfortable.

"Wow!" said Matt, as he scanned the hangar. "You could fit a whole bunch of spaceships in here."

"Big ones, too," said Rob, as he looked around.

Kris took off. He walked towards four sleek ships next to a larger, stouter one; all of them pearl-white like the helicopter. The others followed.

Mr Casper had said that the base would unlock on the arrival of the helicopter, so there was no limit as to where they could go. Soon after they had spread out to look around, Socket and Wrench showed up. The robots, now in their humanoid form, walked with the children as they explored.

Kaya found the living quarters, which, though simple, were comfortable and inviting and, as could be expected, were sleekly modern. There were enough rooms for everyone to have their own; each room contained two sleep-tubes – otherwise known as mind-link chambers – so the children paired up between three rooms.

Down a long passageway from the living quarters, Rob found the Pacific outlook. They all stood there for a while, looking across the ocean at the waves which were breaking on the rocks below. A cloaking field made the cliff face look solid from the outside. No one from the ocean side, therefore, could see the outlook or the children standing there. The base was thoroughly hidden inside the cliffs.

Will discovered some food, or rather, the machine called Food-Mack which served it. It was just like a sci-fi movie: one asked for what one wanted and, moments later, it appeared behind a clear door, which then lifted to allow the food to be taken. Will put the machine to the test and asked for a banana split. There was no limit. Food-Mack even produced an orange for Kaya.

Eventually, they all found the control room, which was larger and more modern than the one at the old base. At the centre of the round room, was a large command chair set on a platform three steps above the floor. With the exception of the doorway, a continuous control console wrapped its entire circumference. Well-padded, high-backed chairs were positioned around the room as though awaiting technicians to man the consoles. Above the console, forming the wall itself, was one continuous video monitor spanning console to ceiling.

Kris strode around, taking it all in. Then he walked over to the large chair on the platform in the centre of the room, sat at it, paused for a moment, then said, "I'm Kris Roar."

"Hello, Kris Roar, welcome home," said a kind, female voice that seemed to come from all around him, as though spoken from the air itself.

The others all looked around as they migrated to stand near Kris.

"Do you know who the others in this room are?" asked Kris.

"I know the sons of Rob and Mara Roar: Rob, Will, Matt, and Kris," said the voice. "I do not know the other two except by the names you have called them since your arrival – Kaya and Shani – and a name Will has used; one of which I am not familiar with."

Everyone stared at Will, Kaya and Shani critically, with narrowed eyes. Will looked at his brothers and said, "Well, I don't think they should be here." When his brothers failed to respond and everyone just continued to stare at him – except for Kris, whose attention was otherwise occupied. Will shook his head, grunted, turned, and left.

After a moment, Rob said, "He'll chill out. He's just being protective."

With a cacophony of blips and bleeps, the console lights flickered on and the room became alive as though someone had plugged in the world. The expansive monitor flickered then filled with images from all over Earth, along with several others from outer space. Looking at the blue marble floating in a sea of black, Kris sat back and swivelled the command chair to scan the images on the monitor.

There must have been cameras all over the world, in each and every part of Earth: deserts, savannas, forests, mountains, tundra, oceans, and even an image of a coral reef. It also seemed that every human culture was represented. Every so often, the monitor changed images, showing someplace different. From this room, one could watch the world – part of a galaxy ranger's job.

Kris asked, "What do we call you?"

"Your parents call me KNIA."

"KNIA?" said Matt. "What kind of name is that for a computer?"

"KNIA is an abbreviation for Know It All," said KNIA.

Matt giggled, and then said, "Kris is a KNIA, too."

"I know of Kris's unique mind," said KNIA. "In fact, I know what makes each of you boys unique and special in your own way. Shall I learn about Kaya and Shani? It would not take long to ask each girl a set of specific questions."

Rob, Matt, and Kris looked at Kaya and Shani, who glanced at each other, then nodded.

"Sure, KNIA," said Kaya.

"Good," said KNIA. "I will enjoy getting to know you two. It is best to speak with you individually. We can do that anywhere you wish, including outside at the Pacific outlook. I noticed you both enjoyed being there. Which one of you will go first?"

Kaya raised her hand, "I'll go first." With a perky stride and her long, dark hair swaying from side to side as she walked, Kaya left the control room.

As the door slid shut, Kris's attention was drawn to one of the images on the huge monitor – the Earth, as seen from outer space.

"KNIA," he said, "I assume you can talk to us at the same time as you talk to Kaya?"

"Yes, Kris. I can simultaneously execute all tasks whether scheduled or not with no impact on my performance."

"So, you could conduct a million conversations all at once, without making a mistake?" asked Matt, a mischievous smile lighting up his face.

"Yes, Matt."

Still with a mischievous smile, Matt moved to one of the console chairs and asked, "Do you have a sense of humour?"

"I have a sensation that could be considered similar to a human's response when experiencing humour," answered KNIA.

"OK, here's a riddle," said Matt, sitting up straight. "What do you call a tick on the moon?"

KNIA was silent for a moment, and then answered, "I do not know the answer to your riddle, Matt. Very good."

Matt eyed the console in front of him for a moment as though that was where KNIA was, and then said, "How do I know you aren't just being nice to me? I mean, you're a know it all. Shouldn't you be able to figure out anything, including a joke?"

"I learn by analysing data," said KNIA. "If the data is not already logical then I must make it logical. The punch-line to a joke or the answer to a riddle is not necessarily, logical. By my analysis, that is why it is funny. The answer is unexpected. I have analysed your riddle and have not arrived at a logical answer. I believe that means I am stumped."

Satisfied, Matt said, "A tick on the moon is a luna-tic."

Kris and Rob had heard the riddle before and thought it was pretty lame, so they just smiled, but Shani giggled sweetly.

KNIA was quiet for a moment, and then said, "I, too, have experienced a sensation similar to a human's pleasurable response upon hearing a good joke. Thank you for sharing that riddle with me, Matt."

Matt had hoped to hear KNIA laugh, but not even a chuckle came. All in all then, telling a joke to a computer seemed rather pointless. He was about to try again, when Kris spoke.

"Speaking of the moon, KNIA, can we see Katia's ship?"

"Yes," said KNIA, "but the image will have to be enhanced because the ship is on the dark side of the moon."

The next moment, a section of the vast monitor was filled with an image of a sleek, silver spaceship resting on the lunar surface. The ship looked all right until Rob pointed out a dark area just behind where the swept wing met the fuselage.

Nervously, as he looked around at the others, he said, "This doesn't seem real ... "

By the time Mr Casper arrived, the sun was burning an orange glow across the Pacific ocean. Shani had just completed her interview with KNIA. Everyone was feeling a bit tired as they sat around the table in the dining area eating various treats from Food-Mack. Having given even Rob the cold shoulder, Will was sitting apart from the others eating his second banana-split of the day.

At the same time, Socket and Wrench were checking over the spaceships making sure that they were in perfect working order. Mr Casper knew he had not needed to tell them to do so because Rob and Mara's sons would be flying them, but he had, just to make himself feel better. But he did not feel better as he was consumed with worry for the Roar brothers' safety.

Whilst, thanks to KNIA, the children slept soundly in their sleeping-tubes, Mr Casper worried incessantly, late into the night. Katia now had less than 187 hours of air remaining on her ship. That gave Mr Casper and KNIA less than eight days to make boys into something resembling galaxy rangers. He and KNIA had their work cut out for them. And so did the Roar boys.

A Hamburger Helper

The first to wake up the following morning was Rob, who walked from the room he shared with Will towards the dining area. The only sound he heard was that of the quiet pat-pat of his bare feet on the floor. He ordered scrambled eggs, bacon, toast and a tall glass of orange-juice, which Food-Mack promptly delivered. The quietness continued as he ate, leaving him feeling a little lonely, so when he was done he set off to look for Socket and Wrench, who, of course, never slept.

He found them in the hangar; or rather heard them amongst the five pearl-white spaceships. He headed in their direction. The amazing helicopter had been moved off to the side leaving the vast hangar empty in the middle, which left him feeling very small as he crossed it.

Four of the spaceships looked like futuristic, military fighter-jets, although, they differed from their Earthly cousins in that their fuselages were perfectly smooth and they had no air-intakes for the engines. The fifth was like the others, only larger. Probably for transporting passengers, Rob thought. He and his brothers would learn how to fly these ships, although how, remained a mystery.

There was a clunk, followed by a fix-it's clicking, clacking, and blip-bleeping coming from inside the passenger ship. Rob headed straight for it. Just then, one of the robots appeared at the top of the gangway extending out from the side of the spaceship. As he approached, he became somewhat awestruck by the actual size of the craft. He supposed the immense volume of the hangar had made all the ships appear small when seen from a distance. But now, it seemed the size of a small house.

The fix-it saw Rob, stopped midway on the gangway, and waved as it made a whistling 'hello' sound. Then Rob saw a long, thin metal beam come slowly out of the ship from behind the fix-it. He could see what was going to happen and tried to give it a warning, but was too late. The beam came fast enough to knock Socket, or Wrench, whichever one it was, off its feet. The robot tumbled the remainder of the way down the gangway and landed on its head.

The other fix-it, apparently unaware of the accident, appeared, carrying the beam midway along its length. Seeing Rob, it greeted him much as the other had. Reaching the hangar floor, the second fix-it walked straight past the first, which still lay on the floor, and then stared back at it, blipping and bleeping in what sounded like admonishment. Something like: "What are you doing lying around? We have a lot of work to do."

The fix-it then hopped up and, catching up with the other, began its own series of blips and bleeps; a scolding of sorts. Rob chuckled as the apparent fix-it argument continued as the two robots walked from the hangar.

Then it was quiet again for a moment, as he stood there looking over the ship, feeling nervous. His chest was tight and his breathing shallow. Everything seemed so strange, like a dream. Taking a deep breath and shrugging off his uncertainty, he walked up the ship's gangway. It was even quieter inside. Having looked around for a moment and counted the passenger seats – sixteen in all – he walked through a short, narrow passageway to the cockpit. Without hesitation, he sat in the pilot's seat.

As he sat there staring forwards through the cockpit viewscreen, a thrilling excitement filled him. He was going to learn how to fly a spaceship! Rob could imagine his mother and father sitting in the same cockpit, flying to other planets. He could clearly remember his parents' faces as though they had only been gone a day; although he worried that someday, he would forget what they looked like. With his worry came a feeling of desperation and an overwhelming desire to find them.

"You ready to get to work?"

Mr Casper's voice startled him and he jerked to look back. He had no idea how long he had been sitting there, or how long Mr Casper had been behind him.

"Ready for what?" he asked, already knowing the answer.

"Ready for what!" said Mr Casper, humour filling his voice. "Ready for your first flight lesson."

Shooting a look towards the ship's controls, Rob said, "Here? Now? In this ship? Isn't there ... ?"

Leaning forwards and patting Rob on the shoulder as he chuckled, Mr Casper said, "No, Rob. Not here. In the simulator. Didn't you guys find that thing, yesterday?"

They had found the simulator. And Kris had identified it as such. But Rob's words were lagging behind his thoughts.

"Have you had breakfast?" asked Mr Casper.

Too nervous to talk, Rob nodded.

"Great. Then let's get you started."

The simulator was in a large room near the hangar. It looked like a stripped-down spaceship with no windows, no wings, and no real length to the body. Actually, now that Rob was standing next to it on a new day with a new perspective, the simulator looked small; like a ride he had seen in an advertisement for a theme-park.

Mr Casper helped him into the simulator pilot's seat. Rob's brothers, one after the other, would soon have their turn. Kaya and Shani would not – much to the girls' disappointment. Mr Casper had promised and would, of course, honour their mother's condition not to teach the girls how to fly. No point in it anyway as they were prohibited from leaving Earth.

Once Mr Casper had given Rob a briefing of the simulator, KNIA took over. There was a mind-link with KNIA during training and, at night, whilst sleeping in the sleep-tubes, the boys would learn from it at an extraordinarily accelerated rate. But first, Rob learned just how maddening the highly-structured lesson on piloting a spaceship could be. KNIA refused to veer from flight school protocol: there was no skipping to the fun part.

He crashed the first time, right into the hangar wall, which left him shaken because it seemed so real, and frustrated because he figured that flying in the simulator would be simple, like playing a computer game. Upon leaving the simulator, he stormed through the passageways to the Pacific outlook, convinced that he would throw himself to his death once there.

Will had his turn next and fared no better than Rob. And, like Rob, after leaving the simulator, Will found himself staring out at the Pacific feeling the same sort of frustration.

Perhaps the two brothers were also a bit scared. There was an overwhelming sense of responsibility as reality was setting in. This was no game.

Next, Matt, and then Kris, had their turns in the simulator. But unlike his older brothers, Matt was good at laughing at himself when he was not yet very good at something. And Kris took crashing into and blowing up all the other spaceships with an attitude of: 'Oh well, maybe next time I'll only take out one or two, rather than the whole squadron'.

The days went by all too fast. The Roar boys and the girls were too consumed with learning to notice the differences in themselves, or in each other. Mr Casper could see it though, and he worried that Adia would be concerned over her daughters' newly-acquired maturity. They were less like little girls now; not that they had been any less tenacious beyond their years beforehand. The Roar boys were still the same Rob, Will, Matt and Kris; but Mr Casper could see the vast increase in their intellect. They were smarter and sharper and now, they knew how to fly spaceships. With the exception of not yet having actually experienced the galaxy, they were fast becoming children of the galaxy.

Of course, none of this could have happened without KNIA. It was during the night when they were all sleeping in their sleep-tubes, that KNIA fed extraordinary amounts of information to the childrens' minds. At the same time, anything they had seen or heard during their daytime lessons was etched into their memories.

And although the others spoke with Katia on occasion – Kris more to get a look at Keb than to talk with the girl – Will took it upon himself to check-in with her on a daily basis to see how she was doing. Though there was no speaking of the cargo she and Keb carried – the cause of her need for help – she told him about her home world of Peridia and the other places in the galaxy she had seen, and Will listened with rapt interest. It was also the case that Will could not tell her – as per Mr Casper's strict instructions – why it was taking so long to rescue her. The story was kept simple: that they were having a problem with the shuttle. Though Katia was assured that the ship would be ready in time to rescue her before she ran out of air, everyone could tell she was nervous. Sometimes, she seemed on the edge of desperation, and even panic.

With Katia now with only three days of air remaining, the air at the coastal base was thick with tension. The children were feeling the pressure, especially Will, who, even more so than the others, was determined they would not fail to rescue Katia and her robot.

While Will was in the simulator, Kaya, Shani, Rob and Matt were in the control room watching a holographic image of a professor of galactic politics lecturing about how to associate with the beings living on a planet called Jawbone; beings that tended to eat anyone that unwittingly visited their planet. Kris studied a complex electronic text concerning the various kinds of power sources for everything from a Polinthian oven, to a robot, to a spaceship, to the power-plant technology used by the more advanced societies of the galaxy. And nearby, Mr Casper sat with his feet kicked up on one of the computer consoles, reading a National Geographic with an image of a flying-saucer racing across a dark star-lit sky on the front cover, with the words, "Are they out there?"

"Mr Casper," said Kris, "why is it that only Polinthia has advanced the power source technology? Not to mention that they make some pretty cool appliances. Why would one civilisation out of so many millions, have a monopoly like that?"

Upon hearing his name, Mr Casper promptly lowered the magazine and listened intently to Kris's question. Placing his magazine on the console, he stood, saying, "There you have stumbled on another one of the great mysteries of the galaxy." He walked over and sat in a chair beside Kris.

Having become bored with the professor of galactic politics droning on about how one society must respect another's way of life, the others swivelled their seats to face Kris. By now, Kaya and Shani had learned what his brothers already knew – that Kris always asked excellent questions. Therefore, a question about technology from Kris might just be more interesting than a boring talk about the beings on Jawbone eating visitors, especially since the stupid visitors had to pass several warning beacons before even reaching the planet. It's just a perfect example that if one fails to pay attention to directions, one could be eaten.

"Let me see if I can make this simple," continued Mr Casper. "The most important technologies must also be closely guarded secrets. A society must be chosen, having proven itself worthy, to hold the secrets to specialised knowledge. Once a society has been chosen to be the stewards of knowledge, like Polinthia's power plant technology, it becomes responsible for the safe-keeping of the knowledge and the subsequent technology with which it has been entrusted. The technology must be safeguarded against copy by others. It is said that this is the best way to keep the millions of diverse galactic societies from spiralling into chaotic bickering."

Mr Casper looked around at his listeners, then leaned in closer to Kris with his elbows resting on his knees, and continued, "And it is not just technological knowledge, but all knowledge important to the well-being of all of societies of the galaxy combined that should be closely guarded. That is why the Polinthians have a monopoly of the power plant market, not to mention the residual benefit of owning one heck of an appliance business. Does this make sense?"

Kris was thoughtful for a moment. Smiling, Mr Casper watched him, as did the others.

"That's why the Mindinee are the only robot masters," said Kris, matter-of-factly.

"Exactly," said Mr Casper, with a nod.

"But who decides who gets to be the keepers of knowledge?" asked Kaya. "You make it sound like there's someone who controls everything."

"Ah!" said Mr Casper, as he swivelled to face Kaya. "Not a someone. Best to call it an entity of sorts, because no one really knows what it is. Few have even seen it. Most just call it 'The Sphere'. Some call it the 'Sphere Of Knowledge' as it controls all the knowledge in the galaxy."

The control room was quiet for a moment. Then Kaya asked, "Well, what does it look like?"

"Yeah, how big is it?" asked Rob. "It must be huge if it holds all the knowledge in the galaxy."

Shrugging, Mr Casper said, "Those who have seen it don't talk about it much. All I've heard is that it's a white sphere. There are no texts about it worth mentioning, even in the Galactic Library on Torset – the seat of the galactic government. A number of scholars have suggested that The Sphere is just a device, and that there is really an advanced civilisation well-hidden someplace in the galaxy that acts through The Sphere as a means to remain hidden."

After a moment, Kaya said, "Maybe, someday, someone will find the hidden civilisation and solve its mystery."

Mr Casper broke into uproarious laughter. With uncertain smiles, the children exchanged glances. His laughter subsiding, Mr Casper said, "Spoken like a person who isn't keeping in mind how very old the universe is." He sat forwards in his seat again and continued, "Galactic scientists estimate that the universe began with the big bang about twelve billion years ago. No one really knows for sure, but it's estimated that there has been interstellar travel for twenty million years or so. The reason no one really knows for sure, is because civilisations have come and gone: sometimes through natural causes, sometimes through unnatural ones ... Huh ... then again, it could be argued that even those that are perceived as unnatural causes are actually perfectly natural." Mr Casper raised a finger, "But there, we end up with philosophy."

Taking a deep breath, Mr Casper then continued, "With the loss of a civilisation, comes the loss of its history. And there is no way, with the loss of perhaps millions of civilisations over millions of years, and even sometimes the loss of the worlds they lived on, to know what knowledge has been lost. So, The Sphere may represent the oldest surviving intelligence in the galaxy, maybe even in the universe; a lone surviving entity from a distant past."

Captivated, the children continued to gaze at Mr Casper.

"That means," he continued, as he sat back in his seat and clasped his hands behind his head, "that any number of millions of beings could, at one time, have known the secret of The Sphere. The knowledge may then have been lost with the death of a single individual or an entire civilisation. Therefore, there may be nothing in existence more important, yet, at the same time, nothing less documented."

"So," said Rob, "we're not going to find out anything about The Sphere from KNIA."

"Not anything much past folklore and conjecture," said Mr Casper, a white, toothy smile spreading across his ebony face.

Blong-blong-blong.

The sound of an alarm broke the calm of the room as the lights repetitively dimmed and brightened, accentuating the ear-piercing, rhythmic noise.

Mr Casper jerked upright and asked, in a commanding voice, "What's wrong, KNIA?"

"Will has become frustrated. He is on his way to the hangar. I believe he intends to attempt actual flight at this point in time."

Mr Casper launched to his feet and ran from the room, leaving the others scrambling to get through the doorway behind him. He sprinted down the corridors, passing through doorways which KNIA opened for him, and arrived in the hangar to see Socket and Wrench each hugging a shuttle landing pad – shuttle engines screaming – as though they could keep the ship from lifting off. There was nothing like a fix-it when it came to tenacity, bravery, and caring.

"Socket!" Mr Casper yelled, as he moved into position to gain eye contact with Will in the cockpit. "Get me some headgear."

One of the fix-its let go of its landing pad and, with a flash of speed that astonished even Mr Casper, shot out of the hangar.

It was back in seconds with a small device. Mr Casper fumbled to hook it on his ear while waving to Will in the cockpit. Rob, Matt, Kris, Kaya, and Shani poured through the hangar doorway and stood to one side, watching. The shuttle was ready for flight.

Will wanted nothing more than to pull back on the joystick and fly the shuttle through the tube and straight up to the moon. But there was Mr Casper, un-fazed, pointing at the communicator … calm, as ever. And there were his brothers and Kaya and Shani standing there against the hangar wall, staring at him, concern etched on their faces. And even the fix-its looked worried in their own robotic way.

Will reached forwards and picked up the ship's communicator. As he placed it on his ear he heard Mr Casper's voice.

" … isn't the way to do this, Will. I know you want to save that girl. I know it's eating away at you but you have to be patient. It's not going to do her, or us, any good if you kill yourself."

Mr Casper moved a little closer to the shuttle and, in a calm, quiet voice, continued, "A galaxy ranger has to remain calm, Will. You have what it takes to be a great ranger, like your mother and father. But you have to trust me. You have to be patient."

Without saying anything else, Mr Casper waited for the boy to make his choice, with Socket beside him. Wrench was still lying on the floor hugging one of the landing pads.

It seemed as though Will hesitated forever, then he reached forwards and switched off the power. As the engines wound down, even the fix-its sighed with relief. Wrench relaxed his body and lay motionless under the shuttle, exhausted if a robot could be.

Under his breath, through pursed lips, Mr Casper said, "These children need a break."

A break meant hamburgers at a café in Sixes; one of the small towns down the coast from the base. The children were too hungry at first to talk much, but as the burgers and fries disappeared, moods improved. Even Will was smiling, as though just being away from the base was all that was needed to raise his spirit. He even seemed to have forgiven Kaya and Shani for barging in on the adventure.

As they talked and ate, Mr Casper pulled the communicator from his shirt pocket and quickly tapped a series of buttons. That done, he kept the communicator in his hand and shot a quick glance at the sky.

"You know," said Rob, "Food-Mack makes pretty good food. Not bad burgers, either. But … " he held up what was left of his burger, "there's something you can't beat about this."

"Speaking of Food-Mack," said Matt, as he looked at Mr Casper, "where does that thing get the food from, anyway? I mean, how does it all work?"

The town was bustling with tourists enjoying the day's warm, dry air. Mr Casper was now watching people as they walked by and seemed to have missed Matt's question.

"Mr Casper?" said Kris. "I think I see that man … "

"Shhh, I know," said Mr Casper. "By the tree in the park. Don't look at him. He was also hiding in the fields near the old base when you guys flew out of there."

Rob remembered now, seeing something below in the fields as the helicopter had banked to the west. He was bothered he had thought so little of it at the time, though it didn't seem to matter now as Mr Casper had showed no surprise at seeing the man.

"OK, listen up," began Mr Casper. "We have to get back to the base without our friend following." He checked his communicator and tapped a few more keys. Then he continued, "Kaya, Shani, you two come with me. Matt and Kris, you two head to the playground at the park. I'll pick you up there. Rob and Will, you go to that arcade down the street. That's close to where our friend's car is parked so I think he'll follow you. I'll pick you up in front of the arcade at … " he looked at his watch, "one-thirty."

Just as Mr Casper was about to send the brothers on their way, something caught their attention, It was a large man walking beside an even larger woman, both wearing suitably large white shorts, Hawaiian shirts, wide-brimmed hats – which Socket and Wrench would have liked very much – white socks pulled up to their knees, and white sneakers with very white laces. Bunched up around the well-endowed couple, were three equally well-fed children dressed much like their parents.

All five were rosy cheeked and smiling gaily, and each was making good time with a four-scoop ice cream cone. The family spanned the pavement from the street to the store fronts, making it impossible for anyone to get by without walking off the pavement and around the moving blockade, oblivious in their bliss.

But oblivious behaviour can have unexpected consequences. And thus it was the case then, for, at that moment, one of the chubby children licked a little too hard on his towering ice cream cone. Moving to counter the motion of the toppling treat, the large child crossed paths with the even larger father, who veered to avoid certain collision but ended up crossing paths with the mother, who was oblivious of the pending disaster because she had noticed a pizza place across the street. Somehow, the other two chubby children also became tangled up in the mess and the fat five got themselves tied into a fine knot. As they toppled with their ice creams, they attempted to save their precious treats as each one of them, in turn, realised that all was lost. They lay on the ground in various manners of embarrassing composure, coated in the ice cream their mouths had missed.

Before giggles and laughter from the Roar brothers and the girls could erupt, Mr Casper shot a glance at them with the sternest look he had ever given and held up a finger.

"First, we help. Then, we get out of here."

As the suited man by the tree in the park across the street stood on his toes trying to see what everyone was doing, Mr Casper and the children all rushed over to help the tangled tourists back to their feet. Moments later, the fat five filed off down the pavement and Mr Casper and the others split into their respective groups and took off.

Later, having left their follower behind, they all headed back to the coastal base in the SUV. Only this time, the vehicle was not following a road. Its wheels had retracted into the body and it was now flying two feet off the ground, at a substantial speed, cloaked, to hide it from searching eyes.

Out of the blue, Mr Casper said, "The machine collects the food from the ocean."

After a moment's pause, while the children realised that Mr Casper was answering Matt's question asked prior to the family's pavement collision, Matt asked, "You mean, everything is made from fish?"

Looking in the rearview mirror, Mr Casper said, "No. Everything is made from sea plants."

"We're eating seaweed?" asked Shani, grimacing from under her red NASA baseball cap.

Looking again in the rearview mirror, Mr Casper said, "It's good food, right?"

They all nodded, "Yeah, very good."

Suddenly, Socket and Wrench appeared outside the windshield, keeping pace with the vehicle. Flying backwards, one of the fix-its held up a small metal device with a short wire sticking out of it.

Mr Casper chuckled, "It appears our friend's car is missing a rather vital part."

Everyone laughed.

"Who is he?" asked Kaya.

"His name is Joe Millin," said Mr Casper. "He's an FBI agent assigned to a division specialising in the paranormal."

"You mean, like the *X-Files?*" asked Kaya.

"Yep. And it appears we're his X-file."

"Do you think he knows where the base is?" asked Will.

"He hasn't been anywhere near the base," answered Mr Casper. "And I don't think he knows exactly what he's looking for, either."

"But what got his attention in the first place?" asked Rob, knowing already what the answer was and feeling guilty about it.

Mr Casper eyed Rob in the rearview mirror. He said, "Someone probably got a look at Socket and Wrench one of those times when they helped you guys out of a tight spot."

Rob looked worried. "Sorry."

"Don't worry about it. He's probably a patient guy that's used to dead ends. We'll just have to be sure he reaches another dead end."

Out of This World

The next morning, everyone rose with the sun, revitalised. There's nothing like a good meal, preceded by a student pilot trying to steal a spaceship, to bring everyone back into focus. The children met with Mr Casper in the control room, as they had on all the other mornings since their arrival at the coastal base.

"So," he said, clapping his hands together, "Rob, Will, you two ready to fly this morning?"

Nodding, the two brothers said, "Yep," as they jumped to their feet and headed for the door.

"Hey, you need flight gear."

Rob and Will stopped and looked at each other, astonished, then turned to face Mr Casper.

"KNIA says you're ready to do the real thing ... "

Smiles appeared on Rob and Will as their eyes lit up. Then they gave each other a high-five.

"Yeah!"

" ... but you're not going all the way to the moon today. This is just a practice flight. Tomorrow is the day you guys go and get Katia. That's a full twenty-four hours before she runs out of air."

Will had a feeling those last words were for him.

Socket and Wrench walked in then, each holding up a pale-grey, one-piece suit just Rob's and Will's size. Because the robots were so short, each had an arm held high holding up the dangling clothing to keep the legs from dragging on the floor. Curious, Rob and Will stared at the suits. There was something about the material: it shimmered as though it was breathing.

"Socket and Wrench made these suits specially for you guys," said Mr Casper. He looked around at the others, "And they made one for each of you, too." The robots stood straight and tall. Mr Casper was sure that if the fix-its had been built with mouths, the two of them would have been beaming with pride.

"They sew?" asked Matt, his face all screwed up as though he had just tasted something bitter.

Glancing at the boy and chuckling, Mr Casper said, "Fix-its can do anything, Matt. They seem to particularly enjoy making clothing; in this case, your flight gear. And they look quite proud of their accomplishments, too … don't you think?"

At the mention of pride, it seemed as though Socket and Wrench's chests swelled magnificently, as they stood there holding the suits.

"Now," began Mr Casper, "you're probably all noticing the shimmer of the material that the suits are made of."

Rob nodded and said, "Yeah, what is it?"

"A very special fabric. They're called skin-suits and they're worn like long johns. A few seconds after you put them on, they'll contract and fit like a second skin."

"Wow, coool," said Matt.

" … then you wear your clothes over the skin-suits."

"What if we want to wear shorts?" asked Will, glancing at Mr Casper.

"Good question," said Mr Casper, pointing at the boy. "And not an unexpected one coming from a boy that likes to wear shorts so much. There's a seam at the top of each leg and arm so you can pull them off. There are also booties, gloves, and a liner to wear over your head in case you need more protection."

"Won't we get hot wearing those all the time?" pressed Will.

"What I've described so far, is only the beginning of what skin-suits can do. Those suits," Mr Casper pointed, "will maintain a comfortable temperature even in extreme environments; hot or cold. Believe me, guys; you won't even know you're wearing them. Look, there's really too much for me to go on about right now." Mr Casper took a deep breath and sighed as he exhaled. "If we weren't running out of time, I would have you study the information about all the stuff in your flight kits before your first flight. You're just going to have to squeeze in some study-time later on, when you can."

Walking over to Rob and Will, Mr Casper said, "Now, why don't you two go and get those suits on. Socket and Wrench will go with you. They also made you clothing more suitable for space travel."

With eager anticipation, and with Socket and Wrench following, Rob and Will took their skin-suits and left the room.

Looking at Kaya and Shani, Mr Casper continued, "They made clothes for you girls, too, even though there won't be any space travel for you." He looked kindly at Shani, who, as usual, was dressed in her baggy clothes with her long, luxurious hair tucked up underneath her red NASA baseball cap. "Socket and Wrench made your clothes to fit the body of a young girl. Your mother would probably approve," he smiled, "but don't let that keep you from liking them."

Shani returned his smile.

Mr Casper then turned to find Matt and Kris looking – as he figured they would – left out. "There is a real danger to what Rob and Will are doing this morning," he said. "It doesn't make sense to have all four of you up there on your first flight at the same time, just in case something goes wrong. So, Matt, as you practice in the simulator this morning, KNIA can make it seem like you're flying, right there with Rob and Will. You'll even show up on their scanners, so for them too it will be as if you're really there."

Though Matt understood what Mr Casper was saying about the risk, he was disappointed at being left behind. He wanted to fly as much as the others. But what was really bothering him, was that Mr Casper had said that Katia's rescue would take place tomorrow, and he had a feeling that only Rob and Will would be going.

"Kris," continued Mr Casper, "While your brothers are doing their thing this morning, I think it would be a good idea for you to study flight procedures; including emergency evasive tactics. A galaxy ranger is always prepared for the unexpected to happen. You'll find some stories in your father's computer logs about some of the problems he's run into. Your father was never really surprised about anything because he was always prepared."

Kris nodded. Though he was eager to fly with his brothers, he was alright with staying behind. He could wait, but he could tell that Matt was bummed-out about it.

A little later, Rob and Will returned dressed in their new clothes and looking every bit the galaxy rangers – albeit, a little young.

Mr Casper reached out, lifted Rob's left hand, and put what appeared to be some sort of an arm guard on his forearm. Rob studied the device as Mr Casper moved on to Will. The arm guard turned out to be a computer and it spanned from his wrist to his elbow. He peered over at Will, who was studying an identical device on his own arm.

"These," said Mr Casper, "can be the most important devices a galaxy ranger can have. They are a compact computer we call an arm-comp. Everything KNIA knows, you can know; even when you're out of range of KNIA."

Next, Mr Casper placed a communicator on each boy's ear. The devices seemed to mould to their ears and become a part of them, surprising both Rob and Will.

He continued, "These are how you will communicate with KNIA. The communicators work integrally with your arm-comps. You can also speak with each other, and others, through them. And, they're also translators."

Perplexed, Rob and Will looked at each other, then back at Mr Casper.

"Translators?" asked Will.

"As you know by now, guys," said Mr Casper, "there is so much to learn about our galaxy. Remember, there are an uncountable variety of languages out there. The galaxy is just like Earth in every way when it comes to diversity between cultures. Only, there are many more different cultures on the galactic scale. What you can expect to find here on Earth, you can expect to find out there, and many times more. So, as well as being a basic communicator," Mr Casper pointed at the device on Will's ear, "that thing can translate foreign languages. When a foreigner speaks, you will hear the words as though they were spoken in your own language."

Mr Casper reached out and touched Will's communicator. There was a slight audible hiss as a small microphone extended to his mouth. "You don't need this microphone unless you want to whisper," continued Mr Casper, "or unless you're speaking to someone who speaks another language and does not, himself, have a translator. With the microphone extended, the communicator translates your words as you speak them, so that what the foreigner hears is in his own language. Now you guys can go anywhere in the galaxy and communicate with anyone."

The room was quiet for a moment, while Mr Casper eyed Rob and Will. They certainly looked the part, he thought, so now let's see if they can play the part.

"Ok, guys," he said, clapping his hands together. "Let's get you into the air."

"Yes!" Rob and Will cheered as they shot from the room.

Kris, Kaya, and Shani followed. Matt hung back, walking from the control room at a subdued pace.

As he walked along the passageway to the hangar, the others getting further ahead, Matt felt a hand on his shoulder and realised he had forgotten about Mr Casper. He stopped walking but was unable to look up at the man. Instead, he found himself an undefined point on the floor at which to stare. Mr Casper's hand slid off his shoulder.

"KNIA says you're almost ready, Matt. Maybe tomorrow."

Matt shot a glance up at the man and quickly looked away, not wanting him to see the disappointment on his face. Frustrated, he said, "I'm ready. I could fly now."

"Yeah, I know you could. But KNIA thinks we need to make sure you're more careful."

Matt peered up at Mr Casper and said, "I only just knocked that light off the Golden Gate Bridge. And KNIA said there wasn't any damage to that ship that the light fell on."

"Yeah," said Mr Casper, nodding, "but then there was that sailboat you capsized ... "

"Oh," said Matt, searching for that undefined spot on the floor again. "I forgot about that." Then he peered up again at

Mr Casper. "But no one was hurt. And it was just the simulator, anyway. I wouldn't do that in real life. I was just having fun."

"And there was that incident with the F-14," said Mr Casper, with a raised eyebrow. "I doubt the United States Navy would appreciate a boy in a space-fighter picking a fight with one of their fighter-jets, even if it was just fooling around."

Again, Matt searched for that spot on the floor. "Oh, yeah. I forgot about that one."

Mr Casper placed his hand on Matt's shoulder again. "After we watch Rob and Will take off," he said, "why don't you go take your turn in the simulator. Like I said, KNIA can have you fly with your brothers from there."

After a moment's hesitation, still disappointed, Matt nodded.

By the time he and Mr Casper arrived at the hangar, Rob was climbing aboard one of the space-fighters and Will was preparing to board another. Socket and Wrench had paired up, one with each boy, keeping an eye on them like big brothers.

Seeing Mr Casper coming towards the spaceships, Will, a mischievous grin on his face, called out, "Don't we get laser guns or something?"

Coming to a stop nearby, Mr Casper said, "You'll have weapons training someday, Will. For now, focus on becoming the best pilot in the galaxy."

Will shrugged and started climbing the fighter's fuselage towards the cockpit, but when he heard Mr Casper call, he paused and looked down. Mr Casper was smiling as he said, "Science-fiction movies have laser guns. We have blasters." Will smiled widely, and continued his climb.

The cavernous hangar came alive with the shrill sound of Polinthian plasma engines powering-up as first Rob, and then Will, prepared for flight. All the while, Socket and Wrench remained close, keeping an eye on things.

With a hand cupped over the ear on which he wore his communicator, Mr Casper said, "OK, guys, be safe. See you in a few hours."

The noise from the engines intensified as the two young pilots ratcheted forwards the throttles and gave a quick wave to their audience. The space-fighters lifted off the hangar floor, turned slowly and then moved towards the tube. Rob's fighter reached the tube first and, with an ear-splitting roar, was gone. Will swiftly followed and the hangar was left in silence, as though the ships had vanished. From the speed with which they left the base, vanish was not far from the truth.

Mr Casper peered down at Matt, and said, "KNIAs waiting for you."

Matt nodded and turned to leave.

"Matt?"

Stopping, he twisted to look back.

"Make it real today."

With a determined look on his face, Matt nodded and left.

Rob and Will were both experiencing the same, intense thrill. Their hearts were racing and their minds light from the excitement of moving with such incredible speed through the tube; far faster than when they had passed through it in the helicopter. Everything they had learned about flying and all the practice in the simulator failed to prepare them completely for the real thing. With the restraining fields holding them in comfort and safety in their cockpit seats, the brothers felt weightless: they had no physical existence; they were at one with their machines.

With such blinding speed, it was impossible to see any detail outside the cockpit; it was all just a blur. Rob wondered what a spaceship flashing through the tube looked like from the water beyond. As he checked his flight controls, he thought that although this was his first time as pilot, somehow, it seemed so right. He wondered whether the familiarity he felt was KNIAs influence, or something innate in him. He also wondered what Will was making of it all.

Will wasn't thinking about much at all. He just had a smile which spread from ear to ear. With the memory of this ride, he would surely not be able to keep his feet on the ground for the rest of his life. No theme park ride could ever compare to this. Not a chance. Not ever.

Bang!!!

Rob's fighter exploded from the tube. KNIA had explained that even with the powerful field that made the inside of the tube a vacuum, like that of outer space, when a ship entered or exited there was a sound like that of a supersonic rumble. Anyone who heard it would think it was thunder.

Due to its cloaking field, Rob's space-fighter appeared as just a shimmer in the air as he pulled back on the joystick. In spite of his seat's restraining field, he could feel the machine's astronomical power as the fighter arced up and shot straight towards the upper atmosphere. Rob decided then, that there was surely nothing in the galaxy like flying. It was purely awesome!

Bang!!!

Will, too, was out and pulling back on the joystick, his ear-to-ear grin still fixed on his face. It was then, that he, like Rob, became utterly convinced he would never find anything in the galaxy as exhilarating as flying a space-fighter. He saw Rob's ship on his scanner and followed, straight up.

Because the very awareness of being in flight has a powerful influence on the mind, a simulator could never create flight exactly as it was. But the simulator at the Galaxy Ranger coastal base on Earth was something else altogether – even by galactic standards – for, as KNIA enhanced the experience via a mind-link, the sensation of simulated flight seemed so very real. So, as Matt, too, now shot from the tube with a bang, the sensation of flying thrilled him beyond his every expectation and his face beamed. He saw his brothers on his scanner and gave chase. And it all seemed so real.

The brothers never passed through the ionosphere to outer space. Mr Casper had forbidden it. They were to stay within 100 miles of Earth although, even at that altitude, they got the sense of what it was going to be like to leave Earth's atmosphere. At one point, they could see the moon so clearly that it seemed to be within reach, and the temptation to go and rescue Katia at that very moment was almost overwhelming.

When a cloaked spaceship is in motion, a cloaking field can cause the fuselage to overheat because it adds friction during flight and absorbs the heat itself. And the added friction slows the ship. Therefore, whenever it was safe to do so, Rob and Will deactivated their cloaking fields and got to go faster. As they flew around the world, their space-fighters' onboard computers jammed any systems that might have tracked them. Although Matt had no need for cloaking and jamming any probing radar, KNIA created simulations that required him to do so.

Although Rob and Will could only see Matt on their scanners, in the simulator, Matt could see Rob and Will as though he was with them. After spending an hour practising fighting manoeuvres, each boy at one time or another getting the better of the others, it was clear that Will was the best of the three. Will had the knack of anticipating the others' moves and, in a split second, taking advantage of an opportunity.

They practiced more manoeuvres by flying low through a length of the Chilean Andes Mountains in South America, and did so without mishap, mistake, or mischief. From Chile, they flew south to Antarctica, and across the frozen continent just feet above the ice. They raced to Australia and crossed from the south coast to the north, over the desolate outback, in just minutes. They raced over the Indian Ocean low enough for their ships' supersonic shockwave to crease the water's surface. They blasted through the Sahara stirring up their own little sandstorm. They even cloaked their ships to fly over the great pyramids at Giza – Rob had always wanted to see them.

On their way home, they flew north through China, and then north-east through Russia, and crossed the Bering Strait into Alaska. They played a little bit more, flying through the towering mountains along the Alaskan/Canadian coast before Will grew serious about what all this was about – Katia.

He led Rob and Matt up to the ionosphere to take one more look at the moon. There was no Earth shadow on it; seen from that high up, it was full and fat. Tomorrow, they would go there and rescue Katia; an adventure like no other before. As the brothers took one last look before heading home, a feeling struck each boy that there was something wrong but neither said anything. Each figured he was just nervous. Tomorrow, it would be all over and Katia would be safe.

Upon landing in the cavern, having shut down their ships' engines and climbed to the hangar floor, Rob and Will's excitement was infectious as the others met them, though Will's cold mood towards Kaya and Shani had returned. Socket and Wrench joined in, hovering at chest height and extending their little hands for a 'high-five' with each boy.

In the simulator, Matt set his ship down with a barely discernible bump.

"Very good, Matt," said KNIA. "As you sleep tonight, I will help your mind assimilate all you have learned today."

All four Roar brothers and the two girls had become used to hearing this from KNIA. They had become accustomed to waking in their sleep-tubes and discovering that things they had read about or seen, or had otherwise been taught the previous day – which they thought they would never remember – had become etched in their minds. This is how the Roar boys learned, in just days, how to pilot spaceships, among other things.

"Sorry I messed around so much, before," said Matt, feeling both exhilarated and tired from flying around the world with his brothers. Even though he had been in the simulator, it had seemed so real.

"It is part of who you are, Matt, to succumb to the urge to push the limits," said KNIA. "However, you have the capacity to judge when it is an acceptable time to joke around and when it is necessary to be serious."

"Well," said Matt as he hopped out of the simulator's pilot seat, "I'm going to go have lunch." He opened the hatch as he continued, "I'm thinking about an ice cream sundae for dessert. Too bad you can't have ice cream, KNIA."

"Matt."

As though KNIA could be seen there, behind him, Matt stopped and looked back.

"Always keep in mind that a person's perception of reality can become blurred. A person can become confused as to what is real and what is not, and to what is right and what is wrong. Sometimes, even something as simple as what is up and what is down can be difficult to discern. A good sense of humour can be useful during a difficult time, but it must be used with care and tact. If not, things can be made worse for you, and others."

Matt thought for a moment about what KNIA had just said. He could keep things straight. He could tell when things were real or not, though, he was uncertain he knew exactly what KNIA meant by all she said. Yeah, he knew when to cut loose and when not to. No problem.

"All right," he said, "I'll remember that."

"I have confidence that you will."

Hesitating, Matt stood there in the open hatchway for a moment, and then said, "Bye, KNIA."

"Goodbye, Matt."

And he was off for lunch and that sundae ...

That night, Kris woke, abruptly. He lay there for a while not really thinking about anything particular, partly wishing he could go back to sleep, partly feeling like there should be something to think about ... something to figure out.

He found himself getting out of bed and walking along the passageways towards the control room, noticing, as he went, a timepiece recording that it was 1:37 in the morning.

Today was the day they would be going to the moon to get Katia. Even if they were not deemed completely ready, they would have to go. But KNIA and Mr Casper had said they'd do well. They had faith in them and, because of their exceptional young minds, the accelerated training had worked better than expected.

The control room lit up when Kris entered. He walked to one of the console chairs and flopped down. It was quiet. He sat for a moment, thinking. Then ...

"KNIA," he said, "did you send us that e-mail?"

After a moment's silence that left Kris wondering why KNIA was not answering his question, KNIA said, "I do not have a reason to send you an e-mail, Kris."

Kris wondered why that answer seemed odd. He was quiet again, and then asked, "Where are you, KNIA ... ?"

"I am here."

"Well, where is 'here'?" Kris pressed. "The base computer seems to be a self-contained system that you tap into the same way we do. I've looked all around the base and I haven't found your system hardware, anywhere. So, where are you kept ... ?"

"I am somewhere else, Kris. Because of my nature, your parents think it best my whereabouts remain unknown."

Ahhh! Now he knew.

After a moment, his brows knitted, and Kris asked, "Can you read minds, KNIA ... ?"

"I cannot read minds in a sense of knowing a person's thoughts. But I can analyse a mind's structure and chemical balance and, with that information, tell which parts of the mind are most active."

"Is that how you help us learn?"

"Yes. The brain is much like a computer, though much more complex because thoughts do not always follow a logical path. This intuitiveness is especially so in the human mind above all others in the galaxy. The human mind is unpredictable and for that reason, highly adaptable. Do you recall, on your arrival at the base, when you first entered the control room ... ?"

"Yeah," answered Kris, a puzzled look on his face.

"How did you know that I existed? How did you know to speak to me?"

Kris thought about it. He clearly remembered that after looking around the control room, he had decided the computer would be voice activated, but how he had known that was a mystery. However, now that KNIA had just told him she was hidden someplace else, confirming his suspicion that she was a separate system, he knew, now, that it was KNIA and not the base computer he had initially talked to. He and the others had just assumed that KNIA and the base computer were one and the same thing. KNIA had made it seem that way when she powered up the control room. For Kris, the KNIA mystery had just been fully realised.

"I think I just guessed," he said.

"Otherwise known as intuition," said KNIA. "And you and your brothers have excellent intuition. So do Kaya and Shani. It is fortunate they have joined us. Intuition, combined with intelligence, can be a powerful tool. Please consider these questions now: Why are you awake? And why are you here?"

Kris thought for a moment, then shrugged, and said, "I don't know. I guess something just doesn't seem right."

At that moment, the control room door slid open and Rob burst in, with Will on his heels, closely followed by Matt (a bowl of ice cream in hand), Kaya, and Shani. Somehow not surprised to see the others, Kris stared at them.

Matt put a spoonful of ice cream in his mouth, swallowed, and said, "Maybe everyone should just have some ice cream and go back to bed."

All eyes turned on him.

"I knew it," he said, "something's wrong ... isn't it?" Matt scanned the others with a concerned look on his face. "It's not Katia is it?"

At that moment, Mr Casper rushed in. Seeing everyone there, he paused to finish pulling on his outer shirt. He then looked around at them and said, "KNIA told me you were all awake. What's going on?" Mr Casper stared at Matt and smiled. "A little ice cream break from sleeping, Matt?"

Matt held up a spoonful, "It's always a good time for ice cream," he said, as he stuffed a spoonful in his mouth.

Socket and Wrench arrived at a run. They were followed by one more person – Adia.

"Mother!" Kaya and Shani called out as they rushed to hug her. "When did you get here?" asked Shani.

"About two hours ago," said Adia, as she glanced at Mr Casper and each Roar boy in turn. Her gaze settled on Matt who had frozen, staring at her with his spoon sticking out of his mouth. "Is it time for a snack?" she asked.

Matt pulled the spoon from his mouth and grinned.

"Someone, please tell me what's going on," said Mr Casper.

"Will and I woke up," said Rob. "And we don't know why, but something's bugging us."

"Yeah," said Kaya, "same with Shani and me."

Mr Casper looked at Kris, who nodded and raised his hand, "Same here."

While cradling his bowl of ice cream in one hand and holding his spoon aloft in the other, Matt looked around, shrugged, and said, "I just thought I was hungry."

Turning to glance at each one in turn, Mr Casper said, "Maybe you're all a little on edge about our big day."

Rob said, "I feel like I do when I'm sure I'm forgetting something."

"Yeah," said Will, "like I just missed the bus or something."

Again, Mr Casper glanced at each child, then at Adia, then towards the ceiling as though that was where KNIA could be found. "What do you make of all this, KNIA?"

"Kris and I were just speaking about intuition," said KNIA. "It appears something of concern has awakened the children."

"KNIA," said Mr Casper, "please contact Katia."

Instantly, a section of the wall monitor was lit with the image of the inside of Katia's ship and Keb staring back. Katia appeared, looking very sleepy, then very worried. "You're not going to be able to come and get me, are you?"

"We're coming to get you right now," said Mr Casper.

Katia looked away and said, "Keb, please check for other ships." Everyone in the control room tensed.

Returning her attention to the screen, she said, "There is no threat showing on our scanner. And we still have just over twenty-four

Earth-hours of air remaining," Katia added, looking away again, presumably at Keb. Again, she returned her attention to those in the control room. "But I do feel like something is wrong."

Mr Casper looked around at the others, then back at the screen. "Katia, prepare your ship. We're coming to get you now."

She nodded, "We'll be ready."

Mr Casper looked down at the two fix-its and said, "Socket, Wrench, get the shuttle and two fighters ready." The robots shot from the control room.

Studying the faces of the Roar boys, Mr Casper continued, "Sending all four of you up there worries me, because the reality is, regardless of how good the technology is under your seat, it's dangerous out there." Mr Casper breathed in and blew out through pursed lips. "But if I don't send all of you and there's some kind of problem ... " Again, Mr Casper took a deep breath, then continued, "Whatever happens, remember this: you boys must stick together. And always watch out for each other."

"Rob, Will," Mr Casper stared at them, "you two take the fighters. Go."

Rob and Will bolted from the room. Kris walked to stand beside Matt.

Mr Casper studied the younger brothers and said, "You two take the shuttle. While Matt pilots, Kris, you should review docking procedures."

The boys started for the door but Matt then stopped, turned, and handed his bowl of ice cream to Adia, saying, "I promise I'm not asking you to do my dishes. There's a really cool machine in the dining area that takes care of that. I just hate to see good ice cream go to waste."

He looked up at Adia with big bright eyes that could melt a tub of ice cream. She grinned and accepted the bowl. Matt started for the door again but turned to peer back at Mr Casper.

"What does that machine do with the dishes, anyway? I've been putting a little scratch on each dish I use but I haven't seen the same one again ... and I check everyone's dishes."

Kris rolled his eyes and took a deep breath. His brother was hopeless.

"Matt," said Mr Casper, holding back a smile, "go rescue the girl. The mystery of the disappearing dishes can be investigated when you get back."

"Right," said Matt, as he turned, and, at a dash, led Kris out.

"So that's why Matt's been clearing our dishes," said Shani. "I thought he was just being sweet."

"He is sweet, Shani," said Kaya, "but that's sort of weird."

Taking a bite of ice cream, Adia chuckled as she shook the spoon at Mr Casper. She swallowed and said, "How is it, that there seems to be an emergency, and yet we've just been discussing a sweet boy, lost dishes, and … " with a guilty smile, she took another bite of ice cream and continued with her mouth full, "this is really good ice cream."

By the time Mr Casper, Adia, Kaya, and Shani arrived at the hangar, the brothers were already in the ships, prepared for flight. Socket and Wrench buzzed around making last minute preparations as engines were powered up. The fix-its retreated and the fighters lifted off. Rob gave a quick wave and was gone down the tube. Will waved and followed, in swift pursuit. The shuttle, being a larger ship, lifted off more slowly. Then Matt and Kris waved and the shuttle pitched, turned, and slipped into the tube.

"Jumping jitterbug!" said Kris, his eyes as wide open as they had ever been as the shuttle accelerated, blurring the tunnel.

Excited, Matt nodded, "Oh yeah, Kris, jum-ping-jitterbug … "

Bang!!!

Rob was out of the tube, pulling back on the joystick, heading straight up, just like his father, out for adventure.

Bang!!!

Will was right behind him. The day had finally come.

Bang!!!

The shuttle blasted from the tube and Matt pulled back on the stick.

"Yeeehaw!" he said, steering the shuttle straight up.

Kris clutched his seat's armrests, his voice stuck in his throat.

Moments later, Rob and Will flew side-by-side as they blasted through the ionosphere and, for the first time, entered the star-scattered blackness of space. Each boy was instantly awestruck by the absolute immensity of the universe. With the naked eye, from Earth's surface the universe looks one-dimensional. But it is an entirely different thing when one finds himself surrounded by it and humbled by the simple realisation that space is so very aptly named. The moon was growing larger with each second.

As the shuttle also broke free of Earth's atmosphere, Matt and Kris were struck with a profound sense of lightheartedness over entering the great dark beyond. Somewhere, out there, were their parents. Somehow, finding them now seemed quite possible. The lights on the shuttle's control console reflected in Matt and Kris's wide-open eyes. The scanner showed the two space-fighters approaching the moon ahead.

They were close, and would be there, soon ...

A short while later, with Rob and Will having taken up tactical defence positions, the shuttle raced from the sunlit side of the moon to the shadowed side. Matt and Kris's eyes took a moment to adjust to the dark.

Soon, Katia would be safe.

Matt sent the shuttle into a dive and flew just above the lunar surface towards the broken Peridian spaceship. Once there, he landed as close as possible and Kris leapt from his seat, ran to the shuttle's hatch, and prepared for boarding.

With the airlock extended almost to its limit and attached to the other ship, Earth's shuttle was ready to receive its new passengers. Kris opened the airlock door ...

Eee! Eee!

The warning signal screamed. At first, he thought he had done something wrong and panic began to set in. But then, Matt was by his side speaking in a startled voice, "Quick, it's a Boargen ship!"

Out of This Solar System

Matt and Kris could hear Rob and Will's alarmed voices, "Get out of there! It's the Boargen!" Then, "They're launching fighters! Three of them!"

Kris turned from Matt to head down the airlock extension but quickly ducked when … whoosh … a brilliant-white ball about six inches in diameter flashed by. In the split-second it took Matt and Kris to turn their heads to see what it was, it had vanished. For a moment, Kris thought they were under attack from Katia's ship, but when he shot a look down the airlock extension he saw a girl running towards him, followed by a robot.

Looking fearful, Katia rushed past Kris and Matt and into the shuttle as the two boys stared, wide-eyed, at the tall, silver robot following her. Kris punched the buttons to retract the airlock extension and close the hatch. As Katia and Keb wasted no time settling into seats, the two brothers bolted for the cockpit.

With Kris in the co-pilot's seat beside him, as though he had done it countless times before, Matt powered up the shuttle, pulled back on the stick, and thrust the throttles forwards. The ship leapt from the lunar surface in a burst of dust and slipped through the blackness of the night side of the moon, away from the Boargen threat, bound for Earth.

Boom!!!

An explosion hit the moon's surface below the shuttle. The blast rocked the ship and set off that ear-piercing alarm again.

Eee! Eee!

Matt grimaced at the noise.

"Kris, would you shut that thing off. We know we're in trouble."

The signal silenced.

Rob was seeing it but it was incredibly difficult to believe it was actually happening. The huge ship was chasing the shuttle and had just shot at it. How could this be? Less than two weeks ago, he and Will were running through a tunnel to get away from some punks. Now, they were running from something he could only have imagined in his wildest dreams. And they had no weapons training. In fact, no training whatsoever as how to deal with what was happening. They were just supposed to rescue Katia; not to fight the Boargen.

All four brothers knew there would be no communication from the Earth base unless there was something Mr Casper and KNIA could contribute in dealing with the dangerous events. As Mr Casper had said several times during the last week, "If you're ever in a tight spot, having me or KNIA screaming advice in your ear when you're trying to figure out what to do, could make matters worse. Trust yourselves. KNIA and I will help if it looks like you need it."

The giant ship fired at the shuttle again, coming closer this time, disturbing its otherwise smooth, swift flight.

"They're shooting at them!" said Rob in desperation, as he and Will blazed trails in their space-fighters to catch up with the shuttle before the enemy ships could surround it. "What are we going to do?!" But no sooner had he said those words, he then knew what they had to do. They had to fight.

Adrenalin surged through Will as he, himself, worked to figure out what next. His and Rob's space-fighters were armed. So was the shuttle. Could firing the weapons be so hard? The reality of the severity of their predicament then rushed into his lungs as he gasped. He then understood, without the slightest doubt: it was fire the weapons or one, or all, of his brothers could die. He, himself, could die.

At that moment, a text message came from KNIA, blinking in green letters on his cockpit canopy against the star-speckled blackness of space beyond: GET OUT OF THIS SOLAR SYSTEM. Will knew his brothers were seeing the same message.

The shuttle changed course, no longer heading for Earth. To Will's astonishment, it headed straight for one of the enemy fighters bearing down on it. Orange bursts fired from the shuttle and the enemy fighter exploded, and was gone.

Will turned his space-fighter, aiming it towards a second enemy, and pulled the trigger on the joystick. Bursts of orange traced a line from the nose of his fighter to the target, which then vanished in a puff of flame. Seconds later, out of the corner of his eye, he saw another explosion. Only when he willed himself to look, did he see Rob's space-fighter rejoining him, and he sighed with palpable relief.

The Roar brothers had figured out weapons training!

They had destroyed the Boargen fighters, but the behemoth was still bearing down on them. It proved its threat by landing a blast so close to the shuttle that, in spite of the protection provided by the shuttle's repulse field, Matt and Kris thought they would soon be skidding on their butts through space.

There were three main options for dealing with a threat like the one at hand. One was to activate the cloaking field and vanish from sight. But cloaking fields were best used to remain undetected rather than to disappear after detection, because an intuitive captain could find a cloaked ship once he knew it was there. The second option was to stay and fight. But given the brothers' inexperience, the chances of winning a battle against such a large ship was slight. The third option was to run. And that is exactly what KNIA had said to do.

Without knowing exactly why, Kris chose a coordinate from the navigation computer and sent it to Rob and Will. Instantly, he received a reply from both. He looked at Matt and said, "Let's go."

At that, Matt pushed the throttle forwards, past a slight resistance at the top, and in a blaze of light, three Earth spaceships slipped away from Earth's solar system.

If Socket and Wrench had been able to arrive at the moon fast enough, they would have thrown themselves at the enemy ships to save the Roar brothers.

The scanner at the coastal base now showed only the Boargen space-destroyer behind the moon, and it was now leaving. Apparently, the Boargen were not yet bold enough to come all the way. Whatever was going on outside Earth's solar system, whatever

Katia carried with her, the Boargen wanted it bad enough to break a number of galactic settlement treaties. This was bad for Earth, and the galaxy.

It had been the longest five minutes of Mr Casper's life. During those minutes he had realised, over and over, that his worst fear could come true: that one or all of the Roar brothers could be killed. For those five minutes, while the Boargen ships bore down on the youngsters, Mr Casper had hated himself, for he had been sure he would have time later, to provide weapons training. However, KNIA had assured him that the brothers could figure out the weapons controls and that technique would come naturally. So, when one after the other the enemy fighters had disappeared from the scanner, Mr Casper was grateful that KNIA had never been wrong, and that the Roar brothers were marvellously capable.

Now, because he had had KNIA tell them to go, the Roar boys were gone. He had no idea where, but they were alive. Although he was concerned for their well-being as he lowered himself into one of the control room chairs, he felt confident that the brothers could take care of themselves. Using a method for cross-galactic communication, which was difficult to achieve, they would contact him, eventually, when they felt it was safe. For now, he consoled himself with the knowledge that the next time he saw the Roar brothers they would be a little more grown up. They would be boys of the galaxy.

Mr Casper looked around for the others. Adia was still there, where she had stopped, cold, upon entering the control room. Kaya and Shani stood, one on either side of her. Socket and Wrench stood in front of them.

He had a weak smile when he said, "Well, they rescued Katia and Keb."

Of course, Katia had been through thin-space many times. But not the Roar boys. For them, it was an exhilarating experience travelling through an instant passage; a limitless boundary that took them from one solar system to another. Like Mr Casper had said: "Travelling through thin-space is like opening a door and walking through a void from one room to another." If space contained no stars, no planets, nothing, and if space was a black texture-less void, thin-space was just that, only a pure white field.

It is said that travelling through thin-space is an art. Some pilots can do it better than others. Those who can do it best, have an instinctive knack for it. Even for those with the knack, however, travelling a great distance across the galaxy requires several passes through thin-space. But for the roar brothers, their first journey from Earth to a distant solar system was accomplished in just one pass; partly because the system was in a desolate region of the galaxy, and partly because Kris and his brothers had the knack for striking out through thin-space; though they didn't know it at the time.

In a flash of light, the three Earth spaceships appeared near a single desert planet circling a large, lonely sun at the outermost rim of our galaxy.

Like Will in the other space-fighter, and Matt and Kris in the shuttle, Rob took a deep breath and oddly enough, relaxed, in spite of there being nothing in sight that he considered familiar. Even his own hands, grasping the space-fighter's controls seemed alien to him.

They had escaped. But to where? To his right, the galaxy spread out across space in a brilliant mist of billions of stars. To his left, the stars, some so far away that they were barely visible, were scattered thinly across an endless black space. Before him, was a pasty-orange planet, still small so far away; and off to the side and behind him, was a massive sun – just one of the few scattered stars in that part of the galaxy.

"Where are we?" came Will's voice through Rob's communicator.

"This is Sundee," replied Kris.

"Not that it really matters," said Rob, his communicator relaying his words to his brothers in the other ships, "we had to get out of there. But what made you pick this place, Kris? We must be right on the edge of the galaxy."

"While you guys were on your first flights, I hung out in the control room and studied emergency evasive tactics and looked through Father's computer logs for examples. The logs mentioned this place. Father wrote 'Sundee is an awful place to get away to'." His voice growing excited, Kris continued, "You guys should check out Father's logs! He's seen some really crazy stuff! Had lots of close calls, too!" His voice mellowed, "Anyway, he also wrote that a good pilot could reach Sundee with just one pass through thin-space from just about anywhere in the galaxy. So I figured Father was saying in a round-about way, that Sundee was a good place to escape to and a safe place to hide, because it's so awful that no one wants to go there."

All was quiet for a moment, as the three ships drew closer to the planet, which, from that distance, continued to be just a pasty-orange ball in a sea of black.

Then Rob said, "Good thinking, Kris. I hope you're right. It does look like an awful place; awfully hot, even from this far out."

Later, the Earth spaceships converged in orbit around the desert planet. Their arrival went unnoticed but by one, and he was not expecting visitors; and nor did he want them.

As the three Earth ships – joined, as one – orbited Sundee, the Roar boys were seated in the shuttle's passenger area near Katia, who, it had been noticed, had a communicator tucked to her ear; one not unlike those the brothers wore. Matt had been experimenting by pulling his communicator from his ear when Katia had spoken. He had giggled at the sound of one of her words and Katia, disapproving, had frowned at him.

Towering above the seats, Keb was standing next to where Katia sat, something Kris was glad of – all the better to study the robot. But while listening to the conversation at hand and studying Keb, Kris was also looking for something: the white ball that had entered the ship and then vanished. With all the excitement, he had forgotten about it, until now. Had he imagined it? He didn't think so. If the white ball was real, it was someplace in the shuttle … but where? And what was it?

" ... granted, you did a fine job of rescuing us," said Katia. "But this is your first time off your planet. With all due respect to your father, who my mother would say is the most skilled and trusted ranger in the galaxy, Earth is not known for producing galaxy-savvy citizens. In fact," Katia glanced up at Keb, and then returned her attention to the brothers, "as far as I know, your father is the only citizen of Earth to travel out of Earth's solar system." She glanced up at Keb again, "Or even further out than Earth's planetoid satellite."

"The moon," Will snapped. "And we know more than you think we do. The rest, we can figure out."

"Will," said Rob, "don't take what Katia's saying personally. She's right to be concerned about whether we can help. There's an entire galaxy out here we don't know much about."

Breathing out as he slowly shook his head, Will looked away, bothered that Katia thought so little of their abilities. He had thought that after all his conversations with her, that they were friends. But now, she was acting like a snob.

"Sorry," she said. "I don't mean to offend you. I am grateful for your help. I owe you my life, and so, perhaps, my trust as well."

Will returned his attention to the group.

Smiling, Katia continued, "You are very skilled pilots." She looked at Will. "Boargen pilots are among the most vicious and relentless, and you bested them."

The Roar brothers exchanged sorrowful looks. There had been no time to consider the pilots in the fighters they had destroyed.

That was a good sign, thought Katia; the Roar brothers did not rejoice over the death of even one aggressor. She knew it could be a confusing mixture of emotions: relief if you survived, yet sorrow if your survival was at the cost of another's.

"We may have a lot to learn," said Rob, "but if you want our help, we'll help. If not, I suppose we should take you where you want to go and then head home."

"Or we could go look for Mother and Father," said Will.

"We do have the summer off from school," added Matt, a mischievous smirk blossoming on his round face.

"Shouldn't we try to contact Mr Casper?" asked Kris.

"I thought about that," said Rob. "But if the Boargen ship is still in Earth's system, they could track us through our signal. Besides, communicating from this distance through a tight-beam would be very difficult. I think we're on our own, for now."

"Well, someone needs to get on the ball around here and invent a better technology for cross-galactic communication," said Matt, feigning outrage.

At Matt's mention of a better technology, Kris became subtly alert. The robot noticed. Kris noticed the robot noticed. He had suddenly realised what the mysterious white ball must be; though how he realised it was more like finding a lost memory than experiencing a revelation.

"Katia," he said, "from my understanding of The Sphere, the Boargen can't make it give them knowledge. What would they do with it if they got it?"

Stark silence overtook the shuttle. Everyone stared at Kris, who noticed Keb's eyes seemed to bore into him. He knew there was no need to fear the robot, but its stare was unsettling.

After his revelation sank in, Katia said, "How do you know about The Sphere?"

Kris took a deep breath. "As Will mentioned," he said, grinning, his bright, hazel eyes scanning the inside of the shuttle, looking for what he now knew was there with them, "we know more than you think we do." He looked at Katia. "I'd like to see The Sphere, if I could."

From the cargo hold at the back of the shuttle, a bright, white orb showed itself and slowly flew towards Kris. It was the most pure white one could imagine, and although it seemed as though it should radiate light, it did not. It was like a crisp hole punched in the dark.

Motionless, the others watched as The Sphere came within inches of Kris' face. He reached up with both hands and grasped it. It felt like ... nothing. He felt nothing. Yet there was something in his hands because he could not have closed them further if he had tried.

Letting go, Kris uttered, "Thank you."

The Sphere visited Matt next, who giggled, but thought, seriously, that there was something familiar about it. Then it visited Will, who thought the same thing. Finally, it came to Rob, who, like his brothers, found it familiar but in a comforting way.

"I think I know why the Boargen want it," said Rob. "I'm guessing they can't make The Sphere give them technology, but they could keep it from sharing knowledge with others."

Katia looked at Keb, realisation dawning, and said, "So that's why they're after it. The Boargen don't need to gain knowledge to control the galaxy. They could gain control of the existing knowledge and … "

"As long as they kept The Sphere trapped," Rob broke in, "they might be able to rule the galaxy by controlling the flow of the technology that exists."

"May I offer advice, young miss?" asked Keb.

It was the first time Keb had said anything in the company of the Roar brothers, and Kris was thrilled. There was no dragging his gaze from the robot. Socket and Wrench were awesome, but Keb was a miraculous accomplishment. The robot moved with grace, with precise perfection, and with pure purpose. There was no wasted motion, even when it spoke.

Smiling adoringly, Katia said, "That's Keb's way of saying he knows what we should do." She looked up at the robot. "Isn't that so, Keb?"

The robot looked down at Katia. It seemed to Kris that if Keb could, he would have been smiling, returning the adoring gaze.

"We do not, at this time, have a choice from whom we receive help, young miss," said Keb. "And I do not believe we could have more capable help than we will receive from the sons of Rob and Mara Roar. They have, after all, already proven themselves very capable."

"You know it, dude," said Matt, jumping to his feet and reaching forwards to give Keb a high-five.

Keb looked at Matt's hand, then at Matt, then back at Matt's hand, and gave him his high-five.

Satisfied, Matt returned to his seat as he said, "You're all right, Keb."

"Thank you, young sir. As, I am sure, are you, too."

Katia stood, looked from Roar brother to Roar brother, and, in an authoritative voice that would have made her mother proud, said, "The Boargen attacked us. My mother was sure it was Admiral Slatter himself; their leader, a hideous man. She told me to keep The Sphere as far from the Boargen as possible. But now that Keb and I have escaped the attack, I think we need to find out what happened to my mother and her ship first, before we do anything else."

"Why did The Sphere come to you in the first place?" asked Rob.

Katia shook her head, "I don't know. Neither does my mother. It just showed up. It is said that The Sphere shares information when it's ready. But it hasn't done so with us yet. I just think we need to find my mother."

Rob nodded, then said, "I think you're right, Katia. We should find your mother. But I think the first thing we should do is find out about this place. Kris brought us to Sundee on a hunch, and I think it's no accident we're here." Rob glanced at Kris, "Father's logs … "

"I disagree," Katia burst in. "We need to find my mother. She'll know what to do."

Dragging his gaze away from Katia's stubborn stare, Rob looked around at his brothers.

"May I, again, offer advice, young miss," said Keb.

Deflating a little, Katia turned to face Keb. Crossing her arms, she said, "You think I'm wrong … don't you?"

"On the contrary, young miss. I believe you are correct that we must find your mother. However, I think young Rob is also correct. If young Kris chose these coordinates for a reason, it is logical then, to discover what we may in this solar system before we continue on. We may find help on Sundee."

She pointed. "On that lifeless planet?" She shook her head, "No man could survive down there."

"Nevertheless, young miss, I believe … "

"Fine!" she said, looking back at Rob, frustrated. "Then what is our next move, Galaxy Boys?"

"Well," said Rob, as he looked around at the others, "I think a couple of us should go down to Sundee and see what's there. Keb might be right. Maybe we'll find something, or someone, that can help us."

After all, why else would the Roar brothers' father have written that "Sundee is an awful place to get away to" The words were too cryptic to not mean something. But what if there was something truly awful awaiting them down there?

They would soon find out.

Katia jumped to her feet, "I'm going with you."

"But we can only fit two in a fighter," said Rob. "And I'm not sure it's a good idea for ... "

Katia crossed her arms and looked at Rob with a "don't go there" look. She said, "I'm as capable as any boy of handling myself in a dangerous situation, Rob Roar. I'm going with you."

Rob looked around at his brothers and rested his eyes on Will, who said, flatly, "Looks like we're all going, Rob."

Later, with the two space-fighters left in orbit, Rob turned the shuttle towards Sundee. Will sat beside him in the co-pilot's seat, and Keb stood behind them, watching.

With Keb there, Will was thinking about robots. He twisted in his seat and stared up at the metal man for a moment, then said, "You can't fly this ship, can you? Because it's armed."

Keb stared down at him. "I am able to pilot any transport, young sir. But my programming forbids me to pilot any vessel armed for combat."

Staring up at the robot, who stared back, Will hesitated, and then returned his attention out the cockpit view-screen – the desert planet loomed large. After a moment, he looked back up at Keb who had resumed watching their approach.

"You can't pilot an armed ship because you can't kill people ... right?"

Again, the robot lowered its gaze. "That is correct, young sir. I may not harm any being."

Will thought for a moment, then asked, "What about a bug, can you kill a bug?"

"Robots are programmed to respect all life, young sir. I may not knowingly kill any creature."

Will hesitated, and then returned his attention forwards. Keb studied the boy for a moment before doing the same. Sundee was now so close that it was a bright orange arch against the pitch black of space.

Several hours later, the orbiting shuttle was on course, circling Sundee for the third time. They had passed over the night side of the planet three times and had seen no lights; no sign of civilisation. Rob was looking for something: a place to land that came with a reason. Maybe his father had mentioned Sundee only as a safe solar system to get away to, rather than as a planet on which to land. Indeed, the pasty-orange Sundee was all desert. It appeared wholly inhospitable. There were no clouds whatsoever and no sign of surface water.

Kris then burst into the cockpit saying, "I think I've found another hint. There's an entry in Father's computer logs that says, 'Sundee is an inhospitable place' – no kidding – 'anyone who wanted to live there would have to avoid the blistering heat by residing in a cave.' And then it goes on to say, 'While landed on Sundee, there was a most horrendous sandstorm in a deep valley, which I have named Rafjur. But only a man wishing for death would set foot on Rafjur.'"

Rob looked beside him at Kris. "Are there coordinates?"

Kris nodded.

"Punch them in," he said. "We'll go there."

"That's weird," said Kris to Rob. "The coordinates are already in the navigation computer ... "

Rafjur was a long, narrow, deep valley sunk between two razor-edge ridges. Rob plunged the shuttle towards the valley floor and set it down near a rock outcrop; a place scattered with a maze of ledges and gorges.

As the dust settled, the boys and Katia followed Keb off the ship. Not that there was any real concern the Boargen would find them on Sundee, but The Sphere was well hidden in the shuttle's cargo bay just in case.

The Roar brothers worried, even if only for pride's sake, that they might be wasting their time on Sundee – Katia was sure of it. They had no idea what they might find there in that desolate valley on that planet out of the way of everything. But because the coordinates for the very spot on which they had just landed had been set in the shuttle's navigation computer, probably by their father, combined with the cryptic words in their father's logs, the brothers believed Sundee was worth checking out. They hoped things would become clear soon though, because man, it was sure hot.

In fact, Sundee was hotter and drier than any desert on Earth. Keb set a steady pace towards the rock outcrop where there would be a welcome shade cast by it by the time they arrived.

Rob suddenly felt uneasy and shot looks all around. Kris was also on edge. Then Will and Matt, too, became alert and Will moved close to Katia. Keb stopped abruptly, the Roar brothers in sync with him, and Will grabbed Katia, halting her. Puffs of dust where each final step had hit the powdery sand, hovered above the ground as though time had stopped. It was quiet, and eerie.

Keb turned his head from side to side, scanning the area. Then, in his ever calm voice, he said, "I cannot explain how it is so, young ones, but creatures are appearing all around us."

Rob looked back towards the shuttle which seemed so far away now. And there were, indeed, creatures scattered around it, sniffing the ground.

"They're at the ship," he said, "lots of them."

"Great jumping jitterbug!" whispered Kris.

The creatures – beasts – looked a little like alligators, only they had stubs for tails and their thick legs held their bulky bodies further off the ground. They had no necks to speak of and their heads were huge, almost as large as their bodies, which, of course, meant their jaws – and probably their teeth, too – were monstrous.

"There is a cave entrance close by," said Keb. "We can make it if we move quickly. From there, I can fend off the creatures. But we must go now, young ones."

A few of the alligator-like beasts noticed the children and the robot and broke into menacing-growling run, and headed straight towards them. Their action drew the attention of the others. The dust from the ground was now a swirling storm of thundering feet. More of these monstrous creatures appeared from the sides, one so close that the children could see its bumpy, brownish-orange skin and beady red eyes.

They all turned and broke into a run, Keb in the lead. More beasts began to appear from nowhere. Each would hesitate and then launch into a lumbering run to intercept Keb and the children.

Matt and Kris were close on Keb's heels. Rob, ever the protective older brother, brought up the rear.

Keeping pace with Katia just ahead of Rob, Will spoke through his heavy breathing, "Weapons training ... would have been ... a good thing ... for this problem ... huh, Rob ... ? We ... need ... blasters!"

"Do not stop running, young ones," said Keb. "I will remove the creature from our path."

There was, indeed, a massive-sized beast ahead, square in their way. Its open mouth revealed grotesque, black teeth. No one stopped. In spite of the huge bulk of the creature – it stood on all fours as tall as Rob – the robot dipped as it met the animal, and without breaking its stride, swiped at it with one arm and the monster was airborne. It landed some distance away, thrashing awkwardly on its side.

It was a torturous run for all the children, but especially for Rob. Being at the rear of the group he knew that if the creatures caught up to them, he would be the first to be ripped apart and eaten. It took tremendous effort to refrain from hysterical screams as his desperate fear mounted.

The mouth of the cave to which Keb was leading them loomed large. But beasts now flanked the sprinting group, keeping pace with them, and many more took up the rear. Katia glanced to the side, let out a short breathless scream – the monsters were a living nightmare – and jerked her attention forwards. Keb swiped one after the other of the creatures from their path, but each, having landed sprawled on the ground, righted itself and re-joined the chase at the rear.

With the children still close on Keb's heels, exhausted, mouths dry, and lungs burning, they reached the cave. They could hear the monsters squeezing amass in behind them, their heavy bodies slamming against the cavern walls. Their deep growls and their jostling with each other for position, echoed through the cave's depths.

Rob couldn't help it; he simply had to glance back. What he saw chilled him to the bone: the monsters were close, close enough for him to see their red eyes; so many, that their eyes cast a terrible red glow, illuminating the beasts' massive, ugly heads and the cavern walls in blood-red. At this sight, a fearful whimper broke loose from Rob's gut.

Hearing Rob's desperation, Keb dropped back taking up the rear, and said, "Do not slow, young ones. There is something man-made, ahead."

They could all see something through the dark … a light! A red light! Their desperation grew, forcing their numb legs to keep pumping. As they approached, the red light turned green and a large, steel door opened.

That's when the worst thing happened: Will fell. It is quite something, if you think about it, their luck at having made it that far in the cave without mishap, even though blinded by the dark. But Will's luck had run out. He hit the ground, hard. His hard-earned breath was forced from his lungs. He had no chance as he flailed on the gritty ground, to inhale again or he would have got a breath full of thin dust. Keb scooped him into strong, metal arms and robot and boy just made it through the doorway before the beasts were upon them.

Instantly, the door closed and the cavern lit up in a dim light. There was an unbearable, thunderous noise as many massive bodies rammed the thick metal door in turn.

Will breathed in, shuddering as he did so, while uncontrollable tears of relief filled his eyes. Will's tears showed just how desperate the situation had been, because Will's eyes never filled. As the others wiped away their own tears, Keb scanned their new surroundings.

Quickly, the robot adopted a protective stance between the children and what he saw standing nearby.

Rafjur, Blasters and Rockhunds

"Children!" a deep, base voice bellowed. "Rafjur wants to know what in great space are children doing on the worst planet in the galaxy? Rafjur hoped when you arrived in orbit, that you would leave!"

It was a man who spoke to them. He was tall, muscular and thickly-built. Standing in the shadows as he was, he looked part animal. He approached, coming into the dim light. The animal part of him was his face, much of it covered with a thick beard and a moustache. His hair was long and messy. He looked every bit like what one might expect of a prehistoric hunter, brought forwards in time from Earth's past. He walked right up to Keb which illustrated just how big this man was, because Keb looked slight standing, unmoving, before him.

"Move out of Rafjur's way, robot," the man said, in a deep, commanding voice.

Keb stood firm. But he also remained speechless as though he had to struggle to stand against an order from a human.

"Rafjur will not ask again, robot. Move out of Rafjur's way."

Keb shuddered, and then moved.

Rob tried to grab Katia but she moved too fast towards the giant brute.

"Don't talk to Keb like that!" she said, stepping right up to the big man, stopping him in his tracks. "We just had to run for our lives from your awful pets out there and now, you're being rude!"

The man glared down at Katia from dark eyes. Her usually straight, long brown hair was ruffled. Her eyes were wide with anger in a face smudged with Sundee's dust. All this would have struck any other adult as adorable, but apparently, not the giant of a man.

"Look," continued Katia, crossing her arms and staring at the man while she tapped a foot, "either stomp on me and get it over with or show me to the bathroom. After being chased by your monsters, I, for one, have to pee."

The beasts outside continued to ram their bodies against the door, each hit making a loud, dull thud. The activity was dying down though as the man began a deep-throated chuckle.

Kris stepped forwards beside Katia, looked up at the man and said, "Only a man wishing for death would set foot on Rafjur."

The man bent in the middle, lowering his big, hairy head to just inches from Kris's face and eyed him.

"That was written in my father's logs," continued Kris. "Are you my father's friend, or will you be stomping on me, too?"

The man eyed Kris some more, then straightened enough so he could look at the other boys, before straightening completely.

He spoke in the same deep voice, but – as Katia would later describe the change in his tone – he was no longer so grumpy and rude. "Will has his mother's eyes," he said, studying Will. "Rafjur knows Rob Roar best though, and he sees him in all of you." He looked down at Katia. "All except the bratty but brave little girl, that is, who has to go pee. Rafjur thinks she does not look like a Roar."

For each Roar boy, hearing mention of their parents stirred up many questions, but between their own exhaustion and the huge man's intimidating stare, none could speak. It was obvious to each though, that they had come to the right place. This man, Rafjur, would help them help Katia. And maybe, just maybe, he knew where their mother and father were ...

Later, the children sat at a large, elegantly-set table in a room made of rich, dark wood, except for the floor which they assumed was the mountain itself. Regardless of the absence of windows, it was difficult to tell that lunch was taking place in a cave on a most inhospitable planet. Given Rafjur's general manner, his offer to prepare a meal had been a surprise. And what's more, the meal was delicious. Rafjur had seemed to enjoy the children's initial uncertainty in accepting his offer for food, only for them to discover savoury tastes never before experienced by their young palates.

As they ate, though they left out any mention of The Sphere, they told Rafjur about the trouble the Boargen were causing. Nothing seemed to surprise him. Then the Roar boys asked him questions about how he knew their parents and whether he knew where they might be. But, impatiently, the man rebuffed each question and finally told them to stop asking him questions he could not answer.

With everyone having eaten, Rafjur sat back in his chair at the end of the table and picked at his teeth with a large, weapon-like toothpick. He paused, and said, "Rafjur thinks the children are getting involved in things way over their heads." Rafjur's eyes were difficult to read as he surveyed the children. "Well?" he boomed, startling them. "Have the children nothing to say to Rafjur?"

After a moment, Will said, "My brothers and I are not going to let fear or doubt keep us from helping Katia, or from finding our parents, if we can; even if you advise us against it."

Rafjur stared at Will. "Hah!" he said, as he slapped his mighty hand with such force upon the table that it seemed the thick slab would break.

In a flash, Keb was by the table standing next to Rafjur. Although the big man was sitting, the robot looked small beside him. And where Keb looked clean and streamlined, Rafjur, with his wild eyes set in a hairy face framed with unruly long hair, looked every bit the wild-man.

Holding very still, Rafjur slowly and menacingly shifted his gaze from the children, who held their breath, to look at the robot. During their escape to the cave, Keb had tossed several of the large beasts a great distance while others had been swiped away with what seemed like little effort. A robot's strength, therefore, was superhuman. Though Rafjur was gruff and scary to be around, none of the children, even Katia, wanted to see him hurt.

As though he could hear the children's unspoken concerns, Rafjur returned his attention to them and said, in a deep, but calm voice, "Rafjur was going to say he likes and admires Will's courage. Rafjur was also going to say that he encourages the young brats to do what they want … "

"No!" screamed Katia, springing to her feet.

Faster than the eye could track, Rafjur had sprung from his seat and held Keb in a vice-like grip. The robot's limbs were splayed awkwardly and its head was grossly bent to one side, squeezed in Rafjur's massive, muscular arm.

Rob had shot to his feet and grabbed Katia to keep her from running to Keb. Will and Matt had also leapt to their feet, and now stared in fear at Rafjur and the robot. Kris remained seated, though he looked as worried as the others.

"If you have not guessed by now, robot," growled Rafjur, as he glared at Katia, "Rafjur does not like robots. If it ever interferes with him again, Rafjur will rip it limb from limb and use its parts to make himself a fine new toaster. Does the robot understand Rafjur?"

"I understand, Sir," said Keb, "and apologise for my gross miscalculation. I will not cross you again."

Rafjur released Keb and the robot straightened, appearing as though the untoward event had never occurred.

"Rafjur does not need to give a machine assurance of his good intentions. But Rafjur tells the robot he has some help to give the children before they go. The robot will now return to the shuttle before Rafjur changes his mind about a new toaster."

"Thank you, Sir," said Keb, and the robot turned and left.

Upon exiting the cave, Keb would find the area empty of the beasts as though they had never existed, having disappeared in the same way they had arrived. Many things about the galaxy were unknown even to an advanced robot, like the beasts that appeared from nowhere and vanished to nowhere. And then there was Rafjur. Keb had no record of such a powerful being.

After watching the robot leave, Rafjur settled back in his seat as though nothing had happened and resumed picking at his teeth with the weapon-like toothpick. He surveyed the Roar brothers and Katia, and then said, "Rafjur wants the children to sit." They sat. "The children do not like Rafjur because they do not understand him. But he will help them in any way he can. Tell Rafjur what they plan to do when they leave here."

It was quiet while Rafjur waited for the children to speak. He sat there, staring at them as though he had all the time in the galaxy.

Rob spoke up with an uncertain tone in his voice: "Well, we need to find out where Katia's mother is, and, I guess, go from there."

Rafjur was shaking his head. "No," he said. "First, Rafjur says the children must learn how to use a blaster. They should always have a blaster by their side so they are not chewed by vicious creatures like Rafjur's rockhunds."

"How does the mighty Rafjur know we don't already know how to use a blaster?" said Will.

The other Roar boys stopped breathing, but Katia smirked.

Rafjur stared at Will through squinted eyes. In a low, growling voice, he said, "Rafjur says for Will to watch his tone and choice of words, youngster. Rafjur knows a poorly used voice and unwise words can cause one trouble. He says to always speak with a polite and calm voice. This is one thing, among many, that Will's father knows only too well. Rafjur knows it has saved Rob Roar's life many times. And, Rafjur understands that one who knows how to use a blaster, carries a blaster."

"Your voice is not polite and calm," snapped Katia.

Kris and Matt's eyes grew wide. Slowly shaking his head, Rob lowered it into his hand. A smile stretched across Will's lips.

Rafjur eyed Katia. He said, "The little girl has seen Rafjur can take care of himself. For this reason, he will speak as he wishes." Rafjur's voice changed then. It became a gentle one; almost father-like. "It is not with Rafjur that the little girl must watch her stupid tongue. After all, Rafjur is not without knowing childish carelessness. Mind what he has said though, for with poor words and poor actions one may bring danger even to friends."

Katia tried to stare Rafjur down. It didn't work. She lowered her gaze. All except Will breathed a sigh of relief, but he lost his smile.

"Why do you call those things 'rockhunds'?" asked Kris.

Rafjur sounded almost as though he was growling when he began to chuckle. Then he said, "So, curious, little boy. Good! That is good. And little Kris is careful with his questions. That is also good. Rafjur says the bratty little girl and the careless little boy would do well to follow little Kris's example."

Rafjur stood, towering above the tall, thick table. As he walked the length of it towards a large doorway that lead to a long hall, panelled with the same dark wood as the dining room, he said, "Follow Rafjur."

Rob, Matt, and Kris immediately leapt up and did so, falling in at a jog to keep up with the giant man, who continued, "Rafjur says rockhunds have lived on Sundee for hundreds of millions of years ... " In spite of how Rafjur's voice carried through the halls like thunder in the mountains, because of the speed at which he walked, it soon became impossible for Will and Katia, willfully remaining seated at the table, to hear more than a suggestion of the deep voice ... then nothing.

They stayed put too long; stubborn and staring at each other. Then, when they were good and ready, they rose and followed at a pace suitable to them; a pace that ultimately left them lost in a maze of corridors that all looked the same.

By the time Will and Katia found the others, after trying what must have been a hundred identical locked doors in a maze of identical halls, they had become flustered. They were frustrated at Rafjur for leaving them behind, frustrated at Rob, Matt, and Kris for following Rafjur, and, though they would never admit it, frustrated at themselves for being so obstinate.

Standing at one of the tall doors made of the same dark wood as everything else in Rafjur's labyrinthine home, Will and Katia could hear repetitive blaster bursts inside. Will hesitated, then pulled the heavy door lever down and, with Katia following, he entered.

Inside, Rob, Matt and Kris stood side by side, each with a postured stance and holding a blaster ready to fire. Before them was a vast rainforest.

Panicking, Will and Katia both gasped and drew back at the sight of a snakelike creature slithering from the undergrowth towards the armed Roar brothers. Just when Will was about to yell out in panic to shoot, the snake rose up on what, until then, had been hidden limbs, and sprang into the air. The newcomers cringed and ducked. Bursts of orange rays shot from the three blasters and the creature shattered into countless pieces and vanished.

Will had not felt Katia grab him, but he noticed a painful grip on his arm and looked beside him. She looked frightened. He was sure he didn't now look as scared as she did, though he knew he had panicked, too. Their feet remaining planted, Rob, Matt and Kris twisted to look back as Rafjur strode to Will and Katia's side. Towering above them, his thick beard and moustache hiding much of his face, Rafjur was an unsettling sight. In each massive hand, he held out a blaster.

In an even tone, he said, "Rafjur says to join the others if the late ones wish. The computer will teach them the basics by speaking through their communicators."

Will and Katia hesitated, and then took the weapons offered to them. As the man turned and walked away, he said, "Later, Rafjur will teach the children the finer points of a blaster."

Rafjur told them that if they were going to go in search of their parents, they should be prepared to protect themselves. They all knew what their host-turned-teacher said was true, and that they would each have to carry a weapon sooner or later. For the Roar brothers, however, the thought of having to use a blaster to defend themselves was still difficult to comprehend, and, by the end of their lessons they were all exhausted and quite sure they wanted nothing to do with any sort of weapon.

Before leaving the firing range, Rafjur gave each Roar brother and Katia a fine, compact blaster with a holster that strapped around the torso. Rafjur's opinion was that a holster strapped around the waist was cumbersome. "The blaster will get in the way if strapped around the waist if the youngsters find a need to run away," he said, with a knowing grin.

Later, as they watched Rafjur prepare for what would surely be another delicious meal, the children were in various states of quiet, still contemplating what it would mean to be faced with a true circumstance in which they would have to use a blaster. The great man wielded a knife with a deftness that left the Roar brothers and Katia holding their breath. Each wondered how he never cut himself, or cut off a finger, or worse.

Rafjur was mincing a thing which looked like some kind of vegetable so fast, that the blade of the knife was a blur when Matt, who was sitting on the counter nearby, asked, "Why don't you use your food machine? It must make pretty good … " With a final whack, the knife was stuck, deep in the counter. " ... f-food ... "

With the knife anchored fast, the great man peered at the boy and stared at him in a way that was difficult to read.

Matt hesitated, and then continued, "Our … um … machine … back home ... " Under Rafjur's glare he shook his head. "Never mind," he said.

Rafjur yanked the knife from the counter, startling his audience, and continued preparing dinner.

Later, as everyone sat around the huge table spread with empty dishes and the remnants of dinner, Rafjur peered at Matt again, and this time said, "Rafjur likes to cook. It relaxes him. But tomorrow, if the boy wishes to get food from that abominable machine, he may."

"N-no," said Matt. "It's not like that … "

"Rafjur knows what the boy meant," he interrupted. "Rafjur just answered his question, but now the boy knows there is little point in asking all the questions that come to him."

"I guess a food machine falls in the same category as a robot," said Katia.

Rafjur stared at her, and then said, "The little girl's comment is more accurate than she knows."

With that, Rafjur's chair scraped across the stone floor as he stood, and said, "Rafjur says it is time for the children to sleep." He began to walk the length of the table. "Follow Rafjur."

This time, Will and Katia leapt to their feet with the others and followed, staying close, both having decided that wandering the halls all night looking for a comfortable place to sleep would not be much fun.

The following morning began with a fine meal that equalled the previous two. Everyone looked well rested, including Rafjur, though he must have awakened very early to prepare such an elaborate breakfast.

Sitting back in his chair, the great man again picked at his teeth with one of those weapon-like toothpicks as he eyed the children. Then he stopped picking and said, "Rafjur says it is time for the children to leave. But there is another thing they must do before they look for the little girl's mother."

The Roar brothers and Katia looked around at each other, each having assumed that Rafjur would be going with them. There was a deflated feeling of having been let down. After all, even Admiral Slatter would never stand a chance against Rafjur.

Rob looked from Katia to each of his brothers, and then to Rafjur. He said, "I think we were all assuming you would be coming with us."

"This is something Rafjur cannot do," he said. "Rafjur has other things he must attend to. But he will show the children where to get a small space-cruiser; a very powerful ship built of a technology that few have. Rafjur knows the cruiser is Rob Roar's and that his sons will put it to good use. Rob Roar would agree with Rafjur and would want his sons to have it."

"Is the ship close?" asked Matt.

"Hah … no, boy. Rafjur says it is on Kablakia, far away from Sundee. As much as Rafjur does not like to admit it, Kablakia is where all the best ships are built."

"You make it sound like we can just go and pick it up," said Rob. "Do we need money?"

Rafjur shrugged as he said, "Rafjur knows Rob Roar has paid for his space-cruiser in full. Rafjur says it makes sense to take delivery."

"So we can just go and pick it up?" said Rob.

Rafjur looked at Rob with a slight grin and a sparkle in his eye; a look that suggested that acquiring the space-cruiser was going to be full of fun and adventure.

"No, boy. You must steal it."

Jaws dropped. Rafjur appeared to enjoy the moment, as the children were speechless.

Rob looked around at the others, then back at Rafjur and said, "But, you said it was paid for."

"Rafjur will explain. Listen: Rafjur says payments for things of great expense are managed by The First Intergalactic Bank. Rafjur says that the item being built is fully funded and paid for as it is being built. This way, there is no chance of either seller or buyer being cheated. Even though this deprives Rafjur of hearing about good fights, Rafjur says it makes good sense to do business this way."

He paused to pick at his teeth, and then continued, "Rafjur knows the cruiser is complete because when he discovered Rob Roar was missing, he considered taking possession of it before the Boargen took control of Kablakia. This is how Rafjur knows the ship is complete, paid for, and well hidden from the Boargen."

"The Boargen," said Katia, looking around at the brothers. "I remember that. My mother told me about it. Going to Kablakia is a terrible idea."

"Nonsense, little girl. But Rafjur says it is because of the Boargen that the boys must take possession of the ship in a sneaky way."

"Steal it," said Rob, after a moment.

"Steal it," confirmed Rafjur, "in a sneaky way."

"Ugh!" Katia rolled her eyes. "This is sooo stupid."

Rafjur stood. The brothers needed no invitation to follow. Though Katia hesitated, she was out of her seat and keeping pace with the great man before he reached the hall.

The cavern which Rafjur and the children entered was many times more voluminous than the hangar at the coastal base on Earth. And that's really saying something. In spite of man's hand – or whoever's hand it was that had hollowed out the mountain – the surfaces of the cavernous cave-turned-spaceship-hangar looked much like the mountains outside; unfinished and rustic. In the distance were huge, dark voids, leaving it unclear just how far back into the mountain the cavern extended.

It was filled from rough-hewn wall to rough-hewn wall with spaceships of varying types and sizes; some of them quite huge. Most of them appeared very old. There were also towering mounds of scrap scattered here and there, each of them as though an ancient ship had simply collapsed where it had stood.

As the children followed Rafjur through the cavern, weaving a zigzag course between the spaceships, the Roar brothers grew excited at the sight of so many of them. There were hulks that looked like they were in a state of disrepair – some of them absolute junk – but the Roar boys saw promise in them; something to repair. Even those ships that appeared to have fallen apart – as though a toy shaken by a giant baby until every piece had loosened and fallen off – looked to the brothers like something to piece back together. As for Katia, she had a look of disgust on her face as if she was walking through garbage.

"There must be a hundred ships in here," Matt whispered to Rob and Will, as they walked side by side.

"Rafjur says there are one-hundred and nineteen functional ships here," said Rafjur, his voice echoing. "Rafjur does not know how many ships could be built with the spare parts; perhaps another ten or twelve."

Rob, Will and Matt exchanged glances, astonished. Rafjur was ahead of them, but in spite of his and their combined loud, echoing footsteps through the cavern, somehow he had heard what Matt had said.

Under his breath, Matt added, "He probably has x-ray vision, too."

"Rafjur can still hear you, boy. Rafjur does not have x-ray vision, but his hearing is exceptional."

Rob, Will and Matt again exchanged glances, only this time, rolling their eyes. Rafjur also had an exceptional ego.

Walking a short distance behind the others, Kris giggled. Nothing got past Rafjur. Curious, he thought.

Echoing words and footsteps were a distant sound to Katia. She, like Kris, was consumed with the growing mystery of Rafjur. Though she disliked considering the brute as such, he was intelligent; like no intelligent being she had ever heard of. How did a man, even as huge and strong as Rafjur, move so fast and muster so much strength to overwhelm a robot – a robot that easily had the strength of ten men? And what about his small fleet of spaceships: many of them warships, some of them quite large and some of them quite ancient? It was like something from out of this galaxy, or from another time.

Though none dared say it, each one thought that with all the spaceships they saw, Rafjur could have his own military fleet except that there was no one to fly the ships, or at least, so it appeared. Though there was no sign of anyone else on Sundee, the complexity of Rafjur's endless halls and locked doors surely had room for hundreds; maybe even thousands.

Just as they were wondering if their host was going round in circles, he stopped at a large spaceship – one that looked as though, with a good shake, it would become like one of the several huge piles of scrap they had just walked by. While Rafjur pushed a button that opened a small keypad and tapped in a code, Will craned his neck to look down the length of the old ship. It looked to be about a football field in length. It was huge.

The spaceship stood on four large landing pads like a giant beast, high enough for a man of average height to walk under. As there was so much of the ship to look at, Will lost track of Rafjur and the others. Before long, from out of the corner of his eye, he caught an image of a thick piece of steel passing by which shifted his attention. It was Rafjur carrying a pipe about the size of Keb. As the great man approached, poised to swing, the children dodged for cover, their hands over their ears. With a deep, loud growl, Rafjur swung the pipe and landed a solid, booming blow against the ship's hull. There was a sigh and the hatch opened.

Like Mr Casper had said, sometimes, brute force gets results. Apparently, Rafjur held the same opinion.

With the hatch open, through a long, wide gangway leading into the belly of the ship, the inside could be seen; or at least a very small bit of it, anyway. There was only a sliver of light bleeding in through the hatch opening. There appeared to be no power or life to the old beast.

Grunting, Rafjur heaved the Keb-sized pipe into the air and again, whacked the ship with it. Lights flickered on and the beast began to hum. Looking around at the children, who still had their hands over their ears – for the sound of a massive pipe being swung at a hollow, old spaceship is a noisy thing, to say the least – Rafjur snorted and nodded once … a note of finality. Then he led the way into the ship.

Later, sitting in well-worn seats on the old spaceship's command bridge studying the flight controls – as per Rafjur's orders – Rob and Kris both wondered what adventures had befallen the crews that had manned the ship during its long since past voyages. Will and Matt had gone with Rafjur to inspect the engines. Having not been invited to do anything and feeling put out by it, Katia had wandered off.

Something must have scared her pretty well though, because a short time later, breathing heavily and eyes full of fear, Katia came rushing back and grabbed Rob's arm.

"He's a pirate!" she said, trying to catch her breath.

Rob pulled his gaze from the panic-stricken girl and exchanged a curious stare with Kris. She tugged on his sleeve and he looked at her.

"Who's a pirate?" he asked. But he knew who she was talking about. It certainly fit.

"Rafjur! I think he must be a pirate!" she said, in a rushed voice, as though the next thing she would do is bolt.

"Yes," growled a familiar voice, "Rafjur is a pirate."

Katia reeled, wild eyed, and faced the giant man as he ducked through the doorway, entering the command bridge.

"What have you done with Will and Matt?" she breathed out, panic-stricken.

It began as a low growl from his gut – which brought poor Katia close to tears – worked its way up to his throat, and burst out as a laugh, more jolly than the Roar brothers had ever heard. For the first time, it seemed to Rob and Kris – Katia was too scared to notice – that they could see through all the hair on Rafjur's face to the man himself as he entered a state of uproarious laughter.

"Why, little girl," he said, "Rafjur has given the little boys to his rockhunds as toys to chew on. A pirate thing to do … wouldn't you say?" Rafjur's laughter kept him from saying more, for, at that moment, who should walk in but Will and Matt, both with uncertain smiles.

Rob and Kris could not help then but smile at Rafjur's good-natured joking; now that Will and Matt were present, that is. For there had been a few moments that they, too, had been concerned for Will and Matt's well-being.

Having gathered her wits, Katia said, "You're no better than the Boargen."

At Katia's mention of the Boargen, Rafjur's laughter tapered off. He said, "Rafjur knows the Boargen cause trouble for power. Boargen kill without reason; even women and children and those who do not fight. Rafjur does none of these things and does not cause trouble for power. Rafjur has spent his life seeking riches. That is all, little girl."

Looking sad and walking forwards to leave, Katia looked up at Rafjur and said, "My name is not 'little girl', it's Katia. And a pirate is a pirate no matter whether he thinks he isn't as bad as another or not." And with that, she left.

It can't be said that each brother was not concerned, to some degree, about Rafjur being a pirate. But if their father trusted him, and it appeared he had, then so could they. After all, Rafjur was showing them how to steal their father's space-cruiser – since it was paid for, anyway.

A Toaster, After All

Morning came too soon, ending, for the Roar brothers, what had turned to be a bit of a rest between the first part of their adventure and the second. They now had a number of tasks to accomplish: to steal a spaceship, find Katia's mother, and all while evading the Boargen, who, Rafjur had said, were undoubtedly searching for them. Rafjur had no way of knowing that the Boargen were actually searching for 'The Sphere', which, of course, at that moment, was in the shuttle on Sundee.

After breakfast, Rafjur lead the children, each packing a blaster in a torso-holster, out through the cave.

"Rafjur reminds the children what he told them the other day," he said. "Rafjur says to stay close and do not worry about his rockhunds. He says they will not be aggressive if the children are with him."

That was the day that Will and Katia had remained behind, so they had missed Rafjur's account of the rockhunds' history: that the beasts had lived on Sundee for hundreds of millions of years. This is why, as the group exited Rafjur's complex, Rob, Matt, and Kris were only slightly nervous, while Will and Katia were downright scared.

The walk through the dark cave was uneventful, but, as the group emerged, the beasts were there, enmasse, as though dogs eagerly awaiting their master. With ease, Rafjur pushed away the rockhunds that got too close. Occasionally, he would reach out and, with a strong hand, he would pat one of the creatures which would then respond with apparent pleasure.

"Rafjur," said Will, feeling fearful, "Katia and I weren't with you when you talked about the rockhunds."

Rafjur stopped and, scowling, he looked down at Will. He said, "Rafjur had forgotten this." He pushed a curious rockhund away from the children as he continued, "Rafjur tells you rockhunds are both rock and creature. He says they live for thousands of years scattered across parts of Sundee. Rafjur says sometimes rockhunds are hungry and so wake up and become creatures that eat."

Will hesitated, and then said, "I thought you said it was only you and the rockhunds on Sundee. What do they eat?"

"Rafjur was right to say it is only Rafjur and rockhunds on Sundee," he said. "Rockhunds eat rocks."

Again, Will hesitated, and then continued, "But if rockhunds are rocks, does that mean they eat each other?"

"No. Rafjur says rockhunds only eat rocks, not rockhunds."

Will looked at one of the creatures sniffing the ground close by. He said, "But they chased us."

"Rafjur says the rockhunds chased the children because rockhunds are curious. Rafjur knows they would have chewed on Will but not eaten him. Rockhunds would not like to eat Will."

Rafjur moved past Will and pushed away one of the rather larger beasts from Kris. No one noticed that this separated Katia from the group. This shift in positions was made worse by a small rockhund which managed to slip in and approach Katia, who was quiet from fear and too much pride as she backed away from the beast and the safety which Rafjur provided.

A high-pitched scream and a blaster discharging brought everyone's attention to the crisis at hand. Even Rafjur's eyes grew wider as he jerked around to see Katia surrounded by rockhunds, one of which she had shot. The beast had shattered into many small pieces – pieces of rock that now lay strewn on the ground at her feet.

As fast as he had when subduing Keb, Rafjur moved to Katia, disarmed the alarmed girl, grabbed her up off the ground, and placed her on his shoulder where she clung desperately to his thick vest, bunching it in her fists. Rafjur looked towards the shuttle. Keb was standing at the bottom of the gangway as though a statue.

"Go back in the ship, robot," he boomed. "The girl is safe."

Keb abruptly did as he was told.

The Roar brothers made their way towards Rafjur and Katia, pushing through the rockhunds, sometimes hitting, with a balled-up fist, one and then another of the huge beasts to send home the message for them to move. They had watched Rafjur punch them out of the way and it seemed not to hurt the dense creatures in the least.

Rafjur kicked the closest rockhund away from him and Katia, and bellowed, "That is enough! Rafjur says you have worn out your welcome!" He pointed to the horizon, "Go!"

At that, the rockhunds waddled away, all except for the beast that now lay scattered across the ground as many pieces of rock, that is.

Glancing at Katia on his shoulder, Rafjur spoke in a calming, baritone voice. "Rafjur apologises to Katia. He was not watching after the girl as he should have."

Wiping a tear from her cheek, Katia said, "At least you know how to say my name." She looked down at the pieces of rock. "I'm sorry I blew up one of your rockhunds."

Chuckling, Rafjur quickly set Katia down; a ride that took her breath away. As he stooped to pick up one of the pieces of rock, he said, "But Rafjur tells you this is not a terrible thing." Cradling the rock in his open hand, he continued, "Rafjur wants the children to look closely."

The Roar brothers and Katia leaned in, each expecting to see a rock. But it was no rock. It was a small rockhund. While Rafjur chuckled, they all surveyed the ground around them. Every piece of the rockhund was moving.

"The children see," said Rafjur, with a glint in his eye, "that rockhunds multiply in a most amazing way."

Later, Rafjur, Rob and Kris watched the shuttle depart. In it, Katia and Keb would drop Will and Matt off in the Kablakian system, where the two brothers would then abscond with their father's space-cruiser, right out from underneath the Boargen noses. Katia and Keb, with 'The Sphere', would then head for a point in space far away from Kablakia, to await the others. From a swirl of sand, the shuttle emerged, soared over the onlookers and shot through the glare of the sun towards space.

Having said goodbye to Rafjur, Rob and Kris were strapped into their seats on the command bridge of the old spaceship – no seat restraining fields on that old beast. The brothers had noticed that saying goodbye to the ship had been a little difficult for Rafjur, probably, they figured, because it had served him well. They wished he could come with them and help, but Rafjur had insisted that he had other important things to attend to.

From the pilot's seat, Rob flicked on one after the other of what seemed to be an endless number of toggle switches. Repetitive beeps ensued. After a pause, during which time the two brothers wondered whether the old ship would even power up, the engines roared to life, shaking the ship.

Rob ratcheted forwards the throttles. The beast lifted off the ground in a cloud of cavern dust, vibrating violently as it did so. The brothers glanced at each other, concerned. As Rob ratcheted the throttles further forwards, the shuddering subsided and the great ship began moving towards the open hangar door.

As they cleared the cavern, Rob thrust the throttles full on. The old ship paused with a deadening silence. Rob and Kris shot panic-stricken looks at each other. It felt like they were falling, but then their heads were snapped back as the beast returned to life, belched, and blasted off down the valley.

Pulling back on the control wheel, Rob was surprised to feel the power in the old ship as it left the Rafjur Valley behind and arched up towards its final run through space. Before leaving Sundee's system, they would make one stop to bring aboard the two space-fighters left in orbit a few days earlier. Then they would be on their way to a point near Kablakia where they would await word from Will and Matt.

Meanwhile, the shuttle with Will, Matt, Katia and Keb aboard had just completed its sixth pass through thin-space. In all, it would take seven passes to reach Kablakia's solar system. Will and Matt would be dropped off on one of the distant moons. And from there, they would take a labour shuttle to Kablakia.

"I'm sorry that big brute handled you like that, Keb," said Katia, looking up from the co-pilot's seat, "but how did he do it?"

Keb looked down at Katia and said, "Rafjur does not fit the description of any known galactic beings, young miss, although he appears to be human. I am unable to explain his extraordinary abilities."

Will stared up at Keb as he climbed out of the pilot's seat to go and find Matt. He stopped to look back at Katia, and said, "It seems like there's a lot about this galaxy that can't be explained ... " he looked up at Keb again, "even by a robot."

Matt was sitting in one of the passenger seats studying a holographic image of the plans to a Kablakian factory; the one where their father's space-cruiser was kept. The Sphere flew by slowly, moving about the ship as though exploring. Matt paused to watch it. He and his brothers had talked about The Sphere but each had been left with yet more questions, and no answers.

Walking from the cockpit and continuing down the aisle at a brisk pace between the rows of seats, Will called to Matt, "We should deactivate the shuttle's weapons now. We only have one more pass through thin-space."

Touching a button on his arm-comp, the holographic image vanished and Matt sprang from his seat and rushed to join Will, as he said, "And we wouldn't want to forget, or Katia would be stuck without a pilot."

Galactic law prohibited robots from piloting armed craft, so the shuttle's weapons would be made inoperative.

From space, the Kablakian moon was an uninteresting grey ball with a sprinkling of lights. Upon landing, however, it was exactly as the computer text had described: a thronging spaceport.

As Will and Matt watched the shuttle with Katia, Keb and The Sphere aboard depart, they were filled with excitement, tempered a little, however, by the fear that they would be caught. But Rafjur had said that although the Boargen closely guarded Kablakia, they would never expect two young boys – unarmed – to sneak in. Also, the Boargen knew nothing of Rob Roar's space-cruiser hidden away in a secret factory hangar, so they had no reason to be on the lookout for intruders.

Surveying the spaceport from where he stood, Will was taken aback by the masses. Matt had the same awestruck look on his face. There were a few humans, even some youths, both human and not, so Will and Matt fitted right in. But mostly, there were a vast variety of what – to them – looked like alien beings; many of whom looked anything but human. There were also Boargen guards, dressed in sharp, black uniforms, human but with greasy-looking, pitch-black hair and pasty-white skin.

The first thing the brothers had to do was get a job, for that was the only way to get to Kablakia, the security was that rigid. If you didn't have a job on Kablakia, you couldn't go to Kablakia; it was as simple as that. It took a couple of hours for the brothers to find employment, during which time they were so paranoid that they would be caught, that they were on edge and jumpy.

Because Will and Matt were small in stature, they were to work as helpers to the waste engineers, known on Earth, as plumbers.

As they walked from the employment office, the clerk, who Matt thought resembled a cow's udder, began chuckling, a sort of choking sound, and called out to a co-worker, "The little runts will be very helpful unclogging the waste lines after gargrosses take their monthly relief."

As the door closed behind them, Will and Matt both stopped and stiffened, suddenly realising what 'monthly relief', meant. They stared at each other, each trying to imagine what a gargross must look like. Both grimaced.

By the time they had secured their employment, they had become used to the tension of uncertainty, especially whilst avoiding the Boargen guards. They became used to the idea that, at any moment, they might have to think fast and flee. Soon, they were minorities walking among so many alien beings, that they began to feel like members of the galactic community. They headed for the public transport.

Once there, they purchased tickets to Kablakia from a nice fish-like being. Both boys had some trouble refraining from staring at the agent, when she handed them their tickets with what looked like a tentacle. And when she smiled, she had no teeth but a mouth, which Will and Matt agreed later looked like that of a baleen whale; a thing that exacerbated the staring problem.

They took their seats on a Kablakian labour shuttle, but there was something wrong with their seats. The brothers fidgeted and squirmed, trying to get comfortable. They would find out later that they had sat in the multi-being section, rather than the humanoid section which was further forwards. In a sad sort of way, the discomfort was worth it, because they heard a couple of rather scary-looking aliens with fat heads, bulbous noses and tiny eyes, speak about something and someone that concerned them: Katia and Keb.

As one of the aliens put it: the Boargen had caught a girl and her robot interfering in Boargen affairs. Will and Matt stared at each other, stunned. The plan had been for Katia and Keb, after dropping them off on the Kablakian moon, to go to a designated rendezvous point; a location where it was very unlikely they would run into anyone. After stealing their father's space-cruiser, the Roar brothers were to meet them at that rendezvous point. That had been the plan, anyway.

Katia had been upset that they were not going to look for her mother first. And she had thought that stealing the space-cruiser was a really stupid idea. But was she stubborn enough to risk everything by going back to where the Boargen had attacked her mother's ship? Rafjur had said that the Boargen were the type of animals to wait for the scared food to return; in Katia's case, to wait for her to return to see if her mother's ship had been destroyed.

If what the two aliens had said was true, Katia's punishment for interfering in Boargen affairs was a trip to Jawbone, where she would either be immediately served as dessert, or kept around as a slave until adulthood, by which time she would be thoroughly fattened for a main course. And the robot, which had apparently been damaged beyond repair, had been sent to the Galactic Space

Academy in orbit around Moxy, to be disassembled for study. There was no mention of The Sphere. No surprise there.

For the remainder of the flight to Kablakia, Will and Matt refrained from looking at each other for fear of crying. Looking downtrodden, they stared forwards at nothing. It seemed as though all had come to an abrupt end for the grand young team that had departed Sundee in a rush of promise.

There was no way to contact Rob and Kris, because arm-comps lacked the power to focus a tight-beam at such a great distance. Of course, Mr Casper and KNIA were also out of range, by far. Besides, there was still the problem that if a Boargen ship remained in Earth's solar system, it could intercept any communication. Will and Matt were stuck. They were alone. And, for the necessity of passing themselves off as simple workers, they were unarmed and therefore unable to defend themselves if need should arise.

During that long, depressing ride on the Kablakian shuttle, Will and Matt were sure they would spend the rest of their lives unclogging the waste lines after the gargrosses had used the latrines. Rob and Kris had probably already blown up in Rafjur's old spaceship. The Boargen undoubtedly had The Sphere. Katia would be served as a Jawbone meal. And Keb would be turned into a toaster, after all.

The Spaceship Switch

"Hey!" said a gruff voice.

Will and Matt awoke with a start, opened their eyes, and looked up. He wasn't human, but close. Rather than hair on his head he had what looked like scales, and his face had an aquatic appearance. He stood on two feet ... well ... then again ... maybe they weren't quite feet.

"Nobody's gonna carry you off this heap!" he said. "Get going!"

Slipping their packs on to their backs, Will and Matt dragged themselves out of their uncomfortable seats, and through the crowded spaceport passageways. As they walked, each boy fought with his own sense of helplessness. Everything had gone wrong. What could they do?

Suddenly, Will stopped walking. Noticing, Matt turned and stared back at him. Both barely noticed the passers-by.

"What are we doing, Matt?" asked Will. "We don't know that everything is messed up. But even if Katia and Keb went where they weren't supposed to and even if they are in trouble again, Rob and Kris will be waiting for us. We can't let them down."

His face brightening a little, Matt said, "We rescued Katia and Keb once." He gave a weak smile. "We can do it again."

"Exactly," said Will, stepping forwards to stand next to Matt. "I think I'm feeling as down as I am because I'm worried about Rob and Kris. You, too, I bet."

Matt nodded, "Yeah, and I've been thinking about Mother and Father."

Will put his hand on Matt's shoulder. "First, we have to get Father's ship. Like Rafjur said, we're going to need it to find Mother and Father, anyway. Then we hook up with Rob and Kris. Then we go and get Katia and Keb back."

"And we're going to have to get The Sphere back, too," said Matt, now standing straight. "Even if we have to steal it back from the Boargen."

"You got that right, dude," said Will, giving Matt a quick squeeze on the shoulder. And as he turned to leave, he added, "Let's do our job."

"Will?" Will stopped and looked back. Matt hadn't budged. "What if Rafjur is tricking us?"

Will cocked his head and squinted. "What do you mean?"

"What if Rafjur is having us get this ship so he can take it from us? What if it was him, who got Katia and Keb caught?"

"You think this is a trap?" asked Will.

Matt shrugged.

Will continued, "I don't think so. I think Father would trust someone like Rafjur above others, because even though he's a pirate, he seems honest ... like he has nothing to hide. Still, you could be right. We'll just have to be careful."

Just then, Will noticed Matt staring at something, his face paling, and turned to see what it was. A Boargen guard was watching them, his black uniform establishing his authority.

Will turned back to Matt and said, "Maybe you're right about that trap. But look, we just have to get to the ship and we're out of here." Will glanced down at the map on his arm-comp. "Let's go, nice and easy."

The boys moved on, aware that they were being followed. It was difficult for each to refrain from panicking and bolting, but they both managed to set a normal, steady pace.

The planet of Kablakia was almost entirely roofed over, a worldwide city, with skyscrapers jutting high above the main roof in some places and deep crevices piercing the surface in others, making for a dramatic mixture of both a gleaming silver and deeply shaded landscape. Much of what was housed inside this man-made shell was sprawling spaceship factories and hangers. Each level of the world-city was dedicated to a primary mode of travel. Will and Matt maintained a brisk pace along one of the levels dedicated to pedestrian traffic.

It was the middle of the night, and what they had read about Kablakia was true: the planet never slept. This worked to their advantage, as, due to the crowded corridors, their pursuer had fallen behind. It was at that moment that Will saw their chance to lose him, and, with Matt following closely behind, he shot into a thick crowd of tall, thin beings who had beaked noses and who were wearing long, oversized robes. Within the crowd, they doubled back, crossed a wide passageway, and vanished amongst the throngs of pedestrians.

Now that they had lost their Boargen shadow, Will and Matt realised how much the spaceport on Kablakia's moon had only been a taste of the diversity of life on Kablakia itself. What Mr Casper had said about evolution's possible variations appearing to be endless, was right on the mark. And it seemed that there was a sample of every possibility right there on Kablakia, although each boy knew in his own mind that was unlikely. A maze of both wide and narrow passageways went on forever, and hoards of galactic citizens never ceased to fill every one.

Later, when no Boargen guards were in sight, Will and Matt dared to stop and rest. Standing to the side of a walkway filled with a bustling crowd, Will glanced beside him and noticed for the first time that the pack hugging Matt's back looked like it had more in it than his own. He pointed at it and asked, "What do you have in that thing?"

Craning his neck to glance back at his pack, Matt then looked at Will and said, "Kris's saucer."

As Matt resumed watching the bustling scene, Will studied him for a moment. Then, with an eyebrow raised, he said, "Better not lose Kris's toy."

Matt dragged his gaze from the throng of Kablakian pedestrians to stare back at Will. "I won't."

By the time Will and Matt reached a transit system, having to sift through endlessly thick crowds as they did so, it seemed that they had been walking for hours. The transit system was much like any subway on Earth, and they rode it the rest of the way to their destination.

A short time later, they found themselves standing in the main lobby of the factory. Here, there were far fewer beings moving about, probably because it was not during a shift change. Will and Matt stood there, wondering how best to continue. From where they were, their father's space-cruiser was still a long walk through a maze of factory corridors and up a few levels to what showed on the arm-comp map as a mysterious void in the factory complex; otherwise known – Rafjur had said, with a rare grin – as a hiding place for a spaceship. Rafjur had said that their father had a knack for making friends in useful places. It was with apparent pride, that he was certain that only Rob Roar would have been able to hide a state of the art space-cruiser right underneath the Boargen noses.

"Hey, you, little ones," a deep voice bellowed, striking fear in the boys that the Boargen guard had found them.

They turned. It was not a Boargen but a man with a very square head – as square as a head could be without actually being a block. The rest of his features suggested the same square theme all over. He was dressed in a uniform – that of a police officer or a guard.

"If you're here to work, you're late for your shift." He held out his hand and added, "Give me your papers."

Will and Matt each dug into a pocket, pulled out what they hoped were the proper papers, and, nervously, handed them over.

The guard began walking away, giving the brothers another moment of panic. But just then, he turned to look back. "Well," he said, "don't just stand there. You're late. Follow me."

As the two boys jumped to follow, the guard spoke, in a deep voice, into a handheld communicator.

"Your de-clogs are here. I'm bringing them down."

Will and Matt exchanged worried looks. They had not figured that they would actually have to work in their chosen career.

Worrying all the way, the brothers followed the blockhead through a maze of glossy-black corridors, still dark in spite of continuous strips of lighting running the length of them. Eventually, they stopped at a door. There was writing on it but Will and Matt were unable to read it. However, below the writing, was a depiction that said it all: it looked like a torpedo with arms and legs and it was in a section of pipe, pointing towards an unnatural-looking pile of debris otherwise known as a clog.

The guard swiped a card through a groove in a small console beside the door and the door opened, slipping into the wall. They entered. Inside, he pointed at the torpedo suits hanging on the wall and said, "Get suited up. The engineer will be along to help you to the waste system access." He grinned, nastily. "If those gargrosses weren't so darned good at installing those Polinthian engines, you little ones wouldn't have so much fun swimming in the pipes." With nothing more to say, the blockhead turned and left. As the door slid shut, the guard emitted a low, heavy chuckle.

Matt turned, wild-eyed, to find Will looking at the monitor on his arm-comp. "Will," he said, "we have to get out of here, fast."

Pointing up at a large vent in the wall, Will said, "And that's our way out." He looked down at the map on his arm-comp and continued, "Good thing we have the plans to this place … " he looked at Matt, "or we'd be looking at a swim in a torpedo suit through poop-clogged pipes."

Hopping up on to a bench beneath the vent, Will studied the vent cover for a moment, and then thrust his hand out to Matt and said, "Hand me that power-driver."

Shucking off his pack, Matt dug into it and pulled out a toolkit. From the kit, he handed Will the power-driver, then alternated between watching Will make quick work of removing the vent cover and watching the door.

Within minutes, and with Will in the lead, Matt, with his pack replaced, followed his brother who was crawling through the factory ventilation system.

Soon, they heard a voice yell, "You stupid clogheads! Come back here! You're in the wrong system! And you need your suits on besides that!"

Glancing at his arm-comp, Will continued his fast-paced crawl with Matt following closely. It was difficult to move through the ventilation system with any sort of stealth, as the weight of each boy's body stressed the rectilinear metal ducts and caused an occasional loud, hollow drumming; a noise that had each boy concerned that they would be tracked and found because of it.

Then an alarm went off; a repetitive buzzing that seemed to drill straight through Will and Matt's ears to their brains. There was little doubt that someone at the factory had finally decided that the two young humans crawling through the ventilation system were a threat. But, in spite of the building fury in the factory around them, Will remained focused and continued, following the promptings from his arm-comp. Less calm but still holding his nerve, Matt stayed right behind him. In time, the buzzing stopped, probably because it was so obnoxiously loud that it hurt the ears of those searching for them.

There was light visible at the end of the maze of ductwork. But there was also a grill, well attached, barring their exit to a storage room. Managing to turn around in the duct, Will lay on his back and, with both feet together, he gave the grill a swift kick. It didn't budge. Next, he felt a tap-tap-tap on his shoulder and looked back. Matt was smiling and holding up what Will would discover was a small cutting-laser.

Matt squeezed past and cut around the perimeter of the grill. Once done, he scooted back and Will gave the grill another swift kick. It was at the very moment of Will's kick, that a blockhead, who looked much like the one who had escorted them to the torpedo dressing room, entered the storage room.

Now this series of coincidental events had the potential of developing into a real problem. However, Will had kicked the grill so hard that it flew from the vent opening, across the room. It hit the blockhead square in the head with such force that the brothers were uncertain whether it was the grill that reverberated like a musical instrument on impact, or the guard's head. Either way, the blockhead's eyes rolled up as though he watched his consciousness float away, and he fell in a heap, forcing the door closed, leaving yet one more obstacle for the brothers to get through to reach the space-cruiser.

Matt stared down at the guard as he said, "Space! You really grilled that guy."

Will slid to the end of the duct and dropped to the floor. After glancing at the guard, he looked up at Matt, who stuck his head out and peered down.

"Come on, Matt. We better get going before that blockhead wakes up and squares off with us."

Matt turned in the duct letting his legs dangle, and pushed off, landing beside Will, staring at him, afraid. Oblivious, Will turned and strode to the blockhead, out cold on the floor.

After the two boys dragged the unconscious guard out of the way, Will took the guard's cardkey and was about to leave when Matt grabbed his arm. Will peered back. Matt looked spooked. In fact, the reality of their predicament had been pressing in more now, making him feel on the verge of panic.

"Aren't you scared?" he asked. "They've got to be all over the place looking for us. I think we're close to getting caught."

Will hesitated, not wanting to admit fear, but then he said, "Yeah, Matt, I'm scared, too. But something tells me we need to have Father's ship. Besides, now it's our only way out of here. Do you agree?" Matt gulped and nodded.

They made their way down more dark passageways to a large door. Beside the door, was a scan-lock. Will swiped it with the cardkey. Nothing happened. He did it again. Again, nothing. Matt took the card and turned it over and over, inspecting it, and then swiped it. Again, nothing happened.

Tossing the card back to Will, Matt whipped off his pack. He pulled out the cutting-laser and looked at Will for reassurance. Will hesitated, then scrunched up his face and shook his head. It wouldn't work. Then the brothers heard something ...

Matt stashed the tool back in his pack and dodged with Will to the corner beside the door, just in time. The door opened and what emerged, each brother figured, had to be a gargross. His horrendously fat body brushed both sides of the wide doorway as he passed through. The gargross shuffled down the hall with his huge feet scuffing on the floor. The brothers dodged through the doorway just as the door closed behind them.

Inside, they found themselves on a catwalk, high above the hangar floor. Will abruptly grabbed Matt and pulled him behind some storage containers. Upon entering, Matt's attention had been grabbed by the incredible sight which he saw below: his father's ship! It was about as large as the old beast Rafjur had given them – a football field or so long. Like the helicopter and the Earth spaceships, the space-cruiser was pearl-white and smooth. Will had seen it, too, but he had also seen a couple of guards.

The brothers peered through a space between the containers to get another look. At the sight of the ship, Will had an intense feeling of excitement that made his heart feel light. He couldn't wait to fly it! But first, they would have to get past the guards. Fortunately, from where they were, they had a bird's eye view of the entire hangar lending them an unencumbered view of the two blockheads below – the perfect set up for sneaks.

Matt glanced at Will and whispered, "I thought this was a secret hangar. Only a few are supposed to know about it."

Will whispered back, "Maybe they found it just now, while searching for us."

"Then we better get Father's ship and get out of here quick, before it gets really busy," said Matt, feeling braver.

He shrugged off his pack and pulled Kris's toy flying-saucer and the remote controls out, then peered up at Will.

"Kris won't like it if we lose it," Will whispered, a doubtful look on his face as he stared at Matt.

"Yeah, but it's for a good cause," Matt whispered back.

Will continued to stare at Matt, and then said, "I guess I can't think of any other way to draw the guards' attention."

With that, Matt flicked the toy's power switch on. The saucer began a subtle humming. Gripping the controls, he adjusted the toggles. With a rise in the pitch of the humming, the silver saucer rose off the catwalk. Matt fiddled with the toggles a little, getting used to the controls again.

Will watched as the object floated down towards the blockhead guards. Matt was masterful with the controls as he steered the saucer, placing it on a trajectory that would take it just above the guards' heads. Once close, he pushed the left toggle all the way forwards and the toy's motors whined as it picked up speed, darting forwards.

The guards heard it, and as they searched wildly for the foreign sound which the flying-saucer made, it streaked past them, just inches above their heads. Taking the bait, the blockheads sprang to the chase and Will and Matt took off, running along the catwalk towards an elevator, Matt with a clumsy gait as he was also steering the flying-saucer, sending it into a far corner of the hangar.

Just as the boys reached the elevator that would take them down to the hangar, a guard entered from the same doorway the brothers had a few minutes earlier. This guard, however, was not a blockhead; he was the very Boargen guard that had followed the brothers earlier. Upon seeing the confusion in the hangar, the Boargen said something similar to what Mr Casper had said a few weeks earlier, when he first saw Kris's toy flying-saucer; something like, "What on Kablakia?!"

Before the new arrival caught sight of Will and Matt, however, the elevator had reached the hangar floor. The brothers sprinted towards the ship – Matt, miraculously maintaining control of the saucer – hoping dearly, that they could gain entry before they were caught.

It was at this time, that the two blockheads, having chased the flying-saucer to the far corner of the football-field-sized hangar, realised they had been duped and headed at a fast, barrelling run, to intercept the boys. Matt managed to make the flying-saucer give chase.

Just as Will was beginning to doubt Rafjur's theory that their father – always planning for life's endless chances – would have the ship's computer programmed to recognise any Roar and allow entry, he saw a thin, dark line form on the cruiser's hull: a hatch was opening with a welcoming yawn, along with a gangway. The fear both boys felt at that moment, racing the blockheads to the ship while the Boargen guard on the catwalk barked orders, made it difficult for them to catch their breath. But all the while, somehow, Matt maintained control over the saucer.

That was a good thing because, as he ran, he looked back up at the Boargen guard on the catwalk and saw him drawing a blaster. Thinking fast, he steered the flying-saucer towards the catwalk and, at the same time, caught enough breath to call out, "Will, the Boargen has a blaster … "

These words probably saved Will's life because, at Matt's warning, Will dived under the open gangway, which was then hit by a blast.

Stopping in his tracks, Matt adjusted the flying-saucer's flight-path. Just as the Boargen guard was aiming his blaster at him, the saucer streaked by threatening to shave a strip of hair off the guard's head, making him dive for the catwalk. Matt pushed the directional toggle to the right and the saucer responded with a glancing blow off the hangar wall and headed – Matt hoped – straight towards the space-cruiser's hatchway.

The blockheads were close when Will crawled out from under the gangway and shook off the hard knock to his head which he'd sustained from diving to the hangar floor. He waited the few moments it took for Matt to reach the ship, and fell in behind him, sprinting up the gangway on his brother's heels. On the way in, Matt passed his hand over a control panel and the gangway began to retract. Dropping to the floor in exhaustion, the boys watched with bated breath, to see if the blockheads would make it to the ship before the hatch closed. If so, Will and Matt could still be caught.

That's when two miraculous things happened: the first was that just as the hatch was about to shut out the light coming in from the hangar, a streak of silver shot through what remained of the opening and skidded across the space-cruiser's floor. Kris's toy had made it. The second was that of a familiar female voice, which said, "Welcome, Galaxy Boys."

Astonished, Will and Matt shot looks at each other, eyes wide. Together, they said, "KNIA?!"

"It is unexpected that you have found the Tenacity," said KNIA. "However, it is ultimately pleasing that you have. As soon as you have moved the ship from its present position, our connection will be broken. But you will easily be able to re-establish contact when you are once again on a stable, calculated course. It is now recommended that you leave Kablakia."

As though an exclamation mark, the muffled sound of a blast was followed by a slight vibration ... which the boys felt from where they sat. Someone was firing a weapon at the Tenacity.

Springing to their feet and throwing off their packs, Will and Matt looked around and then stared at each other. The ship was huge, and they each wondered which way they needed to go to reach the command bridge.

Will called out in desperation. "KNIA?"

"Go through the doorway on the left," said KNIA, "and follow the corridor."

They rushed to the door, which opened at their approach, and upon passing through the doorway, they broke into a run.

"Turn left ahead," prompted KNIA.

Turning left, they ran along a short, straight corridor at the end of which was another door. The door opened on their approach, revealing a command bridge that made Rafjur's old ship look like the antique it was. Will and Matt stopped just inside the doorway, taken aback at the splendour of their father's ship. Another subtle shudder sent Will to the pilot's seat and Matt to the co-pilot's seat. It was time to leave.

Will set into studying the controls, during which time another blast hit them making the vessel shudder. He knew that even when his father's ship – what had KNIA called it? The Tenacity? – was at rest, the repulse field was minimally active. It was the same with the other Earth ships and the helicopter; a trait of a more advanced technology.

Just as KNIA had used a tight-beam to reach the Tenacity, so could Will and Matt now reach Rob and Kris in Rafjur's old ship which was at a previously established set of coordinates on the fringe of the Kablakian system. So while Will was familiarising himself with Tenacity's flight controls, Matt busied himself by using his arm-comp to tap into Tenacity's system. He typed a message and waited. An answer came. Matt smiled, looked over at Will, and said, "Rob and Kris are ready."

"Good, so are we."

With an odd sense of familiarity, Will tapped a series of pads on the control console and the ship came smoothly awake; the bridge lit up. And as Will touched a few more pads, the engines roared into life. Tenacity's surveillance cameras showed blockheads and Boargen guards scattering. They all knew what was about to happen. There was no chance of stopping the space-cruiser, and the young humans from stealing it. At that moment, someone somewhere in the factory was probably saying, 'Those young humans are fired!'

"Will," said Matt. Will looked at him. "The hangar door's not open. How are we going to get out of here?"

If all the Boargen officials on Kablakia did not already know about the secret hangar, they soon would.

A mischievous smile grew on Will's face. He returned his attention to Tenacity's controls and ratcheted the throttles forwards. In a storm of dust, the huge ship lifted off the hangar floor. Will pushed a button that opened a panel to the weapons controls. He looked beside him at Matt again, and said, "Ready?"

With his own mischievous smile, Matt said, "Ready."

And then, as Tenacity turned slowly in place, Will let go a torrent of plasma missiles that, upon hitting the wall in front of them, turned the hangar into a violent wind-tunnel that rocked the ship. Not a thing could be seen out of the bridge view-screen with all the dust and debris, but the scanner showed a clear path, so Will thrust the control stick forwards and the ship exploded from the hangar.

Matt gasped, and then exhaled, "Space!"

It took every bit of concentration for Will to weave the ship around a few tall buildings in Tenacity's flight-path – a hair-raising experience, making him wish he had thought about dodging buildings before blasting out of the hangar. As the cityscape of Kablakia slipped behind them, Will remembered a crucial detail of their plan. He reached forwards and throttled back the engines, slowing Tenacity's ascent.

Even with the seat's restraining fields, Will and Matt had been surprised at Tenacity's incredible power when they shot from the hangar. There had been no way they could have known that such a large ship could spring into motion with such an unstoppable deliberateness. What they also could not have known at that time, was that there were no spaceships in the galaxy that could do what the Tenacity could. It was a one of a kind, and, like the hangar in which it had been built and stored, a grand secret.

A sudden shock rocked the cruiser, jarring the boys from their satisfaction. Will glanced beside him at Matt, who stared back through wide eyes.

Will shrugged, and then said, with confidence, "We have to let them hit us. It's part of the plan."

Then an alarm screamed and the lights throughout the command bridge turned red. The scanner showed three large ships converging. Another blast hit, only this one was more powerful. The boys exchanged concerned glances.

With his confidence now gone, Will said, "I wonder whether, when Rafjur came up with this plan, he figured a whole fleet would be after us." He craned his neck to peer out the corner of the view-screen. "I hope this thing can take the hits."

At that very moment, Rob and Kris were on the command bridge of Rafjur's old spaceship making final preparations to abandon the old beast to its final pass through thin-space.

"Alright," said Kris, glancing at Rob in the pilot's seat beside him. "I have the coordinates and the time figured for the switch. I sent them to Will and Matt. They're probably blasting out of Kablakia right now."

Rob tapped a series of keys on the control console. Hopping up from his seat, he said, "OK, I set the timer. The old beast will pass through thin-space and then vaporise in just under fifteen minutes." He turned to leave. "We better get off."

Kris leapt from his seat and followed, but, before abandoning the command bridge, they took one last look and felt bad for the old ship. But with the clock counting down, they left and swiftly made it to the cargo hold where the two space-fighters they had picked up before leaving Sundee's orbit sat waiting for them. They split up, Rob to one fighter and Kris to the other.

As they had made their way to the cargo hold, Rob and Kris had both been running the spaceship switch plan through their heads, over and over: first, they would fly the two space-fighters off Rafjur's old ship. Then, in the space-fighters, they would leave Rafjur's ship behind, pass through thin-space to the rendezvous point, and there, meet up with the others; Katia and Keb's fate was still unknown to Rob and Kris. Meanwhile, heading to a precisely set point in Kablakia's orbit, Will and Matt, in the Tenacity, would leave at that precise moment, passing through thin-space to the rendezvous-point. Rafjur's old ship, emptied of Rob and Kris and the two fighters, would, as programmed, pass through thin-space at the exact same time as the Tenacity left Kablakia's orbit and appear in its place. A split second afterwards, the old ship would blow up, vapourising into an unrecognisable cloud of debris, leaving those who chased the Tenacity believing their chase was over. For, as far as they would know, the ship had been shot out of space, therefore stopping it and the two human boy thieves from escaping.

This would be Kris's first time piloting a spaceship. He knew how to do it. He knew he could do it. But he was still very nervous; in part, because he realised that just over two weeks ago, he could never have imagined truly flying a spaceship. It was like he was now a different Kris living a different life.

He set to, powering up his space-fighter's engines ... what a thrill! He could hear Rob's ship next to him roaring to life. Then he heard Rob's voice through his communicator.

"You ready to go, brother?"

Kris nodded, "Yep, ready."

In the other fighter, Rob tapped a button on his arm-comp, and then said, "As soon as the cargo hold is depressurised, I'll open the hold doors and we'll get out of here."

With a beep, a green light on Rob's arm-comp began blinking, signalling to him that everything was ready. He pushed a button, sending a signal to the old ship's computer to open the hold doors.

The huge doors separated down the middle and began to open.

Then they stopped.

Rob and Kris shot stricken looks at each other, and then stared down at their arm-comps. The seconds on their timers ticked by unnervingly fast. They had just over five minutes remaining until the old ship passed through thin-space, and then vaporised. That meant that anything remaining on board would also be vaporised; blown into nonexistence.

"Rob!" Kris called out, desperate for reassurance.

Until this moment, Kris had been consumed by the wonder of his new life: of all the possible adventures ahead and the prospect of finding his mother and father. He had felt in control, even when faced with danger while rescuing Katia and landing on Sundee. He had felt in control because, in that time of danger, he had been filled with something to do – run. Now, staring at the doors open only a crack, he was helpless to do anything. Tears welled up in his eyes as he looked around the cargo bay, wishing, more than anything he had ever wished before, that his mother and father would appear, gather him up in their arms, and whisk him away back to Oregon where he could be a little boy again.

Rob pushed buttons on his arm-comp, directing Rafjur's old beast to close the cargo doors. The doors closed the little bit, sealing the opening. Tapping on his arm-comp again, he directed the ship to open the doors. Same thing; the doors began to open, and then stopped. He tried again, desperation rising. Each time, the doors began to open and then stopped.

He stared over at Kris. The mind-links with KNIA had given him and his brothers much more than just the knowledge to fly ships. Rob knew that without the mind-links, he and his brothers would be, for the most part, lost little boys; lost in a galaxy that seemed to have no limit to the dangers one could encounter. At that moment though, even Kris looked like a lost little boy. Rob had never seen him look so afraid.

"Kris! Think! Help me figure out what to do!" Rob pleaded. "We don't have time to pressurise the cargo hold and get back to the bridge to stop the countdown! And if we blast the cargo hold doors, we might blow up the ship with us in it! There has to be another way to get out of here!"

Kris's face scrunched up; physical proof that he was thinking.

Rob looked down at his arm-comp: The time remaining before he and Kris would vanish forever with Rafjur's old spaceship, was just under three minutes. He closed his eyes and took a deep breath, hoping something would come to him. All he could hear was the muffled roar of the engines echoing in the cargo hold.

Then, at the same time, Rob called out, "Kris!"

Kris with his equilibrium regained, called out, "Rob!"

At the same time, the two of them said, "I think I've got it!"

Excited, Rob began, "We're moving with Rafjur's old spaceship, right now … "

"And," Kris cut in, "if we program our fighters' computers with the coordinates for where we're to meet up with Will and Matt…"

"And we also program the computers to direct our ships to pass through thin-space at the very moment that Rafjur's ship passes through thin-space … "

"Then Rafjur's ship will go one way … "

" … and we'll go the other."

The timers on the brothers' arm-comps read less than two minutes by the time they began feverishly reprogramming their ships' computers.

Once finished, Rob looked over at his brother and said, "Kris." Kris looked up. "I think there's one more thing we have to do."

Thin-space was one of the more profound of the unexplainable mysteries the boys had encountered. The most accepted theory was that it was an alternate dimension; an opposite of the known universe. Any attempt at measuring it or collecting a sample from it as a ship passed through had always been met with failure. And a ship could only pass through it; it could never stop. It was believed that to stop was to stay for eternity. The Roar brothers would know this intuitively, but question it endlessly.

Both at the same time, said, "A split second before we enter thin-space we have to have our ships' throttles full-on."

Rob continued, "Otherwise we might get stuck in thin-space."

"I agree," said Kris, "but how do we know about that?"

"Intuition," said Rob.

"Curious," said Kris.

It was time.

"Ready?" asked Rob, exhilarated.

"Ready!" answered Kris, excited.

In a finite second, four spaceships passed through thin-space at the same, precisely coordinated, time.

The Tenacity, with Will and Matt aboard, passed through from Kablakia's orbit to the planned point of their rendezvous. Rob and Kris, in the space-fighters, passed through from the old beast's cargo hold and re-emerged near the Tenacity. And Rafjur's old ship passed through and took the place of the Tenacity in Kablakia's orbit; then, promptly blew up. Every part of it vaporised into space dust.

There was not a person or an alien, wise to the spaceship switch among the boys' Boargen pursuers. In fact, upon the complete annihilation of what was believed to be the fine new ship – the same one that had blasted its way out of a secret hangar and had raced away from Kablakia without any legal clearance – on Kablakia, two blockhead weapons technicians glanced at each other with looks of concern.

One of the weapons technicians said to the other, "I think we were just supposed to stop it."

The other replied, "Well, it's stopped."

Jawbone

Within the same split second that Rafjur's ship had met its end above Kablakia, the Tenacity and the two space-fighters appeared on the periphery of the Heavensa system – the rendezvous point. The three ships then made one more pass through thin-space and arrived in Heavensa's orbit, together.

Heavensa, a wildlife sanctuary complete with dinosaur-like creatures, looked a little bit like Earth had 200 million years ago, when Pangaea was the main land mass, before breaking apart into smaller, more familiar shapes. Arriving at Heavensa, therefore, was a bit like arriving home to an Earth of a distant past. At seeing the blue planet, the Roar brothers felt a little like one might feel upon finding a shady tree in a green field after a long hike through the mountains on a hot day.

The finest Kablakian engineers had designed the Tenacity. It had been built using the most advanced Polinthian engines, the most advanced Mindin computers, and the most advanced and powerful Quadoran weapons. Everything had been assembled by the most accomplished in their field, including the gargrosses who were the best at integrating the Polinthian engines with the rest of the ship's systems. But had any of the Kablakian engineers had a chance to review Tenacity's construction before the ship had been spirited away and hidden, they would have discovered that Rob Roar's space-cruiser was unexplainable. Those who had built it had improvised. The ship was, in fact, ultimately an invention far adrift from the original plans.

The space-cruiser had a large cargo hold which would have held the shuttle had it not been missing along with Katia, Keb, and The Sphere. On each side of Tenacity's hull, built into its thick, stubby wings, were ports into which the space-fighters could dock and become integral with the larger ship.

With a space-fighter on either side of the Tenacity, they moved in close to the larger ship and fitted neatly into the wing ports. Upon entering through the airlocks from the fighter docks to the interior of their father's space-cruiser, Rob was met by Will on one side of the ship and Kris was met by Matt on the other. The boys beamed with palpable relief at being together again.

A fast-paced tour of the Tenacity ended on the command bridge. Gawking as they turned in place, Rob and Kris were thrilled by what they saw. The command bridge was packed full of purpose: aside from the pilot's and co-pilot's seats, were four control seats, each surrounded by command consoles. In fact, the entire ship was filled with purposeful design. And, in the same way that the outside of the cruiser was a clean pearl-white, so was the inside. In fact, according to each brother, it was even a bit stark.

While Will and Matt remained standing, Rob and Kris collapsed into seats – Rob at the navigator console, Kris at the weapons – both still shaken from their narrow escape from Rafjur's old ship. Rob noticed that the excitement of being back together seemed to wear off all too soon. Where Kris looked exhausted, Will and Matt looked solemn. Something was wrong.

Because he and Kris had yet to know about Katia, Keb, and The Sphere, Rob looked towards the command bridge entrance as though expecting to see them enter. He had been so consumed by his own relief and delight at seeing the Tenacity and knowing that Will and Matt were all right, that he had forgotten all about the others. He looked over at Kris, who had just realised the same thing and who was now staring at him.

They were both about to say something when a familiar female voice said, "Hello, Galaxy Boys."

"KNIA?" said Kris, as he leapt to his feet.

Rob sat up straight and Will and Matt brightened a little.

"Yes, Kris. I am very glad you have all made it and are well. You have accomplished a great deal; much of it, unexpected. I am beginning to realise how much I may have underestimated you."

"Is Mr Casper there, too?" asked Rob.

"Yes, I'm here," said Mr Casper. "You've pretty much blown all my expectations out of the galaxy, guys. I didn't bother mentioning the Tenacity because I figured it would be impossible to get it out of that hangar. But do tell, how in the galaxy did you guys find out about it?"

"Rafjur," answered Rob.

"Rafjur!" barked Mr Casper. "Guys, that's not possible … "

"What's not possible about it?" asked Rob.

"Rafjur's dead, that's what's not possible about it. He died saving your father's life. He got sucked into a black hole."

"Are we talking about the same guy?" asked Matt. "Arms as big as me? Hates robots? Talks in third person? That Rafjur?"

"Sounds like him, but there's no way he survived a black hole. No way. Not even Rafjur. Where did you guys go?"

"Sundee," answered Rob.

"Sundee! Guys, no way. Sundee went into the black hole, too."

"Well … " Rob hesitated. This was the first time he had heard such a sharp inflection in Mr Casper's voice. "Well, maybe there's another Rafjur."

"And another Sundee I suppose, too," said Mr Casper. "Where was this Sundee you found?"

"Way out towards the end of the galactic outer arm," said Kris.

They could hear Mr Casper take a deep breath. Then he said, "OK, guys. I can't tell you you didn't go to Sundee and find Rafjur. But I can't figure out how it can be so. I'll leave it at that for now because you guys are a long way from Earth and we could lose the tight-beam connection at any second. KNIAs sending Tenacity's computer enhanced images of that UFO that Adia and her daughters saw snooping around the old base."

Then KNIA spoke up: "It is important that you all know about the unidentified craft. There is no record of one like it existing in the galaxy. Therefore, it cannot be known if whoever was on board has friendly intentions or not."

"And to make the uncertainty about it worse," added Mr Casper, "somehow, whoever piloted that thing knew the base was there."

"Should we be keeping a lookout for that FBI guy, too?" asked Matt, a mischievous smile blossoming.

Everyone laughed, except for KNIA, relieving the tension.

But the topics discussed, however captivating, had left out that which was bothering Rob and Kris the most. Where were Katia and Keb? And where was The Sphere?

Cutting off Rob as he was opening his mouth to speak, Kris asked the nagging question, "What happened to Katia and Keb ... ?"

While Will remained at the Tenacity's controls to take them to Jawbone, and Kris worked to find out where Katia might be on Jawbone, Rob and Matt were sleeping. Each slept in their own ship's cabin, resting up for what they were sure would be a very scary trip. Will and Kris would have to rest later. Since space travel and the inherent adventure that came with it required long, sleepless hours, the Tenacity was uniquely equipped with a means for helping one get eight hours of sleep in two. This gave a whole other meaning to being fast asleep. So a sweet smelling sleep gas added to the air in their cabins helped Rob and Matt rest well; in spite of the thick fear in the air over heading to a place where the inhabitants ate unwary visitors for dinner.

Though he worried about Katia – and Keb and The Sphere, too – Rob was downright angry that she would do something as stupid as going where Rafjur had strictly told her not to: back to where the Boargen had attacked her mother's ship. There was a part of him that wanted to be done with it all and just go home. But he knew they had to rescue Katia from Jawbone; she would die there, otherwise.

And although Keb was a robot – a fancy, human-shaped machine – he was now the Roar brothers' friend. He had even saved Will's life back on Sundee. Having apparently been damaged, maybe even beyond repair, and taken to the space academy in orbit around Moxy, it would be heartbreaking if Keb was scrapped and turned into a toaster. Even though Katia had to come first – no need for Mr Casper to have stressed that – Keb was on each boy's mind. They would save him, too, if they could.

As for The Sphere, the Boargen undoubtedly had it. Mr Casper had only been able to guess they had taken it to the Boargen system: a group of three habitable worlds orbiting a single sun. It was becoming increasingly apparent that The Sphere, the single most comprehensive repository of knowledge in the galaxy, could be negatively exploited. It was The Sphere that chose a society to be the guardians of a given knowledge. That meant that it had the power – through sharing knowledge – to bring wealth and prosperity to a chosen few. But that also meant that it had the power – through inaction – to limit prosperity. And that meant a society with evil intentions – if resourceful enough – could use The Sphere to gain control of the galaxy, by simply keeping it from others.

Kris halted his search for where Katia might be, to join Will. He sat in the co-pilot's seat watching as the Tenacity pulled away from Heavensa and prepared to make its first pass of six through thin-space, to Jawbone. With the cruiser streaking through the cosmos at a tenth of the speed of light, Will pressed the throttle levers against a slight resistance all the way forwards and the Tenacity slipped through thin-space to a galactic location nine thousand light-years away.

Each time Kris had been through thin-space, he had made sure not to blink, hoping he would see something. But each time it was the same; a pure-white field of nothingness which only lasted a moment. There was no glare and no physical feeling other than a slight disorientation; like the feeling that one might get from sitting up too fast after lying down for a while. The only other time he had ever seen a white as pure as thin-space, was when he saw The Sphere, and he wondered whether there might be a connection between the two. Then again, The Sphere also seemed similar to something else he knew – KNIA – as The Sphere was very much like the vastly intelligent computer. Or maybe KNIA was more like The Sphere, though it shared its information through images only. But KNIA was a computer network…right? And The Sphere was … well … what it was. And thin-space was just another dimension through which spaceships travelled in order to traverse the galaxy. But isn't all of life connected in some way? Kris could think about this for hours on end.

The Tenacity appeared from thin-space about 95 million miles from Jawbone and raced to catch up with the planet. With Jawbone shown as a large holographic image at the centre of the command bridge, Will and Kris could see all too well that it was a terrible place. Like Earth, most of Jawbone was covered with water. But unlike Earth, the land masses were smaller, mostly grouped islands, and the coasts were jagged, like a rockhund's row of teeth. The planet was covered in a thick fog, lending a rather spooky, lifeless appearance.

Upon waking, Rob and Matt grabbed a quick bite, and then found Will and Kris who were studying the hologram.

"Do we know where the Boargen dumped her yet?" asked Rob.

"No," said Kris, as he strode around the hologram. "But there has to be a way to find her without knocking on every Jawbonee door and asking." He walked back to one of the two library consoles as he said, "I'll figure it out."

Feeling grumpy, Rob walked over and plopped down in the pilot's seat, followed by Will landing beside him in the co-pilot's seat. Matt ended up leaning on the seat behind Will. A gloom set in amongst the three whilst Kris became absorbed by his search.

"We should be helping him," said Rob, feeling gloomy.

"We are," said Will, staring out at Jawbone which was growing nearer with every second. "We're thinking."

Rob exhaled in frustration, and then said, "Why are we doing this, anyway? She got herself into it ... ! Besides, we're not galaxy rangers. We don't know what we're going to find down there."

The ship's computer described Jawbonee inhabitants as having a level of technology that was not yet far enough advanced even for rudimentary exploration of their own solar system. Although they had a simple radar system that could detect intruders in orbit, Jawbone had no indigenous fuel supply; a necessary ingredient for an advanced industry. The Jawbonee, therefore, still used sailing vessels on the sea, and on land they used creature-drawn carts. But they, unlike Earth's inhabitants, did, somehow, know about the galaxy at large.

The galactic senate had ordered beacons to be set around Jawbone to warn would-be visitors from landing on the planet, as a visit there could be the end of a traveller's journey. The Tenacity passed the outermost beacon and continued on, in spite of the warnings, which gave the Roar boys chills in their spines.

Pausing in his search, Kris looked over at the others with a fearful gaze.

Will nudged Rob. "Scared?"

Rob glanced at him, and then went back to staring out the view-screen at Jawbone, which now loomed large, and said, "Yeah, you think? Three weeks ago we were stuck in that orphanage dreaming of the day Mother and Father would come and get us." Rob glanced at Will, and then Matt. "Now, we're twenty-three thousand light-years from Earth, zipping along through space in a machine as big as a football field heading for a planet where we could be eaten as a meal; or as dessert, if we're lucky."

"Space, the final frontier," said Matt, in a low, quiet voice.

"It's not funny, Matt," said Rob, glaring at him. "We could die out here, or down there … " He pointed at Jawbone. "And you're coming with me; so be serious."

Matt sobered and said, "Sorry."

Rob continued, "We can go anywhere in the galaxy we want and risk our lives in doing so, but what are the chances that we will ever find Mother and Father?" Rob pointed out the view-screen. " … I mean, look, guys, they don't call it space for no reason. There's a lot of it. It's endless." Rob stared at his brothers. "How are we ever going to find our parents in all that space out there … even if we do survive Jawbone?"

"You know, Rob," said Will, "you always tell me to lighten up. You always tell me I can't control everything, and that I have to learn to roll with the punches. Mother and Father know where they can find us. And even if we're not on Earth they know how to find us … Do you want me to go and find Katia?"

Rob glanced at Will. "No," he said. He looked at Matt and continued, "But maybe I should go alone."

"No way," said Matt. "I want to help. And we need Will up here in case we need him to rescue us ... "

"I found her!" announced Kris, barging through the hologram of Jawbone. Excited, he smiled. "Hearing that warning beacon scared the bejeebers out of me. But it gave me an idea. I figured that maybe the beacons kept a record of the traffic around here and I was right. A Boargen ship landed on one of the larger islands." Kris beamed, "That has to be where Katia is."

Matt reached out, nudged Rob, and feigning bravery, said, "So let's go crash the dinner party, big bro."

Rob and Matt boarded one of the space-fighters, separated from the Tenacity, and then shot towards Jawbone. Will and Kris remained behind, keeping a watch for the Boargen, prepared in case Rob and Matt should need rescuing. The Tenacity's computer had already been jamming the Jawbonee radar, keeping the ship hidden, and now the space-fighter's computer did the same as Rob set a course for a large island near the planet's equator.

As the space-fighter streaked along a jagged coastline, the fog was so thick that Rob and Matt rarely caught sight of anything solid. Only once did they see scattered lights through the grey mist along the coast at the base of a silhouetted knife-edge mountain range. But in the waning light, the sight seemed only an illusive image; like something one would see in a nightmare.

Though the space-fighter's cloaking field hid the ship from view, the whisper technology failed to completely mask the rumble of the powerful engines which reverberated across the ocean. As the fighter shot by, however, a number of Jawbonee citizens simply thought they heard thunder, assumed they would soon experience a deluge, and headed indoors.

Finding a suitable location to land where inhabitants were unlikely to witness the event, became the first great risk to the rescue effort. With this in mind, Rob chose a small rocky outcrop about a mile down the jagged coast from where they believed

Katia had been dumped off. As the engines wound down, an eerie sound of the sea slipping along the uneven shore closed in on the two boys and they hesitated to leave the safety of their ship.

As the canopy opened, Jawbone's moist, chilled air flooded in with the roar of the ocean pounding the coast some distance away. It was fast growing dark, although it was uncertain if it was solely because of Jawbone's expected turn away from the sun, or whether it was also because a storm was moving in. A look at his arm-comp told Rob it would be completely dark in an hour, regardless of the cloud-cover.

It was so bitterly cold that Rob pulled up the hood of his coat. Matt did the same. As they set out on their arduous trek along the coast, each boy was grateful for the skin-suit he wore as the suits warmed them up a bit, making up for the chill felt on their hands and face. Though they had known Rafjur would disapprove, Rob and Matt had chosen not to pack blasters as each feared having to use one. But Rob now worried that Will would be right, and that he and Matt would regret not having weapons.

Once the dark had descended, not only did it get colder but the journey over the uneven, jagged rocks along the shore became more treacherous. They had only been hiking for just over an hour which was a long time considering the small distance they had covered. Rob and Matt had already agreed that if the whole of Jawbone was like that one mile, it truly was a wicked planet and not a place they would ever want to live, or visit, by choice. Both boys began to understand why the Jawbonee could be so awful.

When they reached the town – if the rock-bound settlement could be called that – there was just enough light bleeding out of dwellings' windows for Rob and Matt to see as they snuck around, but also, little enough for them to hide as they went from shadow to shadow. Who would have thought that the skills learned sneaking about New York at night would come in so very handy on a distant, alien planet?

There were no large buildings in the settlement, probably because there was scarce level ground on which to build anything as the rocks were so jagged and the mountains so steep. In fact, it appeared as though most of the town was underground. The visible construction of the domiciles – where most of the doors and windows were – were scattered across the rock-face, and seemed as though cave entrances had been expanded with sheer walls of stone. Narrow paths – some of them so steep they required steps – were cut into the face of the mountain, weaving, without pattern, here and there to connect entrances.

Few Jawbonee moved about in the chilly, night air, which made it easier for Rob and Matt to slink from window to window and peer inside. Though inefficient, this method of searching for Katia was, under the circumstances, the only apparent way to find her. It appeared to be dinnertime; the thought of which made each boy quite sure that he would never eat again.

"I wonder what they eat when they're not eating visitors," whispered Matt, shivering as they crouched under a window.

Shrugging, Rob whispered back, "There must be a lot of seafood here," he grimaced and shivered, "or they have a really disgusting way of controlling population growth."

Matt was just looking away from Rob in disgust when a movement caught his attention. But before they could react, rough, bony hands grabbed them by their necks and squeezed. Their heads were twisted to face their captors, which was painful, and fearful. Fearful, not just because they worried their heads would be twisted off, but because the sight of their two Jawbonee captors was a nightmare-come-true. Rob and Matt would have screamed had they had a single breath between them.

Apparently, there had never been a decent photograph taken of a Jawbonee – perhaps because the photographer was always running away – so available images paled in comparison to the actual horror of reality. Each skeletal man's eyes bulged grossly, as though the eyeballs would pop out of the sockets with a smack to the back of the head. With their necks gripped painfully under their chins, Rob and Matt each found themselves drawn to within inches of a face that consisted of a skull with strands of muscle and skin intertwined with bone; the jawbone with teeth bared, being the most prominent bone protruding. It was now all too clear to the fearful boys as to how the planet got its name, 'Jawbone'.

With the Jawbonee holding him by the neck, Rob was dragged from the ground so that his feet dangled in mid-air. His hood was whipped off, leaving his head bare to the chill breeze. He assumed Matt was being handled in much the same way, as he could hear him struggling to breathe. This must have been the way that their captors were able to get a better look at what had been caught.

This was also the way Rob could see more of his Jawbonee captor; a thing which he very much regretted because of the nightmares it would cause him later. The monster that choked him appeared to be made entirely of woven bone, muscle, and skin; not just his face as he'd first thought. Rob strained to look down at the hand which held his neck. It looked as if the skin had been stripped away to the muscle in some places, and the bone in others.

Matt – as brave a boy as he was – struggled to remain conscious. Of course, it might have been because he was being choked that he was about to pass out, but the fear that gripped him at the sight of the part-skeleton part-human made him scream; a scream that was released as a gross, choking sound.

It was at the sound of Matt choking – or screaming – that Rob furiously kicked his captor in the groin. This was a step that one would have hoped would have an impact. Instead, the Jawbonee just chuckled cruelly, and in a deep, guttural voice, said, "I like it when my dinner fights back ... "

Bones and Other Gross Stuff

On Jawbone, it appeared that all the food was taken to the same place because, the next time Rob and Matt hit the ground, they were thrown on to a pile of deceased sea creatures which smelt awful. This did, however, take their minds off their own terrible predicament: that they, too, would soon be dead in a most horrible way.

"Ugh! That is a really nasty smell," said Matt, his face all scrunched up as he tried to get off the stinky stuff. But he slipped and slid and became even more entangled with lifeless fins and tentacles.

Although the awful stench was nauseating, Rob remained seated, albeit uncomfortably, trying to figure out how they were going to get out of staying for dinner. The Jawbonee were strong and not pushovers, so there was a slim chance that he and Matt would walk out of the front door.

It was at that moment – when Rob was thinking and Matt was slipping and sliding, and the fish were stinking – that the only door to the room opened and Katia entered.

At the sight of her, forgetting what was underneath him, Rob leapt up, lost track of his feet, and landed, sprawled on his back on top of a fish, whose eyes popped out and soared into the air. He saw them coming back down, and they hit him in the face; plop-plop. Rob never looked at seafood in the same way again.

In the meantime, Matt had mastered the art of walking on the slippery stuff, so he made it to Katia at the same time as she made it to the pile of dead things and fell into her arms. Rob sort of slipped along on his back until he reached Matt and Katia, and he stood and exchanged a hesitant hug with the girl.

"How did you find me?" she whispered.

"Luck," snapped Rob, venting his frustration towards Katia for getting them into this mess. And it had been luck, too. If it had not been for what Will and Matt had heard on that Kablakian shuttle ...

"They shot Keb," she said.

"We know," said Rob, coldly.

"And they got 'The Sphere'," she added.

Rob looked away, "Yeah, we figured that."

Wrinkling her nose, with a weak smile, Katia said, "You guys smell really bad." Then, taking on a serious tone and, as Rob noticed, a haunted look, she whispered, "I hope you have a plan for getting us out of here, because I think they're planning on having you two for breakfast. Where are Will and Kris?"

"They're on the Tenacity," said Rob.

"The what?"

"The Tenacity. Our father's ship."

"Oh, good, you got it," said Katia, her face brightening a moment.

"Those creeps didn't notice our arm-comps under our coats," said Matt. "Maybe we can call Will and Kris to come down here and blow something up as a diversion so we can escape."

"I bet they don't let us live a minute more if they think they might lose us," said Katia, looking more haunted. "I have a feeling anything that comes from off this planet is a delicacy. I'm sure they'll guard their food like wild animals."

"So the only way out of here is to sneak," said Rob.

"And we won't be going out of the front door," said Katia. "There is always someone guarding the exits."

Whilst listening, Rob was looking around the room. There was no window, just the door through which they had come and a small square hatch in the wall at the end of a large sink set in a long cutting-table. He now regretted not having a blaster.

"Hey," said Rob, returning his attention to Katia, "not that I'm not happy to find you alive ... " he noticed that she looked close to tears, "but if we're such a delicacy, why haven't they ... why are you ... ?"

"I don't know. I think they're fattening me up." She scrunched up her face, " ... because all they feed me are really gross, sweet things." She pointed at the pile of fish, "I have a feeling they're feeding me fish pastries."

"Ugh, that's disgusting," said Matt. "And you mean, you've just been free to walk around, all this time?"

Flustered, Katia nodded, "Uh-huh."

"And the only way out is through the front door?" asked Rob, as he stared across the room at the hatch in the wall.

"Well," said Katia, "there is a maze of tunnels and some of those lead to other exits, but there are always guards. They didn't seem very concerned that I would get away when I wandered into the tunnels and got lost for most of the day. They came and found me eventually, as if by smell," she shuddered.

As if he had not been listening to Katia, Rob walked to the thick counter, leaned over it, opened the hatch and poked his head in, but immediately jerked it back out. "Ugh, that's where the worst of the smell is coming from."

"Uh-huh," said Katia. "That's where they dump the bones and other gross stuff."

Rob was pretty sure that Matt and Katia were depending on him to be the brave one and come up with a way out. There was to be no failing them; especially Katia, after all she had been through, even if he was angry at her for getting them into this mess. He could do it, he thought. He just hoped it was the right thing. If not, what more was there? It seemed implausible that Will and Kris could rescue them, given that the Jawbonee were no doubt on guard for more intruders. It was get out now, or ...

Pulling off his coat, Rob tapped out a quick text message on his arm-comp, and then replaced it, shrugging it on to his shoulders. He glanced at Matt and Katia before turning to stare at the hatch and said, "You guys ready?"

Alarmed, Matt walked forwards and grabbed Rob's arm.

Mustering as brave a look as he could, Rob turned to face him.

"Tell me we're not going down the hatch," said Matt, his eyes wide with the very fear that Rob felt.

Rob glanced at the hatch, then at Katia, saw the stark fear in her eyes and brought his attention back to Matt. He said, "Time to muster up that good sense of humour. The more time we spend talking about it, the less chance we have of getting out of here."

He hopped up on to the cutting-table next to the hatch. Looking back at Katia and Matt, he said, "Don't hesitate to follow me unless I say otherwise. They might hear me landing in whatever crud is down there and come running."

"Uh, Rob?" said Katia, shaking, "What if there is no way out?"

He shrugged, "Then I suppose they'll dig us out."

The thought that he could be dinner scared Matt more than the thought of swimming in really gross stuff, so he stepped closer to the counter. He looked terrified as Rob slipped into the small opening and pushed off.

There seemed a long pause until they heard the splash, then they heard Rob say, "It's alright."

Matt hesitated.

Katia did not. Desperate, she moved with unwavering purpose to the counter, hopped up, slid to the hatch, and pushed off. Matt was right behind her … there was no way he was going to be left behind.

He heard a splash, then Rob say, "Alright," and he pushed off. The fall seemed to take forever, then, Splash!

In his worst nightmares Matt could never have imagined, the absolutely gross, semi-liquid gunk in which he was immersed. It was a cold, chunky stew of slippery, gelatine-like slime in a chilled broth of what he could only imagine was water. Immersed in this goop as he was, he struggled to reach the surface for breath, but there was no up or down … KNIA had been right …

Stricken with panic and flailing, Matt struggled to find an exit. It was as if there was no surface. And if there was no surface, there could be no air. Life usually seemed fun. Things usually seemed funny. But a thing like this – whether he would survive or not – could never be funny. There would be times in the future when Matt's mind would wander back to this moment and all his good humour would drain from him for a time.

Then, hands grasped at him, got hold of his clothes, and pulled him up. As soon as he felt clear enough of the oily sludge, he gasped for air and then vomited. There was no being quiet in the dark whilst swimming with dead fish.

Rob still had a hand on Matt's collar as he began to swim a sort of crawl, bringing his brother with him. Katia hung close as they moved through what seemed like an endless, chunky sludge in endless darkness. Then it seemed like the gunk was thinning, mixing with what each child hoped, was water. There was a gentle flow as though they were entering an underground stream.

As the stench dissipated and the flow of what they now knew was definitely water – fresh water – quickened, their spirits grew a little. However, improving spirits were about to be dashed on the rocks. And so were their bodies. By the sound of it, the stream was being squeezed into a tighter, and yet tighter, cave.

In the absolute darkness of the tunnel, the worst thing one could imagine – aside from being dropped on to rocks at the bottom of a waterfall – was for the water to be squeezed through a cave in which there was no longer room for air. And that is exactly what happened. Rob, Matt, and Katia barely had time to take one last gulp of air before their heads were painfully forced under by the cave roof closing in.

It seemed like forever before they bobbed to the surface gasping for air. The water was colder…and so was the air. As Rob cleared his eyes to look around, he was astonished and relieved to see jagged rocks amidst thick, grey fog. He could also see the lights of the Jawbonee cliff-side town above him. They had been dumped into the ocean. Surely, the danger was almost over. Now they just had to get back to the space-fighter and off the nightmarish planet. That was when Rob felt something large and bulky brush against his leg.

The three escapees were bobbing in scattered, rotting sea-creature parts. And it took less than a genius to figure out that there was probably something that ate these leftovers. In as calm a voice as he could muster, Rob said, "We need to get out of the

219

water." Then Katia's eyes grew wide as she gasped; something had brushed against her legs, too. And he added, "Fast!"

Who knows whether it would have been better to swim towards the shore slowly or not; if only to keep from attracting undue attention from whatever the creature was that was bumping up against their legs. But panic took over, so there was no real use in wondering about fast and furious, or slow and easy, swimming techniques. In a flurry of arms and legs splashing, they made it to shore. Rob, pretty much swam up on to the sharp rocks, cutting his leg painfully. Katia made it, too, and Matt was right behind Rob, who turned to yank him out of the water just as a sizeable creature with a sizeable, gaping mouth, full of sizeable teeth, took a slow swipe at Matt's legs. At its failure to achieve a sizeable chunk of food, the creature slipped, harmlessly, away.

As he regained his breath, Rob stared at Katia. Though it was dark and foggy, he could see the look of terror in her eyes. At that moment, as a stiff breeze chilled the wet girl to the bone while his skin-suit kept him warm, Rob grew very angry at her and said, "I hope you're happy making us risk our lives to save you ... "

"What?" she said, looking shocked as she shivered.

"If you hadn't been so stupid and gone off looking for your mother," said Rob, "we wouldn't be here, on this miserable rock, with everything trying to eat us."

The two glared at each other.

One might now question the fast and furious swimming technique that the children used to get out of the water, as that method is also rather noisy, because at that very moment came shouts from the town above. The escapees had been discovered.

Looking around, Rob leaped to his feet. "Follow me!" he said.

Just as a few Jawbonee reached the waterfront, they reached what on any other planet would have been considered a quaint marina. As Matt and Katia jumped into a small sailboat, Rob loosed it from the dock and, climbing in, he pushed off. As the boat drifted away, something hit the water nearby.

"Arrows!" said Matt. "They're shooting arrows at us!"

There were splashes all around them and a few hollow sounds from arrows hitting the sailboat's wooden hull. Having grabbed a line that looked like it would raise the sail, Rob pulled hard, but there was no give.

Katia pushed by him, saying, "Maybe the stupid girl can help."

She grabbed a coiled line and, leaning into it with all her weight, she pulled, arm over arm, to raise the sail, which then filled with a breeze.

Matt leapt to hold the rudder just as an arrow stuck in the side of the boat near where he had been sitting. Making the line fast, Katia then moved to take his place.

It was then that Rob, with a vicious look on his face, grabbed a metal bar and lunged towards Katia, who screamed and ducked. Unable to understand how he could be that angry at her, cringing, Matt yelled, "Rob don't … "

But Rob swung with every bit of strength he could muster. The pipe hit the mark all right, but not Katia. It knocked the Jawbonee climbing aboard so hard that the skeletal-man made not a sound of pain and tipped back into the water with a splash.

Katia sat up and glanced astern at the floating, unconscious Jawbonee before turning back to glare at Rob, who scowled as he returned to the bow saying, "Head down the coast. That's where we left the ship."

After a moment, Matt said, "Good shot, Rob." But it was a weak attempt at a compliment as he had felt a little guilty for figuring that Rob was about to whack Katia with the pipe.

Though soaked and shivering, Katia began to breathe easier as the boat picked up speed and left the harbour, leaving behind flying arrows and swimming Jawbonee. As if a ray of hope, the clouds cleared leaving a light fog, and the stars set Jawbone aglow.

Scattered torches of Jawbonee in pursuit on foot played along the shore. Then an explosion hit near the little sailboat, spraying the children with water. Something was emerging from the fog behind them. It looked a lot like an old, square-rigged vessel from Earth's past, and it was coming on at a good clip. Feeling panic closing in on him, Rob searched the sky for help. He knew that

Will and Kris had received the message he sent before jumping into the gross stuff, but he had lost track of how long it had been since then.

There was little they could do but run and hope that whatever the Jawbonee were firing at them, would miss. Katia trimmed the sail to get the most out of the breeze. Another blast hit close, spraying them once again. Then, as they rounded a small point, Rob caught sight of a familiar shape in the mist – the waiting space-fighter, close now and glowing white, like everything else reflecting in the starlight.

But now, the large sailing vessel had drawn close enough for the three prospective entrées to see the sailors aboard. One rode on the bowsprit like a jockey whipping a horse. Another stood in the crow's nest like a cat ready to pounce. The ship was a haunting sight, for the faces and hands of the Jawbonee glowed like the sails. Their glowing bones made them look like the nightmarish skeletons from so many horror stories told back on Earth. And then came angry growls, echoing across the misty waters, followed by another close blast and yet another spray of water as the children's fear thickened.

The space-fighter lit up and the canopy opened. Rob pushed another button on his arm-comp and the engines began powering up. Desperate, Katia ran the little sailboat right up on to the jagged rocks and continued the forwards motion by rushing to the bow, jumping to the shore, and hopping from rock to rock to the spaceship; Rob and Matt followed close behind. Rob scampered up the fighter's fuselage footholds right behind her and leapt into the pilot's seat as Katia settled in the rear. Following, Matt stopped short of clambering in ...

"Katia," he said, "you can sit on my lap."

Looking at him as though his head was on backwards, Katia said, "Don't be ridiculous!"

"Matt, get in!" Rob barked, glancing back.

Another blast landed in the water nearby.

"I don't want to sit on a girl's lap," Matt complained.

"What?!" said Katia. "Don't be an idiot!"

Matt breathed out impatiently, and said, "It's just that … "

"Matt!" Rob roared, as he pointed behind them at the ship now looming large, "Get in or we're all dead!"

They could see the weapon on the sailing vessel's deck was being loaded again, much like an olden-time Earth cannon.

Without further delay, Matt leapt into the space-fighter and sat on Katia's lap as he said, "Go-go-go!"

The canopy shut. Rob pulled back on the stick and jammed the throttles forwards and the fighter shot straight up.

The sailing ship ran on to the rocks, crushing the little sailboat into splinters. The cannon was being raised straight up in preparation to fire on the space-fighter.

Then there was a rumble of thunder and the magnificent Tenacity appeared, glowing-white, in the distance through swirling fog. Orange blasts shot out and the great sailing vessel shattered into countless pieces in every direction.

The Jawbonee that had been riding in the crow's nest was propelled by the ship beneath him exploding. With his arms outstretched, he flew towards the space-fighter just as Rob thrust the joystick forwards … the children never saw what they left behind.

Away from Jawbone, on the Tenacity, the children re-grouped as a course was set for the space academy in orbit around Moxy. This was where Will and Matt, while on the Kablakian labour shuttle, had heard that Keb had been taken. With the need for seventeen passes through thin-space to get from Jawbone clear across the galaxy to Moxy, the trip would normally take three days to give one time to breathe between passes. However, understanding that a day – or even an hour – could mean the difference between finding Keb whole or in pieces, they all knew that they had no choice but to compress the trip into as short a period of time as possible; even if it made them ill.

Since Will's last sleep had been on Sundee, now almost twenty-four hours past, he went to bed, spent, knowing that with the help of the sleep-gas he would be awake rejuvenated, within a couple hours. Rob, Matt, and Katia took three showers each to get the Jawbone stench off them, and then they, too, headed for a quick sleep.

Having taken time to rest while Rob and Matt were on Jawbone, Kris was wide awake. He sent a quick update to Mr Casper and KNIA but did not want to take the time to stay a course for a tight-beam connection, so there would be no reply. As he took the Tenacity towards its first pass through thin-space, he felt driven to get to Keb. There was no way he was going to allow his new friend to be turned into a toaster.

Later, Rob, Will, Matt and Katia arrived on the command bridge to join Kris, who was bursting with excitement.

"Hey, guys," he beamed. "I've been thinking about 'The Sphere'."

"Go, little brother," said Will, as he flopped down in the co-pilot's seat beside Kris. "What's with that thing?"

"Well," said Kris, as the others found seats, "I've been looking into some things." He shifted in the pilot's seat so he could better see his audience. "Do you know … there is never any mention of how 'The Sphere' comes and goes. I doubt it arrives through the standard postal service, so how does it get around?" Kris peered through squinted eyes at Katia, and continued, "I bet you don't know how your mother got 'The Sphere'."

Shaking her head, she said, "No. My mother didn't tell me. Maybe there's someone who takes it from place to place."

"But it moves around on its own," said Kris. "When we came to get you off the moon, 'The Sphere' shot from your ship into the shuttle faster than my eyes could follow."

"Look, Kris," said Rob, growing impatient, "what are you getting at? What does it matter how the thing gets around?"

With eyes wide, Kris said, "How it gets around means everything, Rob. Because if it moves from place to place on its own, then why are we worried that the Boargen have it?"

"Huh … good point," said Will. "If it comes and goes as it pleases, then it can just leave the Boargen anytime it wants."

"Then why are we so worried about keeping 'The Sphere' from the Boargen?" asked Matt, confused. "I thought we decided they could seriously mess with the galaxy if they had it."

"Maybe we're wrong," said Kris. "No one understands why The Sphere does what it does. Everyone just accepts it; almost like it lulls those it visits into not caring about the details. Why isn't anyone questioning what it does?"

"Wait a minute!" said Katia, frustrated. "You sound like you think The Sphere is as bad as the Boargen."

Kris shrugged, "I don't mean it that way. But look, The Sphere has complete control over who gets what knowledge ... right? It seems to me that if the societies of the galaxy are conditioned to wait around until The Sphere brings them knowledge, then it has too much power. Because the technology that exists could have been discovered by intelligent beings without its help; by design, there's no competition; healthy or unhealthy. And the way things work, a technology could be lost if a ticked-off bunch of evil guys like the Boargen come along and mess things up; which is pretty much what is happening."

"I'm sure plenty of conversations have taken place about all this stuff," said Katia. "And they have probably always come to the conclusion that the way things work with The Sphere is ultimately good for the galaxy."

"It seems that the Boargen aren't so keen about this sphere-utopia galaxy that you guys have out here," said Rob, glaring at Katia. "And do you want to explain to me where those sick creeps on Jawbone come into the big spheroid plan? Because I for one, don't see the use in a bunch of skeletons wanting to eat a stupid, ungrateful girl and the suckers that risked their lives to save her."

By this time, Will, Matt, and Kris were glancing back and forth between Rob and Katia. The experience on Jawbone had definitely rattled some nerves, and some bones.

Katia stood, glared at Rob, and said, "You've got the suckers and the sick creeps right. Nothing's perfect, Rob Roar; not even a galaxy full of mostly good beings. If you don't like our way of doing things out here, you can always go back to your silly, backward planet."

Rob leapt to his feet, and said, "Fine, Katia! We'll drop you off somewhere; you can go and get your tin-can robot on your own and we'll just get on home!"

"Fine!" she said, "Go!"

With that, she turned and left.

Rob looked downright angry at the whole galaxy as Katia left the command bridge and even Kris looked slightly bummed out. Will and Matt sat, subdued, looking as though they were counting their fingers.

"Rob, we have to find Keb," said Kris, after a moment, "even if he's already scrap metal. We have to at least try to save him."

"Yeah, I know."

"And we should also find The Sphere, in spite of what I just said about it. I can't explain why, but I think it's important."

"I know."

"And we should help Katia find out what happened to her mother," added Will.

Rob took a deep breath, and said, "I know that, too."

"And then we can go and find our parents," said Matt. The others smiled a bit and nodded. Then Matt asked, "How many more passes through thin-space?"

Kris beamed, "Three." His brothers looked at him, astonished. "I figured out a shortcut," he continued. "We'll be there in about an hour."

Now the older brothers understood why they were feeling a little nauseous. Kris had been making passes through thin-space in extraordinarily quick succession.

As the Tenacity made the final three passes, Kris explained to his brothers that although he had to chart a course across the galaxy that avoided celestial bodies, because of the sheer size of the galaxy there was an infinite number of route options; some faster than others. Kris had begun to discover – like his brothers would – that he had a profound, intuitive knack for striking out across the heavens, and, indeed, through thin-space.

The Moxy Gorp

The Tenacity entered the Moxy system at the outermost limit near a large, lifeless planet where it was left. Making one last pass through thin-space, the Roar brothers and Katia in the two space-fighters continued on to the Galactic Space Academy. This time, Katia was sitting, somewhat awkwardly, on Matt's lap, behind Will who was piloting.

From a distance, the academy, orbiting the lushly green planet Moxy, looked a bit like a fix-it in its saucer form, only it bulged more at the polar ends. As the two space-fighters approached, however, it became apparent how large the academy really was; about a mile in diameter.

The Galactic Space Academy was where one could study anything to do with life as it pertained to the galaxy as a whole. Here, one could learn anything from botany to galactic politics. Also, would-be galaxy rangers could train here, as well as those interested in the refuse removal business, which, as one can imagine, is a big business in such a populated galaxy.

Having been granted a visitor's pass, Rob and Will landed the fighters in a hangar just large enough for both ships. The boys were, once again, awestruck by what they were doing and what they saw – it was all still so new. The hangar door closed and the hangar pressurised. Upon climbing down from the cockpits, they were approached by a tall, slender, sturdy-looking man. Each boy decided that Mr Casper would approve of him before having heard him speak, as he was immaculately dressed in a pressed academy uniform and his bald head was polished to a subtle sheen.

Glancing at Katia and each brother in turn, the man said, "My name is Mr Sorell. I am the academy headmaster." His gaze rested for a moment on the closest space-fighter before returning his full attention to the children. "You are an odd group, rather young and arriving in two rather unusual ships." A hint of a smile revealed itself as he said, "Someone sat on someone's lap. Perhaps a shuttle would have been more comfortable." But the Boargen had taken the shuttle when they captured Katia, so this had not been possible.

Although they believed that Keb was somewhere at the academy, it was a huge place; like a small city in space. Finding a robot – an inactive one at that – in a place so large would be nearly impossible. Compounding the challenge, they knew no one they could trust. So although Mr Sorell was well dressed, he failed to make it on to the 'trust' list.

Accepting the headmaster's invitation for a tour, they followed him through passageways that grew increasingly busy with students and the occasional teacher. Though a younger crowd, it was as diverse as Will and Matt had seen on Kablakia. Mr Sorell had been asking them pleasant questions as they walked, such as where they lived – a question that the Roar boys avoided answering – and what they thought they might be interested in studying, but then he stopped, abruptly, and turned to stare at them.

"What are you children mixed up in?" he asked.

Concern had been building in Rob that they were walking into a trap and he now wondered whether he was about to find out that his concern was well founded.

"Really, Mr Sorell," he said. "Like we told you, my father let us come to see what the academy was like. After all, we may want to attend classes here soon."

Mr Sorell frowned, and then said, "It is unwise to lie about one's intentions; especially when you have arrived here in fighting ships of a most exceptional manufacture, and especially when you smell of Jawbone."

Confused, Rob, Matt and Katia each lifted an arm and sniffed.

"Do we really smell like Jawbone?" asked Matt.

A look of disgust crossed Mr Sorell's face, as he said, "I have been on Jawbone. One never forgets the smell."

They remained mistrustful of the headmaster and Rob did his best to cover their tracks.

"We got into some mischief, but now we're here to do the right thing."

It was unlikely that Mr Sorell believed it was that simple, but he grunted and let it go, saying, "We can only hope there are enough galactic citizens that will do the right thing … "

Later, the Roar brothers and Katia were sure that Mr Sorell had let them off much too easily from explaining themselves. But why? Rob would later share his growing suspicion that Keb might be bait in a trap. The others would all agree it was possible, but what could they do differently? They would not abandon Keb; even if he was now only scrap. Although the Boargen might not know the identity of those who had foiled their attack at Earth's moon, if Mr Sorell or anyone else at the academy was spying for the Boargen, the space-fighters would be recognised and the identity of the pilots would then be known.

Heightening their concern that the academy could turn out to be a trap, Mr Sorell offered rooms for them to stay for a few days. In spite of their concern, they accepted and were grateful for the invitation to stay because there was no telling how long it would take to find Keb. Not knowing where to start searching and because all five were hungry, guided by the academy map on Rob's arm-comp, they set out to find food.

The expansive dining hall was filled with students of all ages. Most of them appeared to be older than Matt and Kris. Although Katia was used to such things, the Roar brothers were astonished to see so many youths that appeared similar to them; human, yet some with subtle differences – and others with greater. A few were small with pointed ears and some were skinny beyond belief. But Rob, Will, Matt and Kris all felt as though they fitted right in and received no strange stares. It was, however, difficult for them not to stare, even though they tried not to.

Seated and eating, Matt felt a nudge on his back, and when he turned to look he saw that there was a youth sitting down next to him.

"I am sorry I bumped you. I am sometimes clumsy," the youth said.

"Oh, no worries," said Matt. "Sometimes I'm a little clumsy, too. I'm Matt ... " he hesitated, and then held out his hand, unsure whether the youth would know the gesture.

"I am Yobe of Yorem," he said, engulfing Matt's hand with his very large, thick one and shaking it vigorously.

Yobe looked much like a human, though with a very round face, a round, puffy nose, big round eyes, very large ears partly covered by his long hair, and two sizable front teeth that showed a little when his mouth was closed and a lot when he spoke, smiled or laughed. Although Yobe was about Matt's height, he was thick in the body. And what had really caught his attention, were Yobe's very large, thick hands. Matt resisted peeking under the table but he was sure that given Yobe's features, his feet must be huge and perhaps the reason for him being a little clumsy.

Yobe seemed endlessly cheerful as he always had something to laugh about, leaving the brothers and Katia glad to be sitting with him. But there was also a deep sense that they should be spending their precious time searching for Keb. Since they had no idea where to begin, Rob decided he might as well ask Yobe if he had heard about any recent, unusual events. Yobe's answer had more to offer than Rob dared expect or even hope for, for Yobe was one to keep abreast of matters, especially when they were not his own.

Chuckling, Yobe looked around, checking for eavesdroppers, and then said, "It is not an accident I am sitting here. Do you want to know about a robot? Or do you want to know about a senator?"

The brothers and Katia all exchanged glances, hopes rising fast with their heavy-beating hearts. Yobe confirmed that a robot had been delivered in secret to the base, but its whereabouts were unknown. All he knew was that it had been snuck in by a boy named Mulkin, a youth whom he knew little about but he was trying to find out more. But Yobe did know where the senator, Katia's mother, had been taken, and, indeed, her ship and entire crew and he was able to share this information with them.

Yobe understood the urgency of finding Keb and offered to help, but first, he had an idea; something to check. And yes, his feet were huge, and he went barefoot so every bit of them could be seen, including his large, thick toes. Yobe rushed from the dining hall, propelled by his giant feet, moving with unusual speed to the point of being almost a blur.

Katia and the Roar brothers got up and headed for the dining hall exit. Kris saw them first: three human youths, each of varying height with jet-black hair and dressed all in black, each of them a little taller than Rob. They were approaching, appearing as if they wanted to talk but they had bad intentions. When the black-haired youths intercepted them at the doorway, everyone stopped. The shortest of the three seemed alright at first, but then a little slippery when he spoke.

"I'm Mulkin," he said, sizing them up from dark, calculating eyes.

Upon hearing the boy's name, the brothers and Katia straightened a bit and were instantly wary. Each was sure that Mulkin knew who they were and why they were there.

Mulkin pointed at the other two boys, who looked greasy, and continued, "And this is Ecner and Retsel. I haven't seen you around before."

"No," said Rob, "we're just here to see if we might like to attend the academy."

It was clear that the boy knew otherwise.

"Oh yeah? It's not all bad," said Mulkin. "Learning's no fun but you have to do it to get what you want in the galaxy – right, guys?"

Ecner and Retsel, not appearing to be the brightest stars in the galaxy, grunted and shrugged. Ecner scratched his head.

"I guess you just have to find out what you enjoy doing to make learning fun," said Katia, not knowing what else to say, and looking a little disgusted as she studied Ecner and Retsel.

"Well," said Mulkin, "since you all seem to be so interested in learning, me, Ecner and Retsel are heading down to Moxy; check the place out; do a little exploring. I hear there's a lot to learn about down there. You want to come with us?"

"Oh, thanks anyway, Mulkin," said Rob, suspicious that the conversation was heading for a bad end, "but we won't be here very long and we have a lot to do before we leave."

"Yeah, like find a robot?" Mulkin sneered.

The Roar brothers and Katia glanced at each other. When they looked back at the dark gang they saw the blaster which Mulkin held close to his body.

"You're not going to shoot us," said Katia, praying that was so. "You would spend the rest of your life on a prison planet."

Mulkin smiled with a vicious look, then sobered, and said, "Since the academy is a no weapon zone, they have practically no security here. Too many do-gooders trying to make the galaxy a better place. I could kill all of you and be off this trash-heap before anyone knew what had happened."

Mulkin was positioned so that youths entering and exiting the dining hall were unable to see the blaster, but there were still some curious glances.

"What do you want?" asked Rob, in a forced, steady voice.

"I wouldn't mind dumping you in space. But I'm just supposed to take you to Moxy." Ecner and Retsel pressed in as Mulkin said, "Now move. Your ride is leaving ... "

Mulkin was in a hurry so the flight down to Moxy was quick. The Roar brothers and Katia sat, subdued, each figuring, in an oddly accepting way, that their lives were over. Even so, as they approached the densely forested planet, their curiosities perked up. On the other hand, Ecner and Retsel looked like they couldn't care less; they seemed bored.

Moxy was a difficult planet to imagine without seeing it first from space. Where Sundee had been entirely desert, Moxy was completely covered in thick, green forest. As they entered the atmosphere and drew closer to the planet's surface, hints of water could be seen occasionally – perhaps a river or a swamp – sparkling in what sunlight seeped through the thick forest canopy. There were no large bodies of water anywhere; or at least none that were clear of the planet-wide forest.

Either Mulkin was a crack pilot or he was lucky, because as the small shuttle breached the forest canopy, piloting it became a hazardous task flying around and between the massive tree branches that dwarfed the ship. Only after they landed on the forest floor did the brothers and Katia release their firm grip from their armrests. They were slightly consoled when they noticed that Ecner and Retsel had to pry their hands free as well. Though grudgingly, each Roar boy, to some degree, aspired to Mulkin's piloting prowess.

Mulkin leapt out of the pilot's seat and pointed the blaster at them as the hatch opened and the gangway extended.

"Time to get off," he said, with his familiar greasy sneer.

As the Roar boys stared straight ahead and walked from the shuttle, followed by Katia, each wondered whether they would experience intense pain before they exploded and vaporised, if shot in the back by a blaster.

Then they heard Mulkin say, "You should have stayed on your primitive planet, Earth Boys. Have a nice stay on Moxy."

He, Ecner, and Retsel laughed obnoxiously as the hatch closed.

Katia and the brothers backed away as the shuttle powered up and took off. They watched it slip through the forest canopy high above, and stared after it until they could no longer hear the rumble of the engines. Then they exchanged worried glances and, without speaking, they began milling about looking around.

The majestic trees around them towered to dizzying heights, making up a colossal forest that left each child feeling like a tiny creature. Sunshine seeped through the forest canopy in some places, and poured through in others, setting a stage with a field of shadow dotted with spots of light. Like the Roar brothers, Katia, too, was astonished by the place. As she looked around, consumed by the sights, she tripped on a small root and stumbled into Rob. Still angry at each other, they exchanged hard looks and moved apart.

All the information that could be found about Moxy failed to prepare one for the actual immensity of life there. Some of the trees were so large in girth at their base that it was an investment in time just walking around one. And the gargantuan trees had gargantuan roots that were twice the height of Rob – and stretched along, partly submerged in the ground. There were valleys of open ground between the roots that were littered with leaves, the size of which were befitting the trees from which they fell. It became apparent how easily one could find himself misplaced in such a forest. But probably not misplaced enough to avoid the Boargen, who the brothers and Katia all figured must be coming to get them.

'The only creature on Moxy that one need be concerned about, is the gorp. No matter what its size, the gorp should be avoided at all costs.' It was a warning that every tour-log contained. Other than that, there were no other creatures to worry about. But being in no immediate danger failed to be of any comfort.

As each fought a nagging, internal despair, they discussed, sometimes heatedly, what they could do to escape their trap. They had no way of contacting Yobe. And although they could contact the academy, they had no way of knowing who they could trust. They had the ability, through the arm-comps, to remotely pilot the space-fighters, but the fighters were closed-up in an academy hangar. And the Tenacity was too far away.

They were stuck. They had no choice but to wait for whoever was coming to get them. Then Rob had uncomfortable thoughts. What if they were to be left on Moxy? He looked around. What would they eat? Where would they find shelter? They would die a slow and painful death down here. Maybe that was the plan for them. Moxy ceased to be majestic then, at least for Rob, but he decided not to mention this to the others. Why make them worry even more than they already were?

Rob walked to a large root and sat on the ground, leaning against it. The others followed, one after the other, joining him until they were all sitting in a row against the root; one bunch of long-faced, forlorn children.

"At least there's nothing down here trying to eat us," said Matt, breaking the pensive silence.

It seemed, for a while, that no one had anything to add. But then Kris's focus became absolute, as he thought he could hear something in the distance. He was concentrating very hard, thinking perhaps a gorp made a sound like that – a tinny sort of singing sound. One after the other, the others noticed Kris's intensity and watched him. Then …

"Kris," began Rob.

"Shhh," Kris held up a hand.

The sound drew closer until it could be heard clearly. Suddenly, everyone dived for cover all at once, Katia behind a bush that was a little too small. The sound was very close. It was someone singing, but not very well. They exchanged confused stares; questioning looks cut short by movement in the bushes nearby. A straw hat with a large, yellow flower skimmed along just above the thicket; a hat, underneath which was surely a strange man who could not sing very well.

Breathing in some dust, Katia sneezed and the hat-wearer abruptly stopped singing and turned to look straight at her, who, as already mentioned, was not very well hidden. That's when it was noticed that it was not a man under the hat, but a robot. It was a hat-wearing robot with a large, hinged jaw that also wore a flower-print apron over a white, button-up shirt and khaki trousers. It probably couldn't find shoes to fit its large metal feet, or it would surely have worn them for its walk through the woods. Holding a basket of assorted picked things, the robot stood there looking astonished, if it was possible for a machine to look astonished.

Katia stood and brushed herself off. The robot gasped when Rob stood, and gasped again with each brother's subsequent appearance, an awkward moment, for sure. Looking all around him, the robot then resumed staring at them.

Astonished, in a tiny, expressive voice, it said, "Usually when there are people there is a spaceship! Goodness! Are you lost?"

"That's a question for you," said Katia. "Are you lost?"

"Oh no-no-no," said the robot, waving a hand, "I live here!"

The children exchanged curious glances.

"What's a robot doing on Moxy?" Will asked.

The robot looked around again, turning on the spot to see behind itself, and then it returned its attention to the boys and Katia.

"Did you see a robot?" it asked.

After further curious glances, Rob asked, "Aren't you a robot?"

Gasping, the robot then chuckled, and said, "My singing is a little monotone ... isn't it?" Then, holding out the basket it asked, "Would you like to have lunch with me?"

Again, after more curious glances and on the verge of giggling, Matt said, "Um, no thanks. We just ate. But please ... go ahead."

With that permission, the robot looked down at the basket, dipped a hand in, fiddled about looking for just the right item, found some berries and popped them in its metal mouth, and began chewing. Berry juice dripped everywhere, much of it down the robot's apron. As they looked on, astonished, the metal man glanced down, noticed the mess, and said, "Berries can be so messy!" Looking up, it continued, "Can't they?"

Jaws dropped, and the children all nodded.

Smiling and holding out his hand, Kris stepped forwards and said, "I'm Kris. Pleased to meet you."

Shaking Kris's hand, the robot replied, "Very pleased to make your acquaintance, Kris! My name is ..." The robot stopped, leaving the boys and Katia wondering if it had blown a circuit or something, then continued, abruptly, "Goodness! I don't believe I have a name! Isn't that odd!"

It was an older model robot, perhaps very old, but it had no clue as to its age, or even how or when it arrived on Moxy. It just assumed it had always been there. Although initially there had been some hope that the metal man might be able to help them escape, maybe on an old ship it had arrived on, there was no way, because, above all, the robot was quite sure it was human and never acted anything but.

After some time, with the children finding out very little more about the robot, Matt announced, "I'm thirsty. Why don't we go to that stream we flew over just before landing? It shouldn't be that far. Besides, if the Boargen are coming to get us, we don't have to make it easy for them by staying put."

Excitedly, the robot said, "Great idea! I'm parched ... ! What's a Boargen?"

No one answered the robot. Instead, there were a few passive shrugs and everyone began drifting in the general direction of the stream together. They were all thirsty. Then there would be hunger to consider.

When it is quiet and there is a lot to think about – as was the case during the walk to the stream – a person may realise that there is something he had not thought about, at least, not in a while. It is at a time like that when a person realises he may be experiencing a sort of sixth sense; perhaps even an intuitive warning of something he is not thinking about but should be, or something that might happen soon.

Rob was having one of those sixth sense moments when he saw movement on the giant tree, right next to where Katia was walking along the top of a large root. Running forwards and yelling, "Katia!" Rob shoved her off.

Katia screamed, both from the shock of the shove and because it was a bit of a fall to the ground below the root.

With Rob yelling Katia's name and Katia screaming, Will, Matt and Kris looked, just in time to see what happened; which was not what Katia thought was happening. They believed that Rob was finally taking out his anger and frustration on her. Rob's first thoughts were becoming real, as he realised that the movement had been from a gorp – a large one – one capable of expectorating enough to thoroughly cover a person with the most awful sticky gunk one can imagine.

What happened was not the least bit funny for Rob, who was now coated from head to toe with gorp gunk. But as the gorp shuffled off, Will, Matt and Kris saw the funny side and burst into side-splitting laughter because it appeared as though the gorp had just blown its nose all over Rob. Yep, really gross.

As Katia sat up, her long, brown hair was tossed and tangled, blocking her vision. Turning to find her tormenter through furious, blazing brown eyes, she was sure Rob – for pushing her – and his brothers – for laughing – had all gone mad. She began to say, "That was completely … !" But as she caught sight of Rob through her tangle of hair, she realised what had happened and her tone changed, abruptly, "Oh!" she said.

The robot ran to help Katia to her feet, then looked up at Rob and said, "Goodness! You're drenched!"

Rob wiped his eyes as he said, "Thanks for noticing, genius."

From that moment, for lack of a better name, 'Genius' stuck.

Feeling sore at everyone, Rob left a gooey path all the way to the stream where he then sat in the water and began picking off the sticky stuff, watching it float away. He knew his brothers would keep their distance for a while to give him time to brood. But Katia approached him, took off her shoes and waded into the stream. She knelt beside him, stripped off a dripping piece of goo from his back, and tossed it downstream.

"I am sorry for getting us all into this," she said.

It was quiet for a moment, save for the sound of the stream slipping through the forest. Then Rob said, "Sorry I've been so mean to you."

Katia pulled another sticky strand from his back. As she flicked it into the stream and watched it float away, she said, "I'm really scared we won't get out of this."

He glanced at her. "We're not done for yet."

She smiled, and said, "Thanks for not giving up on me," then continued plucking goo from his back.

Later, when Rob was wetter from the water than from the gorp gunk, he wondered whether he would ever get all the sticky stuff out of his hair. They were all – including Genius – now sitting together on the bank of the stream. It was then that everyone perked up. There was a new sound in the forest; the sound of a spaceship. They all leapt up, dived behind a thick root and covered themselves with the huge leaves scattered on the ground; a thing of great joy to Genius. They waited with bated breath, peering over the root, searching for the ship. Surely the Boargen would find them.

It came into view across the stream, weaving slowly through the massive trees. The ship was small, shorter than one of the space-fighters and thick in the body. Maybe a shuttle or a tiny cargo ship? When it got closer, it hovered for a moment and then landed between two large roots just at the other side of the stream. A hatch opened and …

"Yobe!" the boys and Katia called out in unison.

Perking up as he saw everyone, Yobe smiled and then laughed loftily as he waved his large, thick hand. He sped to the stream, where, without missing a step, he splashed right through with no apparent concern about getting wet.

As they all met at the stream's edge, Yobe pointed at Rob, laughed uproariously, and said, "Rob, you got gooped by a gorp!" Yobe also found great humour in meeting a robot that thought it was a human. He burst into jovial laughter every time he looked at Genius, whose straw hat now sported a crunched yellow flower, damaged from diving behind the root.

Yobe grew serious when he described how he had figured out what was happening and had become very worried. He had thought the worst had happened when he saw Mulkin and his gang of two return, alone.

"So I came looking for my new friends on Moxy," he said, laughing jovially. "And I am glad I have found you. But now we should go. I have found your robot."

Katia wanted Yobe to tell her more, but then …

"Shhh," said Kris, pointing across the stream.

Near Yobe's ship was a small gorp moving ever so slowly through the short grass. A Moxy gorp looks much like a slug, only they are lime green and they have four very short, stubby legs. A gorp can move a lot faster than a slug, but not as fast as a person can walk. And, as Rob had discovered, they can climb trees – that had not been mentioned in the tour-log.

"I think we should share a gorp with Mulkin," said Rob.

Yobe turned and smiled at him, then abruptly crouched and tiptoed across the stream, barely disturbing the water as he did so, astonishing the others with his stealth. Everyone gasped when, without slowing, Yobe dived at the low bank beside the stream as one would dive into water, and, before they knew what had happened, he had vanished into a fine round hole of his making.

They all watched with rapt interest. After tunnelling quickly through the ground, Yobe appeared, with his head poking out of the ground beside the ship's hatch and quickly slipped inside. The gorp remained oblivious. Heartbeats later, Yobe re-emerged with a box and slipped back into his hole. Suddenly, the gorp dropped out of sight and was replaced by Yobe's smiling face as he held aloft a small box containing the grorp.

Soon after, Yobe deftly manoeuvred his small ship through the forest canopy. Convinced he had never had an experience such as flying in a spaceship, Genius plastered his face to a window as though he would never remove it. And he didn't, until the shuttle entered Moxy's orbit. It was then, that Genius pointed out of the window and asked what that big thing coming towards them was.

At that very moment, an alarm sounded and Yobe said, "Boargen!"

The Roar brothers and Katia all rushed to look out, squeezing Genius out of the way as they did so. They could hear Yobe chuckling to himself in the small one-pilot cockpit.

"Mulkin Slatter set you up," he said.

Everyone squeezed together to peer into the cockpit at Yobe.

"Mulkin Slatter?" Rob asked.

"Yes," said Yobe, laughing as he did about everything, "When I found your robot I also found out that Mulkin is Admiral Slatter's son. Admiral Slatter, the Boargen leader. I understand why you were left on Moxy, out of sight of the academy."

Rob leaned in to get closer to Yobe, and asked, "Will we be in view of the academy before the Boargen reach us?"

Yobe looked at his control console, and then chuckled, "Yes."

"Yobe," Rob patted his shoulder, "you came just in time."

"Oh yes," Yobe chuckled, "I did come just in time, and we will soon be safe."

Once back at the academy, it was obvious that no one there knew about the Boargen ship on the other side of Moxy; except for Mulkin and his two grunts, that is. Yobe had discovered that Keb was being kept in Mulkin's personal quarters; hopefully, in one piece.

Their first challenge was that the greasy Boargen boy had to be lured away from his room. He had a blaster and the Roar brothers were unarmed, so he had a potential advantage, but the Roar brothers had a Moxy gorp, and, they had a plan ...

Yobe remained on his ship with Katia to do their part in setting a trap for Mulkin and his gang. Will and Matt set off to Mulkin's ship with the gorp, and Rob and Kris set out to get Keb.

With Katia's help, Yobe sent a message – disguised as coming from the Boargen ship – to Mulkin, who, at that time, was in his quarters with Ecner and Retsel. The ruse was successful. Mulkin received the message and replied that he would leave immediately to assist finding the Earth losers who must have got lucky and found a good hiding place. Katia then headed off to prepare the two space-fighters for a quick escape, and Yobe sent a message to the brothers.

Will and Matt, with the gorp – and with the help from an arm-comp to pick the electronic lock – gained entry to Mulkin's ship. After receiving a message from Yobe telling them that Mulkin was on his way, Will carefully opened the gorp box just enough for the creature to take a stroll. Then they closed up Mulkin's ship and left to catch up with Katia.

Having just received Yobe's message, Rob and Kris watched from a distance as Mulkin, Ecner, and Retsel left for the hangar level. With a hover-cart in tow, Rob and Kris reached Mulkin's room, picked the electronic lock, and entered. They found Keb in a heap, stuffed in a corner with an ugly hat on his head and a thing which looked like a cigar sticking out of his face where a human mouth would be. There was a blaster burn on his chest and a bull's-eye painted around it – no respect.

Yobe would have a dangerous job later, that involved collecting the unharmed gorp from Mulkin's ship and returning the precious, helpful creature to Moxy. He would return him, safely, undiscovered in gorping the troublemakers.

A short while later, Rob and Will were under one of the fighters preparing to load Keb into the ship's cargo hold when Mulkin, followed by Ecner and Retsel, stormed into the hangar. All three were soaked with gorp goo, laying a gooey trail as Mulkin screamed, "That's my robot!"

Without hesitation, Will jumped out from under the fighter to face the dark-haired lads, with Rob right behind him.

Through gritted teeth, Rob whispered, "Will, no trouble."

Will nodded but stood his ground, noticing that none of the Boargen boys were armed. If it came to it, it would be a fair fight, even though Will and Rob were several inches shorter than the gorp-gunked trio.

With Matt on her heels, Katia rushed over from the other fighter, where Genius remained, cowering. Kris strode leisurely towards Keb who was still on the hover-cart. Sizing things up, Rob decided that it might be Katia who would have to be held back; Mulkin would be in real trouble as she was fuming about Keb.

It was then, that Mr Sorell entered. He wasted no time in approaching to intervene, staring at the slimed three with some humour, as he asked, "What seems to be the trouble, Mr Slatter?"

In a huff, Mulkin said, "That's my robot!"

"It is not your robot you ridiculous clop!" said Katia.

"Now-now, you two," said Mr Sorell, giving Katia a stern look. "You will all be quiet." He sized up the three Boargen boys, holding back a smile as he did so, and then asked, "Have you three been on Moxy?"

Mulkin glared at Mr Sorell, who glared back with a look that appeared to unsettle the boy. But Mulkin regrouped and blurted out, "I found that robot adrift in space …"

"That's just not so!" said Katia in frustration.

"Ms Quarin," said Mr Sorell, "please!" Katia demurred. "I think it highly unlikely that Ms Quarin came all this way if she did not believe this robot belonged to her," continued Mr Sorell.

"Then she should prove it," said Mulkin, growing in confidence.

Mr Sorell sighed, then looked at Katia and asked, "Is there any way you can prove this robot is yours, Ms Quarin?"

"Everyone knows only too well that the only way to prove ownership of a robot is to ask the robot," said Katia, exasperated.

"See!" said Mulkin, triumphantly. "She can't prove ownership."

"Yes, she can," said Kris, standing beside Keb.

Kneeling, he pulled out a small tool that looked like a fat pen and used it to unseal Keb's chest plate.

"Hey, tell him to stop that," said Mulkin, now looking worried.

But Mulkin's complaint was too late, for, at that moment, Keb's head turned with some difficulty. In a weak voice, the robot said, "I am Keb, property of Senator Quarin."

Kris resealed Keb's chest plate, turned the robot's head back towards the centre, and stood to see everyone staring at him with looks varying between astonishment and confusion.

"That's a trick!" said Mulkin, dripping goo.

"Will you please explain, Mr Roar?"

Shrugging, Kris said, "Sure. You see, I took a quick look at Keb and figured that maybe the only problem was that his power supply was damaged. So, just now, I supplied enough power with a mini-plasma laser for Keb to function enough to speak ... "

"Very good," said Mr Sorell, staring Mulkin down again. "That will be all, Mr Slatter. Perhaps you three should go and clean up."

Mulkin sneered at the Roar brothers and said "I'll see all of you again."

With Ecner and Retsel following, he stormed from the hangar.

With the Boargen boys gone, the Roar brothers and Katia stared at the door for a moment before, one after the other, each of them noticed Mr Sorell watching them.

"That boy is a dangerous one," he said, "and not just because of who his father is."

Back aboard the Tenacity, Rob, Will and Matt headed to the command bridge to begin searching Grimmin for Katia's mother – Grimmin is the home planet of the Boargen command and the place at which Yobe had heard Katia's mother was being held. Using the ship's computer, the brothers could hack into the Boargen systems and download any desired plans of buildings. In this case, buildings in which they thought prisoners might be held.

Elsewhere on the Tenacity, with Katia watching, hopeful, Kris took a long, nervous, deep breath and set to replacing Keb's power source. This was a tricky undertaking even for an accomplished Mindinee technician, as the inside of a robot is full of billions of parts, many of them microscopic. Kris knew what he was getting into, but somehow he knew he could do it. He figured that it must be in his blood, handed down to him from his Mindinee mother.

As for Genius, convinced he was human, he had announced that the trip in the very cramped and airless cargo hold was such a harrowing experience that he needed to go and take a nap to calm his nerves.

Sneaking In

"Have you guys noticed that The Sphere looks like a little ball of thin-space?" asked Kris, as he held an apple aloft.

The Roar brothers, Katia and Keb – who was now fully repaired except for the blast mark on his chest – and Genius – who, after a nap was now fully recuperated from his traumatic experience of being stuffed in a cargo hold – were all on the Tenacity's command bridge. They had sent an update to Mr Casper and KNIA and now had only one more pass of three through thin-space to get from Moxy to the Boargen planet, Grimmin. And from there, to the city of Dagam.

"Yeah," said Matt, cradling a bowl of ice-cream, "it does sort of look like that."

Will was nodding as Rob said, " I think we've all been thinking the same thing. If The Sphere is from thin-space, that could explain how it gets around. But I still think we need to find it."

"I agree," said Katia. "We should find The Sphere after we've found my mother. But you guys are too inquisitive. There are some things in life that we just can't explain. And maybe we shouldn't try."

"More blind faith, huh, Katia?" said Rob, smiling slightly.

"I'm comfortable with not knowing all the details. And I don't want to fight with you again," Katia added, sweetly, "so can we just be like adults and agree to disagree?"

"As if there are any adults like that," Rob answered, wryly.

"Alright, everyone," Will announced, "here we go."

He pressed the throttles forwards, past the slight resistance, and in an instant of pure white, the Tenacity passed through thin-space and appeared near Grimmin, cloaked from view. Although the Roar boys were now used to the odd sensation of passing through thin-space – a feeling like cresting a hill in a car at a high rate of speed – it took a moment for each boys' gut to settle. It was the same for Katia, though she was used to it, but robots, being machines, never felt queasy.

The three life-sustaining planets in the Boargen Group: Grackin, Grossen and Grimmin suffered from abuse at worst and neglect at best. For the Boargen were a civilisation with a purpose which did not include environmental concerns. Having become almost completely covered by cities and factories – not unlike the factory planet of Kablakia – Grimmin was downright dismal, as was its dingy capital city of Dagam. Once there, the Roar brothers' ability to move about New York unnoticed would be put to a new test. For being discovered in a city like Dagam could mean the end.

With Kris now piloting, his small stature making it difficult for him to reach some of the controls, the Tenacity streaked through Grimmin's orbit and entered the planet's atmosphere. Keb sat in the navigator's seat, watching over the computer as it kept pace with Grimmin's scanners, making sure the cloaked Tenacity remained hidden on all accounts. Genius sat in one of the auxiliary console seats watching everything, apparently intrigued by the operations of a spaceship.

Kris held a finger to the communicator on his ear as he said, "Thirty seconds."

When Rob had suggested to Katia that she stay aboard the Tenacity with Kris and the robots as Dagam would be very dangerous, Katia had shot him a warning stare, one which Rob knew to mean, 'don't even go there'. Therefore, as Rob, Will and Matt prepared to leap from the spaceship to Grimmin's surface, Katia was right there with them when they heard Kris's thirty-second warning.

The space-cruiser would be vulnerable to discovery for a few moments whilst touching down, for, in addition to the rumble of its whispered motors, the cloaking field would have to be dropped to allow for disembarkation.

As the cruiser came close to Grimmin's surface, it suddenly became visible as it swooped and landed with a slight bounce in

Sneaking In

an abandoned area of Dagam. Four shadowed figures ran from the ship to crouch beside the nearest building, and the Tenacity then shot back into the air with a whispered rumble and vanished.

The brief, subtle disturbance went unnoticed by all but one, as he was expecting it.

While searching for where the Boargen were keeping Katia's mother, Senator Quarin, the brothers had discovered that the senator's ship was in Grimmin's orbit. The ship was being used as a jail for the crew, so while the others would free Katia's mother, Kris would free the crew.

Back in Grimmin's orbit, Kris brought the Tenacity to within a few miles of Senator Quarin's much larger spaceship, where it would remain until he returned from rescuing the crew. With the cruiser cloaked and its computer jamming the Boargen scanners, it would remain invisible and undetected. With the help of Keb and Genius, Kris prepared to leave for the senator's ship.

The Tenacity still had a few surprises for the brothers, the most recent being the discovery of the space-bikes. Because the bikes were so well designed to fit neatly in pockets in the cargo bay walls, they had remained undiscovered until Matt saw them mentioned on the ship's computer. The sleek machines looked a little like an Earth jet-ski, only a little longer and with a small cockpit for space travel. The space-bikes were used for transporting one short distances, including to a planet's surface if need be.

The ride was thrilling, as Kris zipped from the Tenacity towards the senator's ship; much like riding a motorcycle. Held to the seat by the restraining field, he felt like he became the machine itself. The space-bike was nimble and instantly responded to changes in direction. With the bike having the same cloaking technology as the large spaceships and being too small to show up on any scanners, Kris arrived undetected.

He raced along the length of the foreign ship and although he knew there were much larger vessels, he was impressed by its size. Kris knew exactly where he was going. He reached an emergency hatch near the engines and wasted no time in linking the cockpit of his space-bike to the senator's ship. Then he was in.

247

He glanced at his arm-comp. The monitor showed a schematic of the senator's ship. Yep, he was in the right place. The ship's brig was close and that was where he headed, carefully looking around corners for Boargen guards as he went.

It was very quiet, leaving Kris worried that he might not find anyone aboard, or worse, that he had been detected and the guards lay in wait for him. Kris had a small blaster strapped to his torso like his brothers did down on Grimmin. He knew how to use it but he dreaded having to. Reaching the brig, he entered and in an odd way, was relieved to see that the brig was full.

As he moved to one of the doorways with a shimmering barrier-field blocking passage through, the prisoners, in turn, became alert and squeezed in on the other side. He met their curious looks with an innocent smile befitting his age; a smile that hinted at nothing that would suggest he was there to rescue them.

Sobering, Kris said, "I don't suppose you know the codes."

A distinguished-looking grey-haired man in uniform moved in until he was just inches from the barrier. He looked at Kris severely, and said, "Yes, we know the code, but who are you?"

"I'm Kris Roar. I'm here to get you out."

The man studied him for a moment, then said, "Even if we get out of here, son, we can't leave without the senator."

"Oh," Kris smiled, "we certainly won't be leaving without the senator."

The older Roar boys, with Katia in tow, had wound their way through the streets of Dagam. There was a general look of filth and decay in the city, even with the lack of lighting on that pitch-black night. But for the lack of light, sneaking through the city was easy; though spooky. There had been a number of close calls where the four had almost run into rather terrifying Boargen creeps; creeps that smelled of decay even from a distance; creeps that would have made the worst of beings in New York seem as if they were out looking to help an old lady cross the street.

They stood now in the extreme dark of the shadows beside a tall, blank wall, behind which somewhere, was Katia's mother. Rob turned so that Will could reach the rope in his pack. On the end of the rope was a circular pad about the size of his hand. As the Tenacity had been built for a galaxy ranger, it had been equipped with everything one could imagine, from blasters and space-bikes, to a very special rope.

Will handed that very same rope to Rob, who then twirled it like a lasso as he stepped back from the wall. He let go and the pad stuck to the wall, but it wasn't high enough. He gave it a yank and the padded end dropped back to the ground. Again, he tried, but again, the pad stuck too low. He tried, yet again, and yet again, but it was still too low. Frustrated, he held out the rope to Will.

Will tried three times to no avail. As he held the rope out to Matt, Katia grabbed it whilst eyeing the boys, and said, "Time for the girl to try."

It looked like she had done it before. The padded end of the rope sailed over the top of the wall and stuck. Katia stared at Rob and Will, expecting praise. Matt chuckled quietly.

"Well, we weren't trying to throw it all the way over the wall," said Will, looking at Rob for reassurance.

Exasperated, Rob breathed out as he shook his head and strode to the dangling rope. He gave it a good, firm yank – the rope held – and said, "Never mind, Will, she showed us up."

Will glanced at Katia, but only for a second because she was staring at him with a raised brow and a smug smile.

Pulling himself up along the rope, Rob walked up the wall hand-over-hand. When he reached the top, he lay face down on the thick crest and moved a little along its length, making room for the others. Katia followed, then Matt, then Will. Together, on the top of the thick wall, they remained low. The pad on the end of the rope was stuck on the inside face too far down to reach, and Will said, "Now how are we going to get that?"

Katia breathed out impatiently and, holding out her hand, said to Will, "Give me your arm."

Will extended his arm.

"No," she snapped, "the other one."

He switched, holding out his arm-comp. Katia tapped a button.

A barely discernable high-pitched squeal sounded and she gave a quick yank on the rope, releasing the pad. Rob took a deep breath, Will groaned, Matt giggled, and Katia said, "I took the time to read the instructions all the way to the end."

From the top of the wall which bordered a large complex, they could see much of their surroundings. There were no security towers, no roving patrols to be seen, and the complex was poorly lit, so the Boargen apparently had no concern about intruders. Rob began to worry that they might be at the wrong place. Perhaps Katia's mother was elsewhere.

But, in spite of the appearance that there was no one around, the four intruders stayed low as they crawled along the top of the wall. They reached a huge building and again used the rope; this time, to climb to the expansive, flat roof. Once there, they took a moment to steady their nerves, for the next leg of the break-in would be more difficult, maybe even a little more unnerving, and probably more dangerous.

The air seemed dirtier up on the roof than on the ground, and that, combined with the darkness of night, made it impossible to see very far. Glancing first at his arm-comp, Rob then pointed at one of many large, round pipes sticking straight up from the roof. As he walked towards it with the others following, he said, "That's our way in."

Once at the pipe, Rob and Will removed the vent cover.

Matt rose up on his toes to peer inside, then looked at the others and said, "You know, in the past three weeks we've spent a lot of time in pipes." He shivered. "When we get through this I'd like to stay out of cramped places for a while. Maybe we could actually explore space," he pointed upwards, " … out there."

Will gave him a pat on the shoulder, and said, "The next adventure, no pipes." He took a deep breath, "I'll go first."

With the hand-sized pad holding the rope fast to the inside of the pipe, Will climbed in, as he said, "Wait until I get to the bottom. The last time we crawled down a rope in a pipe we almost died."

Katia gave Rob and Matt a curious look as Will descended.

After a signal from Will, Katia followed. A few minutes later, so did Matt. As Rob climbed in, he lifted the cover back on to the pipe, covering their tracks. Then he joined the others.

There was a foul smell seeping through the pipes and a coating of gunk that was both sticky and slippery. With the light flipped up on his arm-comp, Will shone it first one way, and then the other. Though a bright beam, there was no end visible either way. With Will leading as they crawled through the dark maze, they did all they could to keep their hands and feet as high up on the sides as possible because the sticky-slippery coating was also thick in places on the bottom.

However, by the time they reached the last leg of their journey through the pipes, they were all feeling pretty gunky. Each of them was also feeling a certain sense of claustrophobia, mostly because of what they had already been through. But now, they had to drop a short distance down a pipe that was just about large enough in diameter to allow a boy in without his pack on, making the final descent more difficult. There was no way of knowing if the room below was occupied. Will stopped.

Keeping his voice low, Matt said, "Maybe we should have tried the front door."

Although Will hesitated, he did so not because of the narrowness of the pipe or the gunk coating that would make it slippery, but because he had just figured out that the only way to go down the pipe was headfirst – upside down – for if the room was occupied, he would have to use his blaster.

Although Rob and Matt had armed themselves with a blaster each, Will had armed himself with two, and Katia had chosen not to have one at all. Will figured that if carrying one was being well prepared, then carrying two was being even better prepared. However, he learned that not to be the case, as two blasters strapped around his torso had made it more difficult to move through the ventilation pipes.

Drawing one of his blasters, without further hesitation Will slipped headfirst down the pipe. Because of the gunk, he almost overshot but with some effort, he managed to stop himself before he clonked his head on the grill below.

Then he realised his shortsighted plan of coming down the pipe headfirst, as even after dislodging the grill barring his entry, he would still be upside down. How was he going to land on his feet?

The room was dark. No sign of anyone. There was a sense of relief as they would at least gain entry without being discovered.

Above, Katia realised the same thing Will had and whispered to Rob and Matt, "How is he going to get out of the pipe without breaking his neck?"

Then she gasped and her eyes grew wider as there was a bang, followed by a crash, which in turn was followed a moment later, by a grand finale of bangs and crashes.

Only Will knew exactly what had happened. Holding on tightly to the grill, he had put all his weight on one side of it. Without warning, the grill had broken free and he had slipped from the pipe while hanging on to the metal grid with the intention of swinging to the floor. It had worked well enough at first, but then mid-swing, the grill had broken free from the ceiling – predictable given hindsight – and he had landed on his back on the floor whilst the grill hit some shelves. The shelves had then broken, sending their contents to the floor, much of it landing on top of Will.

Rob slipped down the pipe as fast as he dared and dropped to the floor with blaster in hand. He scanned the room with the light on his arm-comp. Seeing no threat, he ran to Will, who, lying on his back on the floor, looked up at him and said, "I'm not sure what hurt more; the fall, or the falling things."

As Katia and Matt dropped from the pipe, Rob helped Will sit up and said to him, "Not that I don't feel for you, brother, but we should keep moving."

Staring up at Rob, Will said, "I guess it's good news as I can feel the pain. But I could still outrun a rockhund."

"That would be very macho of you," said Katia, as she and Matt joined Rob and Will.

The plans of the Boargen complex indicated that they were in a supply records room. It was remotely located amongst large storage rooms. The assumption that it would be empty during the night had, fortunately, been correct.

"The computer consoles are over there," said Rob, pointing towards the other end of the room.

While Katia rushed to a console, Rob and Matt each held out a hand for Will, who accepted the help and crawled from the floor. While Will brushed himself off and looked around, Rob and Matt caught up with Katia. The computer monitor flickered on and the system began to hum; a bit loud for comfort.

"The Boargen don't spend much on their technology," she said, lowering herself into a grungy black chair.

"Or on cleaning," Will added, as he stepped up behind the others. "I think this room must be coated with the same grime we just crawled through."

Will looked over at an empty computer console, hesitated, and then went to it. Sitting as he booted the console, he realised how right he had been about the filth. The seat felt clammy, greasy and sticky, all at once. Everything about the Boargen was dirty. The monitor flickered on.

"Shoot!" Katia looked up at Rob and Matt standing beside her. "Access to prison records requires a code."

The monitor blinked with its demand.

Rob reached forwards with his arm-comp and pulled out a small lead. "Here," he said, "plug this into that port."

Katia took what Rob handed her and studied it. "It doesn't look like it's going to fit," she said.

"Just put it in. Trust me."

She did. Although at first the end of the lead was loose, it then morphed to fit and Rob's arm-comp became linked with the Boargen system. Moments later, the arm-comp chimed "complete", and Katia was allowed access to the prison records.

"Thanks," she said, glancing up at Rob.

"No problem. I read the instructions all the way to the end."

At the other console, Will plugged in his arm-comp. As Rob's had, Will's, too, began calculating in order to solve the access code.

"I found her!" said Katia, relieved and excited all at once. "She's not on the prison levels though. They have her locked in quarters." She tapped a few keys. "In fact, she's not far from here."

Rob reached forwards and unplugged the lead. As he turned to leave, he said, "I've set a course."

As Matt turned to follow and Katia stood, they heard Will say, in a surprised but subdued voice, "He's here."

Matt and Katia stopped and stared at him. Almost reaching the door, Rob abruptly stopped and turned. Still seated, Will exchanged stares with the others. In a shaky voice he said, "Father's here ... He's on prison level three."

Katia thought she could imagine what the Roar brothers felt at that moment, as she, too, was terribly worried about her own mother. But she had been born into the greater complexity of galactic life. Unlike the Roar brothers, she believed a single life weighed less on a galactic scale than on a planetary one. But the Roar brothers would risk all their lives combined to save a single one, whether it was for their father, or for Katia's mother.

The brothers had known nothing of galaxy rangers. They had thought their parents were farmers. They had been separated from their mother for a year; and their father for two. The many long months had been confusing. Life had been like a bad dream with their whole lives on hold until some light switched on and some door opened. And that is exactly what happened: Mr Casper had turned on a light and opened a door. He had shed light on the bad dream. With that door open, the brothers escaped the great pause in their lives ... and now they had even found their father.

The others converged on Will only after the slightest hesitation of disbelief. It was true. The name 'Rob Roar' was on the list of prisoners being held several levels below the main complex.

After a moment's paralysing doubt, Rob said, "We need to split up. Will and I will go for Father. Matt, you and Katia go for the senator ... "

"No," Matt complained. "I want to go with you."

"No, Matt. It's a lot further to the prison levels. Will and I can get there the fastest. You have to help Katia."

Matt's eyes showed how much he wanted to disagree.

Katia knew she needed help to rescue her mother but the confliction that each brother was experiencing at that moment was obvious.

She sucked in air, and then said, "I can go on my own. My mother and I will meet you at the pick-up point."

"Katia, you don't even have a blaster," said Rob. "What if you run into trouble?"

Beginning to feel some resentment brought on by the fear of going alone, Katia stared at Rob while thrusting her hand out towards Will and said, "Then give me a blaster ... "

Misinterpreting Rob's look of concern for one of doubting Katia continued, "I can handle a blaster as well as any boy," she said. Then she thrust her hand insistently towards Will while glaring at Rob.

"That's not what I'm thinking. We're not going to let you go alone." Rob looked at Matt. "If you insist on going with Will, I'll go with Katia. But I don't think it's the way to do it." Returning his attention to Katia, he asked, "And why didn't you bring a blaster?"

Staring back, she said, "I don't like them."

"Alright," said Matt. "I'll go with Katia."

After a moment, Rob said, "Thanks, Matt." Then to Will, he said, "She needs one of your blasters."

Moments later, with Katia wearing a torso holster packed with a blaster, she and Matt went one way while Rob and Will went the other.

The two older Roar boys sprinted along the passageways, slowing only to creep around corners. They hadn't seen anyone when they reached the lift to the prison levels. Rob pushed the button, calling the lift.

Each boy knew what the other was thinking as they stared at each other, waiting. Eventually, there would be guards. Rob licked his lips and drew his blaster. After a moment's hesitation, Will did the same. With lips licked and blasters drawn, they faced the lift door. The lift arrived. The door opened ...

Empty.

Simultaneously, they breathed a sigh of relief and got in. By the time they were descending to prison level three, both were filled with stark fear. As the lift settled, Rob and Will exchanged quick glances, then licked their lips again and stared at the door, blasters at the ready.

As the door slid open, two charcoal-haired, uniformed men filled their view. The sight of two alien, blond-haired boys with blasters drawn was obviously an unexpected one, for their eyes widened just before Rob and Will shot them.

Once recovered from the double-dosed hits, the guards would later discover that the two foreign children had shot them with blasters set to stun.

Rob found an electronic key in one of the guard's pockets. With Will on his heels, he bolted, sprinting across the halls as he followed the promptings from his arm-comp. There was a beep and Rob slid to a stop at a door: Cell 3149.

Feeling a dizzying rush of anticipation at seeing their father, both boys holstered their blasters, and again, licked their lips. Rob thrust the key – a small, handheld device with two prongs – into the lock beside the door. The door opened ...

Breaking Out

His hair was long and he was unshaven. He stood, staring at the boys through wild eyes. They stared back. It had been two years since Rob and Will had seen their father, but they were certain they could remember what he looked like.

"You're not our father," said Will, scowling, sounding rather put out.

"I think you're probably right about that," he said. "I don't believe I have any children." He smiled, which was odd coming from a man with such wild eyes. Then he squinted as he said, "But how in mother galaxy did you get in here? And who is your father?"

After a moment's hesitation, Rob said, "He's a galaxy ranger, Rob Roar." There was a tinge of pride in his voice as he said it.

The man's eyes widened as he rushed to the boys and said, "Great mother galaxy!"

He stooped and grasped each by the shoulder, looked at them square in the eyes, and continued, "You boys came all this way for nothing. Your father is nowhere near this system." The man stood. "Let's get out of here before … "

Too late. Faint footsteps echoed from down the hall.

Shooting a wild look at the boys, the man said, "Do you know how to get out?" They nodded. "Good. I'll draw them away. It's likely we will not see each other again." The man released his grip and ran from the cell.

Rob and Will stood there alone, all hopes of finding their father dashed. But then they were stirred from their depressed state by the startled yells of guards giving chase. Returning to reality, they poked their heads out of the cell and, seeing a clear way, they bolted back towards the lift.

Having sprinted across the halls, they rounded a corner; having almost forgotten about the two guards out cold on the floor they jumped over their bodies. Rob then pressed the two-pronged key into the lock beside the lift and the boys waited for its arrival. As the lift settled, the doors opened and Rob and Will gasped at the sight of two more guards.

The boys froze and the guards drew their blasters. One of them said, "Move and it will be your last."

Will and Rob were searched, packs and all, and though the guards took interest in their arm-comps, they were too impatient to figure out how to remove them. Finding the electronic key in Rob's possession, the guard said, "And what did you think you were going to do with this? Free someone?" They obviously knew nothing of the very recent escapee, as they both chuckled.

By that time, Matt and Katia were in a quiet, deserted passageway outside the senator's locked quarters. It was shortly after midnight and everything was still going well for them. Matt's arm-comp beeped. Reading the blinking code on the monitor, he entered the numbers into the keypad beside the door and the door opened. Katia ran into the darkened room calling, "Mother?"

A woman's startled voice called out, "Katia?" and a light came on.

The woman leapt from her bed as Katia reached her and the two embraced. "But what ... ?" she began, as she pulled Katia away. She stopped when she noticed Matt standing by the open door. "I gather we had better move fast," she continued, as she rushed into the other room. She re-emerged moments later, dressed for escape and pinning up her long hair.

With Matt in the lead, following his arm-comp promptings for direction, the three raced from the room. The passageways remained deserted as they headed for the nearest building exit, thankful for their good luck. Matt had a feeling, however, that sooner or later, someone was going to confront them, and he dreaded it. Though he had not enjoyed the pipes which he had crawled through lately, he now wished they could just crawl back up the one through which they had arrived. But there was no chance of getting Katia's mother out that way. As he jogged, Matt glanced at his arm-comp, hoping to see a message from Rob and Will.

Then an ear-piercing alarm went off, finally disrupting their luck. For at that very moment, the Boargen complex came alive with the sounds of many feet hitting the halls. Panicking, Matt, followed closely by Katia and her mother, slipped, unnoticed, into what turned out to be a storage room.

As they crouched in a corner behind some crates, Matt was so unsure of what to do next that he felt on the edge of being overwhelmed. Had the alarm sounded because the Boargen had discovered Katia's mother missing? Or had Rob and Will been caught? And what of his father? Matt noticed Katia and her mother staring at him and wondered how long he had been paralysed?

A group of guards passed by in the corridor outside, their footsteps echoing loudly. From where he crouched, he could see a door at the other end of the storage room. Hearing no further footsteps, without giving it a second thought, he ran across the room. Carefully, he opened the door and peeked out.

To his astonishment, on the other side of the door was a hangar full of spaceships, which brought him some relief from being on the edge of despair. Then he saw something that gave him a thrill and refilled his hope: the shuttle, the Roar brothers' shuttle. It was unmistakable. The pearl-white spaceship was on the other side of the hangar; a beautiful sight among ugly, grey Boargen bulks.

At that moment, Matt's arm-comp beeped. He tapped in a code and a text message from Rob filled the monitor. Much of his recovered hope vanished at the words he read: 'Caught. Get out'. He closed the door and rushed back to Katia and her mother.

"The shuttle's out there," he said, mastering his voice in spite of everything. "We should go now."

As he turned to leave, Katia grabbed his arm …

"What about the others?"

Matt glanced back and said, "They've been caught. That's why everyone is awake." He walked to the door, grasped the handle, and looked back. "We should go before they find out about us."

As Katia and her mother followed, Matt slowly opened the door. He drew his blaster. Katia did the same, but her mother held out a hand. No words needed to be said; it was all in the look: 'Hand it over, young lady'. Katia hesitated, and then did so.

With Matt leading, the three made their way across the hangar, staying close to the Boargen spaceships wherever possible. They were half-way towards the shuttle when several blasts hit nearby, causing them to dive for cover behind a large ship's landing pad.

While Katia remained low nearby, her mother began returning fire. Matt moved so he could see out from behind the landing pad and shot at the first figure he saw, closing his eyes just before firing. His shot, missing the mark, did, however, blast a corner off a large storage container.

In order to reach the shuttle from where they were, they would have to cross an area of the hangar free of cover from spaceships. It seemed impossible. But then, several blasts were fired at the Boargen guards from somewhere else in the hangar. Matt shot a look at Katia's mother, who stared back, surprised. More blasts hit near their attackers. Matt surveyed the hangar, figuring and hoping that Rob and Will must have escaped.

Whoever it was, there was no time to waste. With the guards pinned down, it was time to make a break for it.

"Let's go," said Matt.

With Katia and her mother following, he ran for the shuttle. When he slowed to allow them to enter the ship ahead of him, he caught sight of a single, tall figure in the shadows. The figure waved at him to go. He almost refused to budge because he thought it must be his father, when a blast hit the shuttle just above his head and he shot inside.

By the time Matt had reached the cockpit, slipped past Katia's mother and leapt into the pilot's seat, Katia was already in the co-pilot's seat powering up the engines. He peered sideways at her, and said, "I didn't know you knew how to pilot a ship."

"I don't. But I've watched Keb do it plenty of times." Looking as shaken as Matt now felt, Katia forced a smile. "I can start it," she said.

A blast hit the shuttle. And another. Boargen were converging on them from all directions. Matt knew then that whoever had helped them was gone, making his own escape, or maybe, he hoped, off to help Rob and Will.

He glanced back at Katia's mother and said, "Mrs. Quarin, you should … "

"Find a seat," she finished, as she rushed towards the back of the shuttle.

Matt pulled back on the stick as he ratcheted forwards the throttles. As the shuttle lifted and turned, it was hit with fast, repetitive blasts; blasts too weak to harm the ship but enough to shake its occupants. It was then that he saw the mysterious black ship; the very one that Mr Casper had told them to watch out for; the very one that Kaya and Shani had seen snooping around the old base in Oregon. The Boargen were firing at it, too, as it lifted off. Matt watched as it turned in place, blasting away at the guards who dived for cover like scattering cockroaches. Then, everything was quiet and the mysterious black spaceship was facing him ...

"Matt! I think he's waiting for you to leave," Katia said, as she broke his paralysis.

Shaking it off, he thrust the throttles forwards and the shuttle shot out of the hangar and raced skyward. Matt craned his neck, looking back to see if he could spot the mysterious ship.

"He's over here," he heard Katia say. "He's heading away from us."

The black speck shot across the sky to the horizon.

"It must be him," added Katia, "the one that helped us."

That meant that it was not his father. It also meant that Rob and Will were still caught and without help, and that they had perhaps never even reached their father. It was a diluted relief to be free of the dingy Boargen planet, because the further the shuttle got from Grimmin, the tighter Matt's heart became.

Kris was just getting ready to leave the senator's ship for the Tenacity, when Matt contacted him. The plan had been for Kris – once the senator had been rescued – to fly the Tenacity back to Grimmin and whisk everyone away. So when he heard Matt's voice, he was surprised, then ecstatic, to find out that they had Katia's mother and were on their way in the shuttle. Matt would drop his passengers off on the senator's ship, and then catch up with Kris in the Tenacity.

But Kris could tell something was wrong. For one thing, why was it only Matt who was speaking with him when Rob and Will usually did, too?

"What's wrong, Matt?" he asked.

Mastering his voice, Matt answered, "Rob and Will got caught."

He decided against mentioning their father. Why add worry?

After a deafening silence where Kris fought back despair, he said, "We'll go and get them, then."

Overwhelmed and close to tears, not knowing how they would rescue them, Matt simply said, "Yes."

"Maybe Mr Casper and KNIA can help," said Kris.

"I think we're on our own," answered Matt.

"Maybe Rafjur could help us now."

Matt hesitated, and then replied, "Like I said … "

" … we're on our own," Kris finished.

Moments later, Matt caught sight of the senator's ship, big and sleek, glistening in the sunlight. The Tenacity was nowhere to be seen, but it was there, cloaked from view. Closer now, Matt saw a small craft darting away – it was Kris on the space-bike.

Suddenly, an alarm blared and the scanner showed multiple small craft rushing towards them. The Boargen were sending fighters; not an unexpected thing, but stressful, nonetheless, and even more so under the circumstances.

The crew was ready for them. Matt slipped the shuttle into the belly of the senator's ship and set it down as the hangar doors closed and the bay pressurised. Muffled, repetitive blasts made the air vibrate – the Boargen ships were attacking – as Matt rushed to get Katia and her mother off the shuttle. He was in a hurry to get to the Tenacity, and from there, to rescue Rob and Will. But under attack as they were, Katia's mother and her crew refused to let him go.

Kris had almost reached the Tenacity when a Boargen fighter came straight at him. He had never in his life felt more pain than when the blast hit his minimally protected space-bike; a craft just too small to have a repulse field powerful enough to completely repel an attack. As he spun out of control – the space-bike all but crushed – he knew he had made a mistake. He knew now, that he should have activated the bike's cloaking field, which would have sapped energy from the engines and slowed him; but better to have got there slowly, than never. Too late, now ...

Think! He had to think! Matt should have already left the senator's ship ...

Matt, however, aware of Kris's predicament and desperate to save him, had only just convinced Katia's mother and her crew to let him go by threatening them with his blaster. Katia had done her part, too, ordering, at the top of her lungs, for her mother and the crew to let him go – Kris was about to die.

But Matt would never make it in time because the Boargen fighter was already heading at Kris again, this time, to finish him off. But ... maybe ... just maybe ...

Kris had to try twice before his voice worked: "Keb ... "

"We are almost there, young sir."

Genius ... ! It had to be Genius because the Tenacity was armed.

Suddenly, the Tenacity appeared between Kris and the oncoming Boargen fighter. The beautiful white ship moved in with its hangar-bay doors wide open, and settled around him. He realised then that he had not been breathing – he was out of air and stunned. Then he felt metal arms lifting him from the destroyed space-bike and he was whisked from Tenacity's hangar.

The robot knew where to take him. As Keb carried Kris to the command bridge, the thundering of the repelled enemy blasts hitting the space-cruiser set everything vibrating subtly. Kris willed himself to relax, for upon reaching the bridge, there would be work to do; work, he hoped, that he could handle on his own. In the meantime, it felt great to breathe again. The air tasted sweet and he could not get enough of it.

Once on the command bridge, as Keb set him down, Genius, wearing his broad-rimmed straw hat, poked his head out from where he sat in the pilot's seat, and said, "Thank goodness you are safe! And best of all, here! This is all setting me a-jitter! I'll have to sleep for a week when this is all over!"

All at once, three distinctly different voices blared throughout the command bridge: one of them was Matt, panic-stricken. Kris focused on him first. The second, Kris recognised, was Rob, but he had trouble in believing it was true. The third was a man's voice that said that they could not stay and be of help. He said that they must get the senator to safety. If Genius's eyes could have widened with fear, they would have, for the robot quickly stood and made way for Kris, who then slipped past and leapt into the pilot's seat.

Through the view-screen, he could see the Boargen fighters buzzing around the Tenacity and the senator's ship like angry bees. All around them, flashes lit up space. The Tenacity shuddered slightly with each impact, but it was too powerful a ship to be shaken much by the Boargen sting.

"Matt!" Kris called out.

"Kris! You're alright?" asked Matt, sounding desperate.

"I'm alright!" he answered.

Kris could see the shuttle being chased by several enemy fighters on the scanner.

"Matt, it doesn't look like you're going to make it to the Tenacity!"

"I forgot; Will and I deactivated the shuttle's weapons so Keb could ... Space!" A blast shook the shuttle.

"Matt, just get out of there!" said Kris. "Go home! I think Rob and Will got away! I can get them on my own!"

The shuttle vanished from the scanner, instantly. Kris was sure Matt was safe ... for now. Then, the Senator's ship vanished, leaving, for a moment, a black void where it had filled part of the view-screen; a void soon filled by Boargen fighters.

Even though there was a frenzy of enemy ships swarming around the Tenacity, since the space-cruiser was stationary, Kris took the time to make a tight-beam connection to Earth. He would send a massage to Mr Casper and KNIA that Matt was on the way and that Boargen attack ships might be following. While the connection was being made, he turned his attention to the other voice he had heard – a hurried voice; Rob's voice. At that moment, Kris still knew nothing about the events concerning the alleged discovery of their father, or of events leading to Rob and Will's capture; he knew nothing about the stranger found in the Boargen prison cell instead of their father; and nothing about the mysterious help that Matt, Katia and her mother had received during their escape.

The Face of Death

At the time Matt, Katia and her mother had been making their way to the shuttle in the hangar on Grimmin, Rob and Will had stared death in the face.

As the guards had escorted them from the prison levels, Rob had managed to send Matt the text message: 'Caught. Get out'. He knew that Matt had received it, but aside from that, nothing else.

After an endless walk on legs stiffened by a sense of loss and helplessness, Rob and Will had been brought to a large, mostly empty room with an unusually high ceiling. Though it was a formal room of sorts with ornamental decorations and tapestries covering the walls, the Boargen trade mark dingy appearance was here, too.

From there, they had been unceremoniously shoved into the centre of the room while the guards went to the doors to stand watch. The boys had been stripped of their blasters and their packs; those things having been dumped on a desk at one end of the room. The guards must have thought that the arm-comps were of no significance as they never tried, beyond an initial tug, to remove them from the boys' arms. And the communicators, of course, were a necessity as language translators.

As each boy wondered how long he would have to wait to find out what would happen next, there was a disturbance outside the room. A door flew open and a tall, bald man stormed in, dressed in a sharp, military uniform with a large blaster strapped to his hips. He carried a box under one arm as he walked straight to the desk while staring hard at them out the corner of his eyes. Having set the box down, he roughly looked through each boy's pack. Then he picked up one of the blasters, gave it a brief, searching look, and then tossed it to the desk as he turned to face them.

Only then, did Rob and Will see the left side of the bald man's face. One of his eyes was robotic: a spooky, silver eyeball with a red iris. But most striking and unsettling, was the long, uneven scar that started from his chin, stretched over his cheek, and wrapped up and over his bald head where it disappeared out of sight. There was something purely evil about the way in which he glared at them; a look that sent a chill through each boy's body.

As the man strode towards them, he said, "So, Rob Roar has offspring. And they are as stupid as he was." He stopped just feet from the boys and stared down at them. "You came all this way for nothing. Your father is dead."

Rob and Will exchanged doubtful, rebellious stares, and then returned their attention to the bald man who gave them a cruel stare and a wicked smile

"You don't believe me," he said, in his deep, hollow voice as he circled the brothers.

"But you should believe what I say," he returned to face them, " ... because I killed him."

Their doubt waning, Rob and Will exchanged glances as the man chuckled, cruelly.

The bald man then turned; his attention drawn by a disturbance at the door. A frenzied meeting with hoarse whispers between the guards and a new arrival ensued. Rob and Will were convinced it was about Matt.

"Your interruption had better be worth it, Captain!" barked the bald man.

The new arrival rushed forwards with submissive, fast-paced strides and bowed. "Please pardon my interruption, Admiral," he said, his voice quaking. "But there are others attempting to escape through the hangar. And ... and Senator Quarin is missing from her quarters, sir."

"Ugh!" The admiral turned and swung his fist out at Rob and Will, slamming them both so hard across their faces that they flew through the air and landed, sprawled on the floor. He turned to face the captain and yelled, "If you value your own life, Captain, kill them, if you can't capture them!"

"Y-yes, Admiral," said the captain, as he ran from the room.

Sprawled on the floor, numb from the fisted blow, Rob and Will both tried to clear their heads. The brothers exchanged fearful stares when the admiral yelled again.

"Get that big, dumb pirate in here!"

"Yes, Admiral," a guard answered, and then left the room.

"And bring me Jaggin!"

"Yes, Admiral," came the departing guard's voice.

"That man you released tried to pass himself off as your father," the admiral said, as he turned to look down at Rob and Will. "He is a common thief and will be caught."

Neither Rob nor Will could think of anything to say. Each felt a painful throbbing on his face and a steady sinking of his morale. Then Will noticed something; the box which the admiral had placed on the desk appeared to have shifted, ever so slightly.

"And who did you bring with you? No warriors? Mere children came to rescue a dead father and a useless politician?" The admiral chuckled, staring at them through his eerie robotic eye, and then continued, "I would respect you for your courage, if it were not for your stupidity. Hah! The galaxy is full of weaklings ripe for Boargen rule!"

Rob and Will's attention was then drawn by the arrival of a being that only Rob recognised.

The admiral turned, and said, "Jaggin, perhaps it is one of these two that stole the girl from you?"

The sight of the alien sent a chill down Will's spine. Rob's, even more so because he had seen the same bone, muscle and skin woven face on Jawbone.

Jaggin strode forwards past the admiral, to peer down at Rob and Will. He pointed at Rob and, in a deep, crackly voice, said, "That one fits the description, Admiral Slatter."

In spite of the pain that each Roar brother felt on his face, the blood that each felt dripping from his nose and the fear of the predicament they were in, both snapped their attention to the bald-headed man. This was Mulkin's father; the feared Admiral Slatter; the Boargen leader.

While his attention was on the admiral, Will thought he saw, out of the corner of his eye, the small box on the table move – again – ever so slightly. He looked towards it.

The admiral noticed, turned a bit, and followed Will's line of sight to the box. After a quick glance back at Will, he strode to the table and picked it up.

"You will step out of Rafjur's way before Rafjur does it for you," boomed a familiar voice from the hall.

For Rob and Will, everything had become a nightmare from which it seemed they may never awaken. But, hearing Rafjur's thunderous voice gave them unexpected and welcome hope; only if it had been their father or mother would Rob and Will have been more relieved. Surely, Rafjur would now set them free from their bad dream.

The boys watched as Rafjur entered and assessed the situation. His eyes rested on them, then Jaggin, and finally, the Admiral. Rafjur's expression was difficult to read, partly, Rob and Will figured, because so much of his face was covered with hair, but he looked unhappy; that seemed their best guess.

"Why have you summoned Rafjur?" he said, as he scanned the room again. "Rafjur does not need to be witness to your sick friend's choosing of his next meal … "

Growling at the giant, Jaggin took a step forwards.

Rafjur pointed a thick finger at him, and said, "Rafjur says to be careful what you do next, Jawbonee."

"Enough!" bellowed the admiral.

Jaggin stood down but continued to glare at Rafjur.

While Rob was switching glances from Rafjur to the admiral and back, Will was watching the box that the admiral had tucked under his arm again. Admiral Slatter took one of the brothers' blasters from the table and tossed it to Rafjur.

"That's among the best of the Quadoran blasters ever made," said the admiral. "A little light for me, but among the best. You tend to trade those from place to place … don't you, Rafjur?" The question came in a suspicious tone.

Unfazed, Rafjur tossed the blaster back to the admiral, and said, "Rafjur knows a number of these went missing about the same time that ship was stolen from Kablakia."

That much was true.

Brows raised, the admiral said, "You know about the ship? It was destroyed."

"Rafjur knows much," he said. Then he pointed at Rob and Will and continued, "Rafjur suspects you have thieves, right there." He glanced at Jaggin, disgusted. "But Rafjur thinks the young thieves do not look large enough to make a meal."

"It disturbs you that they will be Jaggin's breakfast?" the admiral asked, still suspicious.

Will continued to watch the box.

"Huh … Rafjur thinks killing any being unnecessarily is unacceptable; especially young ones, and especially to eat." He stared at the brothers with no evident emotion. "But Rafjur has business to occupy him and no time for worrying about runts; even if they are good thieves." As it seemed that Rafjur didn't care what happened to them, despair returned to the boys. "Rafjur will not lose sleep over disgusting Jawbonee habits."

Jaggin growled but stayed put. Rafjur paid the Jawbonee no heed. Then there was a rush of activity at the door.

The captain was back, looking worried. As he rushed to the admiral with his wimpy stride, glancing nervously at Jaggin and Rafjur, he spoke in a fearful voice.

"Admiral, sir, the senator and two others have escaped in the shuttle we confiscated a few days ago." Admiral Slatter breathed in at length. The captain hesitated, then continued, "Also, sir … it appears that the senator's crew somehow got free and … somehow, reclaimed the ship."

The admiral glared at the captain. Jaggin reached for the hilt of a long knife at his hip and grasped it, squeezing. Rafjur watched everything. Rob noticed this but Will still watched the box tucked under the admiral's arm.

Now desperate and fearful, the captain continued, "That's … not all, sir." He swallowed. "It appears, sir … the ship that was stolen from Kablakia and thought destroyed, sir, has appeared near the senator's."

Admiral Slatter drew in a deep breath, then, in a barely-controlled voice, said, "Tell me the senator will not make it to her ship."

"But, Admiral ... she already has ... "

"Ugh!" The admiral drew his blaster and struck the captain across the face with it, sending the officer sprawling to the floor, out cold. He then turned and, in two long strides, he reached the Roar brothers and pointed the blaster straight at Rob.

In one lightningly-fast motion, Rafjur moved to Admiral Slatter and smacked the blaster away, wrapping his massive arm around the admiral's neck and tightening it like a huge python constricting around its prey, causing the admiral to drop the box. The box clunked to the floor and came to rest near Will's feet as Rafjur turned and grabbed Jaggin's wrist, making the Jawbonee drop the glinting blade he had drawn. Rafjur then threw Jaggin across the room where he landed in a heap against a wall, out cold. The great man swivelled to sweep the room with his gaze, holding on to Admiral Slatter like a child would a rag-doll, and said to the guards, who had only just begun to respond, "If you move from your places I will squeeze your admiral's head off!"

As Rob watched Rafjur and the admiral, Will slipped his foot out and turned the box so he could see how it might open.

"Rafjurrr!" growled Admiral Slatter. "There won't be even an asteroid that will hide you if you kill me!"

"The admiral is thinking that even if Rafjur does not kill him, this will be so."

"You will not be hunted if you let me live," said the admiral, squeezing his words out in frustration.

"Admiral Slatter knows Rafjur will cause anyone hunting him great damage."

The admiral tried to nod in the headlock as Rafjur looked down at Rob and Will, and said, "Rafjur has lost profitable business this day." It seemed almost as though the giant smiled when he continued, "Rafjur tells you to stop sitting there like rocks and move as best you can, like Rafjur."

Will lunged forwards and grabbed the box before he stood, following Rob to the door.

"Boy!" barked Rafjur. Rob and Will stopped and turned. "Rafjur wants to know what is in the box."

"Rafjurrr!" growled Admiral Slatter. "That is my box!"

Having been single-mindedly focused on getting out of there, Rob had not paid heed to the box. He looked at Will, who glanced at him and then fussed with the box until it fell open. The Sphere flashed out and hovered, in midair, beside the brothers. Rafjur's eyes widened at the sight.

"Rafjurrr!" growled the admiral, again, straining to see from the crook of Rafjur's arm, his robotic eye grossly bulging. "Don't let them take The Sphere!"

Rafjur hesitated for a moment, staring at The Sphere, and then said, "Rafjur knows The Sphere goes where it will."

Red-faced, the admiral looked ready to explode.

Rob and Will turned to leave but stopped when they heard Rafjur say, "Rafjur should not need to remind the careless boys to take their things with them." Glancing back, they could see in Rafjur's strong gaze the sincerity of his words, as he continued, "And Rafjur says he knows the admiral lies about your father. Rafjur knows any matter of being or beast would not easily kill Rob Roar. The young Roar boys can believe Rafjur in this, for Rafjur knows these things."

With no time to wonder how Rafjur knew what Admiral Slatter had said to them about their father – as Rafjur had not been in the room – Rob and Will rushed to the table. Each strapped on a torso-holster, then a pack. They grabbed their blasters and wasted no more time in fleeing the room, The Sphere remaining close.

Admiral Slatter growled, "Rafjurrr!"

As soon as they were running along the passageways following the map on Rob's arm-comp monitor, Rob tapped a button, and said, "Kris, we're heading for the pick-up-point!"

Meanwhile, Kris had been rescued by Keb and Genius. Keb carried Kris to the Tenacity's command bridge, where he was then simultaneously bombarded by three voices; one of them, Rob's. Matt was in the shuttle fending off a vicious attack of Boargen fighters as he tried, in vain, to get from the senator's ship to the Tenacity. Seconds later, the senator's ship fled Grimmin's orbit taking Katia and her mother home to Peridia, where they would be safe from Boargen hostility. Kris then turned his attention to Rob's hurried message as he prepared the Tenacity for its rescue flight to Grimmin.

Thanks to Rafjur, Rob and Will's escape went unnoticed by all outside the room until the two boys approached the complex exit at a run. Blasters drawn and set to stun, they blasted their way through, stunning the four guards. That was enough to sound the alarm. As the two brothers rushed from the building with The Sphere still following, they were sure that Rafjur was, at that very moment, making his own escape. It was then, that they heard the blessed voice of Kris.

"I'm on my way. I have you on the scanner."

They made it to the street which was beginning to fill with early morning commuters. The pedestrians were all Boargen, with jet-black hair; not a foreigner in sight. There were also numerous grey, bulky-looking vehicles. Rob let Will set the pace and stayed on his heels. Their passage through the growing throngs left a wake of curious Boargen looking after them, not just because they were alien, blond-haired boys running through the streets, but because there was a pure-white orb flying behind them.

After a few minutes of sprinting, Will felt as though his lungs would seize with his next breath and his legs threatened to cramp. It took every last bit of effort to keep moving. It was the same for Rob.

Then came the sound of pursuit far behind them. Rob glanced back: Boargen guards were closing in. He could tell that Will was on the edge of panic. Through his breath, he said, "We're almost there, Will." Encouraging words that Rob needed, too.

The sound of powerful engines approached overhead and for a moment, Rob worried that it was a Boargen ship. But when he looked up, he saw a beautiful sight: the great, sleek, pearl-white Tenacity swooped down towards a large open area just ahead. Screaming, the Boargen people in and around the area scattered in all directions. A few blasts hit near the brothers – the Boargen guards were firing on them.

The Tenacity touched down in a cloud of dust with its gangway already extended, and the two brothers, still followed by The Sphere, caught their last breath of dirty, Boargen air and sprinted up the gangway and into the ship, falling to the floor at Keb and Genius's feet, exhausted and breathless.

Keb touched the button to retract the gangway and close the hatch and called out, "They are here, young sir ... "

A mere white streak across the sky, the Tenacity blasted out of the Boargen city of Dagam and made such haste to Grimmin's orbit and space beyond, that not a Boargen ship could catch it. But that did not mean the Boargen would not follow. Indeed, they had already guessed where the shuttle had gone, and had given chase.

The Sphere

As he was fleeing Grimmin and dropping Katia and her mother off on their ship, and as he had passed again and again through thin-space, Matt had never stopped thinking about Rob, Will, and his father. Matt was still under the impression that they had found their father. It ate at him that he had left the Boargen system without them, though at least Kris was now safe on the Tenacity. But there had been little choice. The Boargen attack had been relentless and he was in the shuttle, unarmed. Softening his worry, helping him believe it would all turn out right, Kris said that it appeared that Rob and Will had escaped, and that he could get them from Grimmin on his own. Matt had yet to learn that it had been a stranger in the Boargen prison cell, and Kris had yet to learn that his brothers had thought they had found their father.

Upon leaving Grimmin's orbit, the shuttle had made five passes through thin-space, one after the other, in quick succession. Appearing in Earth's solar system about 85,000 miles from Earth, Matt was left feeling very woozy. He felt like he had just ridden a roller coaster a hundred times in a row.

In spite of the uncertain outcome of events he had left behind, he would remember, for evermore, the feeling of relief upon returning home from his first trip away from Earth, which now lay directly ahead, floating in a never-ending darkness; a beautiful blue marble in a black sparkling sea. But that relief was interrupted and postponed as a blast violently rocked the shuttle.

The shuttle's alarm blared as Boargen fighter ships appeared, one after the other, blinking red on the scanner.

"Space!" Matt said under his breath.

He thought about choosing another coordinate and passing through thin-space again, but decided against it, for he suddenly grew fearful of getting lost in the galaxy. Of course, he could activate the shuttle's cloaking field, but the energy required for cloaking would draw power from the engines, thereby slowing the shuttle. And with the enemy already upon him – and so many of them at that – the chances of remaining undetected were slim.

With no weapons to defend himself and no means of hiding or escape above simply running for it, Matt was helpless. All he could do was race towards Earth and the safety of the Oregon base at full speed whilst dodging the enemy. As orange blasts lit up space around him, Matt began to feel a familiar despair closing in.

Hoping that Mr Casper and KNIA could help in some way, he was just getting ready to contact them when salvation came in the form of two blinking green lights on the shuttle's scanner: two Earth space-fighters heading straight for him. Then Matt heard an unexpected voice through his communicator.

"Hey, Matt, get ready to duck," Kaya called out.

A second familiar voice called, "Hi-ya, Matt."

Of course, it was Shani.

"Bet you didn't think you'd see us up here."

No, he did not. And there was no time to ask how Kaya and Shani had got permission from their mother to learn how to fly; let alone, to come up here and risk their lives to save him. But he was extremely grateful to see orange blasts flash past and space light up behind him: two Boargen fighters exploding. Then, the two Earth space-fighters streaked by, one on each side.

Matt could see it all on the scanner. Two of the Boargen fighters remained, chasing him, while the others, eight in all, scattered to wage a fight against Kaya and Shani. The two sisters had learned well from KNIA. Their skill, combined with the superiority of Earth's spaceships, gave them the advantage. With the shuttle unarmed, all Matt could do was dodge the blasts from the two Boargen fighters dogging him. Fortunately, the shuttle's repulse field was still strong.

Just when all seemed to be leaning in favour of the Earth ships, as there were only five of the original twelve Boargen fighters remaining, warning signals blared again. Three large ships had suddenly appeared. The Boargen had sent the big guns, and those ships now bore down on the fight.

Adrenalin had been keeping Kaya and Shani from worrying much about what they were doing, but at the sight of the large ships coming towards them, the two girls joined Matt in his stark fear. The chance of being killed became much more real as the three large Boargen ships joined the five remaining smaller ones and attacked. The fight had now become far outbalanced – now in the Boargen favour.

It continued like that, the three Earth ships being chased, for what seemed forever to Matt, Kaya and Shani; but really, it was only minutes. During this time, Kaya and Shani managed to destroy two more Boargen fighters and even inflict some damage to one of the larger ships. But Matt and the girls were quickly becoming fatigued, making their situation that much more desperate.

Then, as the shuttle made its way towards Earth and the two space-fighters zipped in and out of the fray fighting brilliantly against overwhelming odds, a terrible scenario presented itself: somehow, Shani had become separated from Matt and Kaya and was being chased by one of the large Boargen ships and two fighters. She was exhausted. She was in deep trouble and on the verge of panic, trying desperately to escape. But she was surrounded; trapped between three ships.

Suddenly, a massive fireball lit up space behind her and the large Boargen ship disappeared in a firework of orange streaks fizzing out at the ends. Like Matt before, it was now Shani's turn to breathe a sigh of relief when she caught sight of a huge, pearl-white ship and heard Kris' voice.

"I'm guessing that's Kaya and Shani flying those things."

Shani beamed as she ducked out of the way while the two space-fighters, piloted by Rob and Will, launched from the Tenacity and finished off her last two antagonists.

Everything changed with the arrival of Earth's new space-cruiser. Rob and Will finished off the last of the Boargen fighters while Kris fired at a second bulky, Boargen ship, turning it into space dust. The third large Boargen ship vanished, abruptly, through thin-space and left Earth's solar system quiet once again.

All that time, Mr Casper had been on the edge of his seat, chilled to the bone by what he was witnessing. It had been worse for Adia – with the uncertainty of her youngest daughter's fate – who was now questioning her decision to allow her girls to help by learning how to fly fighting craft. Socket and Wrench had practically been biting their nails – if they had had any. But when the Tenacity had appeared and destroyed the bulky Boargen ship dogging Shani, Mr Casper, Adia and the two fix-its had leapt for joy, cheering the children on.

Though at first, Kris had trouble believing the Tenacity would fit, Mr Casper had reassured him that the tube into the Oregon cavern would expand to allow the cruiser through. With the Tenacity settled to one side of the cavernous hangar, the smaller ships entered, one after the other. As the last of them, the shuttle, set down, Mr Casper, Adia, and the fix-its converged on the Roar brothers, Kaya, Shani, Keb and Genius, who was giddy with delight to be so welcomed as hugs and congratulations came from all directions.

During the remaining weeks of summer, in addition to celebrating Matt's eighth birthday, the Roar boys transported Keb home in the Tenacity, to Peridia. There, the four brothers were lauded as heroes and officially named 'The Galaxy Boys' by the Peridians; a name coined by Katia in orbit above Sundee and a name that would stick from that day forth.

But while on Peridia, Kris was reminded of something and he wasted no time in speaking with his brothers about it. Although Katia had first called them Galaxy Boys, there was another that had also called them by that name: KNIA. When Will and Matt had first boarded the Tenacity in the Kablakian factory, KNIA had greeted them with that name. And later, upon joining Will and Matt on the Tenacity, the first time Rob and Kris entered the command bridge, KNIA had again greeted them as Galaxy Boys. How had KNIA known Katia had called them that?

The brothers also visited their grandmother for a day and a night, during which time she fed them delicious meals and desserts. That day and late into the night, they talked about all sorts of things; like about how wonderful it was to have the farm active again. And Grandma regaled them with details of how, upon Aunt Hilary's weekly phone calls, she had satisfied their aunt's every concern and question; which usually had to do with whether the Roar brothers were working hard or goofing about. Of course, Aunt Hilary never asked to speak with the brothers; she would never waste her time like that.

During lunch, Matt accidentally mentioned the huge trees that he had seen on Moxy, which all took their breaths away as they watched their grandmother absorb what Matt had said with a smile. But she merely chuckled and said how beautiful that must have been and that she had also occasionally travelled to Oregon's coast to see the majestic redwoods there, which she could only imagine paled in size to the Moxy trees.

Before they left Grandma's house, Rob got a chance to peek at her computer; for he still wondered if his grandmother's mannerisms might be a cover for some reason, and that it had been her that had sent that mysterious e-mail. But the computer had been turned off and he dared not invade further, so the brothers had departed from their grandmother's perfect little cottage, still unsure whether she was a bit crazy, or whether she somehow knew more than she let on.

The brothers knew they had no choice but to return to the orphanage. Aunt Hilary could be a problem if she found out about everything. And if she found out, then the entire world would find out; and the world was not yet ready to know about the reality of the galaxy. Mr Casper had explained that all the many governments on Earth were not evolved enough to join as one to avoid petty bickering over the riches that could be made with intergalactic trade.

"The governments of Earth," Mr Casper had said, "must be unified as one before joining the galaxy."

And it was true. Earth's combined societies could implode under the pressure of greed and throw the planet's inhabitants into what outsiders would consider to be a civil war.

But now, Earth – as it was said by some galactic politicians, including Katia's mother, Senator Quarin – was at risk from the growing Boargen threat. Those like Senator Quarin believed that it was dangerous to underestimate the Boargen and their leader, Admiral Slatter. Many others, however, accepted the excuses the Boargen had made for the recent events. The Boargen had simply explained that they had misunderstood the function of The Sphere, and that they had been under the misperception that it had been maliciously kept from them in order to keep their society ignorant, and therefore poorer than other societies; like the rich Polinthians, who had that really great appliance business.

Those that were able to see the Boargen for what they were, understood, all too well, the threat to peace in the galaxy, and what that could mean for simple worlds like Earth that were not yet members of the galactic community; and there were many. It was known that Earth was not yet able to defend itself. An Earth conquered and ruled by the Boargen would make the Boargen very wealthy, and those living on Earth would become slaves.

These things, and more, occupied Rob's thoughts as he looked out the aeroplane window beside him. He and his brothers would be landing in New York in a few hours. Mr Casper was not returning with them. That had been part of the deal with Aunt Hilary. He would remain to watch over the farm while the Roar brothers filled their miniscule minds with a commoner's education, only to return the following summer to toil in the fields. That's how Aunt Hilary saw it. Rob wished he could fly one of the space-fighters to Aunt Hilary's apartment and blast it right out of New York, with her and her two daughters riding the rubble to a deserted planet somewhere far away. The thought of his aunt running from the rockhunds on Sundee made him smile, though he knew he would never wish her listed on a Jawbonee dinner menu. Not even she deserved that.

A glint of sunlight caught his attention in the distance. He stared and saw it again and knew it was one of the fix-its. Socket or Wrench would remain with them in New York; their own personal watch-robot. Rob looked beside him at Will who was sleeping, then looked across the aisle at Matt and Kris. Matt was definitely sleeping as he was snoring. But whether Kris was sleeping, was uncertain. Rob had learned at the beginning of their adventure that his youngest brother slept less than everyone had thought.

He smiled about that. They had all grown a little taller during the summer. They had all changed inside, too. Aside from the vast galactic-level knowledge far beyond that of the average youth, each of them had learned, in one way or another, just how precious life was. And they had learned just how much there was to see in the galaxy. There could not have been a better summer vacation. His brothers agreed with him that there was nothing that would keep them from continuing to explore beyond Earth's confines; not the fear of the unknown; not even Aunt Hilary, especially since there was every reason to continue to do so. One reason, above all others, of course, was to find their mother and father. Rob was sure that someday, they would.

The Roar brothers had heard nothing about where their mother could be. But between Admiral Slatter claiming he killed their father and Rafjur being quite sure that the admiral's claim was wishful boasting, the boys were left believing to the core that their father was still alive. Rafjur had said that if Rob Roar was missing, he was missing for a very good reason. The same would be true of their mother. Rob hoped that wherever his parents were, that they were not alone, and that maybe they were even together, like he was with his brothers. For Rob, that thought made missing his parents more bearable.

There had been a grand dinner to celebrate the Roar brothers return to the orphanage. Aunt Hilary and her two daughters were not there, of course. But between Tic's and Talk's excitement and Mother Superior's knowing, warm welcome, the orphanage had never seemed more like a home; even if it was just temporary.

But the brothers were assured of some intrigue during the winter in New York, because that FBI agent Joe Millin had turned up again at the airport, hiding in the corner, watching, as they got off the aeroplane. Mr Casper had been sure that the agent would fade away after deciding there was nothing to see around the Roar brothers, but apparently, Mr Millin saw it another way. The brothers assumed, therefore, that they would see more of Mr Millin in the future.

Later that night, after everyone else had gone to bed, the brothers were left in their moonlit room grouped together around Rob and Will's beds. Socket, or Wrench – there was truly no way to tell the two apart – had snuck into the room through the open window. Mr Casper had said that the fix-it would stay close to them as much as possible, for who knew whether the Boargen would try to harm the brothers; if they could find them, that is.

They were talking about their adventures and the conversation turned into questioning some of those unanswered mysteries, like Keb's glasseen eyes. Kris had questioned the robot about his eyes but Keb had explained that he was unable to discuss such matters with an unauthorised being. Kris had known not to bother pressing further, for he knew Keb would not answer. And although Mr Casper had been with their father when collecting the robot, Dynak, he knew little about the glasseen eyes other than that the glasseen itself was the hardest known material.

The brothers' grandmother would always come up during these conversations; for she was the closest mystery to them. During their dinner with her that first night in Oregon, she had all but suggested that they should go and search for their parents, in a tone of voice that made it sound as though she somehow knew their mother and father were not on Earth. She had also suggested that the brothers should go and look up relatives on their mother's side. What did that mean? Their mother was from Mindin. Did Grandma somehow know that, too? And then there was that strange text streaming across her computer monitor that night. Yes, Grandma was definitely a mystery, but a comfortable one where others were not.

As for Rafjur: Mr Casper had said that the great man had died saving their father; and that Rafjur and his planet, Sundee, had been sucked into a black hole created by Sundee's sun collapsing. How Sundee was there in its system again, with everything as it was, and how Rafjur was alive, Mr Casper had no idea. Nor did KNIA. But Rafjur had helped them; so whether he was a ghost or alive, he was a friend.

And what of the mysterious man Rob and Will freed from the Boargen prison? It seemed clear that he knew their father. As he had said something to them before bolting from the cell to draw the guards away: 'Your father is nowhere near this system.' – words which also suggested that he knew where their father was. The mystery man also had helped Matt, Katia and her mother escape in the shuttle, escaping himself in the mysterious black spaceship, so it appeared he was watching out for the Roar boys.

Although the black spaceship was of a design unknown to galactic records – as was the Tenacity – if the mystery man flying it was a friend – as appeared to be the case – then there need be no concern that the black spaceship was spotted around the old Oregon base. And maybe, the brothers hoped, the mysterious man in his mysterious ship was helping their parents, wherever they might be, like he had helped them.

As for KNIA: the answer to the KNIA mystery seemed always on the tip of each boy's tongue; like knowing a word but not being able to say it or write it. Although Kris had asked KNIA whether she had sent them the mysterious e-mail, KNIA had replied, in her calm, female voice, "I do not have a reason to send you an e-mail". A very strange answer because it was not an absolute denial, as it answered only for the present, and not for the past. And then there was the mystery of where the KNIA computer system was stored. KNIA would not say. And again, KNIA had called the brothers 'Galaxy Boys' after Katia had, but had not been part of that conversation. Coincidence? All of it, combined?

"Like you pointed out, Kris," said Rob, "KNIA and The Sphere have a lot in common."

In spite of feeling very tired, Kris perked up a little and said, "What if The Sphere gave Mother and Father the technology to build KNIA?"

A question, in spite of exhaustion flooding in, that the Roar boys tackled. The Sphere had departed soon after they returned to Earth; to where, no one knew. They all agreed that there was something familiar about it, but the elusive sense of familiarity was something which none of them could quite wrap their brains around. It was as if they each had an incomplete thought about the mysterious white orb; or that they knew something about it but just could not find the specific item of memory through the thick haze of mystery. It was the same problem with KNIA.

Eventually, exhaustion took over and the moonlit room was quiet with the exception of the soft sounds of sleeping.

Later, the room was still flooded with moonlight when the brothers all woke at once. Rob sat up first, then Kris, then Will, then Matt – his eyes only half open. They all looked around at each other and the familiar room, each feeling like the others – disoriented and unusually groggy.

"I had a really weird dream," Matt spoke up, in a tired voice.

Rob, Will, and Kris each had a sinking feeling then. Each realised, independently, that it had all been a dream, everything: the spaceships, Katia and Keb, Rafjur, Yobe, everything, it had all been just a dream.

With sadness sinking in, for his dream had seemed so real, Rob said, "I had a weird dream, too, about us going on an adventure across the galaxy." Rob rubbed his eyes as he asked, "Was your dream anything like that?"

Matt gave Rob an odd look, as though he had no idea what his brother was talking about, and said, "No! Stop messing with me, Rob. I know all that was real. I dreamt that I was talking to a dinosaur."

Then, suddenly, like a miniature full moon, it was there in the room with them – The Sphere. While all four Roar brothers were a bit startled, for Kris, the haze in his mind cleared as abruptly as

The Sphere arrived. Clarity was slightly slower for the others, but as they looked on, Kris got out of bed and strode to the floating white orb that looked very much like a ball of thin-space.

For a moment, he stood, staring, wide-eyed, at The Sphere hovering mere inches from his face, and then said, "You sent us that e-mail – didn't you?" Kris cocked his head. " ... KNIA ... "

THE END
... OF THE BEGINNING ...